WILLIAM WILDE
⫷⫸ AND THE ⫷⫸
STOLEN LIFE

THE CHRONICLES OF
WILLIAM WILDE

DAVIS ASHURA

William Wilde and the Stolen Life

Copyright © 2017 by Davis Ashura

All rights reserved.

Cover art and design by Deranged Doctor Design

Interior design and art by Mikey Brooks (mikeybrooks.com)

Printed in the United States of America

First Printing: 2018

DuSum Publishing, LLC

Paperback Edition

ISBN: 0-9997044-1-9
ISBN-13: 978-0-9997044-1-7

DEDICATION

To my lovely wife who still lets me hide in my cave and write.
I couldn't do this without her patience.

ACKNOWLEDGMENT

As before, none of this could have been done without the support of so many others. This book is no different. I've once more had fabulous editors, but especially Tom Burkhalter, the Master of Modern Aviation Fiction, and a tremendously gifted writer and a better friend. He accepted my whiny complaints (What do you mean it's not perfect?!) without punching me in the nose like I deserved and pushed me to address flaws I didn't want to see.

CHAPTER 1:
UNREAL NORMALITY

January 1987

ther than the Bangles singing "Walk Like an Egyptian" on the radio, the T-bird remained silent as a funeral while William drove everyone to school on their first day back after Christmas break. Serena sat in the passenger seat, her beautiful face frozen in a look of longing. Her dark hair shrouded her eyes. Seated in the back, Jason stared morosely at the dull winter landscape: gray concrete and gray skies. His ever-present California surfer tan and good looks remained, but his ready smile was absent. Meanwhile Daniel's dark features and gray eyes—aspects inherited from his east African mother and Scandinavian father—appeared troubled. Even Lien, the normally vivacious, Chinese foreign exchange student staying with Daniel's family, seemed pensive.

The quiet was fine by William. He didn't feel like talking anyway. The events of the Christmas holidays continued to swirl in his head like a repeating movie loop, and try as he might, William had yet to come to terms with them. Kohl Obsidian was dead, but there remained times when William felt certain he could sense the necrosed leering at him from some dark place, biding his time and waiting to attack. Then there was the fact that his brother, Landon—who William thought had died in a car accident a year ago—still lived but had few memories of who he had once been. He wondered if he would ever see Landon again.

William drove on with his thoughts in a knot, not paying much attention to where he was going. Muscle memory, though, took him and the others safely to St. Francis. He pulled into the full parking lot and killed the engine, but no one exited the T-bird.

Envy stirred within William as he watched other students greet each other with whistles and joyous calls. A few tossed around a football, and all of them laughed and joked like their vacation hadn't ended. None of them seemed to have a single care in the world.

Lucky bastards.

William wondered again how the rest of the world could be so oblivious to his troubles when everything about his life had changed so profoundly. He knew the answer even before he finished the thought.

Because the world doesn't revolve around you.

William sighed. "Let's go in."

"Hard to believe we're back," Lien said as she climbed out of the vehicle.

"It doesn't feel real, does it?" Jason noted.

"No, it doesn't," Serena agreed.

Her mocking half-smile, that sense of private amusement at the world's foibles, had faltered and faded during the flight from

Kohl Obsidian and had yet to return. Too often nowadays, her countenance held a sense of unfocused worry, with only occasional subtle hints of her prior humor.

They walked as a quiet group toward the school's back entrance, sharing 'hellos' with a few other students.

"There's Jake," William said, bobbing his head in his one-time nemesis' direction. Jake must have sensed his regard because he glanced William's way and gave him a brief nod of acknowledgment. "What do you think he'll do?"

"About what?" Jason asked.

"You know. About Kohl," William said. "He saw him that night in Winton Woods. A whole bunch of his friends did, too. They're bound to talk."

"They won't say anything," Serena said, her tone certain.

"Why?" William asked.

"Think about it," Serena said. "They're going to be scared to death to talk to us after what they saw. And they won't tell anyone else because their story would sound insane."

William had his doubts. "You really think they'll keep it to themselves?"

"They'll have to," Jason said.

"Why?" William asked.

"Mr. Zeus visited all of them," Jason answered, "and he made sure they wouldn't remember anything about Kohl Obsidian or even seeing him."

William turned to Jason in confusion. "Are you serious?"

"Of course I'm serious," Jason answered.

William eyed him in rising horror.

"What? It wasn't like Mr. Zeus hurt them," Jason said with a shrug. "Besides which, it needed doing."

3

William gaped, dumbfounded.

"Why is this a problem?" Lien asked, sounding annoyed. "So what if a bunch of normals forget something horrible?"

"You don't think there's anything wrong with messing around with someone's mind like that?" William demanded. "Stealing their memories? You don't think it's like mind-rape?"

Lien rolled her eyes, and William gazed at her in disgust. How could she not care whether something as private as a person's thoughts were stolen? It was wrong, and Lien's indifference was even worse.

"Like Jason said, it's not like Mr. Zeus hurt them," Daniel said in a tone meant to smooth over the situation. "He only kept people from learning about us. Too many questions mean we—or worse, Arylyn—might be discovered."

"I don't care," William said. "Some things shouldn't be done without asking first."

"You don't have to like it or approve of it," Lien said. "It's done."

"You're not helping," Daniel reproved.

"There's nothing to help," Lien said.

William glared at Lien. "I hope you remember this conversation if someone more powerful than you ever does something like that to you."

"If Mr. Zeus wiped all their memories, then why do I remember?" Serena asked. "Why didn't he do that to me?"

"Because you experienced too much," Jason explained. "There would be too much to erase."

"Hi, William," Sonya Bowyer said.

William glanced at Sonya in surprise. He also flicked his gaze

4

at Jake Ridley, Sonya's boyfriend, and Steve Aldo, both of whom had accompanied her. He'd been so focused on his argument with Lien that he hadn't seen their approach. Strange. Not so long ago, his radar would have captured the slightest motions of Sonya Bowyer's celestial movements. Now he had other things on his mind, and her classical, blonde beauty didn't even rate in the top ten of his concerns.

"Hey, William," Jake said in his typical gruff, football player tone. "How was your break?"

"Quiet and boring," William said, mustering a sigh of disappointment.

"Too bad," Steve said with a grin of commiseration. Steve grinned a lot, and the girls loved his dark good looks almost as much as they liked Jake's all-American handsomeness.

"What did you guys do?" Serena asked.

"Day after Christmas, my dad surprised us with a Colorado ski-trip," Sonya answered. "You?"

"Not much," Serena answered. "I spent most of my time with these losers—" she gestured to William and Jason "—and we ate too much and did too little."

"Speak for yourself," Jason said. "I'm not a loser."

"Sure you aren't." William smirked.

"Then maybe I should have hung out with you guys," Jake said. "After Sonya left—and Steve's family went down to the Caribbean—I was stuck around Cincinnati with absolutely nothing to do."

"Nothing?" William asked.

"Nothing," Jake affirmed. "I mean, before Steve left, he and I hung out, but otherwise nothing." His gaze seemed to sharpen. "I hiked some in Winton Woods."

William stiffened, and he hoped no one noticed. "Winton Woods? Why there?"

"I know it's spooky at night, but it's pretty during the day," Jake explained.

"You're such a girl," Steve chortled.

"Says the guy who likes to paint watercolors."

Steve's grin faded, and William chuckled.

The tardy bell rang.

"Catch you guys later," Jake called over his shoulder as he, Sonya, and Steve departed for their lockers.

Serena, Daniel, and Lien left, too.

"That was weird," William said to Jason.

"What?"

"Jake's crack about Winton Woods being spooky at night."

Jason shrugged. "I'm sure it's nothing."

⸺●⸺

Jake reached his locker and tried to fold himself back into the normal routine of St. Francis. He pretended a senior's disdain for the concerns of tardiness while lower classmen rushed about in a mad dash, grabbing books, shouting final words to one another, and hustling to their homerooms. Jake, though, took his time. As a senior, a certain calm decorum was expected.

More importantly, he hoped the normality of life at St. Francis would settle his mind, and he'd discover a way to make peace with what he'd seen.

Because what he'd seen defied reason, and what he'd seen still had him trembling at night. All through Christmas break, a worm of fear had lodged itself in his stomach. What if that creature came back? And what had really happened to William, Jason, and Serena afterward? Jake had been sure they'd been killed by that thing. Then two days before the end of Christmas holidays, they'd shown up again, haggard and worn, but acting as if nothing had changed.

But everything *had* changed.

Jake knew it. He recalled everything that had happened but wished he could forget. He hid a shudder as he again remembered the hideous creature, remembered it looming in front of him, remembered its metal-grinding voice and long apelike arms that ended in foot-long claws.

"You okay?" Sonya asked, coming up to his locker. Her heart-shaped face was filled with concern.

Jake did his best to hide his troubled thoughts. "What do you mean?"

"You looked worried."

Jake offered her what he hoped was a confident smile, the heart-melting grin that effected girls of all ages, from freshmen to seniors. "It's nothing," he lied. "I was thinking about homework and hoping we won't have any today."

Sonya snorted. "Like that's going to happen." She gave him a quick peck on the lips. "We better hurry or we'll be late."

As always, they strutted down the hall, arm-in-arm, and as they entered their homeroom, Jake tried not to react when he noticed William. Seeing Wilde had him off-center. For so long, he'd always thought of William as a rabbit, and now he half-expected to see a dragon.

7

"You sure you're okay?" Sonya asked.

"I'm fine," Jake reassured her, trying not to stare at William.

———◆———

The utter normalcy of school—the classes, the teachers, the students—helped calm William's mind. By the time school let out, he managed to settle back into his regular routine . . . at least for the most part.

His friends must have felt the same way, because the drive home was far livelier than the drive to school had been. The weather even reflected their brighter mood with the sun breaching the ceiling of gray clouds and beaming down a happy, yellow light. Daniel and Jason argued about something nerd-related, something about which ship would win in a battle between the *Battlestar Galactica* and the *Starship Enterprise*. William figured the *Enterprise*. Serena hummed along to the song currently playing on the radio, "Neutron Dance" by the Pointer Sisters; and as always, Lien sang. She belted out the tune as only she could, and William smiled when she missed a note. Lien was a terrible singer, but during the Christmas break, he'd missed her off-key caterwauling.

They arrived home at their little cul-de-sac, and everyone went their separate ways with promises to check in later in the evening.

"Time for your first lesson," Mr. Zeus said when William and Jason entered their home. With his chest-length white beard, tall, slim build, and unlit pipe held between his lips, Jason's grandfather could have been Gandalf the White. "Your training begins now."

"My first lesson?" William asked, hoping he hadn't misheard.

"You mean with magic?" He scowled an instant later. "As long as you don't do something to my memory."

"He's mad because you erased all the normals' memories about Kohl Obsidian," Jason explained.

Mr. Zeus' face tightened. "I can understand why you might feel that way," he said, "but it was required."

"But it's not right," William said.

"It's done," Mr. Zeus replied with a frown.

William glared, not satisfied by the old man's words or everyone's nonchalance about the matter.

Mr. Zeus face sagged into a sigh. "It's not something we do without great forethought," he said, "but we *must* maintain Arylyn's secrecy. No one can ever know of our existence. It's one of our cardinal laws."

"Why?" William asked.

"There's a long list of reasons," Mr. Zeus said. "For now, you'll have to trust me."

William held a scowl for a moment longer before sighing acceptance. "It doesn't mean I'll ever like it."

"And you shouldn't," Mr. Zeus said, "which is a credit to who you are."

"A doofus?" Jason asked, obviously trying to break the tension.

"Isn't that what you call your private parts?" William asked.

Mr. Zeus smiled, and his blue eyes crinkled. The expression took years off his seamed, ancient face—he'd been born before the Civil War. "Right. Why don't we start with instruction on the basics. For instance, what is truly meant when we say '*asra*'? Right now, all you know are the words. You need to know more."

9

"I'm getting something to eat," Jason said. "You want anything?" he asked William.

"Sure," William replied. "Whatever you're having."

"Teenage boys and their endless appetites," Mr. Zeus said in a tone of disgust. "At any rate, the inner aspect—*lorethasra*—is made of five Elements: Earth, Air, Water, Fire, and Spirit. However, not all are equal. Spirit is the most important of the Elements, and control of all the others flows through its use."

"We'll be able to use all the others if we can use Spirit?" William guessed.

"Up to a point," Mr. Zeus said. "All *asrasin*s can bend the Elements to their will, but most are adept with only two or three. For instance, my talents involve Earth, Air, and Spirit while Jason's are Fire and Earth. It is the rare and very powerful *asrasin* who is a master of all the Elements. Even rarer is the poor soul who isn't adept at anything other than Spirit." Mr. Zeus shrugged. "Then there are those like you."

Jason returned and passed William a plate with a couple of PB&J sandwiches and a glass of milk.

William nodded his thanks. "What's different about me?" he asked Mr. Zeus.

"From what I can tell, you're one of the special cases," Mr. Zeus said.

"He's special all right," Jason said. He twisted his limbs and face into a cretin-like countenance and posture.

William might have flipped him the bird, but Mr. Zeus wouldn't have liked it. He settled for telling Jason to shut up.

"You're a *raha'asra*," Mr. Zeus explained. "*Raha'asras*, if properly motivated and instructed, can become quite skilled in the use of all the Elements."

10

"Then I'm one of those super-powerful *asrasins*," William said, his mind quickening with visions of glory.

"No," Mr. Zeus replied, dashing his burgeoning dreams. "You'll be skilled in all five Elements, but you'll be a master of none."

William's excitement faded. "Jack of all trades."

"The very definition of a *raha'asra*," Mr. Zeus said.

"But what does a *raha'asra* actually do?" William asked. "What do any of you do?"

"Let's stick with *raha'asras* for now," Mr. Zeus said. "At the most basic level, *raha'asras* are the ones who keep the rest of us alive."

William's brow furrowed. "How?"

"All *asrasins*—magi and mahavans alike—create our *lorethasra*. That is, inner magic, but we can only survive and thrive in a *saha'asra*, a place of *lorasra*—outer magic."

"Even then, the *lorasra* must be dense enough, or it's no good to us," Jason added.

Mr. Zeus nodded. "Every time we braid our *lorethasra* to *lorasra*, no matter the source, *nomasra* or *saha'asra*, we drain it. It's a *raha'asra* who fills it back up. They create *lorasra*." He held up a hand, forestalling William's next question. "And before you ask, I can't teach you how to do what they do. Only another *raha'asra* can."

"And only a *raha'asra* can create a *nomasra*?" William guessed.

"No. That's something any *asrasin* can do," Mr. Zeus said. "But only a *raha'asra* can fill it with *lorasra*."

William grinned. "Then I guess I am special."

Jason twisted his limbs and features again.

He looked less funny when a pillow hit him in the face.

———●——

A week after the Christmas holidays, life finally settled into a routine, or as settled as anyone could hope.

But for Serena, she remained haunted by nightmares about Kohl Obsidian. Even while awake, the fear sometimes struck her like an electric shock. She'd lose herself to her imagination, seeing the necrosed lurch out of shadowed corners or dark places. Other times his terrible laugh seemed to taunt her like a whisper of doom chittering on the wind.

As the week went on, her fears slowly faded, and she faced the upcoming weekend, the first one after the Christmas holidays, with a long-missing sense of hope. It helped that she, William, and the others decided to go to Graeter's on Friday after school. A scoop of cookies n' cream always gave life a happy sheen.

Afterward, she and William stood alone on the driveway to his home.

"See you tomorrow night," she said. "Movie night, right?"

"I never thought we'd have one of those again," William agreed with a smile.

"I think your favorite part is listening to Lien complain about your choices," Serena said with an unfeigned grin. She tucked a strand of hair behind an ear, knowing how much William enjoyed that simple motion. However, even in the midst of the movement, Serena mentally chided herself. William thought of her as a friend. Nothing more. He'd been pretty clear on the matter.

Although . . . Serena tilted her head in thought. She'd caught William staring at her a few times, a speculative gleam in his eyes, and she worried he might have started to think of her as something more. For his sake, she hoped not. While such a change in their relationship would likely ensure the success of her pilgrimage, she didn't want to see William hurt.

He'll be hurt no matter what you do, said the reedy voice of her conscience.

"See you tomorrow," William said. Thankfully, he hadn't noticed her distant thoughts. "Or tonight, if you've got nothing better to do."

"We'll see," Serena said. "I've got a lot of homework, and you know how I hate getting it done at the last minute."

"Or maybe you like making the rest of us look bad?"

"Says the guy with straight A's." Serena forced a laugh past her troubled thoughts. "Some of us actually have to work for our grades."

William chuckled. "I guess I'll see you later then. Have fun with your homework."

Serena rolled her eyes before heading home. Regret at what she had to do to William filled her thoughts.

Isha put down the paper he'd been reading as soon as she entered their house. Even seated at the kitchen table, his broad, heavily muscled form seemed to shrink the room. "What's wrong?" he asked with a frown on his bearded face.

Serena wanted to kick herself. She had failed to school her features to stillness, and instead allowed her troubled emotions to remain visible for anyone to see.

"William. I don't want to see him hurt," Serena said, unafraid to admit the truth to Isha.

Her relationship with her mentor had changed after Kohl had entered her life. Serena trusted Isha as she trusted no one since the death of her mother.

"I know your feelings for him have grown," Isha said. "The Far Abroad can be seductive, but it also makes a person fragile and weak, especially for those of us pledged to Lord Shet and his Servitor, your father." Isha held up a cautionary finger. "Neither of them abides weakness."

"Yes, sir," Serena said, accepting the mild rebuke.

"Remember, sometimes we have to do those things we would rather not in order to rise in this world."

"I won't fail," Serena promised, "but it doesn't mean I won't have regrets along the way."

Isha stared at her for a moment. "Sometimes we have to decide whom to hurt if we are to save the ones we love."

Serena settled her features into one of polite interest at Isha's not-so-subtle implication. "Meaning what?"

"It doesn't matter," Isha said. "Word reached me last night. Your father sent a dream."

A flutter of panic winged within Serena's stomach. "What did he say?"

"He says that our time grows short. He demands answers. He wonders why we haven't yet captured William, especially since it was my idea to come here. I was the one who convinced the Servitor that William might be a *raha'asra*."

"We haven't taken him because we aren't yet sure what he is," Serena said. "As long as he wears that stupid *nomasra*—the locket on his necklace—we can never know. Besides, he might contain the blood of a necrosed. I doubt my father would praise us for bringing something so monstrous to Sinskrill."

14

Isha waved aside her concerns. "Even with his *nomasra*, if the blood of the necrosed had entered him, it would have either transformed him into one of them or killed him by now. Since neither has occurred, it means he's overcome it."

"You're sure?" Serena didn't allow her joy to show. While she could trust Isha, old habits of hiding her emotions died hard.

"Of course," Isha said. "As to your other statement, 'never' is a powerful word. You claim we can never know. I disagree. *Nomasra* or not, early on we both knew what William most likely represented."

"We can guess what he is, but supposition isn't the same as knowing," Serena replied, stubbornly clinging to her earlier point.

"You really believe William is nothing more than a potential *asrasin*?" Isha asked, his tone scornful. "You're certain of that? Or perhaps it's your affection for him that drives you to defend him so vigorously."

"It's not," Serena answered, mentally flinching at her defensiveness. She took a breath, and took a second to organize her thoughts. "Logic drives me," she said. "We would look very foolish if we brought a simple *asrasin* back to Sinskrill. We need more than mere supposition."

"We *would* look foolish," Isha agreed with a nod. "But as you said, we won't know what he is so long as he wears that *nomasra*. Which means we have to remove it."

"How?" Serena asked. "It's more than a mere locket hanging from a thin, gold chain. Only William can take it off, or someone incredibly strong, like Kohl Obsidian."

"And we lack Kohl's strength," Isha mused before trailing off into silence as he stared at the tabletop. He looked up after a moment. "Has there been any time when William has taken it off?"

15

"Not that I know of. I even asked to see it one time, but he left the chain around his neck and passed the locket over to me."

"Then we'll have to nullify the *nomasra*," Isha said. "Or, barring that, destroy it or trick him into removing it."

"How?" Serena asked again.

"Allow me to think on it."

A large part of Serena hoped Isha would never find a way. Her father might consider her pilgrimage a failure if that happened, but it would probably be a forgivable failure. *Going against six magi, surviving a necrosed, and seeing the creature killed . . . her pilgrimage already had to be considered some kind of success, didn't it?* In any case, at least she would see her sister, Selene, again.

CHAPTER 2:
MYSTERIOUS STRANGERS

February 1987

I heard Mrs. Clancy is sick," William said to Serena as he slipped into his seat for English. He had to speak loudly in order to be heard over the hubbub throughout the room as other students carried on their own conversations. "She's supposed to be out for the rest of the semester."

"What happened?" Serena asked.

"Something about her pregnancy," William answered. "Bedrest, I think. I didn't even know—"

He broke off when a bowtie-wearing, middle-aged man with a gray beard as long as Mr. Zeus' strode purposefully into the room. The man—he had to be their substitute English teacher—wore a red, argyle sweater that stretched heroically over an ample middle and a cheery, rosy-cheeked grin. He could have been Santa Claus.

The rest of the students quieted down as well, and their din diminished to a general mumble.

"Good morning, class," the man said after the room eventually silenced. "I'm Mr. Cleating, and I'll be filling in for Mrs. Clancy for the remainder of the semester."

He spoke in a clipped, self-important manner, and Serena flashed a smirk and roll of her eyes before she delicately tucked a strand of hair behind an ear.

William leaned forward, distracted and arrested by the motion. Tucking a strand of hair . . . such a delicate, graceful gesture. Her lips pursed, and his pulse quickened.

Serena glanced his way and flashed him a quick smile, and William smiled in response, hoping it didn't come across as sickly, and also hoping she hadn't noticed the interest in his eyes. She could usually figure out what he was thinking without any difficulty.

"We are meant to cover C.S. Lewis during the next few weeks," Mr. Cleating said. He clenched an unlit pipe between his teeth and sat upon the corner of his desk. It creaked ominously whenever he shifted his weight. "However, I would rather read something different. Something still in the realm of the mythic but far more interesting: *The Lord of the Rings*."

William started, not sure he'd heard right. He replayed Mr. Cleating's words in his mind and realized he had heard right.

"You're probably loving this," Serena whispered.

William grinned in response. He'd be *required* to read *Lord of the Rings*? Best reading assignment ever!

"The reason I chose *Lord of the Rings* is because it and C.S. Lewis' master work, *The Chronicles of Narnia*, are both deeply Christian allegories, which is difficult to find in the realm of mythic, secondary fantasy," Mr. Cleating said.

William's brow creased. He'd never noticed any Christianity in *Lord of the Rings*.

"And choosing a Christian-themed mythic novel seems apropos here at St. Francis, yes?" Mr. Cleating continued.

William raised his hand.

"Yes . . ." Mr. Cleating shuffled through his student list. "Mr. Wilde. What is it?"

"How is *Lord of the Rings* Christian?" he asked.

Mr. Cleating smiled, and his entire face lit up, glowing and transformed by his humor. His eyes crinkled with delight as he jabbed his pipe at William. "You'll have to read the book and find out," he said, "but I promise, we'll all discover them together. A word of advice, though. Tolkien sought to create a modern myth containing elements of Christianity, similar to how paganism contains elements of Christianity, or vice versa. Remember that and his vision becomes more clear."

"What do you mean?" William asked.

"Some Christians believe that pagan stories are imperfect representations of the Logos, of the Word of God," Mr. Cleating said, still wearing his eye-crinkling smile. "But a pagan might feel the opposite. As we'll discover, Professor Tolkien played around with those themes in his singular book."

"Books," Steve Aldo said from the other side of the class.

"What did you say?" Again Mr. Cleating referenced his student roll. "Mr. Aldo."

"You keep calling *Lord of the Rings* a book, but it's a trilogy," Steve explained.

William raised his eyebrows in surprise. When had Steve read *Lord of the Rings*?

"It was published as a trilogy," Mr. Cleating said. "The *Fellowship of the Ring*, *The Two Towers*, and *The Return of the King*. But Tolkien intended his masterwork to be read as a single massive, majestic volume. It is, in fact, three volumes in one."

He addressed the rest of the class. "Now, as I said, both *Narnia* and *Lord of the Rings* are definitively Christian, but one obvious difference between the two works is that Tolkien wasn't quite the Christian apologist that C.S. Lewis became. Obvious allegories, such as Aslan as Christ, aren't as easily found in *Lord of the Rings*. Instead, Tolkien's work is multilayered, deeper, and more resonant. In fact, it is deeply Catholic, which again is quite apropos for this institution."

William raised his hand again and was called upon once more. "I still don't get it. I've read *Lord of the Rings*—"

"Nerd," someone muttered, to a chorus of chuckles.

William ignored it. "—and I never saw the Christianity in it."

"You never saw the Ring as an anti-sacrament?" Jake asked, appearing surprised.

William's mouth dropped, and he faced Jake with eyes wide in shock.

"Or saw the symbolism of Morgoth as Lucifer or Satan as Sauron?" Jake continued. "And when Gandalf becomes Gandalf the White, he becomes like the pope. He doesn't have authority over kings, but they still listen to what he says."

William continued to stare at Jake Ridley in slack-jawed amazement. *Jake Ridley had read* Lord of the Rings? And he apparently had an even deeper understanding of it than William did. *What the hell?* In that moment, William would have been less surprised if a dog had walked into their class wearing clothes, like in *The Far Side*.

"You aren't the only one who likes to read," Jake said to William, wearing a smug smile.

William couldn't help but continue to stare at Jake as if the other boy had grown two heads and four arms.

Sonya apparently felt the same.

"What? You know I like to read," Jake said to his girlfriend.

"I guess you have someone else you can talk to about all your nerd stuff," Serena whispered to William with a teasing grin.

"Quiet," he hissed.

Mr. Cleating, though, was smiling broadly. "You are exactly right, Mr. Ridley. The Ring is an anti-sacrament, and in many ways Gandalf is the pope. He has no specific right to rule, but kings and stewards bow to his will. Or at least they try not to annoy him," he added with a dry chuckle and clap of his hands. "There is so much for us to learn."

After class, William cornered Jake in the hallway. Students buzzed past them and Steve, Sonya, and Serena waited nearby. "How'd you learn all that stuff about *Lord of the Rings*?" he demanded.

"I read a critique," Jake said. "It cleared up a lot of things I didn't understand the first time I read the book. And Mr. Cleating is right, it is a single book."

"You read a critique?" William asked.

"Yeah. Once someone points out the Christianity, it's obvious," Jake enthused. "But there's all sorts of deeper stuff Tolkien was trying to get across, like how Gandalf, Frodo, and Aragorn are characters, but they also represent the mind, heart, and will."

"Maybe I should read this critique," William said.

"I can bring it to school if you want."

"Thanks." William felt faint. The world could have tilted on its axis and the sense of wrongness would have been no less. Jake Ridley had studied *Lord of the Rings*, which meant somewhere in that arrogant ass of a person, a decent human might lurk.

"No problem," Jake said.

Jake and his friends left, and Serena and William made their way to Biology. They sidestepped small groups of students damming the hallway like boulders in a stream and bent close in order to be heard over the between-bells ruckus permeating the lengths of St. Francis.

"There were three of us against Kohl," Serena said. "You, me, and Jason. Which roles do you think we played?"

"I never thought about it," William answered, still mulling over what Jake had said.

"I think I was the mind, because clearly I was the only one with a brain."

"Clearly."

"And you were the heart. We went where you guided us. Jason was the will."

"I guess," William said, still troubled by his potential misreading of Jake over all these years.

"You know what this means, don't you?" Serena asked, breaking into his distracted thoughts.

"What?"

"I'm actually going to have to break down and read *Lord of the Rings*."

"I told you to read it months ago," William protested.

"Back then I thought it was nothing but a straightforward adventure story, like Conan or Barsoom."

22

William did a double-take. *What the hell? Had he stepped into some kind of alternate universe?* Conan he could accept Serena knowing about since Arnie and all that, but Barsoom?

"You know about Barsoom, right? John Carter?" Serena asked. "The Martian books by Edgar Rice Burroughs. Don't tell me you've never read them."

"Of course, I've read them. Or at least some of them," William muttered. He made a mental note to check out a few of them from the library when he had time.

• •

A gathering of students, including Serena, William, Daniel, and Lien, shuffled about in front of St. Francis' gothic entrance. They waited to board one of the school buses parked before them. A field trip had been planned for a number of freshmen and seniors as part of their religious studies class.

"I loathe the bus," Lien said, quoting Molly Ringwald from *Sixteen Candles*, as she climbed aboard and stared down the aisle at the disorderly flock of students. A spit-wad almost clipped her in the head, and she grimaced. "There has to be a more dignified mode of transportation," she huffed.

Serena silently agreed. She'd never ridden a school bus before, and based on the behavior of the mixed bag of students, she didn't figure she'd missed much. "Where is this church located?" she asked William after they took a seat.

"Over-the-Rhine. The ghetto," William answered.

Serena made a moue of distaste. "How fun." She stared out the

23

window and let the conversation wash over her as the bus lurched to a start, and they began their journey downtown.

While they traveled, she considered what to do. Thus far, Isha hadn't yet come up with a plan for removing William's *nomasra*, and his lack of success left Serena torn. For William's sake, it would be best if she and Isha failed at their task, but then what about Selene? What would happen to her little sister? Would their father punish Serena by taking Selene away from her?

Her thoughts tumbled over one another, and she couldn't come up with a good answer to any of her concerns. On either path someone she cared for would be harmed, and Serena sighed in frustration.

"It is sad, isn't it?" William asked, gesturing to the people on the streets. He'd apparently mistaken her sigh for an indication of sorrow.

They'd reached the ghetto, and Serena paid closer attention.

Some folk sat on their front door stoops, watching their neighborhood with tired, worn-out visages. Others shuffled by with shopping carts full of stuff and fearful, darting eyes. A few, however, strutted about like wolves on the prowl, deciding which sheep to prey upon.

Serena recognized all the various archetypes represented here. They were as familiar as a hereditary enemy. The ghetto in Over-the-Rhine was a microcosm of her own home.

"It's cruel," Daniel said. "All these people stuck in ghettoes like this. It's only so the rich don't have to see them and can pretend they don't exist."

"Are you saying that because most of them are black like you?" Lien asked.

"Meaning I wouldn't care if they were white?" Daniel asked.

Lien nodded.

"I'd feel the same way no matter what they looked like," Daniel said.

"Besides, Daniel's only half-black," Jason reminded her.

"Everyone's half-something," William said. "I'm a mix of Indian, Irish, and a bit of Carib black."

"Not me," Lien said, sounding proud. "I'm pure Chinese."

"And no one cares," Jason said. "Skin-deep is how most people here see us. None of us are fully white, but that doesn't make any difference, not even to the people in Over-the-Rhine."

"We're foreigners everywhere in the Far Beyond," Daniel agreed. "Some of the folks down there would call me an Oreo, black on the outside and white on the inside."

Jason smiled. "We're nothing like that. We're not white or black."

"Or Chinese," Lien piped up.

Serena felt like an outsider, listening to them. They were talking about their true home of Arylyn, and she wondered again if it was really as free and egalitarian as their descriptions.

"Check out the buildings," William said. "This area is supposed to have more historic buildings than any neighborhood outside of Harlem in New York."

Serena immediately noticed what William meant. Hidden beneath the boarded-up windows, and the crumbling facades stood once lovely buildings. "Why would they let them get this rundown?" she asked.

"Because this is the ghetto," Daniel said.

A sad, but true answer.

A short time after, they pulled in front of the church and disembarked the bus. The anklet William had given Serena for Christmas jingled with every step she took.

He noticed. "Is that the anklet?" William asked.

Serena drew up her pantleg to let him see.

He smiled, obviously pleased, and together they followed the other students into a large parish hall. Windows, yellowed and rippled with age, allowed in some sunshine while gusts of wind rattled them in their frames. Heavy, dark beams held up the ceiling and interspersed amongst them were rugged chandeliers to light the space. Several fragrant candles burned cheerily on a corner table. The floral scent did little to cover the musty odor filling the air.

While the students waited for the teachers to tell them what to do, Serena caught sight of a tall, blonde girl—strong and self-assured—accompanied by an Asian Indian boy, also tall and confident. He moved with a sublime grace.

She inhaled sharply. "Who's that?" she asked.

William looked to where she gestured. "Jessira. You know her. She's a freshman."

"I meant the boy she's with."

Based on his frown, William must have immediately understood who Serena meant. How could he not?

Even with his youthful, unfinished features, the handsome boy standing next to Jessira had an undeniable presence.

"I don't know," William said, his frowning deepening.

Serena suspected he might be jealous, and she paused in her thoughts, wondering if it might be true.

"He moves like . . ." William said.

"Like what?" Serena asked.

"Someone dangerous," William finished.

Serena nodded agreement. William's observation rang true. The Indian moved like no freshman Serena had ever known, like no person she'd ever seen. Next to him even Isha would have seemed clumsy.

"Who is he?" Serena repeated.

"Let's find out," William suggested.

They had only taken two steps before the Indian noticed their approach and assumed a curious smile while he awaited them.

"Hello, William, Serena," Jessira said. "This is Rukh. My . . . good friend."

"Pleasure to meet you," Rukh said. Around his neck he wore a silver chain with a pendant of a calico cat.

"Pleasure to meet you, too," William said.

"Are you new here?" Serena asked.

Rukh quirked a smile at Jessira before answering. "I arrived yesterday. I'm learning what's required somewhat later than I intended."

Serena frowned, trying to parse out Rukh's words. They contained a sense of hidden meaning.

"Gather round," said Father Jameson, their religious studies instructor. "We'll be splitting up into three groups. Each of you will be assigned a different part of the church. As soon as you're done with whatever you're told to do, come back and find me. You'll then get your next task."

William and Serena were assigned to the same group as Jason, Daniel, and Lien, and they were sent to clean out a couple of rooms in the back of the church. Cobwebs curtained the corners, and dust covered every surface.

Serena grimaced, although the work didn't truly disgust her. She'd done far worse. Nevertheless, she knew the others would expect her to respond with an unhappy expression.

"We should make this work last," William suggested. "Take our time with it, like an old janitor friend of mine once told me."

"When did you have an old janitor friend?" Jason asked.

"Back when I worked for the city library a few summers ago," William answered. "He always told me to slow down and take it easy."

"I'd rather get it over with," Serena said, still grimacing. "The sooner the better."

A few hours and a few chores later, the church looked much better. Afterward, they gathered in the chapel. While everyone slowly streamed in, Serena cast her gaze about the sanctuary. The stained-glass windows above the altar immediately captured her attention. One of them depicted the risen Christ with lambs and children at his feet. The image touched a fallow part of her heart, one she wished swelled with more life.

Father Jameson interrupted her thoughts when he began the service. "Come to me, all you who are weary and burdened," he said, "and I will give you rest. Take my yoke upon you and learn from me, for I am gentle and humble in heart, and you will find rest for your souls. For my yoke is easy and my burden is light."

"That's beautiful," Serena whispered. She wished such a loving God was real.

"It's from Matthew, chapter eleven," Jason told her.

Next came communion, and William, Jason, and Daniel all went to receive.

Lien stayed with Serena. "Us heathens need to stick together," she whispered with a half-smile.

During communion, a musician played a soft melody on a guitar, and Serena closed her eyes, praying for her sister.

———————◄ ● ►———————

William leaned back in his chair, feet propped on his desk as he tried to focus on the slim novel in his hands, *Against the Fall of Night*. However, his attention continued to drift, and his gaze flitted about his room. The *Galactica*, the *Enterprise*, and the *Millennium Falcon* had pride of place on a bookshelf. The pennants for the Bengals and the Reds still hung from the wall. The only change was over his bed where a poster from *Blade Runner* had replaced Eddie the Head. Otherwise, his room embodied its nerdish normality, but a new sense of unreality had entered William's life.

Ever since they'd survived Kohl Obsidian attacks, he'd spent many hours reading about the necrosed. Mr. Zeus had brought back several books on the topic, and William had devoured them. Early on, he'd quickly discovered that much of what the magi considered to be settled knowledge was oftentimes grossly wrong. Some of it was poor deduction, while other supposed facts were nothing more than laughable supposition.

For instance, in one book the author had advised that the best way to kill a necrosed was to stab the creature through the heart with a sword made of white-gold. Other than sounding like a cool weapon—Thomas Covenant would have loved such a weapon—it was a stupid idea.

So too, was the explanation of how a necrosed covered such

vast distances so quickly. They ran really fast. Nothing more. Just speed.

How dumb.

But in one book, *The Dying Dead*, the author might have actually come across a necrosed a time or two. That volume contained a reference to what happened if the blood of a necrosed infected an *asrasin*. According to the author, there were three possible outcomes. The blood would transform the *asrasin* into a necrosed, the blood would kill the *asrasin,* or the *asrasin's lorethasra* would purify the corruption of the necrosed. In that last case, the blood became a blessing rather than a curse, but in all of history, only two such cases had ever been documented.

The claim in *The Dying Dead* had sent William's thoughts traveling back to his first meeting with Kohl Obsidian. When the necrosed had confronted them at the *saha'asra* in West Virginia, the monster had snatched William's *nomasra* and the locket had burned the monster, causing him to bleed. That blood *had* mixed with William's own, penetrating through a scratch delivered by one of Kohl's talons.

Until reading that account, William had never considered exactly what had occurred during his first meeting with the necrosed.

Now, he did.

Ever since his parents' death, he'd noticed his increased speed, strength, and stamina, even his improved sense of balance, and those changes had accelerated following that initial confrontation with Kohl.

Had something happened to him?

"Earth to William," Jason said.

30

William snapped upright in his chair and blinked. "What?"

"I've been calling your name for five minutes. You ready?"

"For what?"

"Sparring. It's time for judo," Jason said. "Hurry up."

"Sorry, man. I forgot." William said. He glanced at the digital clock on his nightstand and noticed the time. "Let me change and I'll be right down."

"Be down in five," Jason shouted over his shoulder as he left William's room.

Sparring against Jason.

William's thoughts drifted again. Recently he'd started winning matches against Jason. In fact, of the two of them William was now the faster and stronger, and while he lacked his friend's skill, that too could be changing.

A few weeks ago, Jason had asked about it, but at the time William hadn't known the answer. He now did. Or at least he had his suspicions, suspicions he feared might be correct and which he feared to discuss.

Kohl Obsidian had touched William. Blessed or cursed, he wasn't sure, but he had yet to tell Jason and Mr. Zeus about it. According to *The Dying Dead*, history had never recorded what happened to those two individuals blessed by the blood of a necrosed. Reading between the lines, though, it seemed likely that they had met a terrible end at the hands of their fellow *asrasins*.

Jake plunked his books on the school library table where Sonya and Steve already sat and prepared to get some work done. A mix of old chandeliers and new fluorescent fixtures provided lighting, and circular tables, populated by busily scribbling students, took up the central portion of the large, open room. The edges of the library held the stacks, the odd assortment of books and magazines. They left the place smelling like old paper.

Jake liked it.

Twenty minutes later, though, he hadn't gotten past the first page of the history text he meant to read. Instead, he found himself staring out at the morose weather, a typical midwestern winter day—cold and windy with endless, scudding gray clouds—and wishing for somewhere warm and tropical.

Jake grimaced. *February. The worst month of the year. Utterly pointless, with nothing to do or see.* At least the other winter months had the excitement and joy of sports and playoffs to brighten their dismal days.

But not February.

By February the Super Bowl had ended, March Madness was weeks away, and the sweet smell of fresh cut grass from baseball's Opening Day was a distant hope. The only thing of note in February, that crappiest of months, was the Daytona 500. Speed Week.

Jake sighed. Sunshine, pretty girls, and fast cars all collected down at a Florida beach. How he'd like to be somewhere warm like that. Maybe even farther south. Like the Caribbean. Maybe St. John's. His family had gone there once for Spring Break, and he'd loved it. The sand, sunshine, and warm water. Anything to escape Cincinnati's dismal winters.

And he needed that escape.

Jake frowned as unwanted memories rushed back. He'd tried to forget what he had seen, but every day the same scene recurred in his mind. And he hadn't been the only one to see it, either. All his friends had. They'd all been there in Winton Woods when William, Jason, and Serena had shown up with swords in hand and fear on their faces.

At the time, Jake had scoffed at their concerns, all the way to the moment *he* had arrived. The creature who haunted his thoughts, the monster out of nightmares, a demon with talon-tipped hands, fangs like a bear, and a snarling voice of terror.

Who or what had that thing been?

Weeks later, Jake still had no idea. During the Christmas holidays, he had gone back to Winton Woods—only during the daytime—searching for William, Jason, and Serena's remains. He'd even ventured a short way in to the forest, but he'd found nothing. No trace. No blood. No bodies. Not even the crappy truck William had driven. Nothing to give any sense as to what might have happened to the three of them. They'd simply fallen off the face of the Earth.

And then a few days later, right before Christmas, everyone who'd seen the monster started acting weird, like they didn't know what Jake was talking about. They claimed to have no memory of the fanged horror who had chased them through Winton Woods. It was like one day they knew, and the next day, they didn't. As literal as that.

It hadn't taken long for Jake to figure out what must have happened to his friends. Something had made them all forget about the monster. Someone had stolen their memories, and if Jake wasn't careful, that same someone would come for him, too.

"Jake!" Sonya snapped her fingers in front of his face.

He started and glanced around, relieved to find himself still in the library.

"Where were you?" she asked.

"Thinking about college," he said, managing a rueful smile even while guilt ate at him at how often he'd been lying to Sonya. He took a sidelong glimpse of William and his friends who sat several tables over. He tried not to shiver when his eyes passed over Jason.

"You sure?" Sonya asked, sounding doubtful. "You've been acting weird ever since Christmas break. What's going on?"

"Nothing," Jake said, a touch of irritation creeping into his voice. "I was thinking about college. That's all."

Sonya eyed him with a frown. "Why are you worried about college?" she asked. "You've got your scholarship to Notre Dame."

"I still don't know why you chose that program," Steve said. "They haven't been good in, like, forever. You see how bad Miami beat them a few years ago?"

"They've turned things around since then," Jake replied.

"Whatever. They aren't going to be any good this year or next, and you know it."

"Yeah, they will," Jake said. "They've got me."

Steve snorted in derision. "Sure thing, superstar."

Jake didn't have a chance to reply because Mrs. Menshaw, the librarian, shushed them. Sonya and Steve returned to their studies, and Jake tried to do the same, but he couldn't concentrate on his work. He continued to wonder about William and his friends.

Who were they? They laughed and talked like nothing

bothered them—Lien even sang non-stop—but their attitudes came off as muted compared to how they'd been before Christmas.

William caught him staring, and Jake offered a brief bob of his head. William nodded in return before laughing at something Serena had said. But Jason looked Jake's way with what might have been wary curiosity in his eyes.

Jake quickly shifted his gaze away and suppressed another shudder. He remembered the creature at Winton Woods, but he also remembered Jason, and the lines of fire erupting from his hands.

CHAPTER 3:
TRUTHS AND FEARS

February 1987

Serena shadowboxed in the basement, sparring by herself as she worked the punching bag. She slipped a pretend jab and fired off a right-left-right combo before circling to the left and taking an angle for a high kick. A resounding thud echoed through the basement as the heavy bag rocked on its chain.

Serena instantly brought up her hands, defending and ready to go at it again, but something gave her pause.

Isha. He'd entered the basement on quiet feet and stood behind her.

Serena turned to face him.

His posture and demeanor contained equal parts excitement and wariness.

"What is it?" Serena asked, breathing heavily. She'd been shadowboxing for the better part of an hour, and she leaned over with hands on her knees.

"I've figured it out."

"Figured what out, sir?" Serena straightened, hands on hips now.

"How to break the *nomasra*," Isha answered.

Serena grabbed a towel and collected her thoughts as she wiped off the sweat glistening on her arms and face. She'd secretly hoped the remedy for breaking William's *nomasra* would escape her teacher, but experience should have taught her how forlorn such a hope would be. When Isha searched for a solution, he almost always found it.

"It's only a temporary solution, but it should work," he said.

"What do I need to do?" Serena pushed aside her disappointment. Failure to bring William in might still be forgivable for her, but not for Isha, not anymore.

He handed her a compact meant to hold a woman's face powder. Serena studied it, trying to figure out how to open the container. She'd never applied much makeup before.

"Handle what's inside with utmost care," Isha cautioned. "It's an acid."

"An acid?" Serena paused in the act of opening the compact.

"Only for items imbued with *asra*. Wipe some of the powder on William's locket, and the magic of the *nomasra* will fail for a short period of time."

"What would it do if it got on my skin?"

"A rash if the dose was strong enough," Isha replied. "Otherwise, a little bit of itchiness. Nothing more."

Serena studied the tan powder in the box. "Won't William feel it on his skin?"

"Not with the amount you'll need," Isha answered. "But it took me a great deal of effort to create. I had to drain one of my *nomasras* to make what you hold in your hands." He gave her a stern gaze. "Don't waste it."

"You're certain it won't leave a residue."

"William won't notice a thing," Isha said in assurance. "The powder is undetectable. It's has no smell or greasiness, and best of all, it's temporary."

"Odorless and tasteless," Serena said with a sad smile. She thought of iocaine powder from *The Princess Bride*, a book William had loaned her last semester, back in the fall when things were so much easier. "And if I refuse to do this?" she asked.

"You think you can escape to Arylyn?" Isha asked.

"Of course not," Serena said. "But we could let William escape there. No one would know. We could tell my father that he left for Arylyn before we could secure him."

"And why would we do something so foolish? Because you have affection for the boy?" Isha shook his head before focusing his intense regard on Serena. "You know the love I have for you, but I won't allow William to escape. I won't risk my future—our futures—based on your childish pity for him. We will succeed in your pilgrimage."

Serena felt a part of her die. "Yes, sir," she said. William, her first true friend, and she had to betray him. He would hate her forever, and she would deserve it.

"You will do this?" Isha pressed.

She had wanted to keep William safe, but it had always been long odds at best. Her course had narrowed to a single choice, and Serena shoved down her sorrow and regrets. She lifted her head and met Isha's gaze. "I'll do it."

"Good," Isha said. "If all goes as planned, we'll be home before spring."

"And if I am unable to apply this acid you've created?" Serena asked.

"Must I spell it out?" Isha asked.

Serena watched him with what she hoped was expectant curiosity.

Isha's features hardened. "Your sister will pay the price."

Serena gasped, unable to contain her shock. Her heart pounded, and she silently cursed herself. If Isha knew of her feelings for Selene, then what about her father? Maybe he knew, too.

"The resemblance is obvious—many suspect you are true sisters rather than adopted siblings—but more importantly, you weren't careful enough in hiding your affection for the girl. And if I know, then your father does as well. Why do you think he's brought Selene so close to his side? You must know he won't be kind to her if you fail him."

"I understand."

"Then you'll do this?"

"I already said I would," Serena answered.

Isha gave a satisfied nod. "Then let's have no more foolish talk of failure," he said, sounding genial and pleased. He gestured to the heavy bag. "I'll leave you to your training."

Serena waited for him to depart before resuming her work on the heavy bag. She threw combinations of punches and kicks, gritting her teeth as she sought to replace grief over what she had to do with anger. Weakness could not be allowed. Not now. Not ever.

But despite her best efforts, two tears worked their way down her face. They ruined her composure, and Serena pressed her face into the heavy bag and silently cried.

She allowed the tears to flow for a count of ten before she pushed off the bag and dried her face. *Enough.* She firmed her features, shoving aside the sorrow. *No more weakness.* She would soon have to return to Sinskrill, and there she would have to be hard and strong in order to survive.

Jason approached his grandfather's workshop with trepidation. He grimaced, hesitating a moment before raising his hand and rapping on the door.

"Come in," Mr. Zeus said.

Jason opened the door and discovered his grandfather grinding a newly forged blade and setting the edge. The comforting smell of metal and hot oil filled the air, and a mishmash of tools lay scattered about the workshop: hammers, tongs, and various clamps. The forge lay quiescent, but heat still billowed off it; and the overhead fan flapped gusts of wind. Filings littered the ground and hot oil had spilled onto the floor from when Mr. Zeus had quenched the blade he currently shaped.

Jason grimaced at the mess, knowing he'd have to straighten it up. He mentally sighed. *Might as well get to it now.*

"Decide not to go to the arcade?" Mr. Zeus asked. He kept his attention on his work, moving from the grinder to whetstone, and rasped the newly forged knife against it in practiced, efficient movements.

"Had some homework to do first," Jason answered.

"And?"

Jason shook his head. He should have realized Mr. Zeus would guess something was bothering him. "And I wanted to talk to you about William."

"What about him?" Mr. Zeus tested the edge of the blade on a piece of paper. It sliced through with a hiss. He drew out a leather strop.

"I know he's a *raha'asra*, but I don't get what we're still doing here. We should be back home by now."

Mr. Zeus looked up from his work. "It has to be his choice, remember? It's how Arylyn does things."

"Sinskrill wouldn't care."

"We're not Sinskrill," Mr. Zeus said. "We're better than them."

Jason had no response. He began gathering tools and putting them away while he sorted out his thoughts.

"What's this really about?" Mr. Zeus asked. "Why do you suddenly think we should abduct William to Arylyn?"

Jason shrugged. "I don't think we should abduct him, but I don't know if it's safe for us to stay, either. I've got this feeling . . . things are changing."

"We'll leave when he's ready," Mr. Zeus said. "It's our way. We only take potentials who are willing to come. We don't ever force them."

"I'm not talking about forcing him. Just strongly encouraging."

"Why? We have six magi here. What could possibly endanger William that has you so worried?"

"None of us could help him much when a necrosed showed up," Jason reminded Mr. Zeus.

"You really think another necrosed is heading our way?" his grandfather asked.

Jason wavered. "It's not a necrosed," he finally said. "It might be worse." He had Mr. Zeus' entire attention now.

"It's William himself. His abilities," Jason said.

Mr. Zeus quirked an eyebrow. "What abilities are you referring to?"

"You know how clumsy and weak he was when we first met? Even the simplest sword forms gave him trouble. The weapon was too heavy for him. But after his parents died he immediately started getting better."

"If I recall, Landon had the same growth, did he not? Weak until he wasn't? Sounds like a family trait, if you ask me."

"Which I'd be fine with, except William's gotten even better since our battle against Kohl Obsidian," Jason replied. "He's more athletic than I am now. Before Christmas he wasn't. That kind of improvement . . ." Jason shook his head. "It's not natural."

Mr. Zeus frowned. "What do you suspect?"

"Kohl Obsidian bled when he attacked us at the *saha'asra* in West Virginia," Jason said. "I saw it. It happened when he tore off William's *nomasra*, the one that suppresses *asra*, including the *asra* binding a dead creature to life. The *nomasra* hurt the necrosed, and he bled. But what if Kohl's blood got on William, or in him somehow?"

For once Mr. Zeus was rendered speechless. He opened his mouth to say something, seemed to think better of it, and settled for leaning back on his stool while he stroked his beard in thought. "I don't know," he finally said. "But I've read that the blood of a necrosed is the infection that transforms an *asrasin* into one of those creatures. You think it's happening to William?"

"No. I already looked into that, right after we got back," Jason answered. "The transformation, if it was going to happen, would have already occurred or the *asrasin* would have died. Or . . ." Again, Jason hesitated. "Sometimes the blood of the necrosed can be purified by the *asrasin*'s *lorethasra*, and it becomes a blessing instead of a curse."

Mr. Zeus leaned forward in his chair, his gaze intense. "What happens to those with this so-called blessing?"

"I don't know." Jason shrugged. "The books you brought back don't say anything about it."

Mr. Zeus' gaze turned faraway. "I'll have someone research it at Arylyn's library," he said. "For now, make no mention of your concerns to William. Keep it between the two of us. No one else."

"If William has the blood of a necrosed, we may not be able to take him to Arylyn."

"Weren't you the one arguing about how we should snatch him up and take him there immediately?"

"I know," Jason said in frustration. "I'm contradicting myself."

"Then what is it?"

"William has a chance to be a very powerful *asrasin*. We all know that. And if he's truly as powerful as we suspect, he might be able to do on his own what it takes both of our *raha'asras* to accomplish."

"None of this argues against us taking him to Arylyn," Mr. Zeus noted.

"The book mentioning this blessing says the blessing of a necrosed extends in strange ways. It might make William even stronger, as in the very way he's changed."

43

"Again, you're not offering an argument against taking him to Arylyn."

Now came the heart of Jason's worries. "What if William hasn't been blessed?" he suggested. "What if he's still in the midst of transforming into a necrosed, but the transformation has been halted because of the *nomasra* he's wearing?"

Mr. Zeus lips pursed in thought. "I don't think it's likely. It's not how that particular *nomasra* works."

A wave of relief passed over Jason.

"But as I mentioned before," Mr. Zeus continued, "I'll have someone research it. If none of the texts tell us what to do, we'll ask William to remove the *nomasra* and observe what happens to him."

"And if he's in the midst of transforming?"

Mr. Zeus' visage filled with sorrow. "You know what we'll have to do."

Jason nodded, his heart heavy at what he'd suspected all along would be Mr. Zeus' answer. "I guess this isn't the best time to bring up my concerns about Serena, then," he said.

———◆———

"It's beautiful," Serena said to William, pretending to study his locket. All she had needed to do was ask to look at it, and he'd passed it over to her without removing it.

"I can ask Mr. Zeus to make you one," William offered.

Serena smiled, feigning pleasure. "Thank you. I've got the exact picture to put in it, too. One of my mother." She pretended to frown in concern. "Looks like I smudged the locket. Let me clean it." She reached into her purse and pulled out a tissue, the corner of which held the acid Isha had made. She carefully applied it to the back of William's locket while she supposedly removed her smudged fingerprints. "There." She shoved the tissue into her purse, all the while taking care not to allow any of the acid to touch her skin.

Fifteen minutes later, Serena struggled to maintain her patience and composure while she waited for Isha's acid to eat away at the *nomasra*. She and William shared study hall in the library, and at any moment, the bindings keeping William's *lorethasra* contained would temporarily fade away, but then what would happen? Would he notice? And what would he say if he did? Her thoughts whirled around and over themselves, looping into a knot of uncertainty. Centered within it, though, lay the question of what she should do once she confirmed William's status as a *raha'asra*.

She didn't want to see him hurt, but she saw no way to protect him. She could lie to Isha, but he would see through any deception of hers. Then he'd tell her father what she'd done even as he stole William away to Sinskrill, and Selene would be the one to pay the price for Serena's failure.

Or she could confess her secrets to William and Mr. Zeus, something that carried its own set of risks. After all, she and Isha were mahavans, enemies to the magi. They likely wouldn't overlook that fact, or all the falsehoods Serena had told them over the past few months.

As mahavans reckoned matters, enemies destroyed their weakened foes, and Serena had no reason to think the magi were any different. Mr. Zeus and the other magi of Arylyn would likely attack her and Isha. Strip them even. And why not? Who could stop them? After all, they outnumbered her and Isha six-to-two.

A picture arose in Serena's mind of her sister, innocent and helpless in the clutches of their unforgiving father. Selene's features torn with fear, forced to pursue the life of a bishan. Or worse, Selene with the obdurate gaze of a mahavan. None were images Serena could bear. While the notion of betraying William left her cold and full of sorrow, Selene might not survive Sinskrill without Serena's guidance and protection.

"You okay?" William asked, his eyes crinkled in concern.

Serena frowned in confusion. It took her a moment to focus on the here and now. She flashed a smile. "I'm fine," she replied. "Just thinking about my homework." She demonstrated by lifting her American History text so William could see the cover. This week, they'd started in on Woodrow Wilson, a president Serena had quickly learned to detest. The man had been an authoritarian racist, almost a fascist really. In many ways, he reminded Serena of her own father, all the way down to his belief in eugenics.

William grunted acknowledgement before resuming whatever he was studying.

Serena returned her gaze to her own text, but as before, she couldn't focus on anything but her own worries. The words of the history book swam before her eyes.

It didn't help that William's *nomasra* started flashing its weakness, distracting her further. The black wall blocking her view of William's *lorethasra* briefly flickered a translucent gray. Whenever it did, Serena caught a glimpse of who William might become as an *asrasin*. Thus far, it hadn't been enough to make a definitive determination, but soon she'd have her answers.

Too bad Mr. Zeus had never taught William how to hide his *lorethasra*. If he had acquired such a skill, then Serena might never learn what he could become.

While she waited for William's *nomasra* to fail, she felt someone's gaze upon her, and she searched for the source. Sitting on the far side of the library, she discovered who it was. *Jake Ridley. Again.* Serena frowned. He didn't spend as much time as he used to with his sycophants, not even Sonya Bowyer, and Serena caught him staring at her a lot. She wondered why. His eyes never held the peculiar assessment of a boy interested in a girl, but rather of someone searching for an answer.

Serena frowned further when she caught sight of something odd about Jake. She hadn't noticed it until this very moment, and her eyes widened in astonishment. Pale, white coruscations suffused Jake's being. They pulsed like an arterial tree, moving in time to his heartbeat.

Serena bit back a gasp.

Jake held the unprimed potential to become an *asrasin*.

Serena quickly shifted her eyes back to her history book. Her thoughts cascaded. Locating a single potential in a decade was rare. Finding two in the same city, at the same time, who happened to know one another was unheard of, almost miraculous.

But Sinskrill would only care about Jake if he had a truly sublime potential, and as far as Serena could tell, he didn't. Which meant he had no value to her.

Serena tried to focus on her textbook, but once again William's flickering *nomasra* distracted her.

"You sure you're all right?" William asked again.

47

"I'm fine," Serena reassured him.

"Is that why you've been reading the same page for the past ten minutes?" he asked, flicking his gaze to her book.

Serena looked at the page and realized William was right. "I don't like Woodrow Wilson," she admitted with a sheepish smile.

"You sure it's not something else?" he asked.

"Like what?" Serena asked, finding herself annoyed by his persistence.

"By everything that's happened. Kohl, Aia, Landon . . . all of it. And now we have to act like everything's normal when nothing could be farther from the truth."

"You feel it, too?" Serena asked, the lie regarding her disquiet slipping readily from her lips.

"I'm going to be a magus. I'll have to leave everything I know. My family. Landon. You." He shifted in his chair, wearing a sad demeanor. "It's not as easy as it sounds."

"It doesn't sound easy at all," Serena said. "But after seeing what you'll be able to do, your destiny, it makes me feel even more like a nobody." The lie, though it came as easily as always, filled Serena with guilt.

"In this world or any other, I don't think you'll ever be a nobody," William said.

"You're sweet to say that." Serena answered his kind words with a sincere smile.

"You want to go get some ice cream? The cafeteria might not have Graeter's, but it still tastes good."

"No," Serena replied. "I want to study. For real this time."

William shrugged and bent his head again to his text.

Serena stared at her book as well, and this time she made a

show of turning the pages. However, concentration continued to elude her as William's *nomasra* pulsed, the translucent flashes coming faster and faster.

Hurry up, she urged. Jason, Lien, or Daniel might show up, which would be an absolute disaster. They'd sense the *nomasra's* failure, and wonder why, a question she'd rather not have them ask. Not when she was so close.

The end came unexpectedly. The blackness of the *nomasra* faded away with a sharp snap like a cracked stone. It was a sound only Serena heard, and William's *lorethasra* became clearly visible. It glowed like white fire, pulsing throughout his body, a more potent version of Jake's own pale, unprimed one. William's *lorethasra* held a rustling green tendril of Earth that smelled like ivy; a line of blue—his Water—that swayed and susurrated like waves. An angry yellow flare of Fire carried a mild sulfurous stink, while Air whispered, a clear thread holding a fresh, glacial scent. All were evenly distributed amongst a thick band of bone-white Spirit with a scent that reminded Serena of a pine forest in spring.

There was no doubt. He had the *lorethasra* of a *raha'asra.*

William sensed nothing and kept his eyes upon his book. He had no idea his life as he knew it, his hopes and dreams, had all been gutted.

He glanced at Serena with a questioning smile, one she forced herself to respond in kind even while she wanted to cry.

———■●■———

"He's a *raha'asra*," Serena confirmed as soon she got home.

Isha looked up with a pleased smile from the book he was reading. He carefully marked his page and set the volume aside. "Tell me everything," he commanded, his visage characteristically intense.

Serena explained what she had done, and what she had observed.

"And the *nomasra*?" Isha asked.

"It resumed its normal state a few minutes later. None of the magi will notice any change to it."

Isha smiled wider and steepled his fingers. "Excellent news," he said. "Sinskrill will be pleased."

"You mean my father will be pleased."

Isha waved aside her words. "Is there a difference?"

"No one is greater than Sinskrill itself, but he who gave it life. Those who forget earn my ire," she said, quoting from *Shet's Counsel*, the accumulated wisdom of Sinskrill's true Lord and Master.

"Your father forgets nothing. He knows Shet rules our home, and he serves him with all sincerity," Isha replied. "But understand this. As long as your father has the Lord's approval, he *is* Sinskrill."

"And for my father's approval, we have to sell William into slavery?" Serena asked, letting her bitterness show.

Isha threw his head back and laughed. "Child, we're all slaves, even your father. Did you not hear what you quoted?"

"I don't like being a slave," Serena said.

"Who does? But it is the way of life on Sinskrill. You might as well dislike gravity." Isha snorted. "Was there anything else of note you wish to report?"

"There was one other oddity." Serena hesitated, not sure she should even bother mentioning her discovery.

"Am I to guess or will you tell me?" Isha asked with an expectant arch of his eyebrows.

"Jake Ridley is a potential. He hasn't been exposed to a *saha'asra* yet, but it's there."

"Jake Ridley? The boy who saw Kohl Obsidian?"

"The very one," Serena confirmed. "The greater oddity, though, is I never sensed his potential before today."

"Never?"

"Never."

"How powerful might he become?"

"Not very. Average at best."

Isha tsked. "A pity. Average we have aplenty on Sinskrill. The extraordinary would have been a useful find, the final piece to bring us glory when we return home."

"Glory in someone else's misery," Serena said, twisting the knife.

Isha never noticed. Instead, he stroked his chin in thought. "What's changed about this Jake Ridley?" he seemed to muse more than ask. "You should have sensed his potential long ago."

"So should Jason and the other magi."

"Yet none of you did. Or at least they never mentioned it if they did." Isha's frown deepened.

"Why's this bothering you so much?" Serena asked.

"Because it doesn't make any sense. You're telling me Jake Ridley was a normal person, and now he's suddenly a potential. An oddity such as this deserves thought." Isha's eyes grew distant, and the room fell silent while Serena waited for him to finish his considerations.

"Has anything unusual happened to Mr. Ridley?" Isha asked, breaking the quiet.

"Other than his encounter with Kohl Obsidian? No."

"Did Kohl touch Jake?"

"No."

"And you're absolutely certain he's always been a normal person until now?"

"Yes," Serena said, allowing some of her exasperation to show.

Isha lowered his lids in a gaze of warning.

"I'm sorry, sir, but you're questioning my intelligence, and I still don't know why you find this particular oddity so fascinating."

"This oddity is so fascinating because, if what you say is true, a normal person became a potential in a matter of weeks. That doesn't happen. In fact, it shouldn't be possible."

"And yet it occurred."

Isha stiffened, and he inhaled sharply. "Blood."

"Blood?" Serena had no idea what Isha meant.

"Blood can be transformative," Isha said. "It can turn an *asrasin* into a necrosed, a witch into an unformed, and a *raha'asra's* blood is said to be the most potent of all. History tells it can cure almost any magical malady. And in rare instances, it can change a normal person into a potential."

"You think William's blood somehow got into Jake?" Serena said, not hiding her doubt.

"Perhaps," Isha said, "but that's a mystery for another time." He focused his raptor-gaze upon Serena. "Do you know what abilities Jake might possess?"

Serena shook her head. "No. As I said before, he's average at best, and I didn't have a chance to study him closely enough."

"No matter. Leave him to me. I'll find out."

"And if he's nothing more than an average potential?"

"Then we have no use for him. Arylyn can have him."

Serena nodded silent agreement, hoping for Jake's sake that he proved uninteresting. He deserved a life free of mahavans and magi, a chance to live as he wanted to, somewhere outside this eternal war. Her eyes narrowed as she reconsidered Jake's *lorethasra*. It reminded her . . . She couldn't help it. She gasped.

"What is it?" Isha asked.

Serena couldn't quickly enough conceive a lie to hide her observation, and she also knew Isha would immediately see through the fabrication.

"I didn't make the connection before," Serena said, while she silently prayed to whatever deity might be listening on Jake's behalf. "His *lorethasra* is a pale imitation of William's."

Isha stilled. "You're certain?"

"Yes sir," Serena said, still silently cursing herself. Because of her, two young men would now become slaves to Sinskrill.

Isha noticed none of her self-loathing. "Two *raha'asras*?" he breathed, pleased and awed at the same time. "We shall stride to the highest ramparts of Sinskrill when we return. The Servitor's Chair isn't too high a reach for what we've discovered."

"Yes, sir," Serena agreed. She kept her visage and tone agreeable, but fresh guilt roiled her stomach like a bag of worms.

"We take them both," Isha said.

"Even though Jake's only average?"

"No *raha'asra* is merely average," Isha said as he rose to his feet. "I will test him myself before I inform Sinskrill. But if Jake Ridley is truly a *raha'asra*, then we'll take him, no matter how *average* he may be."

53

Nausea filled Serena's stomach. *She'd ruined Jake's life, too.*

"As soon as I verify the truth, I'll send for a war band. We'll take William and Jake as soon as they arrive."

"I don't want to see William hurt."

"He won't be," Isha said. "However, obedience and a desire to fight for his future is a requirement no one can overlook. Remember, nothing in this life is given. It's taken."

CHAPTER 4:
WHO TO MISTRUST

February 1987

Jake metaphorically girded his loins as he prepared to confront William, who sat alone at a cafeteria table. He held a small cup of ice cream and was reading some book, probably a fantasy. *Typical.*

All of William's friends had left for the day—the weekend, actually—even Serena, which was perfect as far as Jake was concerned. He needed privacy for when he confronted William, and he certainly didn't want any of Wilde's friends around, especially Jason.

Jake grimaced in annoyance, and if he was honest with himself, fear inspired most of his irritation. The image of fire blistering off Jason's hands like a wide-open flamethrower still shook him as much as the memory of that monstrous creature engulfed in those flames.

Right now, secure in the safety of the cafeteria, the power of those terrifying images receded, and Jake judged Wilde to be cautiously approachable. At least no deadly monsters or fire-throwers lurked nearby.

To get to this point, Jake had picked a fight with William, something that had landed them both in jug, in detention.

A persistent niggle of doubt remained in Jake's mind, though.

What if *William* could also throw fire from his hands? Or what if he could mess with a person's head, make them forget things the way Jake's friends had forgotten about Winton Woods? He wasn't sure what he would do then. Jake chewed his lip in worry. Maybe he should forget about confronting William. Tell him it was all a big mistake.

Jake's jaw firmed.

No.

He wanted answers. He needed them, was desperate for them. He had to understand what he'd seen that dreadful night.

Three other students shared jug with them, but the others weren't paying attention to him. Neither was Mr. Callahan, who had watch over them.

Jake approached William's table. "Can we talk?" he asked without preamble.

"You picked a fight with me," William said, his face tight with anger and suspicion. "Why would I want to talk to you?"

"It wasn't a fight. It was an argument," Jake said, taking a seat opposite William.

"Whatever. I'm still stuck here after school because of you." Anger filled William's voice.

Jake puffed up, wormy fear fueling feigned anger. He used his most intimidating voice and posture. "If we'd really thrown down, you'd have ended up bleeding, like you did when I decked you during the Oklahoma drill after football season. You remember that, right?"

William nodded. "I remember. You caught me when I wasn't ready. But try me now. You've got all my attention."

Jake mentally cursed. William sounded serious and pissed off, the last thing he wanted. He'd gone to great lengths to get some answers from Wilde, not provoke an actual fight with him.

"What do you want?" William growled.

Jake started.

"It's written all over your face. You want something. What is it?"

"Answers," Jake blurted. He immediately winced. There went his plan of asking probing questions meant to get William talking.

"About what?"

"About a night in Winton Woods."

William stiffened.

Rising excitement billowed through Jake. He was on the right track. "About a creature trying to kill us all, and about you, Serena, and Jason fighting it."

William pretended to laugh, but he was a terrible liar. His wide-open eyes gave him away.

"I knew it," Jake said, and laughed with unexpected relief.

"I don't know what you're talking about," William huffed.

"Yes, you do. You know exactly what I'm talking about. I remember that night, everything about it."

"Really," William insisted, "I don't know what you're talking about." This time his attempted lie was more believable.

"Steve Aldo remembers, too," Jake lied.

William flushed, and surprise and worry flicked across his features.

"See? You do know what I'm talking about," Jake said, smiling in satisfaction.

William shook his head in negation. "No, I don't. I was only—"

"You know. Stop lying," Jake demanded. He slapped the table in frustration. "Sorry Mr. Callahan," he said when the teacher looked their way. "We're trying to talk out our differences."

"Then do it more quietly," Mr. Callahan ordered before turning back to grading papers.

"Okay. You think you know something," William said. "Now what?"

"Steve saw that thing," Jake began. "Everyone did, and they remembered for a while. But then one day none of them did. The strange thing is, a couple days after that monster attacked us, I met Jason's kooky grandfather."

"He's not kooky," William said, a warning note in his voice.

"Whatever." Jake shrugged. "But it was the day after I talked to him that no one could remember a damn thing anymore. After I saw what Jason can do, I figure his grandfather can do even more, like make people forget about a battle with some nightmare creature in the middle of Winton Woods."

"All right. You remember something. I get it," William said.

A fresh surge of relief washed over Jake. "Thank God. I was afraid it had all been a terrible dream."

"You were hoping this *wasn't* a dream?" William shook his head in disbelief. "Dumbass."

"If it was a dream, then it meant I was going crazy." Jake leaned forward. "What was that thing? Before he forgot, Steve called him the Devilman."

"His name was Kohl Obsidian."

"Was?"

"I killed him." William shifted. "Well, me, Jason, and Landon."

Jake frowned in confusion. "Your dead brother?"

"I thought he was dead, too, but he isn't. He came back and helped me, and we killed Kohl."

Jake stared aghast at William. He said it so matter-of-factly. Killing someone. Like it was nothing. A shiver passed through him. This was the person he'd mocked and jeered for all these years? This was the person he'd bullied? All the while, he'd never known that William Wilde had the heart of killer.

"What are you?" Jake whispered.

"Just a regular guy," William replied.

"No, you're not," Jake said. "You're something else."

William rolled his eyes. "What do you want?"

"I told you, I want to know the truth. I want to know what's happening to me. Why do I remember but no one else does?"

"I'll tell you what I'm allowed to," William said. He held up a cautionary hand at Jake's incipient protest. "And before you start threatening to tell anyone about this, think about whether you want to piss of someone who can throw fire, cause earthquakes, and erase memories."

———•———

Isha wore a tight-lipped frown when Serena arrived home. "Where is William?" he demanded as soon as she entered the house.

"Jug. In detention," Serena answered.

"How did he end up in jug?" Isha asked.

"He got into an argument with Jake Ridley."

Isha rolled his eyes. "I thought those two had reached a truce."

"We all thought so," Serena said, "but apparently not."

"Did they come to blows?"

"No. Just a heated argument."

"A heated argument, no punches, and our two *raha'asras* end up in jug together," Isha summarized.

"Yes to the first two points, but we don't know what Jake is, at least not yet. What's wrong?"

"We do know. I've observed Jake. He's a *raha'asra*," Isha said.

"Oh." A simple, stupid word to ineffectually express Serena's regret. Poor Jake. *His life as he knew it had ended, and he had no notion of its passing.*

"Whatever has you bothered, you need to control it," Isha advised. "We return home soon, and the Walkers hear all."

Serena blinked at the warning. While she and Isha had a unique bond, one of friendship and family, on Sinskrill such ties and concerns would be considered a weakness. Isha nodded as if he could read her mind.

Serena dipped her head in acknowledgement. She understood what her mentor needed from her. For some reason, at this moment, she had to suppress her emotions or risk having others take advantage of her. Or worse, hurt her through those she cared about.

"I think you misunderstand," Serena said. "I like William and his friends, and I've even grown to tolerate Jake, but I'm troubled because I don't know if William or Jake can survive on Sinskrill. Then what would happen to our reputations?"

"Better," Isha said softly. "Is there anything else about Jake troubling you?"

Serena frowned, trying to understand what was really going on. Danger lurked, and she had an odd sense of foreboding. She needed to be very careful with her next words.

As a result, Serena took time to organize her thoughts. "Jake Ridley is of no consequence," she began, "but I don't want him failing on Sinskrill. I want him to succeed. Our reputations depend on it. And, yes, I pity him. Our home is harsh, and as weak as he is, it'll be hard on him. He'll be like a wounded animal we won't put down."

Isha grunted in satisfaction. "An apt description."

"Will you tell me now what's happened?" Serena asked.

"Your father required an update, and I gave it to him," Isha said.

"What did you tell him?" Serena asked, careful that no worry marred her features or her voice. She remembered Isha's earlier, veiled warning, but even before this moment—whatever threat it held—she'd already begun the process of rebuilding her core of hardness, the armor around her heart. Very little could cause her hurt or fear now . . . or so she wanted to believe.

"Everything," Isha answered. "Several days ago, I dreamed to him all I knew about William. Even our suspicions about Jake."

The fortress around Serena's heart shuddered. Pieces flaked off, and she struggled to contain the panic in her heart. "What did he say?" she asked, although she suspected the answer.

"He dispatched a war-band," Isha answered. "They should arrive at any moment."

"What if William leaves for Arylyn before they arrive?"

Isha's gaze sharpened. "Then things will not go well for us," he said. "To lose the quarry at this late stage . . . Your father would not forgive such incompetence. We would pay a high price for our failure."

Serena nodded, and mentally scribed another line of grief and guilt to her ledger of sorrow. "William won't be going anywhere," she said. "We have movie-night this weekend."

"When?"

"Saturday. Tomorrow."

Isha nodded. "Good. This weekend is when we take him," he said. A second later he pierced Serena with his focused intensity. "Understand this: I will stop at *nothing* to prevent William from leaving for Arylyn. Am I clear?"

Serena nodded. Unspoken in Isha's threat was the promise that if William couldn't be brought to Sinskrill, he would be killed. Isha would see to it personally, and he would fight her if she tried to protect William.

"Your father wants William and Jake quite badly," Isha said. "He sent Dalton."

Serena cursed. "Dalton the hunter."

Isha nodded. "No one escapes his clutches once he's caught sight of his prey." He chuckled. "In a way, we've been extremely fortunate in this entire endeavor."

"In what way?" Serena asked. Her voice remained calm despite the storm of her emotions.

"The magi of Arylyn discovered William first. They groomed him for years, earning his friendship and trust. All along, they must have been fairly certain he would turn out to be a *raha'asra*, but before they can claim their certain prize, we'll steal both him and Jake from beneath their noses." Isha laughed. "They should have taken them both straightaway to Arylyn instead of bothering with this delusional notion of choice."

"They thought they had time," Serena said. "And they had no reason to suspect their prize was in danger, especially with six magi protecting him."

"It won't be enough," Isha promised.

"No, I suppose not," Serena agreed. Regret surfaced again, but she quickly suppressed it. She imagined her heart hardening into a stone. "What happens when the war-band arrives?"

Dalton the hunter, a tall, lanky man with narrow features, beady eyes, and the nose of a rat, stepped out of the shadows of the nearby darkened hallway and into the room.

Serena started.

"Then we capture William Wilde and take him to Sinskrill. Or we kill him." Dalton grinned, a toothy smile full of malice.

After his talk with Jake, William sat stone-faced and angry through the rest of detention, and he remained angry all the way home.

How could Jake remember what had happened? His memories of that night should have been erased, and until today, William had no reason to doubt they hadn't been. In fact, Jake had actually confirmed that his friends couldn't recall the events of that fateful evening but, somehow, he could.

How?

The question kept resonating in William's mind as he slammed shut the front door and stomped up the stairs.

Jason and Mr. Zeus sat in the family room, watching TV, *Jeopardy* from the sound of it.

I'll take "Stuff Jake Knows But Shouldn't" for five hundred, Alex, William thought sourly.

"How was jug?" Jason asked with an annoying grin.

"Fantastic," William muttered. He paced about the room, unable to sit still.

"What's got your goat?" Jason asked.

"You're not going to believe it," William said.

"Well, whatever has you bothered can wait," Mr. Zeus declared. "We have more important issues to discuss." He clicked off the TV.

"Yeah, we do," William agreed. "Jake Ridley for one."

"Yes. I imagine you consider him an annoyance," Mr. Zeus said. "Jason tells me the two of you got into a bit of a scuffle."

"More of an argument that got out of control," William said. "He picked a fight with me so we'd end up in jug together."

"I don't get why the two of you were arguing anyway," Jason said. "I thought you were becoming . . . I don't know, not friends, but at least not enemies."

"You're not listening," William said, his frustration bubbling. "Jake picked a fight with me so we'd *have to have* jug together."

Dawning understanding broke across Jason's face. "Why?"

"Because he knows."

"Knows what?" Mr. Zeus asked, his irritation obvious. "Stop being so mysterious."

William told them, gratified when both their jaws dropped open in shock. A weird German word perfectly captured how he felt: *schadenfreude*.

"How could this happen?" Jason demanded of Mr. Zeus.

Mr. Zeus frowned in thought while he stroked his beard and puffed his pipe. "Jake's an unprimed potential," he eventually said, sounding contemplative.

"No, he's not. He can't be," Jason said. "We'd have noticed if he was."

"Only an *asrasin* or a potential *asrasin* wouldn't have been affected by the braid I placed on him," Mr. Zeus countered.

"Braids are spells, right?" William asked.

Mr. Zeus nodded. "Or any type of action using *asra*. In this case I used one geared for normal people, non-*asrasin*s."

"Which is why you think Jake is a potential?" William said.

"Exactly. If I had used a different braid, one designed for *asrasin*s, it would have left normal folk nothing more than simpletons."

"But Jake isn't a potential," Jason persisted. "None of us—me, Lien, Daniel—ever sensed that about him. It was never there."

"Yet it's there now," Mr. Zeus replied. "It has to be." Jason still looked like he wanted to contend the point, but Mr. Zeus waved aside whatever argument he wanted to make. "A discussion for another time. What does Jake want?" he asked William.

"The truth. He wants to know everything about what happened. About Kohl. About how Jason cast fire. All of it."

"What did you tell him?" Jason asked.

"Nothing," William replied. "I told him I had to ask you first before I told him anything."

"Good. Then invite him over for dinner tomorrow. Tell him I'll explain everything then. Leave it to me." Mr. Zeus steepled his fingers. "Now. We have other issues to discuss. Matters are coming to a head."

A prickle of unease worked its way down William's spine. "What else is there?"

"Sit down," Mr. Zeus ordered.

The prickle heightened, and William took a seat on the couch next to Jason. "This isn't like those other times when I found out you've been lying to me about something, is it?"

"No, but we have concerns," Mr. Zeus answered.

"What kind of concerns?"

"We need to test you. Find out if you have the blood of Kohl Obsidian in your veins."

William rocked back in his seat. *How had they known?* The world swam before snapping into focus.

"I'm guessing by your reaction that the answer is 'yes'," Mr. Zeus said, his tone droll.

William stared at his shoes, fear replacing his earlier anger at Jake's revelation. "Is this when you kill me?" William asked, somehow remaining calm. He lifted his gaze to stare Jason and Mr. Zeus in the eyes even as he judged the distance to the front door. He wouldn't go down without a fight.

"Kill you?" Jason's face scrunched up in horror. "What kind of crappy people do you think we are?"

"It's what the book said," William said.

"Well, the book's wrong," Jake replied.

"All we know is that you're a *raha'asra*," Mr. Zeus said. "Or you will be if you don't first turn into a necrosed."

William shook his head. "I'm not going to turn, and I'm not going to die, either," he said. "Both of those scenarios would have already played out by now. I'm blessed or whatever it's called when a necrosed's blood doesn't turn or kill you."

"Take off the *nomasra*," Mr. Zeus said. "The locket with the picture of your parents. It could be slowing the process."

William pulled out the locket and stared at it. He'd never thought it might the reason he hadn't either turned into a necrosed or been killed. With trembling fingers, he slowly slipped off the necklace and unconsciously held his breath. He closed his eyes and waited.

The room remained quiet. After what felt like minutes with nothing said or happening, he cracked open his eyes. Mr. Zeus and Jason stared at him, unblinking.

"Well?" William asked. He unclenched fisted hands grown sweaty with his nervousness.

"I don't feel anything but his *lorethasra*," Jason said to Mr. Zeus. "There's nothing else there."

"I agree," Mr. Zeus said. "Not that I expected there to be," he told William, "You contain no corruption." Mr. Zeus doffed an imaginary hat. "Congratulations. You aren't going to become a demonic killing-machine."

"Then I'm okay?" William asked. His voice cracked, and for some reason he recalled a silly scene of wood thrushes singing to a bright, sunny dawn. Corny as hell, but a perfect description of how he felt.

"Then you are blessed," Jason mused.

"It's kinda gross, though, isn't it?" William asked. "The blood of a necrosed in my veins."

"Well, in this case it hasn't harmed you one bit," Mr. Zeus noted. "According to Jason, you're now stronger, faster, and tougher than he is. In addition, you're also a potential *raha'asra*. You have it in you to become a very powerful *asrasin*."

William puffed up and grinned.

Mr. Zeus shook his head in disgust. "Don't be so proud of your abilities," he warned. "You didn't earn them. They came to you with your birth or by accident. Nothing more than blind luck. It's like being proud of being tall."

William's grin faded. Leave it to Mr. Zeus to make something grand sound stupid. "Is that it, then?" he asked. "Is that what you wanted to talk to me about?"

"Not entirely," Jason said. "We also need to talk about Serena."

"What about her?" William eyed the other two through narrowed eyes. Based on their expressions, it felt like the other shoe was about to drop.

"We believe Elaina . . . You remember the fortune teller we met when we joined Mr. Bill's circus?" Jason asked.

William nodded. "She's hard to forget."

"Well, we think she was a true witch," Jason said. "Witches and warlocks are a race of magical beings descended from *asrasin*s."

"I've had people research what Elaina said," Mr. Zeus said. "She said she's a witch from a place called Sand. It happens to be an actual village of witches and warlocks, but we have no idea where."

William's mind reeled. "You're saying the fortune-teller was an actual, honest-to-goodness witch?" William shook his head in disbelief. "How much magical crap is there?"

"A lot," Mr. Zeus said. "Elves. Dwarves. Unformed. Necrosed. Holders. All of them are woven, the creations of *asrasins.* All magical beings descended from our kind."

William's attention caught on something Mr. Zeus had said. "Holders. You mean like Landon?"

"Yes," Mr. Zeus affirmed. "Holders are also a type of woven. Same as fairies, gnomes, dragons, and a thousand other species. Almost every creature from almost every myth had its origin in truth. We created them. All of them, either directly or through unexpected breeding. But at the heart of it, a*srasin*s were their makers. Our creations once walked and stalked the earth, swam and hunted the sea, or flew and ruled the air."

"All right. Elaina's a true witch," William said, hoping repetition would make the word sound less ridiculous. *Would there never be an end to these unbelievable conversations?* "But what's this have to do with Serena?"

"We think Serena might also be a witch."

"What?"

"Remember what Elaina told you when she read your fortune?" Jason asked. "She said Landon was alive and that me, you, and Serena have magic. True witches know things."

"There's no way Serena could be a witch. We've never seen her use magic or even touch it. Plus, if she has magic it means she's been lying to us all this time. She'd never do something like that."

"She may be a witch and not know it," Jason said.

William's simmering disbelief faded a bit.

"Since we know she isn't an *asrasin,*" Jason added, "that's the only thing that makes sense."

"How do you know?"

"First of all, she's not a potential," Jason said, holding up a finger as though reciting a list, "or her *lorethasra* would have flowered in the *saha'asras* we encountered." He held up two fingers. "Second, she's not a magi. We'd know." A third finger went up. "And she can't be a mahavan. During all the battles against Kohl she never once formed a braid. She should have, to save her life if nothing else, since mahavans are known cowards."

"I don't know," William said, remaining skeptical.

"The other possibility," Mr. Zeus said, "is she's an unformed, a creature who can transform other magical beings into something other than their true form. But if that were the case, *I'd* know."

William groaned. More new words and creatures. He clutched his temples. "I think I've got a headache."

"The reason we're telling you all this is because we need to go to Arylyn much sooner than we thought," Mr. Zeus said.

William's head jerked up. He searched Mr. Zeus' and Jason's features, hoping to see some bend, but their expressions remained unyielding. "When?" he asked.

"Soon. This weekend won't be early enough," Mr. Zeus said. "Arylyn is the only place where we'll all be safe."

"But why now?" William demanded. "I'm not ready to leave. I have to wait for Landon. What if he returns and we're all gone?"

"We told you. Serena may be a witch," Mr. Zeus explained, "and whether she knows it or not is immaterial. Thus far, you've already come in contact with a holder, a necrosed, and a witch."

"And don't forget Aia, the kitten who spoke in our minds," Jason reminded him.

"Creatures of magic seem drawn to you," Mr. Zeus continued.

"It happens, and when it does, it's dangerous. You can't remain here, lit up like a lamp while you wait for some new monster to try to kill you. You barely survived your last such encounter. Do you really want another such meeting?"

William reluctantly shook his head.

Jason ruffled William's hair. "It's not all bad," he said. "At least you get to live in paradise."

———— • ————

Serena quickly regained her equilibrium after Dalton's unexpected appearance. She and Isha moved to stand shoulder-to-shoulder and faced the mahavan known as the Hunter. In this, they were allies. Their family room contained a tension, the kind when two powerful dogs encountered one another for the first time. The three of them silently assessed one another, and Serena sought to break the impasse.

She sneered at Dalton, seeking to set the man back on his heels. "A bit much, don't you think?" she asked, referring to his melodramatic entrance. Her words and demeanor were a calculated insult, a wrist-slap to remind Dalton that while he had power on Sinskrill, she too might one day have similar influence.

Dalton's smile vanished from his rat-like visage. "What do we know of Wilde's habits?" he asked in a curt tone.

Serena hid a smile. The hunter had noticed the insult and didn't appreciate it. "I go to school with three of Arylyn's magi," she said. "After school William goes home, where he lives and trains with one of those magi, Jason Jacobs. He's quite powerful, and his grandfather, Mr. Zeus, is even more so. There are four more magi living across the street."

"Six magi, then," Dalton mused. "I suppose the three of us and the two mahavans I brought with me can handle them."

Serena silently scoffed.

"And Wilde's never alone?" Dalton asked.

"Rarely. Only when he and I go out to see a movie or have dinner together."

"Do you have such a plan coming up?"

"No."

"Then you need one."

"There is another matter," Isha said, wearing a smile Serena recognized as one of relish. "One of equal importance as William Wilde."

Dalton's jaw briefly clenched. "What is it?"

Isha gave the hunter a hard stare. "Reconsider your attitude." His tone remained mellow but the warning was evident. "I bring home a powerful *raha'asra*. You know what this means."

They stared unblinking at one another. Dalton was the first to look away.

Isha gave a grunt of satisfaction.

"There is another potential we've recently discovered," Isha said. "He, too, is a *raha'asra*. We must have them both."

"Two *raha'asras*." Dalton's eyes widened in amazement. "You'll have a Primeship for this," he said, his tone far more respectful.

"I suppose I will," Isha replied in a noncommittal tone.

Serena viewed her teacher with confusion. What higher posting could there be than a Primeship? Then again, he had mentioned the Servitor's Chair.

The phone rang from the kitchen, and Isha tilted his head toward it, a silent command. Serena muttered under her breath. Isha hated using the phone.

"Hello?" she answered.

"Serena? Hey. It's William."

"Hi. What's going on?" she asked, infusing her voice with girlish curiosity. She noticed Dalton watching intently, and she turned her back to him.

"Nothing much," William said, "but movie night's off."

Serena frowned. "Why?" she asked, aiming for a puzzled tone with a tinge of hurt.

"Mr. Zeus got mad about my jug, and he wants me to break figurative bread with Jake tomorrow night."

"Jake's coming over to your house for dinner?"

"If he says yes," William replied, sounding unhappy and resentful.

"Well, have fun with that," Serena said with an involuntary grin.

"Yeah, I'm sure it'll be a blast."

"It won't be so bad," Serena said. "At least Jason and Mr. Zeus will be there."

"I guess," William said, still sounding unenthusiastic. "Anyway, I'll talk to you later. Maybe we can do something on Sunday?"

"Sure. Catch a movie?"

"We'll see. Later."

"Bye."

Isha and Dalton eyed her expectantly when she hung up, and Serena explained her conversation.

"Both of the *raha'asras* will be next door tomorrow night?" Dalton mulled. "And we're certain they're both *raha'asras*?"

Serena castigated herself. She could already see the way Isha and Dalton would plan for William and Jake's capture. Both *raha'asras* would be in one place tomorrow, and she'd told them so. *Idiot!* Why hadn't she lied or remained silent? Anything other than tell the truth?

"I personally inspected Jake," Isha answered, "and Serena did the same with William."

"Meaning only one is truly known," Dalton said.

"Meaning they both are. Serena confirmed William. It's the same as if I had done so."

"It isn't the same."

Their argument didn't matter. Serena had already betrayed the one person in the world who she could have called a friend. There was no returning from what she'd done, and she steeled her heart to accept the burden she'd have to bear.

"It is since I trained her," Isha countered. "She is my bishan. I trust her."

"You trust her." Dalton smirked. "How touching."

"She knows how to do her task," Isha said. "Don't read more into it than exists."

Dalton shrugged. "Regardless, I see a means for us to capture both *raha'asras* tomorrow night."

Curiosity raised its head, but Serena paid it no attention. She didn't care. She felt broken inside.

"How?" Isha asked.

"The reward for the ones who bring the *raha'asras* in will be enormous," Dalton said, sounding crafty.

"Yes, and I'll be sure to share my honor with you and your mahavans," Isha countered.

Dalton grimaced, and Isha laughed. "Did you really think you'd be able to take the lion's share of glory in this endeavor? After Serena barely survived a necrosed and had a large hand in that tainted creature's demise? And never forget it was I who uncovered William Wilde to begin with."

"Fine," Dalton growled. "The glory is yours."

"But I can be generous with those who ally with me," Isha said. "Now tell me your plan."

"Our prey are having dinner together tomorrow night," Dalton began. "We attack them during their meal and secure our prizes."

Despite her inner turmoil and self-loathing, Serena jeered at Dalton's stupid plan. "Those two magi are going to be more than you and your two mahavans can handle," she said. "And what if the other four are present as well? Five of us against six magi? On their ground? We'd lose. Badly."

Dalton huffed in disdain. "You overestimate their chances," he said, "or perhaps your time abroad has weakened your resolve."

"Or perhaps you speak from ignorance," Serena countered. "I saw them fight, remember? They defeated a necrosed. No mahavan in all of history can make such a claim."

"Then what do you propose?" Dalton asked. He crossed his arms. "Ask them nicely if they'll give us the *raha'asras*?"

"No," Isha said. "But Serena's right. Cunning is required here, not brute strength." A moment later, he smiled. "We wreck Jake's car. William is the only one who likes to drive. He'll end up driving Jake home. Somewhere on the way, there's likely to be a stretch of road with no one to witness our actions. We'll take them there."

CHAPTER 5:
PRIZED NEEDS

February 1987

The doorbell rang, and William looked up from where he'd been watching *Wheel of Fortune*. He checked the clock. Precisely six p.m.

"At least he's prompt," Jason noted from the kitchen where he'd organized the pizza for tonight's meeting.

Mr. Zeus set aside his pipe. "One small point in his favor." he said from his place in his ugly plaid recliner.

William opened the door, and Jake stood on the front stoop wearing his letterman's jacket. Shadows from the weak porch light hid half his face, and his breath misted in the winter air. To William, Jake seemed nervous but trying hard not to show it.

"Come on in," William offered. "Glad you could make it."

"Thanks for inviting me."

"Toss your coat on the couch."

"You must be Jake Ridley," Mr. Zeus said, rising from his chair. "Welcome."

Jason nodded in greeting. "Jake," he said.

His simple greeting seemed to carry shades of meaning, some of it threatening, and Jake noticed. He stiffened further.

Jason gave a knowing half-smile. "You're safe. No one's going to hurt you here."

"You say I'm safe, but I saw what you did to that creature," Jake said.

"If you remember that, then you also remember my actions didn't have much effect on it." Jason pointed to William. "He's the one who killed it. He's the one you should fear."

Jake stepped away from William, eyeing him warily.

"Enough. Stop trying to frighten him," Mr. Zeus ordered Jason before returning to Jake. "My apologies for my grandson's behavior. He thinks he's being funny. You have nothing to fear from us."

"Maybe this wasn't such a good idea," Jake said, edging toward the door.

"Then you'll never learn what you seek," Mr. Zeus said. His words halted Jake's retreat. "I meant what I said. You have nothing to fear from any of us. Not tonight. You're a guest in our house. It means something where we come from."

"And where exactly is that?" Jake asked. "It sure isn't Alabama, or wherever you say you're from."

"California, actually," William corrected. "But that's not where they're from either."

Mr. Zeus snapped his fingers. "I understand now."

"Understand what?" William asked in puzzlement.

"You see it?" Mr. Zeus asked Jason, disregarding William's question. "Look at his *lorethasra* and compare the two of them."

Jake looked from one of them to the other, appearing even

more confused than William felt. "What's going on?" Once more he appeared on the verge of flight.

"An explanation for why you were able to resist my braid, the one meant to wipe your memories," Mr. Zeus said. "After you and your friends encountered the necrosed, I erased those memories, and it worked on everyone but you. Only someone with the potential to become an *asrasin* could be left unaffected."

"I have no idea what you're talking about," Jake said, sounding both frustrated and scared.

"You've got a lot to learn," William said with a snort, remembering his own talks with Mr. Zeus and Jason. "Let's talk over pizza. Pizza always makes things better."

Jake gave a hesitant nod. "If you say so."

"I say so," William told him. "You'll thank me after you hear what Mr. Zeus tells you."

After passing Jake a plate piled high with pepperoni pizza and a can of Coke, William got his own food together and they all took seats in the family room. He'd barely settled in when Mr. Zeus launched into his explanation. Most of it William already knew, and he only half paid attention. He did chuckle, though, when Jake's eyes grew wide and his jaw dropped when Mr. Zeus and Jason demonstrated some of their abilities.

"You're saying I can learn to do all this?" Jake asked. "That I can become a magus?"

"Yes. And not any normal magus," Mr. Zeus said, "but a *raha'asra*, a rare and sometimes powerful *asrasin*. In fact, your potential *lorethasra* is almost identical to William's, only less powerful, less vibrant in its colors."

Jake sat speechless.

"A lot to take in, isn't it?" Jason asked, this time with a friendlier grin.

"Yeah," Jake answered, sounding breathless. "How did this happen? Was I born like this?"

"No. You were changed," Mr. Zeus answered. "As I said, your potential *lorethasra* is almost identical to William's, but not as powerful."

"William is powerful?"

Mr. Zeus nodded. "With study and practice, he has the potential to be more powerful than any *asrasin* born in centuries."

William tried to appear modest, but he knew he sucked at lying. "I have the potential," he said. "It doesn't mean I'll actually manage it."

"And I'm like him?" Jake asked Mr. Zeus.

"No and yes. No, you'll never be as powerful as him. But yes, you're like him since your potential *lorethasra* was derived from William's."

"What?" William and Jake both exclaimed.

"The only way your potential *lorethasra* could be so identical to William's is if it had its origin in his. That can only happen if his blood—only the blood of a *raha'asra* can effect such a transformation—somehow mixed with your own. Less than a drop is all that's required."

"You mean he infected me?" Jake asked, eyeing William in anger and disgust.

"He infected you with magic. I think you should thank him rather than curse him," Jason noted dryly.

William, though, felt no less disgust than Jake. He, too, scowled as he tried to figure out how his blood might have gotten into Jake.

They figured it out at the same time. "The Oklahoma drill!" they said together.

"That's why we couldn't sense your *lorethasra* until a few days ago," Jason said. "It was still gestating."

Jake made a sound of loathing. "You make it sound like some kind of creature growing inside me."

"I'm sure this is all quite repugnant to you," Mr. Zeus said with a dismissive wave of his hand. "But since you now know about us, we need to know about you. I couldn't wipe your mind before, but now I know which levers to pull, it won't be a problem."

Jake swallowed. "What do you need me to say?"

"The truth," William advised. "Don't lie to them. They'll figure it out."

"Tell us who you are," Mr. Zeus said, his face grave. "I have an idea, but I want to hear it from your own mouth. Prove you're worthy to receive the knowledge because your reputation says that you're a bully, and Arylyn has no room for such individuals."

"I'm not a bully," Jake said with an obstinate thrust of his jaw.

William rolled his eyes, making sure Jake saw.

"Okay. I mean I might have bullied you a few times, but it's not who I am."

"Then who are you?" Jason asked.

"And why do you care if you won't remember any of this?" William asked. "If you step into a *saha'asra*, you have to leave the real world. You might never get to see your family and friends again. Your life the way it is now would be over, and I think you really like it the way it is now."

"I've got to know the truth," Jake insisted in a dogged, quiet tone. "It's all I've ever wanted."

"What about the rest of it?" Jason asked. "Sacrificing your life here?"

"I think I'll pass," Jake replied. "But can I think about it some before I give you my final decision?"

"Can you think about whether to come with us to Arylyn?" Mr. Zeus asked. "Absolutely, but I've made no such offer yet, and I won't until I know who you are. As I said, word travels that you're a bully. But words spoken about another are often nothing but rumor and gossip. I want solid information. Provide it. Prove yourself. Who are you?"

Jake's face pinched as he seemed to gather his thoughts. "My father owns a large car dealership, so I've always been rich, and I love it. People think I'm conceited, which is probably true, but I'm not selfish."

William snorted and Jason shook his head in disbelief.

"It's true," Jake said defensively. "I'm the one who organizes the football team's food drives."

William blinked in surprise. "You did that?"

Jake nodded. "Even as a freshman, it was me. Every summer since eighth grade I've volunteered at a center for handicapped kids. And most Saturday afternoons I volunteer at a nursing home. I spend time with the residents since their families don't come by much."

William found himself impressed. Last semester he'd made his peace with Jake, but he'd never really come to like him much, even before their most recent disagreement. But if he was telling the truth about all his volunteering, then Jake Ridley did have a generous heart, and William wished he could have known that other version of him better.

"Then there's my brother, Pete," Jake continued. "He's got a type of muscular dystrophy. It means he's always been weak and always will be. Ever since he was little, I've watched out for him as much as my parents have."

The entire time Jake spoke, Mr. Zeus stared at him, wearing an enigmatic expression. William wondered at his thoughts.

"You don't lie. You believe your heart to be as generous as you claim," Mr. Zeus announced. "You've earned your grace period, but you'll never again talk about what we told you, or what you saw of Kohl Obsidian."

Jake breathed out in relief. "I promise not to say a thing," he vowed before quirking a grin. "Besides, who'd believe me?"

"You misunderstand," Mr. Zeus said, his voice growing chill. "You won't speak because you won't be able to, except to another magi. I know where the levers are, remember?"

Jake's lips thinned in anger. "You can't cast a spell on me."

"We prefer to call them braids."

"That's not fair!"

"Life never is," Mr. Zeus replied. "You have your answers. Consider your curiosity sated."

———•———

Jake said his goodbyes to Mr. Zeus and Jason, and William accompanied him out to his car.

"Very enlightening evening," Jake said in as laconic a fashion as he could manage. He leaned against his Corvette and tried to sort out his thoughts. His breath frosted in the cold, night air.

William's neighborhood, quiet and suburban, seemed to mock him with its sense of normality.

"You're handling it better than I did," William said.

Jake grunted acknowledgement, but his thoughts were elsewhere. As usual, they circled back to the monster at Winton Woods, the necrosed. "That thing really killed your parents?"

William nodded. "I thought he killed Landon too, but I guess my new world is one full of miracles."

Jake spun his keyring around a finger. He caught it in mid-flight before spinning it in the opposite direction. So much of what he'd been told sounded ridiculous, fantastical, and impossible. But what about the necrosed and Jason and Mr. Zeus' demonstrations of their abilities? "How do you deal with it?" Jake finally asked. "All these magical things. The monsters. The spells or braids, or whatever. I thought I was ready for anything, but this is too much."

"It wasn't easy," William admitted. "At least not at first, but eventually you get used to it."

"Are you really going to Arylyn?"

"Kohl made me an orphan. There's not much holding me here any more. The only reason we haven't already left is because I wanted to graduate from high school first."

"Then I've got until graduation to decide what to do?" Jake asked.

"Only if they accept you," William reminded him. "But no, you don't have that long. Mr. Zeus says it's gotten too dangerous for us to stay here. He plans on going to Arylyn in the next few days. All of us. Maybe next weekend."

"Wait. Mr. Zeus is worried?"

William nodded.

"About what?" Jake asked in exasperation. "He's a magus. Jason can blast fire out of his hands. You guys fight demons and monsters. What could be dangerous for someone like them?"

"Other creatures like Kohl."

"Oh." Jake fell silent as he considered what to do. "I've got two days to decide my future." He chuckled in grim disbelief before unlocking the Corvette, and sliding into the driver's seat. "That's not much time."

"It's what it is," William answered, offering no pity. "Besides, I still don't get why it's such a hard choice. You've got a great life. Why would you want to give all that away?"

"Why would you?" Jake asked, inserting the key into the ignition.

"I've got no choice," William said. "Once my *lorethasra* was exposed to a *saha'asra*, it became Arylyn or death."

Jake grunted understanding while he considered what he wanted. In the end, the decision wasn't hard. While the lure of magic was great, he liked his life the way it was. He had good friends and a family who loved him. By most standards, his life was already magical enough, or at least blessed. There was no way he'd trade it away for anything, not even magic. "Should I call you when I've made my decision?"

"That's fine," William said. "I'm sure Mr. Zeus won't let you live out the rest of your life wondering if you made a mistake."

"You mean he'd wipe my mind?"

"You know what they say: ignorance is bliss."

"I guess," Jake agreed. He keyed the Corvette's ignition. Nothing happened. Not even a sputter. Again, he turned the key and goosed the gas, but still nothing. "Battery must be dead," he muttered in irritation. "Perfect."

"I'll get my jumper cables," William said. "We'll have you rolling in no time." He backed up his T-bird until it rumbled next to Jake's dead car. He popped the hood and attached the jumper cables.

"Try it now," William suggested after a few minutes.

Jake keyed the ignition, but the Corvette gave absolutely no response. "Shit," Jake muttered. "Can I use your phone? I need to call my parents and have them pick me up."

Jason poked his head outside. "What's going on?" he asked.

"Car won't start," William explained. "I'm going to drop him off at home."

"I'll come with," Jason suggested.

"It's only a few miles. We'll be fine."

"You sure?"

William nodded.

"All right then. See you soon." Jason retreated into the house.

Jake helped disassemble the jumper cables, and climbed into the passenger seat of William's T-bird. "Nice ride." He caught William's eye-roll. "I'm serious. It's a nice car."

"Thanks," William said. He pushed a tape into the stereo, and *Aces High* by Iron Maiden kicked on, blaring through the speakers.

"I thought you only liked pop," Jake said.

"That's Lien. She likes to sing along to those kind of songs. The poppier the better."

"Well, if I'd known you liked cool stuff, I wouldn't have dogged you so bad for so long," Jake said with a grin.

"Yeah, you would," William replied.

Jake had no response. Part of him felt hurt by William's words. He settled into his seat and stared out the passenger window. "I know I've been a dick to you most of our lives, but I really am sorry about how I treated you."

"I appreciate that," William said, "and maybe one day, we can actually get along and be friends."

"I'd like that," Jake said, "but it's not going to happen if you're leaving in the next week or so."

"You already decided to stay," William said, sounding unsurprised. "Can't say I blame you."

William took a turn onto a quiet road that skirted Winton Woods. Up ahead, a van stood unmoving at a stop sign, emergency lights blinking.

William eased the T-bird to a halt. "Should we help?" he asked.

A car pulled up behind them. Seconds later a bright light shone directly in their faces from the side windows.

"Hey!" Jake cried out. *What the hell!*

The windows to the T-bird shattered.

Jake's irritation transformed into fear.

Arms reached into the car.

"Get your hands off me!" William shouted. Someone quickly dragged him out of the T-bird. A grunt and thud followed.

Jake spun about when he felt hands on him as well. He struggled to free himself, cursing loudly. He tried to pry the fingers off. A sharp pain in his head ended his struggles and thoughts.

———●———

William groaned, struggling to figure out what had happened and where he was. His last memory had been of a stopped van, strobing lights, and smashed windows. He'd punched someone, and then . . . nothing.

He couldn't see. He swallowed the tide of incipient panic as he blinked, hoping to clear his vision. A blindfold. A cloth covered his eyes, and his hands were tied in front of him as well.

The fear ebbed, and confusion took its place. *What the hell had happened?*

A hard jolt bounced him around, and he slammed into something hard and metallic. He grunted in pain.

"William?" a voice came from his right.

"Jake?"

"Yeah. You have any idea what's going on?" Jake whispered.

"I don't know. We were driving to your house. There was a stop sign and a van," William said. He focused on everything he could recall. His thoughts came slow and befuddled, as if moving through molasses.

"I remember that," Jake said. "Then those bright lights. Someone grabbed me."

William recalled those details, too. His eyes went wide behind the blindfold. "We've been kidnapped."

"Kidnapped?" Jake laughed nervously. "Who would kidnap us? You sure this doesn't have something to do with Mr. Zeus pranking us or something?"

"Pretty shitty prank, but no, it's got nothing to do him."

William's confusion faded and outrage took its place. *Sonofabitch!* Whoever had done this would get a beating and worse when he got free. "What's going on!" William shouted. "Who are you?"

87

Someone ripped away the blindfold, and William blinked at the sudden bright light. His vision slowly cleared, and the sight greeting him was one he would have never expected. Serena sat facing him. They rode in the bed of a van.

"Serena? What are you doing here?"

She watched him with flat and lifeless features. No bindings constrained her, and Mr. Paradiso, her father, sat beside her. He wore a smile of triumph.

William's emotions whipsawed as confusion mixed with anger. Understanding came to him, and with it his fury rose once again.

"What's she doing here?" Jake asked.

"We're here because of her," William said. He stared Serena in the eyes and dared her to deny his charge.

She never flinched from his gaze, neither repudiating his claim nor affirming it. She simply watched him with a bored, uncaring demeanor before facing forward to where three unsmiling, non-descript men sat.

"I don't understand," Jake said. "Who are you people?"

"William already told you. You've been kidnapped," Mr. Paradiso answered. "You have both been given a great gift, and we require that gift. On Sinskrill, we will learn your true worth."

"Sinskrill?" Jake frowned at William. "Isn't that the island Mr. Zeus talked about?"

"Yeah," William said. "The island of humanity's enemy."

Serena's father laughed. William had only met the man a few times, but every time he'd come away with a sense of unease. He had always felt judged by Serena's father, as if he were a chicken and Mr. Paradiso was a farmer deciding whether to wring his neck for the supper pot. It seemed his instincts had been right.

"Humanity's enemy?" Mr. Paradiso snorted. "So the fools of Arylyn call us, but merely making the claim doesn't make it true. We're a nation like any other, wanting to grow and expand." His gaze focused. "You two will help us accomplish our goal."

"You won't get anything from me," Jake said, thrusting his jaw out belligerently. "I'll never help you or do what you want."

Mr. Paradiso smirked. "For now, that is your choice. But on Sinskrill you'll find that choices have consequences, and those consequences can be quite severe. You'll also discover that on Sinskrill you either do as you're told or you die." His offhand tone indicated, more strongly than his words, how little he cared what they decided or about their ultimate fates.

"What about you?" William asked Serena. "You're one of them? A mahavan?"

"No," Serena replied, not bothering to face him.

William waited for further elaboration, but she said nothing more.

"She isn't a mahavan yet, but she will be elevated to that status when we return to Sinskrill," Mr. Paradiso said. "You'll learn all about it. For now, though, here's some advice: get some rest. We've a long journey ahead of us."

Serena continued to stare forward, still wearing a flat, unfeeling visage, and William glared at her. Rage engulfed all thought. He jerked toward her, not sure what he intended, and she finally deigned to look at him. Serena gestured, a flick of her hand, and a fist of air slammed William against the side of the van.

She'd done that, William realized with shock. *Some kind of braid*. Her action, more than anything else he'd experienced so far, informed William of the utter depth of her betrayal.

Once again, he glared at her, but this time he kept still. Serena sniffed in clear contempt, but otherwise, her face continued to hold a dispassionate mien.

Hatred such as he had never experienced filled William's heart. "I should have let Kohl kill you," he whispered.

Serena met his gaze, and a flicker of emotion passed across her face. Hurt.

Good.

CHAPTER 6:
ABANDONING
THE FAR ABROAD

February 1987

S erena passed the initial hours of their journey with her eyes closed in meditation, but peace eluded her. Nevertheless, with her eyes closed at least she could avoid William's glare.

Leading up to his abduction, she had thought her heart a stronghold, an inviolate fortress from which she could accept his anger and loathing after her betrayal.

Fool.

"You must be strong," Isha whispered to her.

Serena cracked open her eyes. She saw William and Jake speaking softly to one another. "I am."

"Then show no guilt at what you've done."

"Is it so obvious?"

"Only to me, but I know you too well for your own good," Isha said with a smile. "I doubt Dalton or the others have any sense of what you're feeling, but your father, the Servitor, will."

Serena nodded, and her gaze slid back to William. He must have sensed her regard because he glanced her way. She braced herself, doing her best to accept his hatred, to let it wash over and through her. William surprised her. Rather than loathing, his mouth curled into contempt.

Serena blinked. She hadn't expected him to overcome his hatred of her so quickly, or to replace it with a more manageable emotion like scorn. If true, he might actually survive Sinskrill and prosper there.

For his sake, she hoped so.

The drive droned on, growing tedious as the hours passed in silence. Only Dalton and the other two mahavans spoke to one another in brief conversations. Otherwise, the van remained quiet, and Serena stared out at the monotonous winter landscape. Snow covered the ground here, wherever "here" was. Illinois maybe.

The only excitement occurred on the evening after the kidnapping. At a rest area in Wisconsin, William and Jake made a dash for freedom. They ripped their arms free from the mahavans gripping them and sprinted for the highway.

Neither managed more than ten steps before they tumbled, both of them landing on their butts.

Dalton chuckled. "Running isn't a possibility, boys. Not until you learn to undo a braid."

William opened his mouth to shout for help, but no sound came out.

"Nor can you call out to anyone."

Afterward, Dalton leashed William and Jason with braids that allowed them to walk like automatons but nothing more. They finished in the restrooms with no one the wiser at their restraints and returned to the van, silent but furious.

They made no further attempts at escape.

In the van, Serena viewed William's and Jake's scraped and swollen faces with outward dispassion but a stomach full of remorse. She should have told William the truth long ago. Then he'd be safe on Arylyn.

"At least now they know resistance is an empty gesture," Isha told her, noticing her unhappiness at William's and Jake's minor injuries. "This way they'll be more compliant, and we need that, given how far we still have to go."

"Banff, Canada," Dalton said, overhearing their conversation. "A long drive in the Far Abroad. I'll be happy when it's over."

They traveled on, and Serena tried to get what rest she could, but guilt kept her awake and restless.

The next morning, Dalton took a turnoff and eventually had them bouncing along a gravel road. Half an hour later, a few miles away from the town of Banff proper, they came to a halt.

"We're here," Dalton announced.

Serena stepped out into a chill, frosty morning. Mount Norquay's serrated, gray spine soared to the west, dominating the pale-blue, winter sky.

Their breath misted.

"What happens now?" William asked.

"Now we hike," Isha announced. "The *saha'asra* we need is located on the other side of that ridge." He pointed east to a rugged rise.

"And the van?" Serena asked.

"Already dealt with," Dalton answered. "An arrangement with a local. We sold it to him for half its actual worth."

"Do we have to stay tied up?" Jake asked.

"No. Free them," Dalton ordered.

Mr. Paradiso stepped forward and unsheathed a wicked-looking kukri. A single slice to each of their bonds cut them free. "Rub your wrists," Mr. Paradiso advised. "It'll relieve the numbness in your hands."

"Have a lot of experience in tying people up, do you?" William replied.

"You'll want to be careful—" Serena began.

"Shut up. No one's talking to you," William said.

She slapped him, a hard back-hand. "You may become a *raha'asra* and one day earn a place on Sinskrill, but for now you are nothing," she snapped. "I am your better. Remember that and know your place."

William tongued the inside of his lips. They felt bruised where she'd struck him. He glared at Serena but took her advice and remained silent.

"Get moving," Mr. Paradiso smirked, giving Jake a shove.

Their boots crunched on snow, and the hike soon had them panting and sweating despite the cold air.

Dalton didn't let them slow down, though. There were no more rest stops or breaks for food. "We're almost there," Dalton huffed.

———•———

Serena breathed deeply when they stepped onto a bare field cut in two by a winter-frozen stream. The *saha'asra*. She allowed the *lorasra* of the place to fill her, to soothe away all the unremarked-upon aches and vague sense of illness she'd grown used to in her time in the Far Abroad.

"I feel weird," Jake announced. "Everything seems brighter and happier."

"It's your *lorethasra* coming to life," William explained. "It's what happens the first time you step into a *saha'asra*."

"You're bound to us now, boy," Dalton said. "Even if you wanted to escape, you couldn't. Not unless you want to die."

"Remove your *nomasra*," Isha told William. "You know the one I mean."

William's eyes darted about in panic. Serena knew why. The locket. It held a picture of his family. He wouldn't want to give it up.

"No," William said. "I can't."

Isha pressed close, menace radiating off him. "Take it off, or we cut off his fingers." He pointed to Jake.

Glaring, William did as told.

"Good. Now to disable it." Isha concentrated. His *lorethasra* pulsed and he drew out a white thread of Spirit, duller in sheen than William's and smelling faintly of cut wood. Isha gave a satisfied grunt. "It's done." He tossed the *nomasra* to Serena.

She caught it without thinking and tucked it away in a pocket. She couldn't give it back to William, but Selene would like it. She'd like the picture of a family who obviously loved one another.

One of Dalton's mahavans triggered the anchor line to

Sinskrill, and a doorway opened, one filled with a kaleidoscope of colors and geometric patterns. Through the chaotic images a yellow beacon pulsed in a staccato rhythm that Serena hadn't seen in months. The colors swirled about before settling down and fading away. A deep bell tone rang out as the door opened out onto a rainbow bridge extending into infinity.

"You should be proud," Isha told her. "No bishan has ever performed so admirably. A defeated necrosed and two *raha'asras*. We'll be greeted with great acclaim."

"Thank you, sir." Serena managed a false, bright smile even while she tried to force unconcern for William's fate. He'd have to find his own way in Sinskrill . . . or have it found for him.

"Ready?" Isha asked.

Serena stepped onto the rainbow bridge. A mad rushing sound filled her ears. The rainbow bridge filled her vision with coruscating colors. Her body stretched out, feeling as if it might reach a breaking point. With a snap, she came back together and stumbled out of the anchor line.

Sinskrill opened before her like a blooming flower. The late afternoon sun shone on the crystal waters of nearby Lake White Sun, and farther out, the glistening Norwegian Sea. To the north and east, a line of rugged, gray foothills rose towards distant mountains. Her breath plumed, and she inhaled the scent of pine from the nearby forest.

An unexpectedly beautiful homecoming. Serena grimaced a moment later at the sewer-like stench and feel of the island's *lorasra*.

MEXICO

"Good Lord, it's hot down here," Jason complained, pissed off by the humid weather, but more so by worry over what must have happened to William and Jake. The police had found William's T-bird abandoned on a small road near Winton Woods. The driver and passenger side windows had been smashed in, and all their searching—police and magi both—hadn't yielded the slightest clue as to what had happened.

Early on after their disappearance, Mr. Zeus had sensed William's *nomasra* heading northwest and never slowing. Unfortunately, he had no notion as to where they might be ultimately headed.

As a result, a somber group—Jason, Mr. Zeus, Lien, Daniel, and Daniel's parents—stood alone on the same black sand beach in Mexico where they'd gone after the final battle with Kohl Obsidian. Waves caressed the untouched shoreline, and raucous cries filled the jungle at their back. A narrow track cut a wavering path through the trees.

From here they planned on journeying to Hawaii and from there, to Arylyn. While the *saha'asra*s in West Virginia and Arizona could have taken them directly home, none of them knew if any necrosed still waited near those two locations. Thus, this more circuitous route. They'd caught a flight from Cincinnati to St. Paul, Minnesota, and from there, they'd traveled along an anchor line to Mexico.

"You realize the authorities are going to believe we had something to do with William and Jake's disappearance," said Mr. Karllson.

"At this point, that's the least of our concerns," Mr. Zeus said, "and frankly, I don't care."

Jason snorted. "Besides, good luck serving us a warrant on Arylyn."

"What do you think happened to them?" Daniel asked.

"Serena and her father." Jason's lips curled into a snarl. "They're mahavans. They have to be. It's the only thing that makes sense. We found a *nomasra* in their house after they disappeared at the same time as William and Jake."

"It was a pretty old *nomasra*, though," Daniel noted. "And dead. They might have found it in a flea market for all we know."

"And they just happened to vanish at the same time as William and Jake?" Mr. Zeus asked sardonically. "Not likely, especially since we already believe Serena had something of *asra* to her. This merely proves who she truly was."

"We should have listened to Elaina," Jason said with a sour grimace.

"The witch from Sand?" Mrs. Karllson asked.

Jason noticed Lien's mouth twitch and the twinkle in her eyes. "Don't say it," he warned her.

"What?" Lien asked in an injured tone.

"You were going to say Elaina is a Sand witch," Jason told her. "Ha, ha. Good one. Very original."

"No, I wasn't," Lien said, maintaining a hurt tone. "I was going to say—"

"Not now," Jason snapped, frustration making him irritable.

"I'm not in the mood for jokes. We should have listened to Elaina. She said Landon was alive, and he is. She also said Serena had *asra*. We thought it meant she was a witch, but she meant Serena is an *asrasin*, a mahavan from Sinskrill."

"She's not a mahavan," Mrs. Karllson said. Upon noticing Jason's confusion, she elaborated. "Yes, she's from Sinskrill, but she's not a mahavan. More likely, she's a bishan, someone still in training, tasked with delivering William to their island. Only then will she achieve the title of mahavan."

"And we gave her, not one, but two *raha'asras*," Daniel said bitterly.

"A disaster," Mr. Karllson agreed.

"All is not lost," Mr. Zeus said. "Whoever disabled William's *nomasra* didn't do as complete a job as they should have."

"You can still sense it?" Mr. Karllson asked in his deep rumble.

"Roughly," Mr. Zeus said. "But it's an intermittent signal. It comes and goes. I can't get a distinct location. I only get a vague sense of direction."

"Then how does the *nomasra* help us?" Daniel asked.

"I know where William has gone," Mr. Zeus said. "He was traveling steadily west at the normal speed of a car on the interstate. Then, in an instant, he moved thousands of miles away, far east and north of us."

Jason started. He glanced at the others and saw similar surprise on their faces.

"After all these centuries, we might be able to discover the location of Sinskrill," Mrs. Karllson said in a hushed tone.

"It's supposed to be an island like Arylyn," Lien said excitedly, "but somewhere north, somewhere cold."

Mr. Zeus nodded. "We've always suspected it to be the case, and William's rapid movement in that direction proves it."

"But without knowing the key to Sinskrill's anchor line," Daniel began, "how can we get there and save him?"

"There are ways to travel to an island other than by an anchor line. An *asrasin* who knows the correct location can always get there by boat." Mr. Zeus' face grew grim. "And I promise you this: once I learn Sinskrill's location, nothing will stop me from bringing William home."

SINSKRILL

William shivered when an icy breeze blew too hard. The frost-scented wind bit hard, slicing through his winter coat. It gusted, and he leaned forward to prevent being toppled over.

"Son of a bitch, it's cold," Jake muttered.

William didn't bothering responding. Dejection kept him quiet. He didn't even care to look around at the legendary island of Sinskrill. Its dismal charms had long since worn off, within minutes of their arrival.

Rays of sunshine had briefly split the dreary overcast when they first arrived and reflected off a large lake that seemed to fall away into the ocean. However, minutes later the gloomy clouds had shuttered away the golden light, casting the sky in a gloom William hoped might be temporary but suspected might be permanent. This said nothing of the unavoidable wind that insisted on gusting from all directions.

"Let's go," Dalton said. "The Servitor is expecting us."

"Who's the Servitor?" William asked.

"You'll find out soon enough," Dalton replied.

They marched along a crooked, stone-paved road leading to the eastern shore of the lake. Humped hills surrounded the water on all sides, and the trail traversed a serpentine course through them.

William had little time to take in the sights, though. Dalton and Mr. Paradiso—he still wasn't sure which of them was in charge—kept them traveling fast. When they exited a gorge bounded by two rounded rises, a wide valley containing a series of fallow fields opened out before them. Upon the hillsides, a herd of cattle munched on grass.

As their small troop approached the farmland, William made out a motley assortment of people working the land. They wore heavy, tan clothing and fur hats as they leaned into shovels and hoes, digging into the hard ground. Another group of men and women, similarly dressed except for a mohawk-shaped plume of green feathers bifurcating their leather caps, seemed to be overseers. The workers gave their group a cursory once over before resuming their work.

"Is this him?" one of the overseers—a man—called out to Dalton.

"It's *them*."

"Them?" Puzzlement filled the man's features, followed an instant later by an understanding grin. "The Servitor will be pleased."

"We are all pleased," Mr. Paradiso said. "It was my bishan who discovered them and helped me bring them in." He gestured to the other mahavans who had aided in the capture. "Dalton's band was helpful, as well."

"Lord Shet be praised for your success," said the overseer, dipping his head in respect.

"His glory returns," Mr. Paradiso intoned before giving Dalton an indication to move on.

Their road gradually shifted southwest before eventually turning directly south.

There, a village hove into view, clean and well maintained, with large, stone-walled buildings lining the stone-paved streets. Children darted about, playing some sort of game, while a few lean dogs, their ribs showing, wandered about.

Despite the outwardly settled character to the village, William sensed a despondency to the place.

"It looks like shit," Jake noted.

"This is Village White Sun, your new home," Mr. Paradiso announced. "You'll see more of it later, but for now, come. The Servitor awaits."

After the long walk to the *saha'asra* in Banff followed by this hike up and down a series of hills, William's legs burned. He panted, ready to take a rest, but Mr. Paradiso wouldn't allow it.

He led them to a palace standing atop a rocky cliff and overlooking a bay whose indigo waters were mottled with whitecaps. The structure rose like something from a fairytale, with peaked turrets built of white stone. A set of stairs led from the village to the castle but forked halfway up. One side continued onward and upward and the other side headed down to the water, where a handful of fishing boats had been hauled onto the beach where their crews worked on their catch.

Mr. Paradiso allowed them no time to linger. He pressed on, and they soon arrived at the palace. A wide gate split a curtain-wall that embraced the entire structure and its grounds. Guards armed with pikes and swords nodded acknowledgement as they passed beneath the raised portcullis.

From there they entered the courtyard, and William noted servants rushing about, easily identifiable by their clothes. They wore the same tan outfits and hats as the workers in the fields. The focus of the space, though, was taken up by the presence of a man at the far end of the courtyard. He sat upon an ornate chair and wore simple, dark clothing, a thin, gold circlet, and a fur-lined cloak. None of it did anything to soften his thickset features, his spade-like jaw and beetling brow, or lessen the force of his aura. Several people stood near him, some obviously guards. Others, William guessed, must be mahavans, based on their well-dressed, officious demeanors.

"Kneel," Serena ordered.

Jake didn't do so quickly enough for her liking, and she kicked his legs out from under him.

"Two when I expected one," the man in the chair said, his voice deep, powerful, and commanding.

"Yes, my lord," Mr. Paradiso replied, also kneeling. "We were most fortunate."

"Rise and explain," the man ordered.

"Not you," Serena hissed when William made to stand.

He grimaced at her but remained kneeling. Her lips tightened at his defiance, but she did nothing, and he smiled inside. *Good.* Ticking her off might become his new hobby on this crappy island.

"William Wilde is a natural-born *raha'asra*," Mr. Paradiso

began. "Quite powerful, as you can sense, and somehow, his blood entered this other, a former normal by the name of Jake Ridley. That transference changed this otherwise unremarkable boy into a potential. And now that he has entered a *saha'asra*, his *lorethasra* has come to life. He, too, is a *raha'asra*."

The man in the chair smiled. "Well done."

"Thank you, my liege," Mr. Paradiso said.

"And based on this success, it's self-evident that you must have done equally as well in the training of my daughter."

William's head jerked to the man in the chair, this Servitor who obviously ruled Sinskrill. *Serena was his daughter? Did that make her a princess? Then what did that make Mr. Paradiso?*

"It was my pleasure to instruct her as best I could," Mr. Paradiso said. "I believe she has almost achieved mastery of her abilities."

"Almost?" The Servitor frowned.

"It is your judgment to make, my liege."

The man in the chair dipped his head in acceptance of Mr. Paradiso's words. "Is it true that our newest *raha'asra* was involved in the killing of a necrosed?"

"It is, my liege," Serena replied, rising to her feet as well.

The Servitor cracked a smile. "Excellent. Strong, fearless, and powerful. He will serve us well."

Serena bowed before stepping aside.

William found himself the focus of the Servitor's attention. Serena's gaze could often be intense, but it was nothing compared to this man's regard. His interest burned like the sun.

"I am the Servitor, the Liege of Sinskrill, as decreed by our Lord, Holy Shet."

"His glory returns," the others in the courtyard intoned.

"You did not come here of your own volition, and I don't care," the Servitor said. "You will do as instructed, and you will learn your roles. Serve Sinskrill and prosper. Fail, and you will learn the true meaning of suffering."

William shivered, and it had nothing to do with the biting wind.

CHAPTER 7:
THE SERVITOR

Serena paced within her father's study. Nervous butterflies flitted about her stomach, and she fought the urge to pace out her anxiety. Today her status would be rendered by the Servitor, the Loving Servant of Sinskrill, Lord Shet's Voice, her father.

Of course, he had yet to arrive—late as usual—and while Serena waited, she studied the room for changes. She noticed no obvious differences. Floor-to-ceiling bookshelves lined the walls and brimmed with heavy books, histories mostly, while a chocolate-colored leather couch faced the dormant fireplace. A heavy oak desk, dark with age and a surface stained with ink, crouched like an ogre before a bank of mullioned windows. A tall, elegant alabaster case stood next to it. Always locked, it held Shet's Spear, and Serena knew better than to approach the mystical weapon. Only the Servitor could handle it.

Serena stared out the windows, toward the upper and lower courtyards of the palace. In the distance, were Village White Sun, the Norwegian Sea, and the setting sun, now only a vague glow behind Sinskrill's clouds. The view was incomparable since the

Servitor's office stood on the top floor of the palace directly adjacent to her father's private quarters.

Serena mentally chided herself. She had to break her childish habit of regarding the Servitor as her father. Like all children of Sinskrill, she had no true father. Not in the sense that those of the Far Abroad used the term.

The Servitor's servant, Selene Paradiso, interrupted her thoughts by popping in and lighting the fireplace. Serena's sister, a scrawny, little girl of nine, would become a rare beauty when her bony features filled out. She and Serena shared the same dark brown eyes, dark hair, and dusky skin. They even shared the same parents, although Selene didn't know it.

"Will there be anything else, ma'am?" Selene asked, using the honorific accorded a bishan.

Serena smiled warmly and knelt, intending to take her sister in her arms, but at that moment the Servitor entered the room. She quickly straightened.

"Madam," he said, striding into the room and his vision aimed at a sheaf of paper in his hands. He missed Serena's loving smile toward Selene. "Her honorific is madam. She is a mahavan, as of this very moment." The Servitor lifted his gaze to Serena. "We'll hold the public ceremony later, but I've already drafted the orders." He waved the papers in his hands.

"Thank you, my liege," Serena said, dropping a curtsey.

"You earned it. Two *raha'asras* is a rare prize for a bishan's pilgrimage."

"Yes, my liege," Serena replied.

"Why are you still here?" the Servitor asked Selene, who stood frozen with uncertainty.

"I was waiting word from madam as to whether she required anything else, my liege."

"I require nothing at this time," Serena answered, "but make sure my quarters are clean when I arrive."

"Yes, madam," Selene replied with a curtsey. "I already laid out new bedding, and dusted the rooms from top to bottom."

"Leave us," the Servitor commanded his youngest and only other child. He didn't spare Selene any further notice as he turned to Serena. "The *raha'asras* you brought in—William Wilde and Jake Ridley—require instruction. We have no room for the slothful."

"When will you start their training?" Serena asked, hoping the guilt she felt for the plight of her once-friend didn't show on her face.

"I won't. Only a *raha'asra* can train a *raha'asra*. I've sent for Fiona. She was at Village Bliss, cleansing their *lorasra*. The ley lines showed signs of corruption."

Serena mentally frowned. Fiona was an odd woman, brought from England more than sixty years ago at the same age as William and Jake currently were. From Serena's earliest memories the old *raha'asra* had always struck her as someone to avoid. Her whip-like tongue could cut as painfully as a barbed arrow, and she continually railed against her status, somewhere between a mahavan and a Prime. Her arrogance should have long since been punished, but Fiona remained shielded by her importance to the entire island, and she knew it.

"Couldn't a Spiritualist have taken care of that?" Serena asked.

"Yes, but a Spiritualist couldn't have repaired the broken ley line. Only Fiona can."

"I see," Serena replied. "And she went willingly?"

"Of course," the Servitor replied, his eyes hard. "She knows better than to defy me."

He obviously had a means to force Fiona's compliance, a useful lever Serena would dearly love to know. Information was currency on Sinskrill.

"I expect her arrival tonight," the Servitor continued.

"Didn't the troll, Travail Fine, help train Fiona?" Serena asked.

The Servitor nodded.

"Then won't his help be required as well for William and Jake?"

"I don't trust Travail," the Servitor answered. "Hopefully, Fiona will be up to the task."

"What if she isn't?" Serena pressed. Even before the final word left her lips, she stifled a sharp inhalation of worry. One never challenged the Servitor. Serena held her breath.

The Servitor's thick beard rippled as his prognathic jaw clenched.

Serena's worry shifted to fear.

"Then Travail will succeed where she fails," the Servitor responded.

Serena remembered to breathe and relief flooded her. Apparently, the Servitor had chosen to disregard her lapse in respect.

"Now that I've satisfied your curiosity, you may leave," he ordered. "The rest of the night is yours to do as you wish."

Serena bowed. "Yes, my liege," she said, and exited his study.

Downstairs, on the third floor in the family quarters, she ran into Isha. He'd trimmed his beard and changed out of his travel-stained clothes and into dark trousers and a ruby-red shirt.

"How went the meeting?" he asked.

"Well enough," Serena replied with a grin. "I've been elevated."

Isha's face broke into a pleased smile. "Excellent, and perhaps later on citizenship shall also be yours. Boldness will see us become a power here on Sinskrill."

"You already have allies chosen for us?" Serena asked.

"Possibilities only," Isha answered. The glint in his eyes gave away his pleasure, and he held up a cautioning finger when Serena made to ask more. "Say no further. The halls in the palace are not a safe place to discuss such matters. The Walkers hear all."

***

"Welcome to your new home," Dalton said, giving William an unhelpful shove into a single-room cottage. "This is where you'll stay until you earn more."

William stumbled across the threshold and took in the hovel. Anger, disbelief, and depression warred in his mind. *How had he fallen so far, so fast?*

"Good luck," Dalton said with a derisive chuckle before he left.

William stepped farther into the shack, making room for Jake to enter.

The cottage's rotted, thatched roof looked ready to fall in, and an air of dankness, of mold permeated the place. Cobwebs clung to the corners and rafters, fluttering in a breeze that swirled dust-bunnies across the stone floor. A small fireplace took up one corner of the room, and a rough-hewn table, a small lamp, and two chairs stood beside it. Twin cots, pressed against opposite walls and finished the furnishings.

Jake closed the door, and the cottage plunged into gloom. A single window, yellowed and sagging with age, let in some of the gray twilight. As William's eyes adjusted, he noticed multiple cracks lacing the mortar binding the gray stones that formed the walls. Similar gaps surrounded the poorly fitted door, which barely hung from its hinges, and the wind soughed through all the various openings, moaning like a ghost and reaching with chill, insubstantial fingers.

"You see any firewood?" Jake asked with a shiver. "It's freezing in here."

"I saw a pile near those barracks where we had supper," William replied.

"The one where all the single men live?"

William nodded. "I'll go get some."

"We'll both go. I don't think we should be separated around here," Jake said.

Darkness had settled upon the island by the time they finished gathering the wood. A handy set of flint-and-steel atop the mantel quickly got a fire going, and they settled in for the night.

"How do you turn on the lamp?" Jake asked.

"I think you have to use *asra*," William said.

"How do you figure?"

"There's no cord or lightbulb. No place for oil or kerosene, either. It has to be magic."

"Magic," Jake muttered. "I keep thinking I'm going to wake up and this will all be some terrible dream."

"Same here," William agreed. He flopped onto his cot with a groan of weariness.

"What do you think happens tomorrow?" Jake asked, dropping into his cot as well. "And why'd the sun set so soon? It was morning when we left Banff, and that was only a few hours ago."

"We're probably way east of Banff," William said, "and I have no idea about tomorrow." Truthfully, he didn't want to think about it. He wanted to get what rest he could.

"No idea?"

"None. Serena lied to me about who she is, and Mr. Zeus and the others knew hardly anything about Sinskrill."

"Will they be able to find us?"

"I don't know. Maybe. I don't want to talk about it now," William said, irritation creeping into his voice. "Let's get some sleep and see what happens in the morning."

"All right," Jake agreed.

William closed his eyes and tried to sleep, but it eluded him.

Tedium and a sense of unreality had filled the long drive to Banff, but now, after arriving in Sinskrill and meeting the Servitor, reality settled in. The horrible, wretched truth proved impossible to avoid, and William's mind swirled over the events of the past few days. Mostly, he tried to figure out what he could have done differently to avoid this, what signs he'd missed about Serena. Like Jake, he also wished he could wake up and find out it had all been nothing more than a terrible nightmare.

However, the rotted thatch above him, the chill air cloaking him, and the dank odor of decay underneath it all told him otherwise. This prison might be the place where he would live out the rest of his life.

William wanted to howl at his stupidity, his blindness. *How could he have not realized the truth about Serena? Idiot.*

Anger kept him awake, but eventually it faded, and a fitful slumber took over. He woke often, though, shivering beneath his thin blanket. While the fire helped, it couldn't fully warm the cottage or banish the icy wind cutting through the various gaps in its construction.

Hours later, the door slammed open, and William sat up with a shout of alarm.

"Good. You're awake," said an old woman with an English accent. She clutched a lantern in her hands and wore the fur-trimmed clothes of a mahavan rather than the sturdy, tan clothes of one of the workers. Drones were what Dalton had called them after meeting the Servitor. A gold necklace hung around her neck, and a white cap perched upon her head. Her lips turned up in a friendly smile, and with her seamed face, she could have been someone's kindly grandmother.

"Who are you?" William asked.

"Your instructor. Your Isha, if you will," the old woman replied. She strode to the lantern on the table and somehow brought it to life. The cottage bloomed with light. "Your first lecture begins now."

"What?"

The old woman chuckled. "Not too bright, are you boys? Stand up straight."

William and Jake shuffled to their feet.

The old woman's kindly face twisted into a scowl. Her eyes

narrowed, and lines of fire surged along William's veins. He screamed in pain, fell to the ground and curled around his knees. He thought his eyes might boil away. His toes curled, and his muscles spasmed, threatening to tear their ligaments. Jake thudded down next to him, also crying out in agony.

"Be quicker next time you're told to do something," the old woman said. "You'll find me far more forgiving than a true mahavan, but my patience is not endless."

The pain subsided, and William panted in relief.

"Stand up."

William shambled to his feet as quickly as he could, with Jake following suit.

The old woman smiled. "Better. Now. The first one who can tell me who I am gets to keep their blanket tonight."

"Our instructor?" Jake blurted.

"Are you asking or telling?"

"Telling."

"Correct." She gathered William's blanket. He started to protest, but a single, cold glare from the old woman froze him to silence. "This is your first lesson. Never expect help from the person standing next to you. We're alone in this world. Children, siblings, parents . . . none of them are as important to you as yourself. Take what you need, no matter the cost to anyone else. Am I understood?"

She wore an expectant air, and after a moment of silence, sighed in disappointment. "The proper response to those with greater status than your own—which in your cases is most everyone—is 'yes, ma'am' or 'yes, sir' unless you're speaking with a female mahavan. Then it's 'yes, madam'. And the Servitor is always 'yes, my liege.' As I am essentially a mahavan, when I ask you a 'yes or no' question, your response should be 'yes, madam' or 'no, madam'. Am I understood?"

They must not have answered quickly enough because once again fire burned William to the marrow. He writhed on the ground, and when the pain ended, he slowly stood up, face flushed with anger and humiliation.

"Now. Some facts. My name is Fiona Applefield. I was brought to Sinskrill in nineteen twenty-three at the age of nineteen. This island has been my home ever since, and this island will be my home until the day I die. Much like you do now, I once longed to escape, to return to my family in England, but in time, with great pain and loss, wisdom taught me the folly of those dreams. Now I serve. Save yourself the trouble by learning from my mistakes and accepting your fates. Put aside notions of home and family. Sinskrill is your home, and the Servitor is the only family you will ever require. Understood?"

"Yes, madam," William replied. Jake echoed his words a split second later.

"Excellent. Perhaps you have brains within those craniums after all. More information for you to digest. Sinskrill was founded in sixteen fifty-nine B.C. by the followers of our holy Lord Shet—may his glory soon return. We will discuss him in greater detail at another time. The island currently contains one thousand and eleven souls—including the two of you—and is governed through the divine inspiration of Lord Shet by the Servitor." She gave a mocking smile to William. "Do you wish your blanket back?"

"Yes, madam," William quickly replied.

"Then repeat back to me what I said." She held up a cautioning finger. "Miss even the smallest detail, and your clothes become forfeit."

Despite the cold, William broke out in a sweat. The old crone wasn't exaggerating. She meant every word of her threat. William wracked his brain, trying to ensure he remembered everything Fiona had told them.

He repeated her words as best he could, and when he finished he waited with a pounding heart for her response.

The old woman gave him a penetrating stare before tossing him his blanket, shutting off the lamp, and exiting the cottage without another word.

———•———

Over the next week, Fiona took William and Jake on a tour of the island, explaining what they were expected to do. During her time with them, she was by turns surly, jocular, distant, and friendly.

Today was a surly day.

"Don't speak unless spoken to," Fiona snapped when she picked them up from where they had breakfast at the men's dormitory. "We have a long journey ahead of us: Village Paradiso. And to ensure your strength, we walk. No bicycles."

William mentally groaned. Paradiso, the middle village of Sinskrill's three habitations. He hid his complaint underneath a compliant, "Yes, madam."

Jake parroted the phrase in unison with him.

Fiona doled out punishments in the same way as Sinskrill's ever-present clouds doled out rain—randomly, but seemingly every hour of every day—and since his and Jake's arrival, William had begun to unconsciously flinch whenever Fiona spoke. Her commands were never capricious, but it was impossible to tell what would trigger a punishment. An insufficiently obsequious tone could be enough.

"Keep up. I want to be at Paradiso by mid-afternoon." Fiona set off at a mile-devouring pace, and William and Jake kept up with her, maintaining the five steps distance behind her that she'd dictated early on.

The journey passed in silence, except for their dull footfalls upon the stone pavers of the bombastically named Great Way, the rutted road connecting White Sun to Paradiso, and from there to Bliss, the northernmost of Sinskrill's villages. William mentally snorted. The Great Way. *Yeah, right.* There was nothing great about it. It was just a broken, ruined path, barely wide enough for an ox-cart.

William skirted a large mud puddle, one big enough to threaten a wagon wheel. Many more of equal size, or greater, rutted the road, and given Sinskrill's continual rain from its ceiling of perpetual gray clouds, the puddles never had a chance to fully dry.

Overall, the morning proved an apt metaphor of the whole island: crappy weather falling on a crappy road on a crappy island full of crappy people.

William even thought the scenery crappy. White-capped mountains towered to the north, their shoulders forested with alder, cedar, willow, and cottonwood, while stands of pines stood lonely sentinels amidst nearby fields of heather.

William reconsidered his thoughts about the scenery, and

reluctantly concluded that other than the weather, Sinskrill could be considered beautiful.

But not her people. The denizens of the island were universally cruel and evil. Beyond the hundred and fifty or so mahavans and mahavans-in-training, there were a little less than a thousand drones. Every one of them was a lying snake, every bit as vicious, cunning, and cruel as Fiona and Serena. None of them could be trusted. All of them—mahavans and drones alike—sought the approval and attention of the Servitor, the Loving Servant. To further their ambitions, all were willing to go to any extreme, even happily selling out their own family members.

William shivered when the wind blew hard, and he gathered his thin cloak more tightly about himself.

It never really warmed up in Sinskrill, either. Even the summers were said to be cold. Cold and hardship were a way of life for these people, supposedly meant to harden them for war when their god, Shet, returned to reclaim his place as ruler of the world.

Lord Shet, William mused. More like Lord Shit.

Thunder rumbled, and minutes later the interminable rain fell. William grimaced as the cold water landed on his unprotected head. A hood would have helped, but on Sinskrill protection against the weather was considered a liability, a weakness. While the rain poured, William imagined himself somewhere far away and warm, on Arylyn, the island Jason had once shown him: a place of sunshine, rainbows, colored shadows, and happiness. For the thousandth time, he wished he was there right now.

Stupid, stupid jackass. Why had he insisted on returning to Cincinnati after defeating Kohl?

"What are you thinking about?" Jake whispered, too low for Fiona to hear with the splashing rain to muffle their voices.

"I'll tell you later," William whispered.

"Somewhere warm?" Jake guessed.

"Somewhere warm," William admitted. The phrase had become their private mantra.

Ironic, William thought. He and Jake despised one another growing up, but now, on this island of misery, they were each other's only friend.

A steady clip-clopping echoed over the sound of the falling rain, and William looked down the Great Way for the cause.

The Servitor rode toward them on a magnificent, white stallion. The reins and saddle were gilded and etched with fanciful geometric designs, like something from America's desert southwest. They somehow shone in the dull light.

William and Jake immediately pulled off to the side of the road and knelt amidst the pooling water. One always knelt in the Loving Servant's presence. Even Fiona and all the mahavans did.

"Rise," the Servitor commanded before pointing to William. "I will speak to this one alone. Travel on. I'll send him to catch up in due time."

"Yes, my liege," Fiona simpered.

Jake gave William a tight-lipped nod of support before setting off with Fiona.

William faced the Servitor with a leaden stomach.

The Servitor smiled. "You probably think you've fallen far in this world, that there is no basement below your current station," he said in a friendly, conversational tone. "Believe me, you've yet to taste the depths to which I could cast you down if I so chose."

"Yes, my liege," William replied, the only acceptable manner by which to address the Servitor.

The Servitor laughed. "Your words are humble, but they have no relationship with your true emotions. Anger seethes within you." He cocked his head. "Would you like a taste of *my* anger?"

"No, my liege," William quickly replied, a flutter of fear working in his stomach. He knew Fiona's pain, and imagining what the Servitor could do made his knees tremble.

The Servitor chuckled again. "Perhaps you're not as stupid as I was led to believe," he said. "That time your reply was humble, and it was also fearful. It is how you should always speak when addressing me."

"Yes, my liege," William agreed, a wave of relief washing over him.

"Fiona is instructing you in our ways of obedience and obeisance," the Loving Servant said. "Do you think she has been a valuable instructor?"

"She has been an excellent instructor, my liege," William lied, hoping that no hint of the disdain he felt was reflected in his tone.

He apparently wasn't as successful as he'd hoped.

The Servitor wore a mocking half-smile. "I'm sure. And were she here, I'd be interested to hear Fiona's reply to your words."

William mentally cursed himself. *When would he learn? To survive this shithole, he had to learn to hide any hint of defiance from his posture and tone. No other response but bland acceptance was permissible.*

The Servitor smiled. "As to why I wished to speak with you . . . you have two choices, William Wilde. You can either help me by becoming the *raha'asra* I require. Or you can refuse, and I'll slowly destroy your friend."

He spoke in a calm, matter-of-fact tone, and William's knees shook once again. This man would do exactly as he promised and feel no more regret than if he had snuffed out a mosquito.

"You believe me, don't you?" the Servitor asked.

"Yes, my liege," William replied in a truly humble, fearful tone.

"I believe you do," the Servitor said. "I'm glad we had this chance to converse." He heeled his stallion into motion and left without another word.

⸺ ● ⸺

Later that evening, after an exhausting day in the fields of Village Paradiso, they returned to White Sun where Fiona left them to fend for themselves. William and Jake had supper in the men's barracks before retiring to their hovel.

In the week since their arrival, they'd managed to clean it up. The cobwebs were gone, but the cracks in the door and mortar remained. Those they couldn't fix, but after they got a fire burning, the cottage felt warmer than the miserable weather outside.

William flopped into his bed, utterly spent.

So far, their days on Sinskrill remained an unchanging struggle of hard labor followed by a tasteless supper and restless sleep. And during all of it, there had been no chance to clean up because of a typically stupid, arbitrary rule on this island of stupid, arbitrary rules. They could only use the baths in the barracks during the hours between sunrise and sunset. Thus far, William and Jake had yet to get back to White Sun early enough to make use of them.

As a result, their hair hung lank and greasy. Their clothes, boots, and every exposed piece of skin held a layer of dirt or drying mud. William could barely make out Jake's natural skin color through the caked-on grime, and he didn't want to imagine what the two of them smelled like. Thankfully, they'd gone nose-blind to their stink.

Jake fell onto his cot as well. "What did the Servitor have to say?" he asked.

William told him.

"He said the same thing to me when he rode up on me and the B—I mean Fiona."

Jake had been about to call Fiona 'the Bitch', their private name for the crone, but thankfully, he'd caught himself in time. A few days back, thinking they were alone in their cottage, they'd discussed Fiona, mocking her, laughing at her idiocy, and complaining about her cruelty.

No one else had been around, but somehow Fiona had learned what they'd said, and her punishment had been severe with lots of pain.

Later, one of the drones had told them about the Walkers—the Air Masters—Sinskrill's spies who heard everything. Closed windows, shut doors, even deep caverns weren't immune to their penetrating ears. From then on, William and Jake were careful to speak in only the most banal, inoffensive terms about any topic.

"What do we do?" Jake asked.

"What we're told, until we earn our way out of this cesspool."

"Earn?"

"We're both supposed to be *raha'asras*, untrained and all that," William said, "but from what Jason and Mr. Zeus told me, *raha'asras* are powerful."

"Then we get to live like Fiona, with only the Servitor telling us what to do?" Jake asked.

"Sounds as heavenly as somewhere warm," William replied.

"Warm," Jake agreed in a fervent tone.

"Did you notice when Fiona unlocked our *lorethasras* this morning?" William asked.

"I noticed," Jake replied. "There's no way to miss something like that. The way everything suddenly brightened, like all the sounds were prettier, the smells sharper, the air sweeter."

"It's the only part of this nightmare that makes the rest of it tolerable."

"No, it doesn't," Jake disagreed. "Nothing could make up for what's happened to us. I'd trade all of this—I don't care how wonderful you think *lorethasra* or *lorasra* feels—if we could wake up home tomorrow morning in my bed."

His words struck a sympathetic chord, but the phrasing set William to laughing.

"What's so funny?" Jake demanded, sounding offended.

"I didn't know you played for the receiving team."

"Receiving team? What are you talking about? I play defense," Jake said, clearly confused now.

William laughed again. "Think about what you said. *We* wake up in *your* bed tomorrow."

Jake laughed. "Even if I did play for the receiving team, there's no way I'd want to share a bed with you."

"I'm so disappointed," William said dryly.

Jake chuckled again, but a second later he sobered up. "You know what I mean, though, right? I'd give up all the supposed glory of magic if we could go home."

William waited for the wind to whine through the gaps in the mortar before answering. Walkers could supposedly hear anything, but maybe they couldn't distinguish a whisper amidst the sound of a blustering breeze.

A few seconds later he had what he needed. "We will," he vowed in a murmur, while the wind whistled through their cottage. "We know where the anchor line is. Once we're taught how to use our *lorethasra*, we'll open it and get off this hellhole."

"That won't be enough," Jake said.

The wind stilled, and so did their conversation.

"What did they do with your *nomasras*?" Jake asked.

"They took them," William told him. Even as he spoke the words, he understood what Jake was trying to tell him. Yes, they could learn to use the anchor line and flee Sinskrill, but without *nomasras* containing *lorasra*, they wouldn't get far. Which meant they'd have to make what they needed.

Just another obstacle to overcome.

CHAPTER 8:
SCHEMES AND DEATH

March 1987

Y ou used to be faster," Sherlock Carpenter mocked. He was a tall man, young, slender, and with long fingers that played over the hilt of his blunted *jian*. More importantly, he was Village Paradiso's Prime, their ruler under the Servitor's tutelage. Sherlock quirked his eyebrows in challenge. "Again? Or are you tired of losing, little bishan?"

Serena maintained her composure, keeping her face still and suppressing any evidence of her irritation. She calmly retied her hair, gathering stray strands into her ponytail. Her brother sought to annoy her and cause her to lose focus. One of the oldest tricks in the world, since anger rarely aided a cunning warrior.

Even now, Sherlock's thin lips curled in a mocking smirk, another attempt to needle her. "Being away from Sinskrill has made you soft," he said.

"Believe what you want," Serena replied, "but while my skills might have deteriorated during my time in the Far Abroad, you and

I both know how matters between us usually ended before I left. Enjoy your triumph while it lasts."

They sparred in the lower courtyard of the Servitor's Palace. A wall of alabaster stone rose all around them. Barracks and paddocks stood to the east while a viewing stand rose to the north, along with entrances into the Palace proper. South held the raised portcullis and main gate, but the west contained an open space. There, in squares of packed dirt, the mahavans, bishans, and shills sparred and trained.

This was the Crucible. This was the true heart of Sinskrill. This was where all could witness the skills or follies of those seeking greatness. This was where shills gained promotion to bishans, and where bishans earned the opportunity to become mahavans. All the time, those training within understood that failure at any step would end with the stripping of their *lorethasra* and they would live out the rest of their lives as drones.

Sherlock called her forward. "Prove it."

"Not a problem," Serena said. Before setting herself, she took time to adjust the heavy padding protecting her chest and arms.

Sherlock rolled his eyes, but Serena didn't hurry. In truth, she needed the break. Sweat beaded on her forehead, and she tried not to pant. While she had trained in the Far Beyond, it hadn't been with the intensity required of the Crucible. Worse, her protective padding both weighed her down and inhibited her movements. She had forgotten how heavy it was and had yet to fully adapt to it.

"Any time you're ready," Sherlock pressed.

"I'm ready," Serena said. "I'll break the brakes off you." She laughed at Sherlock's perplexed frown. Distraction worked as well as angering an enemy.

Serena attacked before the confusion faded from Sherlock's face. She expected his uncertainty to force him back into old patterns. She swept her blunted *jian* from her waist upward in a diagonal slash. Sherlock blocked. He followed up with a thrust. Serena slapped aside his blade. She stepped into his guard. A knee to the gut, and Sherlock folded over. She set her *jian* against his neck.

"Touch," Serena said. She breathed deep and worked to slow her thudding heart and did her best to hide her fatigue.

Sherlock stood up with a scowl. "Swords are a simple measure of skill, but my talents lie elsewhere," he declared. "Politics, for instance. In that arena, I'll—how did you phrase it? Ah, yes. Beat the brakes off you. Or do you really think the Servitor will displace one of us on your behalf? That you or Adam, your Isha, will gain Primeship over one of the villages? It won't happen," he jeered.

"Not yet, but I'd watch out once I'm made a citizen."

Sherlock scowled further, and Serena secretly smiled. *Fool. How easy he was to tweak.* It amazed her anew how Sherlock had ever gained control of a village, given his lack of control over himself.

"There are only twelve citizens," Sherlock said, "and none of the current holders are old or feeble."

"Then perhaps one of them shall be enfeebled."

Sherlock grinned. "If I didn't know better, I'd think you found a spine, being away from home."

"And if I didn't know better, I'd think you found a brain."

"How droll." Sherlock readied his blade. "Again?"

Serena brought up her blade.

"Ready?" Sherlock asked, his very question an insult.

In the Crucible, a blade in hand was itself an indication of readiness.

"Only if you are," Serena answered with a mocking smile.

Once more Sherlock foolishly displayed his emotions. He grimaced in irritation, and Serena mentally rolled her eyes. *Pathetic.* As Isha had often taught, *Knowledge of your enemy's emotional state gives you control of your enemy's emotions.* Serena believed it a truth as obvious as gravity, but apparently Sherlock had never learned it. Perhaps, she thought, because Darren Pyre, the aging leader of the Fire Masters, had served as his mentor. Maybe the old man had grown lazy in his dotage.

Sherlock rushed in.

Serena slipped a high thrust and parried a low sweep. She gave way when Sherlock pressed forward. She slid under an overhand strike. He blocked her return horizontal slash and lunged in behind his parry. Again, Serena ghosted away.

"Do you run from all your fights now?" Sherlock sneered. "I heard this new *raha'asra* had you running all the time. You sprinted across half a continent, fleeing for your life, did you not?"

Serena maintained focus on Sherlock's blade and stance.

"This William Wilde. I understand you had to feign feelings for him," Sherlock continued. "Perhaps those feelings became true, and you became as soft as he is." He lunged in behind a thrust and carried it into a diagonal slash.

Serena's concentration broke for a moment. She didn't like thinking about William.

A horizontal slice she barely blocked forced her attention back to the match, and she forced aside her guilty thoughts, the weakness that had settled in her heart like pus. Only the living moment mattered.

She studied Sherlock while she slid aside from another vertical slash and slipped a thrust. His horizontal slash met air when she darted back.

Sherlock stepped away with a growl of frustration. "You *have* become a runner," he complained.

In that instant Serena saw her opportunity. She stepped right, cutting an angle. A diagonal slice arched upward from left to right. Sherlock blocked it, but Serena rode her momentum into a straight thrust. The blade skimmed along Sherlock's sword before slamming into his padded chest.

He stumbled back with a curse.

"Maybe I do run more than I once did," Serena said, "but I still find a way to win." She stepped out of the training square, leaving before Sherlock could recall her and challenge her again. There was no chance she could beat him with that maneuver a second time.

⸺●⸺

Much like the raptor's nest for which it was named, the Eyrie stood atop the Wild Peak, the southernmost tower of the Servitor's Palace. Wide windows lined three walls of the room as well as the ceiling and provided expansive views of Sinskrill in three directions.

Leaning off the Eyrie like an accusing finger stood a long, glass-bottomed balcony, the Judging Line. Those deemed treasonous to Sinskrill were tossed off that high platform, with their fate given to the hands of the judging winds. The balcony swayed in the blasts of wind blowing at the Eyrie's heights, and only the most daring, or those with no choice in the matter, such as the drones required to keep the Line clean, risked spending any time out there.

For Serena, the balcony had never brought her unease. She found it peaceful, all alone with no one to bother her. Her comfort at the heights made it all the more surprising that her talents had ended up being Fire and Earth rather than Air.

Regardless, she enjoyed spending time on the Judging Line, or when the weather wouldn't allow it, within the Eyrie itself. Such as this morning when a cloudless dawn had brought bright sunshine streaming down upon Sinskrill, and set the nearby indigo waters of the Norwegian Sea to glistening. Farther, past where the *saha'asra* no longer held sway, the water appeared leaden. Westward, Village White Sun had already risen for the day, and the drones, ant-like in the distance, moved about, doing as they were bidden.

As she watched them, Serena wondered about William and Jake. *How were they doing? Probably not good. How could she expect anything else given the nature of her home?*

A line of drones broke off from the others and approached the Servitor's Palace, and Serena's curiosity piqued. Though her talents didn't include mastery of Air, she could still use that Element to a certain extent. She sourced her *lorethasra*. She sometimes wondered what aroma it carried but no *asrasin* could know the scent of their own magic, and she didn't trust anyone to tell her. They'd only lie.

She drew out a thin tendril of her silvery Spirit and coated it with a thick layer of Air mixed with a touch of Water. Next, she reached for *lorasra*, which ebbed in dendritic pulses along ley lines throughout the Servitor's Palace. She separated it into its component Elements, and to the thimbleful that she extracted, Serena attached her nascent braid, Air-to-Air and Water-to-Water.

The air before her eyes stiffened, hardening into lenses. Binoculars. An old trick, one all mahavans knew. Serena tuned its depth and quality until the faces of those distant drones sharpened into focus.

Though their features weren't identical, the peasants were nonetheless indistinguishable. They all possessed faces frozen in the same dead-eyed expression, a flat-featured, dull acceptance of their miserable fate, a loss of identity and hope Serena had already seen on William's and Jake's visages when she'd seen them yesterday plowing a field by hand.

The morning's bright mood faltered, and Serena stared off in the distance, wondering again what she could have done differently. As always, she had no answer. If William and Jake had escaped to Arylyn, what would have happened to Selene? Serena might have been judged a failure, stripped of her *lorethasra*, and her sister left defenseless and alone.

Serena shook her head.

She had taken the least, worst choice available to her, and she decided that guilt had no reason to find a home in her heart, not when her entire impetus had been to save her sister.

Sweet Selene.

They shared the same parents. The Servitor, of course, and a drone woman whose name should have long since been forgotten, but one Serena remembered. Cinnamon. Their birth-mother had been a woman of great beauty, and it had been that beauty which had captured the Servitor's attention. Upon her, he had bred Serena and then almost a decade later, Selene.

They had been a happy enough family, but like all drones, their lives had been hard with scarcity and persistent cold.

At age ten Serena had undergone and survived the Tempering, the testing all children of Sinskrill underwent to determine their fitness for becoming mahavans. Upon her passage she'd been whisked away from Cinnamon and formally adopted by the Servitor and his wife, childless Alaina, who had never been much of a mother.

Instead, it had been Cinnamon to whom Serena had gone for comfort and love, who had wiped away Serena's tears and kissed her skinned knees. Serena could still remember her birth mother's smell, hear her bright laughter, and feel her loving arms holding her. Cinnamon had taught Serena of gardening, but the love they shared had ultimately doomed her.

Alaina, cruel like all mahavans, had accused Serena's birth-mother of blasphemy, denying the divinity of Lord Shet. As a result, Cinnamon had been killed, eyes gouged out and whipped to death in front of Serena. Toward the end of the torture, Alaina, smiling with vicious triumph, had allowed Serena to speak with Cinnamon one last time. Blood had streaked her mother's face. Her body had been flayed open, and she'd lost control of her bowels. Serena had wept. She had held Cinnamon's hands and promised to take care of Selene, to let nothing terrible happen to her. Cinnamon had smiled then. She'd cupped Serena's face as she died.

Serena shuddered, caught in the whirlwind of her most terrible memory, unable and unwilling to let go of the pain. The pain spurred her, kept her from succumbing to Sinskrill's lurid call of darkness and futility. And any god who listened to her pleas, who helped save Selene from their mother's terrible fate, would forever earn Serena's worship.

A drone intruded on her thoughts, bringing her a meal of eggs, coarse bread layered with butter and cheese, and buffalo milk.

The interruption reminded Serena of why she had come to the Eyrie in the first place, and she took a breath, settling her thoughts before taking an appreciative sip of the thick, buttery liquid. Much better than the flavored, white water that pretended to be milk in the Far Abroad. Serena dug into the breakfast, eating in silence and only looking up when Isha approached.

He seated himself beside her, and a drone brought him a plate similar to Serena's. "What thoughts press so heavily upon you?"

"Alaina died on a day like this," Serena replied, mixing a truth with a lie.

"I didn't realize you were close to her."

"I wasn't, but to have died so young is a tragedy."

Isha shrugged, clearly uncaring, as he tucked into his meal.

Of course, his dismissiveness might have changed if he'd known the truth about Alaina's tragic death.

Serena had been very careful with the poison she had administered to her adopted mother—vengeance for Cinnamon. In addition, with Alaina's death, the Servitor had done exactly as Serena had hoped. She had been put in charge of Selene's upbringing. Together, they had shared a room in the servants' section of the Palace all through Serena's time as a shill and a bishan, but following her elevation, they now shared a mahavan's quarters.

"Your charge . . . how is she?" Isha asked, breaking into her thoughts.

"Well enough," Serena replied, unsure as to the purpose of Isha's question.

"Next year she faces the Tempering," Isha noted. "Have you considered what will happen to her if she doesn't pass?"

"She'll pass."

"Once she does, and becomes a shill, who will have the mentoring of her?"

"Are you offering?" Serena asked with a half-smile.

Isha chuckled. "Certainly not. One shill and bishan is enough for me."

"Then maybe I should take on the role myself," Serena said.

"Is that wise?"

"You don't think I can be hard enough on her?"

Isha didn't reply, which was answer enough.

Serena chewed her lip. If Selene passed her Tempering, she would become a shill. From there, with hard work and luck, a bishan and eventually a mahavan. She would become a truly tempered warrior of Sinskrill, all weaknesses hammered away like a blacksmith forging iron into steel. Was that what Serena wanted for her sister? What their mother would have wanted?

"I have work to attend, but as your once-mentor, I offer a piece of advice," Isha said. "Come down from the Eyrie."

Serena blinked, confused. "I'm hardly ever here."

"I speak metaphorically. You've roosted in this high chamber ever since you've come back to Sinskrill. It's time you lived amongst our people again. You need to. Alliances and factions . . . the game never ends, and if you wish to protect yourself and what you find important, you should remember that."

"Politics." Serena scowled. She hated it, but hating it didn't make it any less real or deadly. "What do you suggest?"

"Make yourself approachable. You're popular right now. You

134

brought in two *raha'asras*. Now is the time to forge your destiny. There are several candidates, low-ranking mahavans, newly risen from drone families or from families who have fallen. Strong and smart. They could help you. Seek them out."

"And protect my flank."

"Yes."

A thought came to her. "And by strengthening myself, I strengthen you?"

Isha smiled. "Of course."

—————•—————

"I've been wondering," said Jake as he dug his rake into the soiled hay and deposited the mass into the nearby wheelbarrow. "You think we should have taken that left turn at Albuquerque?"

"Every day and twice on Sundays," William replied with a grin.

Jake took a moment to straighten up and arch into a long stretch.

William commiserated.

Cleaning the Servitor's stables was backbreaking labor, given the seemingly endless stalls full of grime, piss, and befouled bedding.

At least it was dry. Better than being outside and getting rained on.

William grimaced when a cold breeze swirled into the stall in which they worked.

Maybe the stables were dry, but they still contained the same damp chill as the rest of Sinskrill. Even the dimness—only a few dull lamps provided illumination—reminded him of the island's oppressive cloud cover.

"What do you think that other place was like?" Jake asked, getting back to work.

"What other place?"

"The warm place."

Arylyn.

William paused to consider as he leaned on his rake. His gaze grew distant as he remembered the one vision Jason had shown him of his lovely home, of beauty made real. Words were ineffectual to describe it.

"That pretty, huh?" Jake asked, apparently noticing William's dreamy-eyed stare.

"Yeah."

"When did you go there?"

"Never," William replied. "Jason showed it to me once, like a portrait in my mind."

"No talking," growled Tristan Winegate, one of the mahavan Earth Masters. On Sinskrill, the man was called a Tender, but anywhere else he would have been called a farmer.

William and Jake broke off their conversation, and rolled their eyes after the Tender wandered off.

In the three weeks since William's and Jake's capture, they had learned precious little about *lorethasra* or *lorasra*, but they had learned much about the structure of the island's society.

At the bottom were the drones, the vast majority of Sinskrill's inhabitants, and at the top was the Servitor. Below him were six Primes, one each for the villages of Bliss and Paradiso and four to lead the individual castes of mahavans, one to represent every Element that made up *lorasra*. Next followed the other mahavans, the most powerful ranks being either the Seres—Fire Masters—or the Walkers—Air Masters. After them, the Riders—the Water Masters and then the Tenders. At the bottom stood the Spirit Masters, who lacked a Prime to lead them or a name to indicate command of their Element.

Another oddity about the island: upon birth, every infant, including those conceived by drones, faced testing, and if deemed to have the potential to become a *asrasin*, the child would sometimes be adopted by a mahavan couple. Similarly, if a mahavan couple produced a baby found to be unfit, that infant was immediately stripped of its *lorethasra* and sent to live with a drone family.

Serena had become a minor celebrity in Sinskrill since she was a natural-born child of the Servitor. Only rarely did such individuals go on to become mahavans.

"How many more stalls are there?" Jake asked, breaking into his thoughts.

"Five."

"Then we're done?"

"We're done."

"We might make it back in time to take a bath, then," Jake said in a hopeful tone.

William took a whiff of his ripeness and shrugged. His rough-hewn hemp clothing—itchier than wool—stunk. He stunk, but clean or dirty, what difference did it make? He and Jake would still be slaves. While he'd learned to cope with his life on Sinskrill, it didn't mean he didn't dream of freedom.

"I know. I feel the same way," Jake whispered. "I saw the look on your face," he said by way of explanation. "Freedom."

"Freedom," William mouthed back.

Walkers couldn't hear what wasn't spoken, and over time, he and Jake had become adept at lip-reading.

"How do you work so hard and never get tired?" Jake huffed during a rest period a few hours later as he leaned on his rake.

"Don't know," William said, breathing heavy but with plenty of juice left. "Probably something to do with the necrosed. His blood changed me."

A shadow darkened their stall door, and their conversation halted as they turned to see who it was. William's jaw clenched.

Serena.

Gone was the girl he'd known at St. Francis. In her place stood a mahavan, her hair tied back in a ponytail, and wearing a long, dour, gray dress. She held silent as she seemed to study him.

Though William wanted to throttle her, see the life leave her eyes, he straightened and assumed a bland but respectful attitude. To have done otherwise would have invited punishment. "How can I help you, madam?" he asked.

Serena stared at him, and William imagined her lack of concern at his grime-covered features, the tufts of facial hair trying ineffectually to form a beard, and his lank frame. He'd lost a lot of weight since coming to Sinskrill.

So had Jake.

"I require nothing," Serena replied.

Then get the hell out of here, he wanted to shout at her. Instead, he maintained a civil, servile tone and asked, "May we return to work?"

"Is this what you wish to do? Hoe crap all day?"

"We were commanded to—" Jake began.

"I wasn't talking to you," Serena said. "What have you learned of *lorethasra* and *lorasra*?" she asked William.

"I don't understand the question," William responded in the lifeless affect of a drone.

"What is the basis of *asra*, our magic?"

"*Lorethasra*," William said. "The inner aspect is made of five Elements, Earth, Air, Water, Fire, and Spirit. I'm told the Buddhists may have lifted that last notion from ancient *asrasin*s but got 'void' and 'Spirit' mixed up. Spirit is said to be the most important of the Elements, and control of all the others flows from it."

"And *lorasra*?"

"It contains all the Elements but Spirit," William continued. "It flows along ley lines, and an *asrasin* braids his Elements to the corresponding ones in *lorasra*."

"And the practical application?" she asked. "Tell me."

William mentally scowled. Oh, he had plenty to tell her, but every bit of it would lead to trouble, either for him, Jake, or both.

A second later an idea came to him, and he suppressed a smile. The drones had a way of irritating mahavans while largely avoiding punishment. They pretended to have a cretin's stupidity, and since dull-wittedness was expected of them anyway, it often worked. Best of all, in this circumstance William really had a cretin's ignorance. It would drive Serena crazy. "I don't know," he said.

"What do you mean you don't know?"

"I don't know," William repeated. He pushed it. "Does that mean something else on Sinskrill?"

"Fiona has taught you nothing of worth?"

"I don't know, madam," William said. He looked to Jake. "Did she teach us anything of worth?"

Jake shook his head.

"I guess she didn't teach us, then," William added in his best slow-witted voice.

"I see." Serena's jaw clenched, and William silently rejoiced. Anything that upset her was fine by him. "She never taught you of braids, then?"

"What are those?" William asked. He pushed it again by giving Serena a dullard's slow blink. "For your hair?"

Serena grimaced. "You were never this dense back home," she hissed.

"We're a long way from home, madam," William reminded her, and felt further gratified when she reddened. Her mouth opened as if she wanted to say something else. Instead, she spun on her heel and stomped out of the barn.

William shook his head. *What was she upset about now?* He decided he didn't care. Besides, who could tell what Serena truly felt? She was a consummate liar.

Jake edged closer. "What was that about?" he asked in a whisper.

"Who cares? Let's finish up and get those baths."

———————●———————

Later that evening, William and Jake retired to their small cottage after taking a bath. In Village White Sun, their shack was considered extravagant for only two people. Still, while it might be considered large by some, it lacked much when it came to livability. With Sinskrill's constant drizzle, icy water leaked through the thatch and porous mortar. Some rain blew in sideways and splattered William's and Jake's cots no matter where they placed them. As a result, the fireplace did little more than keep winter's icy claws at bay.

William didn't know if he was becoming inured to the misery of their prison, or if by day's end, he was simply too tired to care.

"Buck up," Jake said.

William gave him a questioning glance.

"We've got it bad, but we're alive. We'll get out of this."

"Yeah," William said, too dubious and downcast to believe Jake's words.

"We have to keep fighting," Jake said. "Otherwise, what's the point? We might as well slit our wrists now and be done with it. We never gave up during the football season, remember? We could have given up and cashed it in, but we didn't. We fought. You fought. You held. I'm telling you to hold now."

"This isn't football," William reminded him.

"I know," Jake said in exasperation. "It's a helluva lot worse. I get it. But at the end of the day it's also the same in all the ways that matter. Back home we had to fight for each other. Same here. We watch each other's backs and hold on."

William exhaled heavily, a modicum of hope taking root. "Thanks."

"You've done the same for me," Jake said. "Especially those first weeks. I might have jumped off a cliff if you hadn't been around."

"Next time you feel that way, let me know, and I'll give you a friendly push," William said with a smile. "At least then I won't have to listen to your snoring any more."

"Ha, ha," Jake said in a sardonic tone.

William's smile broadened.

"That's the spirit," Jake said. "We fight for one another, and nothing in this hellhole will break us."

"I know," William said, "but I wasn't smiling about that. I was thinking about home. You remember how much we hated each other? It was stupid, but at the same time it was simpler."

"You want to go back to hating me?"

William grinned, his mood further lifting. "Who said I ever stopped?"

Their conversation stalled as they silently considered their shared past.

"What do you think they're doing back there right now?" William asked, breaking the quiet.

"Who?"

"Sonya, Steve, everyone."

"Funny you should bring up Sonya," Jake said with a knowing grin. "Everyone knew about your crush on her. Even Sonya."

"Everyone knew?" William asked, stricken with embarrassment. "Even you?"

"Of course, even me," Jake said. "Why do you think I gave you such a hard time? Half of it was because of Sonya. I didn't want you sniffing after her."

"And the other half was because you're an asshole?"

"Well, there is that," Jake admitted. "I can't help it."

William laughed.

"Anyway, then you went and got all dark and mysterious on me," Jake continued. "Badass really, with your sword, and the fact that you knew how to use it."

"You thought I was a badass?"

"We all did. Even Sonya. All through Christmas break, until she forgot about what happened. You know, Mr. Zeus' spell and everything. Anyway, you and Jason were all she talked about. More you than Jason, though."

William grinned. "Really?"

"Really. Now stop looking so smug about it."

"Sorry," William apologized, not the least bit remorseful.

"No, you're not."

William couldn't stop grinning. "Why me more than Jason?"

"Are you kidding? Jason throws fire. A guy like him is *too* badass, if you know what I mean," Jake said.

"I'm not really much of a badass now, am I?"

"I'm not much of a rich jerk now either."

"You're still a jerk," William said. "Just not rich." He laughed until Jake threw his soggy blanket and caught him flush in the face.

"Why exactly are we here?" asked Walker Brandon Thrum with a frown. His blocky features were similar to the Servitor's although they shared no familial ties. "All I see are a bunch of drones doing their normal work." He sat his horse at ease and appeared bored.

Serena viewed him briefly before turning away and not bothering to respond. Brandon could figure it out. Though he pretended to be an idiot—he used his height, thick build, and heavy-set features to promote the fiction—he was actually quite intelligent.

The two of them sat their horses on a rise overlooking Village Paradiso's fallow fields of stubbled stalks. With them rode two other mahavans who Isha thought might be of use to her. Serena had brought them here to feel them out about a possible alliance. They watched a group of drones clear the land in preparation for the spring planting. The warmer weather remained months away, but the fields still had to be made ready.

"Aren't those two down there your parents?" Rider Evelyn Mason, a Water Master sneered at Brandon as she pointed out a couple. Other than Serena, Evelyn was the youngest of the four of them.

Brandon shrugged in eloquent disregard.

His lack of response earned him a scowl. Evelyn's auburn hair—rare on Sinskrill as most tended to have dark hair and skin—seemed to play about her plain face although no breeze blew, and her blue eyes flashed.

Serena mentally shook her head at the interplay. Evelyn was fierce and ambitious but blunt as a butter knife. Had she really thought such a careless insult would have aroused Brandon's ire?

Serena sighed, and she found herself wishing that a better candidate amongst the Riders might have been available to meet her needs. Unfortunately, the others had already forged alliances or were too weak to be of any use. Thus the powerful, aggressive, but stupid Evelyn Mason was the best choice available to her.

"I should be at White Sun instead of wasting my time watching an anonymous group of drones," Tender Tristan

Winegate whined. The final member of their group lay between Evelyn's youth—she was only a year older than Serena—and Brandon's mid-twenties.

"I don't know what you're complaining about," Evelyn said. "If you were in White Sun, you'd be doing the same thing as you are now: watching a bunch of drones. It is what Tenders do, isn't it?"

"We don't *watch* the drones," Tristan said defensively. "We oversee and supervise them." In his annoyance, he lisped, a childhood speech impediment he'd largely overcome, except when angry. Tristan, with his black hair, bright hazel eyes, and even features, would have been a handsome man if not for that.

"The *raha'asras*. We're here for them," Brandon guessed, justifying Serena's faith in him.

"Why?" Evelyn demanded, justifying Serena's scorn for her.

"They work the fields," Serena said, "and I understand they've been taught little more than a fragment of our art. They remain as ignorant as drones."

"A month here, and they've learned nothing?" Tristan asked in disbelief.

"So they told me."

"You spoke to them?" Brandon asked. "I'm surprised they didn't attack you." He smiled. "I've heard they don't appreciate their new lives here."

"Either they learn and earn a place for themselves," Serena said, "or they don't and are stripped. The decision is theirs." She shrugged in dismissal, an action unreflective of her true feelings about William and Jake.

However, this time her plans for them might actually do them some good.

"What are your intentions for the *raha'asras*?" Tristan asked.

"Travail."

"The troll?" Evelyn asked. Her eyes widened an instant later. "You want to have their instructorship transferred from Fiona and given to the troll."

Serena nodded, hiding her surprise at Evelyn's insight. "Fiona has gained allies who block my ultimate goal, but if she's disgraced, her influence wanes."

"Then what?" Brandon asked. "What is your ultimate aim?"

"Citizenship as a start, and then we will see," Serena answered. She knew her words sounded vague, but she couldn't tell them the rest of her plan. If they learned it, they'd hand her over to the Servitor's justice.

The horses snorted, and one of them whinnied in fear.

"They smell something," Evelyn said.

A howl broke the relative quiet, and their horses shifted about, skin twitching.

"Unformed wolves," Tristan said. "It's still the heart of winter. That's when they come down."

"We should have killed them off long ago," Brandon said with a grimace.

"They're unformed," Serena reminded them. "How can we hunt what we can't rightly identify?"

"The Spiritualists can identify them," Brandon pointed out.

"Then why is it that every Servitor for the past thousand years seems to disagree with your logic?" Tristan countered, clearly the most devout of them. "Why haven't they done what you think they should?"

Brandon shrugged. "I don't know."

"Then you should trust the Servitor."

"I do, but—"

Serena cut off Brandon's reply with a slash of her arm. An eavesdropping Walker could easily claim that Brandon's words were treasonous or blasphemous. "We all trust the Servitor, and through him Lord Shet," Serena said, flashing Brandon a glare of warning.

"His glory returns," the others intoned, and Serena breathed a little easier.

Another set of howls had the horses shifting again.

"I think the wolves are getting closer," Evelyn said with a frown.

"We'd better get down there and help keep those idiots alive," Serena said in feigned disgust meant to conceal her worry. The Tenders should have pulled the drones back by now, but the peasants still worked the fields, oblivious to their danger. Closest to the forest and the howling wolves were William and Jake.

———————•◦•———————

"What's that howling noise?" Jake asked, looking up from where he'd been working manure into the soil.

"Wolves," William answered, head still bent to his task as he dug into the ground with his hoe.

Jake glanced around nervously.

"They won't attack a group of people this big," William said. He didn't seem the least bit concerned. "Don't worry about it." He continued to work, wearing the same dull-eyed, placid features displayed by the rest of the broken-spirited drones, but William wasn't broken. Jake knew it. However, William's ability to pretend otherwise was impressive.

Such as the other day, when that bitch Serena had shown up. Jake wanted to break her face, and he knew William felt the same way. Somehow, though, William had kept his composure. He'd stayed calm in the face of humiliation.

Jake wished he knew how William did it, because he was barely holding on. He shook with rage one moment and wanted to weep the next. Sometimes he wished that when he went to sleep, he'd never wake up.

Sad to want to be done with life at eighteen.

Jake couldn't help it. He hated this place, and if it wasn't for William keeping up his spirits, he wasn't sure what he'd do.

"Better get back to work," William whispered. "Tender Thomas is giving you the stink-eye."

Jake didn't bother glancing to where William's eyes had gone. Instead, he grunted his 'thanks' and got back to work, grateful that he had a partner he could rely on. Neither of them had made friends with any of the other drones, all of whom would probably sell them out in a heartbeat if the opportunity presented itself. It was Sinskrill's way: *trust no one.*

"You ever wonder why they have such normal names?" Jake asked William a short time later.

"The people here?" William shrugged. "I heard it was because Lord Shet, may his glory soon return—"

"His glory returns," Jake said with an eyeroll. Stupid phrase, but if he didn't say it and someone found out, the old witch, Fiona, would punish him.

"—ordered them to conquer the world in his name. Part of that meant they had to learn the ways of their greatest enemies, even to the point of taking on their names. For a long time they had Chinese ones."

"And now they have English ones?"

"That's what Fiona told me, but who knows if it's true," William said.

The wolves howled again, the sounds closer. Jake's eyes darted about in increasing worry. He looked to Tender Thomas, whose face wore a sickly demeanor. The mahavan's eyes flitted about in apparent nervousness.

"Drones," the Tender called out. "Retreat south toward the village. We'll wait out the wolves there."

No sooner had he spoken than four lean, gray shapes burst out of the foliage carpeting the low-lying western hills. They streaked toward the drones.

William reacted instantly. He broke the blade off of his hoe and held the wooden shaft before him in a defensive posture. "Get behind me," he ordered Jake.

"We have to go," Jake protested.

Tender Thomas, the mahavan who should have stayed behind and protected the drones, had already taken off. He sprinted away from the wolves. The rest of the drones ran too, dropping tools as they raced for safety. They wouldn't reach it. The wolves were coming on too fast.

Unless William held them off and bought the drones some time.

Jake vacillated. The panicked part of him told him to race after the drones, but his better part wanted to stand and fight with his friend.

"I need you to protect my back, William said. "Get behind

149

me." His voice sounded strangely calm, unhurried and unworried, as if he'd spent his entire life fighting off wild wolves.

Jake did as William instructed. He swallowed heavily as the wolves charged. There was no way to outrun them. Panic again threatened to overturn his thoughts, but with an effort he got his mind working. He snapped off the blade of his hoe and copied William's stance.

Thudding hoofbeats from behind them gave Jake hope. Horses thundered their way, and only mahavans rode. He risked a glimpse back and snarled when he saw who led the charge.

Serena. Great.

She'd probably tie them up and hand them over to the slavering wolves.

The animals peeled off into two pairs. So did Serena and her three horsemen. The earth trembled, and Jake struggled to remain upright. William had no such trouble.

A howling wind blew one wolf off its feet, entangling it with the other running by its side. Both screamed when a stream of fire billowed off Serena's hands and engulfed them.

The last two wolves darted past the two riders facing them. The animals now had a clear path to Jake and William.

"Oh, shit," Jake whispered.

"I've got this," William said, his voice still calm and measured. "It'll be fine."

The wolves lunged, and William spun about. He moved faster than anyone Jake had ever seen. His staff blurred, but the wolves were equally swift. They evaded his thrusts and swings while he batted aside their lunges and snapping teeth.

All the while, Jake stood like a frozen spectator. He held his staff before him, unsure how he could help William. Entering the fight would probably distract his friend rather than provide support.

The mahavans circled back. The wolves snarled as they focused on this new challenge. They flicked their gazes from the oncoming mahavans to William and back again. Their yellow eyes glowed, and Jake inhaled sharply. The wolves' eyes brimmed with intelligence, with thought, cunning, and planning.

As one, the animals raced back toward the forest. At the last moment, one of them hurled itself at a mahavan, Tender Winegate. The mahavan screamed as the wolf ripped his throat open. Both animals fled before the other mahavans could react.

CHAPTER 9:
NECESSARY DECISIONS

March 1987

The Loving Servant, the Servitor of Sinskrill, Axel Carpenter, listened carefully as his daughter stated her case. She spoke in simple terms, explaining what had transpired yesterday. She did so without unnecessary commentary or emotional pleas. Excellent. Axel felt pride at the kind of mahavan Serena had become, poised, precise, and rational. Adam, Axel's half-brother, had done well in her training, expunging all weaknesses but one: Serena's love for her sister, Selene.

Even now, the young girl busily swept the corners of the Throne Hall of Lord Shet with a tied-off bundle of rushes. Those of the Far Abroad would have described Selene as Serena's Achilles heel.

An apt description.

Axel's mind wandered as he considered his youngest child. Scrawny, but destined to be a great beauty, like her broodmare. But appearances meant less on Sinskrill than elsewhere. Here the issue of gravest importance was whether the girl had the hardness of heart, the strength at her core to become a mahavan.

Axel couldn't tell—no one could—but they would learn this summer when Selene faced her Tempering. She'd either pass or fail, the fate of all children who weren't stripped of their *lorethasra* at birth.

A disquiet at the notion roiled through Axel. He wanted Selene to succeed. He hoped she would, but until then, like all children, she had to serve as a drone. Even a Servitor couldn't overturn such a long-standing law, not even for the sake of his daughter.

Axel returned his attention to the matter at hand. Fiona stood beside Serena, maintaining a disdainful posture, but her scornful mien didn't deceive the Servitor. He'd known her far too long. He saw the way her eyes occasionally flitted about, the nervousness betrayed by lips pressed into a thin line. Fiona was rightfully fearful. Her actions, her lack of attention and regard for the *raha'asras* under her care, had brought them to near calamity, and as a result to all of Sinskrill. She would be punished for her poor judgment, and she knew it.

The only question was how harsh a judgment she would face. Axel hadn't yet decided, but given the serious nature of the charges, he had ordered the meeting be held in the Throne Hall of Lord Shet. All verdicts involving a mahavan accused of incompetence were adjudicated here.

Axel's gaze played over the room. He already knew most of the facts of the matter and no longer needed to pay the proceedings much mind.

At the public entrance to the Throne Hall stood a pair of large, gray double-doors twice the height of a man. From there, a wide aisle led through a forest of iridescent, gold-enameled columns ascending from an onyx-marble floor to a ribbed ceiling of glass and mosaics that depicted scenes from *Shet's Counsel*, Sinskrill's holiest book. In one image the god humbly provided knowledge of fire. In another he lifted humanity from the depths of ignorance. A different one showed Shet striving against the endless forces of evil.

Axel shifted in the Servitor's Chair, a richly upholstered leather seat shot with threads of gold and framed with purpleheart wood, which held the noblest of colors. It sat upon a raised dais, two steps above the rest of the floor, while three levels higher brooded the empty throne of Lord Shet. A titanic statue of the god's warrior persona loomed behind it and over the entire Hall.

Six arms reached out from the figure's shoulders, each hand holding a different weapon. The right hands grasped a khopesh, a mace, and the Book of the Dead. In his left ones, Shet held a bow, a spear, and the Knife of Woe. The jaws of a crocodile helmeted the figure's head, serving as a crown, and a sneer of cold command twisted the statue's face.

Justifiably so.

Before his long slumber, the mighty had gazed upon Shet's works and torn their hair in despair.

Fiona began her defense, but Axel knew what she would say. He knew what everyone would say. No plans or schemes remained hidden from him. All events stood out as clearly as the sunshine pouring through the windows lining the Throne Hall. How could it be otherwise with Shet to guide his thoughts, to let him see the truth as no man otherwise could?

Then again, upon ascension no Servitor remained merely a man or woman. All became so much more, masters of all forms of *asra*. Even the mighty Sapient Dormant, the Overward of the necrosed, had once bent knee and pledged obeisance to the unbroken line of Servitors.

"How could I have known the unformed would attack?" Fiona asked. "Always before, they approach at night, seeking those who aren't protected by stone and heavy doors."

"Such as foolish lovers slaking their lust in the fields?" Axel needled, reminding Fiona of an unfortunate incident from her youth.

The old *raha'asra* reddened, and the Servitor smirked. She never had learned to control her emotions, unlike his daughter, who stood unruffled and ready.

"The unformed are an abomination, and we should . . ." Fiona began.

"Enough." Axel cut off further discussion. He leaned forward in his chair. "You have failed. In all ways. Judgment will be rendered."

Fiona stiffened.

Good.

Not including Serena and Selene, the old *raha'asra* had three living grandchildren who had achieved the rank of mahavan, and one of them a Prime. As a result, Fiona had grown too proud and influential. It was time to cut her down.

"You won't be stripped, and you'll retain your rank," Axel said. He noticed Fiona's shoulders slump in relief, but now came the pain. "But Travail will take over instructorship of the new *raha'asras*. He will answer to Serena, and you will answer to the troll. You will serve Travail in whatever capacity he requires." Axel leaned back in his chair. "So says the Voice of Lord Shet."

"May his glory soon return," Serena and Fiona recited.

"Dismissed."

After they left, Axel sat alone in the empty Throne Hall—Selene had gone on to some other task—and he flexed an arm. Fur rippled on his forearm as the appendage took on the form of a bear's foreleg. Long claws extended from wide, heavy paws.

Fiona thought the unformed an abomination.

Axel smirked. On this, as in many other matters, she was deeply mistaken. The unformed were Shet's wild children, much like the line of Servitors.

ARYLYN

Jason sat on the front porch of Mr. Zeus' house in Arylyn and sipped a glass of lemonade as he stared out over the waters down below.

The cascades tumbling over Lilith's Cliffs gathered below as a narrow continuation of River Namaste. The waters flowed north through a canyon of rugged rocks before eventually emptying into the Pacific Ocean. A mile past the river, a golden beach stenciled an aquamarine bay before merging into a soaring glassine, ruddy-black cliff and decorated by a rainbow that arched from sea to stone.

Jason had always loved it here. Even if the views had been dull he would have loved it since this was Mr. Zeus' home, warm and inviting. A white-picket fence demarcated the front of the property and was split by a low gate opening beneath a jasmine-cloaked arbor. A slim walkway of granite flagstone traced a gray line through gardens and a small plot of grass. The narrow path gave way to wooden steps rising to a wraparound porch supported by stacked stone columns, and eventually a front door painted the same robin's-egg blue as the exterior siding.

With no one to maintain the home and grounds during the years Mr. Zeus and Jason had been away, the house had fallen into disrepair. It took weeks of hard labor to bring the place back to a semblance of order, and peeling paint and overgrown weeds had been the least of their concerns. More pressing had been the leaky pipe underneath the kitchen sink, which had rotted most of the flooring in that room.

Now everything was once more in tip-top shape and beautiful. The only thing missing was William.

"You're thinking about him, aren't you?" Mr. Zeus asked.

Jason nodded. "He should be here with us."

"He will be," Mr. Zeus promised. "Both him and Jake."

"You've figured out a way to get them off Sinskrill?" Jason asked, a thin thread of hope pulsing through him.

Mr. Zeus hesitated. His pause meant the answer remained 'no', but Jason felt only minimal disappointment. After all, he had expected it.

"I haven't yet figured out a way, but I will," Mr. Zeus said.

"You really think so?" Jason asked. "Be honest."

"I already have a sense of Sinskrill's location, and eventually

157

I'll have more," Mr. Zeus said. "So honestly, yes, I think we'll find him."

"I still don't understand how knowing Sinskrill's location is going to help us," Jason replied with a frown. "We still don't know the key to Sinskrill's anchor line."

"Getting there isn't the hard part," Mr. Zeus said. "The hard part is the island itself. We don't know anything about it. We don't know how many people live there, how many mahavans, the structure of their government . . . anything."

"From what I've read, they don't have much of a government," Jason said. "They have these people, drones they call them. Slaves it sounds like. Then there are the mahavans, and a ruler."

"The Servitor," Mr. Zeus supplied.

Jason shook his head in disgust. "You'd think after warring with them for as long as we have, we'd know a little more about the enemy."

"Then you'd be wrong," Mr. Zeus said. "After we retreated to our respective islands, the interactions we've had with the mahavans can be numbered on one hand."

"Which does nothing to help William's situation."

"Patience. I know he's somewhere north of us—"

"But how do we get to him?" Jason interrupted, hating his pessimism and whining.

"A boat, remember?"

Jason muttered in disbelief, cursing his stupidity. *Of course, a boat. How could he have forgotten?* The anchor lines made travel between far off places more manageable, but they obviously weren't the only means to journey to distant locales.

"In all the histories of the wars between our people, one thing becomes quickly clear. The enemy hardly ever seeks the solution to a problem through any means other than *asra*." Mr. Zeus wore a crafty smile. "I doubt the mahavans or their Servitor will expect us to simply sail to their shores."

"How do we let William know we're coming?"

"For that we have dreams."

Jason smiled, and hope once more flitted through his heart.

SINSKRILL

Serena stood at the base of Mount Toll, at a spot where the River White Sun leapt down a ladder of waterfalls and rapids as it cut through a set of gorges and chasms. The Servitor had passed word to Travail, informing the troll of her arrival. They had agreed to meet at this rocky place of wind and water.

Serena searched about, seeking out Travail. She'd only met the troll a few times, but never for an extended conversation. Curiosity and nervousness occupied her thoughts.

Travail was a justice, a giver of judgment, which meant that once he made a decision, his verdicts were inviolate. Not even the Servitor could overturn them. Something to do with historical precedents and the magic of a troll. Thankfully, he rarely exerted his authority since Travail had little love for the Servitor or the people of Sinskrill. Mahavans and drones alike did their best to avoid the troll's attention and evade his judging eye.

Movement captured Serena's attention.

Travail.

He leapt down the river's course, launching from one water-slick boulder to another with the agility of a mountain goat. As he worked his way closer, it became apparent how big he truly was.

"Gods," Serena whispered. She'd forgotten Travail's massiveness. He stood even larger than Kohl Obsidian, possibly ten feet tall, twelve when the horns curling off his head were included. With his massive thews and frame, Serena judged him to weigh a thousand pounds. *How did something so massive move so swiftly and with such fluid grace?*

Travail took a long dive into the water, and his coal-black form disappeared in the current. Seconds later, he surfaced and swam strongly toward the shore. Toward Serena.

She took a step back before drawing a steadying breath and stiffening her spine.

This was it.

This was the next ploy in her plan to save her sister, and maybe earn a measure of forgiveness from William. Serena took another deep inhalation and slowly exhaled. Her die would be cast if the troll agreed to train William and Jake.

Travail stepped toward her. Water pooled at his feet, draining from the short, black fur covering his body. He wore a loincloth but no other clothing, except for a thin strip of leather to tie back his long, black braids. The troll's stony face—his spade-like jaw covered by a braided goatee and heavy brows—matched the rocky crags all around them. "Serena Paradiso. You have come," he rumbled, his voice as deep and mournful as the tolling of a church bell. "What do you require? Your father was evasive when he asked for this meeting."

Serena struggled to meet the troll's unsettling gaze. His eyes were pure white and had no irises or pupils. "Thank you for meeting with me, sir," she said.

"Travail," the troll corrected. "I am not your sir, master, or liege. I am who I am, a troll. Nothing more. Nothing less."

"Yes, sir. I mean Travail." Serena fumbled about in unexpected clumsiness. The troll folded his thickly muscled arms and scowled, and she hurried on. "Two *raha'asras* have come to Sinskrill. They require instruction. The Servitor deemed it wise for you to guide their training."

"Because it worked so well the last time?" The troll snorted in derision. "Fiona Applefield has been a grave disappointment to me."

"I cannot answer for her," Serena said. She had finally found her footing and spoke in a more controlled tone. "But Fiona is incapable of doing the work required of her. Therefore, in the matter of these new *raha'asras*, she is to answer to you regarding their training, serving in whatever capacity you deem necessary."

"I want nothing to do with Fiona," Travail declared. "She already betrayed me once and once is more than enough."

Serena blinked in surprise at the troll's bitter feelings toward the old *raha'asra*. In fact, she had no idea that Travail had feelings about anyone.

Interesting. Later on, she'd have to discuss the matter with Isha.

"Is that a judgment?" she asked.

"A request."

"If you will not allow her to work with you, that is, of course, your prerogative," Serena said.

"And Fiona's punishment if I deny the Servitor's request?"

"I don't know," Serena replied. "He recently spoke of stripping her."

"Axel won't strip her," Travail said, sounding sure of himself.

Serena startled. She'd never heard her father referred to by his first name.

"He would lose his only *raha'asra*," Travail continued. "Fiona is too valuable."

"But now we have two to replace her," Serena reminded him. "She is not as valuable as she once was."

Travail dipped his head in acknowledgement. "Though I despise what she has become, I would not wish my former pupil to be stripped. She can serve me."

"Thank you," Serena said, not understanding why she felt such relief. Why did she care what happened to Fiona? Strip her. Punish her. Toss her off the highest peak on Sinskrill. Serena shouldn't care, and yet she did, despite hardly knowing the old woman.

"These two *raha'asras* . . . they come from the Far Abroad?" Travail guessed.

"Yes," Serena said. "They were discovered."

Travail tilted his head. "You discovered them? You brought them here, not of their own volition?"

An odd tone had suffused the troll's questions, and an unnamed worry slithered down Serena's spine. "Yes."

"I see." Travail stared her up and down, and his eyes narrowed.

"Is there a problem?" Serena asked. She maintained a calm posture, trying not to shift in nervousness while she waited for the troll's response. His assessing gaze persisted, and she swallowed in anxiety.

"No," he finally replied. "But it does raise the question as to why you're here. Your purpose," the troll mused. A second later, he smiled, and his square teeth flashed. "You truly think that I'll answer to you?" He laughed when Serena couldn't conceal her surprise at his insight. "I answer to no one."

"The Servitor requires that you *do* answer to me," Serena countered.

"His requirements are not my concern," Travail said. He seemed to loom closer. "I will instruct these *raha'asras* but only under these conditions. They will live with me. Whatever tasks have been set for them end now. I will release them to the Servitor's service when I deem them properly trained. This is my judgment."

The world hushed for a moment, shivering more briefly than a single flit of a hummingbird's wings. Something felt like it passed out of the troll and into the great beyond.

The sensation left Serena confused. "What was that?"

Travail stared at her with his disconcerting, white, iris-less eyes. "Are you certain you want to know?"

Serena decided she didn't.

The troll gave her a nod of satisfaction. "I'll send for the boys in several days."

"I didn't tell you they were boys."

"Yet I already knew it. Consider how I learned that information while you plan the words you'll speak to your father. Also consider this. While I train these boys whose lives you've helped steal, I will do my best to set them free."

His final words spoken, Travail strode away from her.

"I'm counting on it," Serena whispered to the troll's retreating back, knowing the river's tumult would hide her voice from any listening Walkers.

CHAPTER 10:
A TORTUROUS FIGHT

March 1987

Following the encounter with the wolves William and Jake became minor celebrities. It seemed the animals they had fought were actually unformed, a type of woven, deadly and powerful. Even mahavans were cautious around them. Many drones wanted to hear the story of how two untrained *raha'asras*, drones for all intents and purposes, stood their ground against such fearsome creatures.

With the passage of a single day, though, their celebrity faded. Life returned to its normal dull pace, and after another backbreaking day of labor, William and Jake joined the line of drones entering the barracks for the single men of Village White Sun. It was time for supper. While he waited in line, William scratched at his itchy facial scruff. Since drones didn't shave, he and Jake had ugly, half-filled beards and long, lanky hair that left them looking like hippies.

He didn't care. Right now, all he cared about was food and sleep.

They ambled along with the other weary drones into the brick building.

The barracks consisted of two spaces. The back contained the sleeping quarters while the front—the commons—held a number of tables and benches set in rows for the men to have their meals and relax during the few hours when they weren't working. Tall, narrow windows brought in light.

The line shuffled forward, and William and Jake passed inside. As always, the drones' demeanor changed the moment they entered the barracks. Life registered in their eyes and conversations broke out. Laughter. Teasing. Arguments. Hope. Sorrow. Anger. They came alive, although wariness remained in their eyes since Walkers heard all.

Still, at least they had a few hours to let down their guard, William thought.

Inside the commons other drones—those too elderly or infirm to work the fields—prepared the meal, and doled it out along a buffet line. As the young men received their food, they often exchanged greetings with their older brethren, and smiles flashed amongst them.

During his two months on Sinskrill, William had never been able to coax such a response from a drone, young or old, not even after fighting off the unformed wolves. Neither had Jake. They had received only cursory words and explanations during their time here. No slowly warming smiles, sentiment, or acceptance.

Only the cold shoulder.

Maybe it was because they were outsiders. William wasn't sure. Plus, while they shared the same labor as the drones, everyone knew he and Jake were *raha'asras* in training with their own separate dwelling to punctuate the differences.

William regretted many things about being abducted to Sinskrill, but the loss of friendship and fellowship topped the list.

"Why are you here?" a gruff voice demanded. "You don't belong with us."

William searched for the source of the voice. A drone, thin like all of them, with black hair, a thick, dark beard and a short whip coiled at his waist, glared at him and Jake. William mentally groaned. Justin Cardinal, the foreman. Rumor had it he would soon be given the chance to marry.

His intended bride, Mary Clemmons, was a pleasant young woman who deserved better. A few weeks ago, Justin had witnessed her laughing at something William said to Jake. The next morning, Mary had arrived at the fields sporting a bruise on her jaw. She never spoke to them again.

Later, Justin's glare seemed to follow William and Jake wherever they went. He shadowed their every movement, staring at them with ill will, and doling out infractions and punishments for the thinnest of reasons. William had even heard him complain to Fiona about them, trying to get them in trouble with her. Luckily, she hadn't believed the foreman and told him to mind his own business.

"Why are you here?" Justin challenged again. He uncoiled his whip. "You don't belong with us. Leave."

"This is where Fiona told us to go for our meals," Jake said. "You have a problem with it, take it up with her."

"Tender Thomas says otherwise," Justin said.

"Since when?" Jake asked.

Justin cracked his whip. "Since now. Since I spoke to Tender Thomas today. Now step back."

William tugged on Jake's arm. He'd once seen Justin snap a fly out of midair with his whip.

Jake shrugged off William's hand. "I'm not leaving until I've eaten."

"Then you're leaving hungry and bloody." Justin snapped his whip, catching Jake on the top of his head.

Something broke inside William. Red rage covered his vision, an anger he hadn't felt since the final battle with Kohl Obsidian. Distantly, he heard Jake's cry and saw his friend crumple to the ground, arms covering his head to protect against further blows.

William caught the whip as it descended toward Jake. Through the haze of fury, he barely registered the leather cutting into the palm of his hand. He jerked, and Justin stumbled forward. William thudded a front kick into the foreman's chest, sending him crashing backward into a table.

The room grew quiet.

Justin groaned as he slowly levered his way upright. He swayed for a moment and gestured to some of the drones. "Take him. Take them both. Beat them like they've been stripped."

Four men stepped forward, faces grim with a promise of violence. William recognized them as Justin's closest allies.

The drones fanned out, preparing to take him en masse. William didn't wait for their attack. He took the fight to them, launching forward.

He clipped one, a flush shot to the temple. The drone went down. William angled away from a punch and shoved one man into another, where they tangled in a knot and fell to the floor. Pain bloomed in the back of William's head, and he stumbled. One of the drones had gotten behind him.

William ducked another blow he sensed coming. His attacker fell forward, thrown off balance by the lack of resistance and his own momentum. William spun about and delivered a hook to the liver. The man stepped back, hands up and ready, but an instant later the pain hit, and he crumpled.

The drone he'd shoved away clambered to his feet, a shiv in hand. Fear wormed through William's anger. He faced Justin with his whip, this drone with his shiv, and a third unarmed man. And they didn't look like they'd stop with just a few punches.

William pulled back, desperate for an opening as the drone with the shiv swung and thrust wildly.

There.

William got inside the shiv-wielder's guard and caught a thrust. A wrench of the shoulder had the drone braying in pain. A knee to the temple crushed the man into unconsciousness.

A line of fire ripped across William's back, and he cried out. Another line, and he collapsed to the ground. He turtled, covering up as best he could as strikes landed against his head and shoulders. Kicks and punches. A yip of surprise, and the blows came fewer and slower.

William rolled over and saw Jake busily pounding on the unarmed drone. The others remained down, and only Justin still stood. The foreman loomed over William, wide-eyed and fearful although he still held his whip.

Hatred blossomed within William.

He scissored his legs between Justin's and tripped him. He quickly scrambled on top and landed elbow after elbow to the foreman's face, opening cuts and breaking the drone's nose. A moment before Justin had been smiling in triumph, but now his eyes rolled up. His face became a mask of blood. One last blow, and the foreman stiffened, unconscious.

William staggered to his feet.

"What is going on here!" a voice roared.

William's gaze snapped to the speaker. A mahavan, Tender Thomas, stood in the doorway, his face red with anger.

His eyes widened when he saw William and Jake standing amidst five downed drones. "You!" A single gesture, and William collapsed. It was like Fiona's punishments but a hundred times worse. He couldn't even scream. Pain surged along every nerve fiber. He spasmed, jerking as muscles threatened to tear free of their bones. His blood boiled. The pain intensified, and William lost consciousness.

———— • ————

Jake sat upon the floor of his prison cell, resting his head against the stony wall. He closed his eyes and pretended to be back home. He could pretend he and his little brother, Pete, were playing Pole Position. Jake never won, but that hadn't been the point. The point had been to hang out with his brother.

He missed him. He missed his family. His friends. He even missed St. Francis, which he'd always assumed he'd look back upon as a useless part of his life. But he'd actually liked high school. Loved it, in fact.

Then, during the Christmas holidays, a strange longing had stirred his heart. Jake smiled ruefully as he realized what that stirring had meant. William's blood had smeared into a cut on

Jake's hand and he'd gained *lorethasra*. With it had come a vague sense of incompleteness, of an unknown need and wanderlust.

Lorethasra. A curse, as far as Jake reckoned matters. The first of many miseries, starting with Serena Paradiso and continuing with Fiona, the Servitor, and this prison, a perfect representation of Sinskrill as a whole. Sure it was clean, with only a light layer of dust and dirt covering the floor. No rats scrambled about on a carpet of feces and urine, but beneath it all existed the same hopeless pits of hell seen in the prisons of *Ben-Hur*.

Jake sighed. He missed movies and TV, too.

He shifted, and cursed when the movement set off new throbbing in his head. Tender Thomas had worked him over pretty good, but nothing like what he'd done to William. His friend lay in the next cell wearing a blanket of bruises.

"How are you doing?" Jake asked.

"It helps when I don't move," William said.

"It would have helped even more if Tender Thomas hadn't pounded us so much."

"Yeah, it would."

Jake recalled something just then, and he chuckled.

"What's so funny?" William asked.

"I was thinking about the time I challenged you to a fight," Jake explained. "Last fall, remember? The priests' garden, only I sent Mr. Meron instead." He chuckled again. "Sure glad I didn't show up. You would have kicked my ass, and probably anyone I'd brought with me."

William barked laughter before breaking off with a sharp intake of breath. "Guess I shouldn't laugh."

"You going to be okay?" Jake asked.

"I'll live if that's what you mean," William said, "but I doubt I'll want to for awhile." He hissed in pain.

Jake waited for William's breathing to return to normal before speaking again. "How'd you learn to fight like that, anyway?"

"Mr. Zeus taught me. Jason and I used to spar a couple hours every night."

"You were like Bruce Lee or something," Jake said.

William didn't respond, and they fell silent.

"You remember Tyrone Stable?" Jake asked, ending the quiet.

"Our running back? Sure."

"Tyrone and I used to talk sometimes," Jake said. "We got to be pretty good friends, and he used to talk about how white people didn't really understand racism or the reason slavery still holds a sting for people like him."

"Tyrone's the whitest-acting black guy I know," William said. "I'm blacker than he is. Doesn't he listen to The Smiths and Echo and the Bunnymen?"

"Yeah, but that's not all there is to Tyrone. He used to say that for whites, racism ended back in the nineteen-sixties, but for blacks it never went away. He used to say white people buried it underground where they didn't have to look at it. Or think about slavery, and how a person's body, their very personhood, belonged to someone else. It was intolerable, and one of the great evils in the world."

"Why are we talking about this?" William asked, sounding confused. "You realize my mom's people were brought to Trinidad as slaves, right? And I'm not exactly a white guy myself."

"I know, but whenever Tyrone got on one of his rants, I'd nod and agree, but really I was bored and waiting for him to shut up. I was like, couldn't he talk about something else?"

"And now you've got first-hand experience of what it means to be a slave?"

"Pretty much," Jake said. "And you know what I've figured out?"

"What?"

"It sucks."

"Well, I could have told you that."

"Yeah, but that's because you're smarter than me."

"Not that smart. I'm stuck in here with you, remember?"

Jake chuckled. "You know, maybe if we hadn't been so pigheaded, we could have been friends a long time ago."

"Probably so."

"How very touching," a voice quipped in an acerbic tone.

A young mahavan stood directly outside his cell, and Jake swayed for a moment as he rose to his feet. "Thank you, sir," he said, keeping the sarcasm out of his voice and doing his best to mimic the flat, despondent affect that William used when speaking to mahavans.

"Your friend doesn't rise," the speaker noted. "He mocks me perhaps?"

"Sir, I can't rise," William replied. "Tender Thomas made sure of that."

"Oh? I think you'll want to rise for this occasion," the mahavan said with a smile. "You and your friend are about to receive the Servitor's justice. Mercy might still be available." The smile faded. "Or I can administer justice on both of you right here and right now if you don't stand up this instant."

William levered himself upright with a groan. Swelling closed both his eyes to mere slits and misshaped his jaw. Jake thought it might be broken. A large goose-egg throbbed on his temple.

"Good," the mahavan said, smiling again. "Come along. All of Village White Sun has turned out for this."

William stumbled when he exited the darkened tunnel that led from the prison to the lower courtyard of the Servitor's Palace. As usual, clouds obscured the sun, but the light outside shone dazzlingly bright after the cellar-like gloom below. He squinted against the brilliance as a new headache thumped to life.

At the top of the stairs he swayed a moment, struggling to maintain his balance. He silently cursed Tender Thomas' not-so-tender ministrations. The man had taken an inordinate amount of pleasure in inflicting pain when he'd broken up the fight with Justin and his friends. Maybe it was because Tenders held the lowest status of mahavans, and in a place as status-conscious as Sinskrill, that meant something.

"Come along," repeated the young mahavan who had fetched William and Jake from the prison. He led them to a raised, wooden stage, and William rocked back at the sight before him.

The entire village of White Sun had assembled there, but it wasn't their presence that sent a chill down William's spine. It was their silence, their lack of expression. In the old Westerns back home, the crowd at a hanging always had a festive atmosphere, with children playing, and everyone baying for the blood of the condemned. But the drones of White Sun stood in solemn silence, staring with worshipful attention at the Servitor, who waited atop the platform.

Serena stood there as well, a sour grimace of either illness or unhappiness marring her features.

Good. Let her suffer. He hoped she had boils or hemorrhoids and maybe the flu to go with it.

"Up," the mahavan ordered.

Reluctantly, William dragged himself up the stairs. At the top he swayed again, and nausea curdled his stomach. It took him a few seconds, and he worried he might topple over, but Jake steadied him until he could recover his balance. William nodded his thanks and stepped forward to where the mahavan indicated.

The Servitor spoke to the silent crowd, his voice booming through some trick of acoustics or his use of *asra*. "Ours is a culture formed by the instructions of Lord Shet, and amongst his holy declarations is the notion that all should know their place and give way to those of greater worth. Should anyone, mahavan or drone, strike someone of greater rank, that person's life is forfeit."

The last part sounded like a quote, and the crowd finally responded, clapping and shouting with rapturous applause.

The Servitor held up his hands, calling for quiet. "Which is why we are assembled this afternoon. Last night, these two men broke that law."

The Servitor thrust an accusing finger at William and Jake, and the crowd hissed lustily, calling for vengeance.

"They assaulted one of my foreman, Justin Cardinal," the Servitor said, "a good man carrying out my will, and through me, that of our Lord Shet. Had such been the extent of what occurred, there would be no need to deliberate on the fate of these two. But events are not so simple. William Wilde and Jacob Ridley are *raha'asras*, not drones.

"In fact, one day they may stand before you as mahavans of Sinskrill, noble and upright," the Servitor continued, "but that day isn't today, nor was it last night. Today and last night, their station did not truly stand above or below Foreman Cardinal's. Thus, it is unclear who should have answered to whom, and we find ourselves in a conundrum. I've prayed hard on what must be done, and our Lord has answered me. He told me that mercy, his greatest blessing, shall be offered to all who rupture his peace."

"Oh, shit," Jake whispered, and William held in a shudder of fear. He locked his knees. The mercy of Shet was a misnamed abomination.

"For Foreman Cardinal, mercy allows him to live, but he is no longer a foreman. He will live out his life as a drone, nothing more, nothing less. But for a potential *raha'asra*, one who might hold the great responsibilities of a mahavan, a more severe judgment is required. One of these men will be lashed, the one who instigated the melee, but not the other, since he merely sought to defend his friend."

Murmurs arose at his words, and William shared a look of horror with Jake. He had no idea what a lashing meant, but like everything else on the island, it sounded awful.

The Servitor held up his hands again. "It is an uncommon justice akin to stripping, the same mercy offered to those who fail their Tempering. But rather than cull his *lorethasra*, we will cull his body. It won't break him, but he will know pain, and with it, justice."

He gestured, and the young mahavan who had hauled William and Jake out of the prison stepped forward, his face pious and severe, but when no one could see, a vicious smile distorted his features.

"My son, the noble Sherlock Carpenter, Prime of Village Paradiso, shall be the one to administer justice upon this man, Jake Ridley."

William's stomach fell. He remembered the Servitor's promise to hurt Jake. "Lash me," William begged. Broken-bodied though he was, he knew he was still stronger than Jake.

Sherlock addressed the Servitor, his eyes wide with surprise. "My liege?"

The Servitor clapped approval. "What bravery William Wilde shows," he shouted. "It is that bravery that proves the judgment of Lord Shet. The brave should be spared the foolish decisions of their lessers." He nodded to Sherlock. "Begin!"

Sherlock faced Jake, not bothering to hide a nasty grin. A single motion, and Jake's clothes shredded off him. "Now we bring you merciful justice," Sherlock whispered.

Jake's screams began at once. William watched, wide-eyed with horror. He wanted to spin away from the sight, to hide his face and cover his ears, but he didn't. Instead, he made himself watch. He had to remember this. Evil had to be faced.

Jake's skin glowed, a silver luminescence bright enough to light the entire courtyard. It persisted, and Jake's scream seemed to go on and on. The brilliance lessened, but the torment didn't end. Jake's skin grew translucent. His bones, blood vessels, and organs became visible.

⬤

Serena's heart bled. Jake . . . What had she done to him? Sherlock might wield the braid, but it had been her actions that had allowed this to come to pass.

The screams went on, and something inside her shattered. Serena knew she would never forget this moment. She didn't want to. It should haunt her for all the days of her life. Punishment for the evil she'd perpetrated. But no one could know her heartbreak. She leaned on Isha's teaching, keeping her visage blank and uncaring, but her soul wept.

A closed-off box in her mind broke, one in which she'd stored away the truth: Sinskrill could never be home. Evil imbued the heart of this place, included in every aspect of its design, from the lack of anything resembling familial love and devotion to the enslavement of those like William, Jake, and Travail, all the way down to the stripping of the drones. Sinskrill was a sadistic prison.

Serena could no longer remain here. And she'd already decided that Selene wouldn't be raised here. She had to break all of them free of this place.

———————— ● ————————

William saw Jake's heart pounding within his distended chest. A bulge like a balloon filled with gas rolled down his abdomen as if something sought to push its way out of him. A rank smell hit the platform. Jake's bowels had emptied.

William's outrage and fury grew. This was no mercy, no justice, and he vowed to pay these people back for what they were doing to Jake, to kill every last mahavan if necessary. And he would start with the Servitor, his son, Sherlock, and Serena. He'd kill them all.

Jake's cries grew hoarse as his voice gave way, and he panted. His eyes shut tight.

"Enough!" a deep voice roared.

Jake's screams of pain broke off, and he collapsed like a puppet with its strings cut.

William searched for whoever had spoken. The sight meeting his eyes made him blink in disbelief.

Kohl Obsidian had been huge, but this black-furred figure with horns curling off its head was something else entirely. The creature's white, iris-less eyes seemed to glow, and his heavy jaw appeared clenched in resolution. "This one is mine," he declared. "He is not to be damaged any further."

"This is justice, Travail," the Servitor said. "It is not in your purview."

William stopped listening. He stumbled to Jake's side and rolled him over. His friend stared sightlessly at the sky. William pressed an ear to Jake's chest, praying he wasn't dead. Seconds of quiet seemed to pass before a ragged breath and a distant heartbeat reached him. William almost sobbed with relief.

Jake lived.

William cradled his friend's head in his lap, at a loss for what to do next.

The disagreement between the Servitor and the creature—it had to be the troll—continued.

"This may be justice," Travail said, "but it does not supersede my own authority as Isha to these two bishans. Only I can punish them."

179

The Servitor shook his head. "No. Even you serve at Shet's discretion."

"And only an Isha can decipher Shet's will when it comes to the judgment of a bishan."

"Not when your bishans attack my foreman."

"Your foreman attacked my bishan first, after denying him sustenance."

The Servitor grew still.

The troll continued. "Also amongst Lord Shet's instructions is this: *'He who denies his brother sustenance is a coward and a thief. Lose him a finger for his selfishness.'*" Travail's voice held a trace of mockery.

"I had not been made aware of former Foreman Cardinal's transgression," the Servitor said, a lie that even William could discern.

"Then I leave you to administer more appropriate justice to your former foreman while I will take possession of my bishans. But only after this one—" Travail pointed to Jake "—is healed of what you ordered. See to it, and ensure no further harm befalls him." His glowing, white eyes intensified in brightness before flashing once, and their brilliance dulled. "That is *my* judgment."

"I'll see to it myself," the Servitor said, sounding strangely humbled . . . even fearful.

CHAPTER 11:
WORKS AND HEALING

March 1987

S hortly after Serena passed her Tempering, Adam had taken her on as his shill, one of the first things he taught her was sailing. From the very first lesson she'd loved it. The wide-open sea, the wind sweeping past, the salty spray, but more than anything else the heady sense that anything was possible, even freedom. After that first lesson, Serena had taken every chance she had to get out on the water.

For her shill pilgrimage, the project needed to prove her worthiness to advance to the rank of bishan, she had refurbished an old dhow, a single-masted, thin-hulled vessel of ancient design. Some might have thought her decision a risky one, but Isha had believed otherwise. He'd guided her, telling her that any shill could learn to create fire or cause an earthquake, but mahavans were craftsmen as well as warriors. In the end, repairing the dhow had proven to be a wise choice.

Following Serena's success in her bishan pilgrimage—bringing in William and Jake—and earning the rank of mahavan,

Isha had granted her ownership of the dhow. Unfortunately, during their months in the Far Abroad, with no one to care for the small boat, rot had set in. While Serena could have repaired it in a few weeks, she'd never found time to set right what wind and saltwater—the twin banes of any ship's existence—had ruined. Weather or work had always interfered.

Today, though, Serena had no obligations in her way. Today, with the weather unseasonably warm, she had every intention of working on her dhow.

She'd hauled the small boat onto the beach and lashed her into a wooden housing. It was where her father found her.

"Work is coming along well?" he asked.

Serena stopped her repairs and bowed to him. It didn't matter that he was her father. Before all else, he was the Servitor.

"It never ends when it comes to a boat," she said.

"Very true." The Servitor nodded. "But take pleasure in the work . . ."

". . . and your heart will know contentment," Serena said, finishing the quote from *Shet's Counsel*.

"You kept up with your studies," the Servitor said, sounding pleased. His broad features shifted into an unexpected smile.

"Isha accepted nothing less than perfection," Serena explained, ducking her head at the Servitor's praise. Strange how much her father's admiration pleased her, especially given how many days she'd spent hating the old crocodile who masqueraded as a man.

"Look at me, child," the Servitor said. "In this moment I am not the Servitor. I am your father."

Serena did as instructed, hoping her surprise at his acknowledgement of their kinship didn't show.

He laughed. "Your face . . . Normally, no emotion crosses it, but in this you are betrayed. I should take you to task."

He maintained a pleasant smile, but Serena's heart raced. *Betrayed.* A word only one rung removed from 'treachery'. How could her father have seen the treason in her heart?

"Ease your mind and forgive an old man's humor," her father said with a chuckle. "I know you were surprised by my admission of our familial ties. Nothing more."

Serena laughed, hoping it didn't sound as nervous as she felt. "No forgiveness is required, my liege."

The Servitor's eyes narrowed. "Did I not tell you that in this moment I am your father?"

Serena cursed her lapse, and the fear surged once more. "Forgive me, father," she said.

His frown erased. "No forgiveness is required, daughter," he said, an echo of her earlier words. "I am your father and no one else's."

"What about Sherlock and Devon?" Serena asked.

"We all know their ties to me are a fiction. They carry not a drop of my blood, nor did I have a hand in raising them."

"But they are your sons," Serena said, daring to contradict him.

He tsked in annoyance. "Tradition dictated their adoption when I made them village Primes, but I have no deep affection for either of them. Only you provide me hope." He uncharacteristically hesitated. "And in time, perhaps Selene as well."

Serena allowed her confusion to show. "I don't understand."

"Adam—your Isha—and I share the same father," he said.

"But he has no natural children of his own, and only two adopted youth. Both failed their shill pilgrimages, a great disappointment, and both were stripped into drones." He sounded vindictively pleased rather than sad. "Their failures had me worried for our bloodline." Again, her father smiled in pride. "But then you came along and achieved magnificence. Do you know how rare it is for the natural child of a Servitor to become a mahavan? It's uncommon enough to merit note."

"I am glad to have brought you joy," Serena said. She bent her head but allowed her father to see her pleased smile even as she understood that it hadn't been her achievements the old crocodile had come to celebrate. It was his own.

"Bending your head just then, you very much remind me of your broodmare. You remember her?"

Broodmare. Her birth mother. Her true mother. Cinnamon. "I do," Serena said.

"You are every bit as beautiful and graceful as she, and more importantly, you have become a mahavan of note. I am proud of you. I have a father's pride in your accomplishments."

Serena dipped her head again in silent acknowledgement, but her thoughts flitted elsewhere. Though the Servitor was her father, Isha had more properly served in that role.

"And if Selene proves as strong as you . . ." The Servitor trailed off with a laugh. "I will have double a father's pride and achieved something rare and wondrous." He sighed then. "If only your broodmare hadn't proven sacrilegious and fallen ill. How many more mahavans might she and I have been able to breed?"

Serena bit back a snarl. Her mother had not fallen ill. She had been murdered.

184

Her father never noticed her anger. He mounted his white stallion, the Servitor once more, and gave her a nod of farewell. "I will see you at the Palace?"

"I need to check on William first, sir," Serena answered. "He's been a week with Travail and I want to see how he's doing. I may spend the night in White Sun."

The Servitor frowned. "No. Oversee William, but do not attempt to return to White Sun. It's already afternoon. By the time you reach the troll's abode, it will be late. I don't want you traveling alone at night. Not when the unformed so recently attacked in broad daylight. Stay with Travail until the morning."

"Yes, my liege," Serena said. Once again her features hid the truth of her roiling emotions.

Spend a night near William? The man who had more reason to hate her than anyone else in the entire world?

She grimaced at the thought.

———◆———

Travail's home was a broad meadow of heather and grass on a cliff overlooking Lake White Sun. To the east reared a fractured mountain, half its face broken off and tumbled down into a field of massive boulders. North and west rose a forest of pine and cedar that blunted the frequent hard winds from those directions. The area had a microclimate, drier than other parts of the island, but the omnipresent clouds remained as prevalent over Travail's field as they did everywhere else on the island.

But when the sun did shine bright and warm, William liked to hike to the cliff's edge and watch the serenity of Lake White Sun and contrast it with the distant, rolling waters of the Norwegian Sea. Plus, on some days, a rainbow took shape.

William had only been with Travail for a week, but already he loved the troll's home more than any other place on Sinskrill. Certainly more than the miserable hovel he and Jake shared at the village. With no cottage or home—Travail didn't need one given his thick fur—they camped under the stars, and a sense of freedom, purpose, and hope—an audacious belief—was slowly taking root in William's wary heart.

All thanks to the troll, who currently sat with eyes closed in a meditative pose, his back pressed against a boulder standing twice his height.

"You should get some rest," Fiona called out.

William stood and watched the old *raha'asra* approach. He viewed her with antipathy, but made sure to mask his feelings from his features and posture.

An insight occurred to him as he waited for Fiona. He wondered if this was how Serena approached the world: a lying face to hide her true feelings and intentions. He silently vowed to master such deception for himself. Whatever it took to get off the island.

"How's your jaw?" Fiona asked him. "Can you take a measure of healing?"

"I'm fine, madam," William lied. His face remained bruised, a pulsing headache made balance a challenge, and some of his teeth still sat loose in their sockets. For now, he could only eat soup.

Fiona folded her arms and bore a half-smile, sarcastic and cutting. "You think the pain is better than my healing."

"Your healing hurts too much," William admitted.

Fiona used a braid that forced his body to repair itself more quickly than it otherwise could, and while the process worked, it also hurt like hell. At most, William could endure only a few seconds of it.

"How's Jason?" William asked.

"Convalescing in your old cottage," she answered. "But he's coming along. I imagine he'll join you in a few weeks."

"But he's getting better?"

"I said he was," Fiona said with a dismissive shrug before turning to study Travail. "How long has he been sitting there?"

"A few hours."

A flash of fondness passed across Fiona's face so quickly that William wasn't sure he'd actually seen it.

"I am able to answer whatever questions you have about my state without need for an interlocutor," Travail said, opening his eyes.

"Of course," Fiona said with a sardonic dip of her head. "Learn well from him," she told William. "He taught me, too."

"To my everlasting detriment and shame," Travail said. "You are a grave disappointment."

Fiona shrugged. "Nevertheless, you were a fine instructor, certainly better than the old *raha'asra* who was originally tasked with my training."

"I remember him well," Travail said, sounding fond.

"Pang Arun," Fiona added, in a wistful tone of her own. "An old Buddhist from Cambodia, and a sweeter, kinder man I've never known."

William could barely hide his shock. Fiona had actually

sounded tender toward this old *raha'asra*. "What happened to him?"

"The seasons of our lives lead inexorably to winter," Travail said. "Pang died, gracefully and quietly, in my arms."

"I should go," Fiona said, rising abruptly. "It's getting late. I'll let the Servitor know your healing goes well."

"You came all the way up here to check on me?" William asked in surprise.

"It is my task. The Servitor requires my service to Travail, and Travail requires that I see to your healing."

"I will require far more than that," Travail said. "You will come back every day to aid in William's instruction as soon as he is hearty and hale."

Fiona briefly bowed. "Yes, sir," she said before departing.

Several hours after Fiona left, William was standing on the shore of Lake White Sun and testing how far he could throw a rock across the water when Serena came striding up the pathway leading to the meadow.

William groaned. "What does she want?" he muttered.

"No doubt to determine your state of health," Travail said, catching William's eye. "And something else. With this one, patience is required to learn her true purpose. Listen and watch. Speak little."

"Where's Jake?" Serena asked as she drew up.

"At the cottage, madam," William answered, his voice drone-dull. "Fiona is taking care of him. He can't travel yet."

"What about you? How is your healing coming along?"

"Coming along," William said. His face should have been answer enough.

Serena's face, usually expressionless, softened. If William hadn't known better, he would have said regret filled her eyes. Her mouth opened, and she appeared on the verge of saying something before her mouth shut with a snap. Her features became bland and unreadable once more. "I am to stay here tonight," she declared. "Prepare bedding for me."

"You aren't going back to the village?" Travail asked.

"The Servitor ordered otherwise," Serena said. "He fears the unformed might attack a lone traveler this late in the day."

"The unformed never venture this far south," Travail noted.

"And they never used to attack in broad daylight," Serena said. "Yet they did exactly that less than two weeks ago."

Travail grunted. "So be it. You may remain here overnight if you wish."

"Madam, we don't have extra bedding," William informed Serena, "but you can have mine."

Serena grimaced. "Yours is likely lice-ridden. No, thanks."

His bedding wasn't lice ridden! William had fallen far in the world, but not that far. He tried to maintain some semblance of cleanliness when it came to bugs and things like that.

"It doesn't matter," Serena said. "A bedding of pine needles will do. See to it."

"Yes, madam," he replied.

"One other item," Serena added. "The Servitor has a message for you. He wishes to remind you of the sovereign law of Sinskrill. Everything here is property. All of it belongs to Shet. Every human, animal, and plant belongs to our Lord. That includes you, and it is for the Servitor, with Shet's guidance, to decide how best to dispose of his property."

"Yes, madam," William said in his blandest tone although he didn't need the reminder. It had already been pounded into his head.

"The Servitor also reminds you that should you fail in your studies, Jake will be the one made to suffer, and as Shet's property, your friend will be the one who is . . . disposed."

William gritted his teeth. *If it was the last thing he did, he'd see this island burn.* "Understood," he said. He knew anger reddened his face, but he didn't care. Pride could only bend so far. He even left off the honorific 'madam' and wondered if she'd notice and what she would do about it.

She gave him a hard stare, but nothing more.

———◦—

ARYLYN

The trade winds blew cool this evening, and the aqua ocean darkened as the sun set. Jason opened the gate to Mr. Zeus' house, ducking below the jasmine draping the arbor. The clean fragrance of the flowers seemed a perfect complement to the purple-pink sky at twilight.

"How are the new recruits coming along?" Mr. Zeus asked from the front porch.

Jason sagged into a chair with a groan of weariness.

Mr. Zeus chuckled. "That well, eh?"

"Those two would work me to death if I let them," Jason answered. He slumped back in his chair and closed his eyes. Sweat beaded upon his scalp and forehead and slowly dripped down his neck and nose. The early evening breeze playing across his overheated skin felt wonderful. Maybe he'd rest here for awhile. Or forever.

How had Rukh talked him into another round of sparring? Jason had already been tired when the inexhaustible boy had pressed him for another session. *Where did Rukh get the stamina?*

Jake made a sound of relief when another breeze fluttered through the front porch of Mr. Zeus' house.

"Want anything to drink?" his grandfather asked.

"Please," Jason said, not having the energy to open his eyes.

Mr. Zeus went into the house and returned with a tall glass of water. "Those two are certainly proving themselves quite capable," he noted with a smile.

"Capable of making me miserable," Jason grumbled.

"Stop whining," Mr. Zeus said with a laugh. "Show them some compassion. They're orphans like William."

Jason scowled. "That still bothers me," he said. "How likely were we to discover two potentials, orphans whose parents both bequeathed them enough money to afford St. Francis, only a few weeks after William's abduction? Doesn't that strike you as odd?"

"Of course, it does," Mr. Zeus replied. "But remember how Cornelius and Lien all arrived here within months of one another. And Lien then discovered William. With *asra*, coincidences aren't always coincidental. Sometimes it is something else guiding our movements."

Jason gave him a sour grimace. "What? You think God had a role in what's happened to us?"

"I certainly hope so, but who can really say?" Mr. Zeus replied with a gentle smile. "But regarding Rukh and Jessira, I'm not worried about them. I took their measure before telling them of Arylyn and bringing them here. I trust them."

Jason shook his head. "I wish I could trust them like you do."

"Are you sure your feelings about them aren't clouded by someone else?" Mr. Zeus asked, his demeanor now serious. "Don't let what Serena did to us make you overly mistrustful."

"I'm trying not to," Jason said, "but it's hard. Part of why I'm willing to train Rukh and Jessira is because I want to get to know them, learn who they really are. After what Serena did, we can't afford to take any chances."

"None of us will forget what she did, but Rukh and Jessira deserve to be judged on their own merits, not hers."

"I'll try," Jason promised.

"That's all I ask."

"What did the Council have to say about our proposal?" Jason asked.

"They don't approve." Mr. Zeus frowned. "They talk about their normal fears, and don't see how we can actually steal William and Jake away from Sinskrill. They also fear that the mahavans might capture one of us and learn the key to *our* anchor line."

"Didn't you tell them to change it after we leave?" Jason asked. "If we get stranded in the Far Abroad, we can always dream them our location and have them bring us home."

"They threw out the possibility that Sinskrill will capture a pair of us and keep one to threaten with torture while the other is sent to sneak an opening into Arylyn."

"None of us would do that!" Jason protested.

"I agree, but the Council . . . they've always been like this."

Jason shook his head in disgust. "Cowards."

"Don't judge them too harshly," Mr. Zeus advised. "Their greatest concern is Arylyn's safety. For them, nothing else matters, and in many ways, I understand their concern."

"So we can't do anything?"

"I didn't say that," Mr. Zeus said. "Right now the Council may be fearful, but their opinions can be shifted. Lillian Care is already on our side. So is Break Foliage."

"That's only two out of the six."

"Yes, but Bar Duba may also break for us."

"The Councilor for Air?" Jason shrugged. "Even if you can convince him, the vote would still be tied."

"No." Mr. Zeus wore a pleased smile. "Lillian is the Mayor, and since this is essentially a raid on Sinskrill, the Council would have to operate under the rules of war. In such a circumstance, the mayor's vote counts for two."

"Four to three," Jason said with an answering smile.

Mr. Zeus nodded. "We need a more solid plan to convince Bar, though. Right now, we've got nothing more than *'Let's go!'*"

"What do you need me to do?"

"Nothing yet," Mr. Zeus said. "We're going north. I already told you that, and soon enough, we might have a more exact location."

"You've found Sinskrill?" Jason asked, a spark of excitement flaring.

"Not yet," Mr. Zeus said, "but I'm close. My sense is that it's somewhere north of the British Isles, but even when I pin the exact location down, we will need a way to approach without being discovered."

Jason smirked. "I'm surprised those idiot mahavans didn't destroy William's *nomasra* as soon as they took it off him."

"I'm sure they did," Mr. Zeus said with a smirk of his own. "But there were two *nomasras* within the locket, not one. There was the locket itself, but also the picture of William's family tucked within it."

Jason shook his head in admiration. "You sneaky old man."

Mr. Zeus made a mock bow in Jason's direction. "Indeed."

CHAPTER 12:
INSTRUCTIONS
AND CHALLENGES

April 1987

A hard shove rolled William onto his back and into full wakefulness.

"You've rested long enough," Travail informed him as he squatted next to William's bedroll. "You're healed. It's time to begin your training.

"What the hell!"

A slap rocked William's head to the side.

"No cursing."

"Ow!" William blinked back tears. The slap felt like it'd loosened some newly reset teeth. "What was that for?"

"Because you cursed. There will be no cursing during your training," Travail explained. "And I pulled the punch. Stop whining. You're fine. Now get up."

William scrambled out of his blankets. He probed his face, wondering if his jaw would swell.

A sliver of sunshine to the east heralded dawn's imminence, but William's breath frosted in the winter-cold air. "Why do we have to get up so early?" he asked.

"I'm always up this early. You used to be up this early, too, when Fiona had charge of your training. It's time to re-establish old habits." Travail stared at William in obvious expectation.

"Yes, sir," William hastily responded.

Travail settled back on his heels. "Better. Now. Let's go for a run."

He set off at a trot, a ground-eating lope that quickly had William huffing for breath. Much of his stamina from his life before Sinskrill had been robbed during his time here. While a drone's work was taxing, it wasn't the same as running or exercising the way he once had.

Travail must have recognized William's difficulty in keeping the pace. He grunted and slowed down.

They completed several circuits of the troll's meadow home, and by then the sun had risen, a dull glow through the eternal cloud banks enshrouding Sinskrill.

"Are you able to maintain this pace and converse?" Travail asked.

"Yes, sir," William gasped.

"Good. Now your training begins in earnest." Travail took them off the confines of his field. They entered the forest of old-growth pines and cedars west of his meadow and took a path that rose steadily. William's claim of being able to run and talk at the same time was soon put to the test.

"Let us discuss anchor lines," Travail said. "Tell me what you know of them."

196

William didn't know much more than what Mr. Zeus had taught him, and the topic never came up during Fiona's infrequent instructions. "They connect the *saha'asra*s," William said.

Travail waited, and tsked when nothing more was forthcoming. "Your education is sorely lacking. You know the difference between *lorasra* and *lorethasra* at least?"

This William did know. "*Lorasra* is the *asra* within a *saha'asra,* or an endowed object like a *nomasra*, and *lorethasra* is the *asra* within a person. With *lorethasra*, we're able to tap into *lorasra*."

"And the elements that make up *lorasra*?"

"Fire, Water, Air, and Earth."

"*Lorethasra*?"

A cramp directly below his ribs knotted William's side, and he rubbed at the soreness. "Spirit, Fire, Water, Air, and Earth. Spirit is supposed to be the most important of the Elements."

"Not supposed to be. It *is* the most important," Travail corrected. "Spirit is the foundation upon which an *asrasin* weaves a braid linking the Elements of his *lorethasra* to those of *lorasra*."

"Yes, sir," William said. Any other time, he would have been fascinated by the troll's teachings, but right now he would have paid real money for a rest. His legs burned, and the cramp under his ribs throbbed. He stumbled and had to work to regain his balance.

Unfortunately, Travail showed no signs of slowing. They broke from the trees, and their path finally leveled off. William gasped in relief. *Thank all that was holy!* He couldn't have kept running uphill much farther.

"With the absolute basics behind us, perhaps we can progress with your instruction," Travail said. His pace slowed further when they reached a tumbled slope of rocks and boulders. "Choose one," the troll ordered as he picked up a massive boulder.

"You want me to pick up a rock?"

Travail frowned in feigned confusion. "Did I not say that?"

"Yes, sir," William said, unsure what he'd have to do with the rock but certain he wouldn't like it. His suspicion was confirmed an instant later when Travail started up the hill with his boulder.

William mentally groaned. He found a basketball-size stone but could barely lift it. He dropped it and found a lighter one. *Much better.* William hefted the rock up to his shoulder and followed Travail. "Why are we doing all this running and lifting, sir?" he asked between pants.

Travail waited for him at the top of the hill. "Because you are weak, and I sense you can be strong. You'll need that strength if you wish to accomplish that which you long for."

William hesitated, wondering what the troll meant.

Travail smiled. "You long for freedom," he said, "as do I. Perhaps together we can achieve our shared dreams."

"You don't want to be here?" William asked in surprise.

"No," Travail said, his voice curt. "I am a prisoner, no different than you."

"And you're not worried about Walkers listening in on us?"

"Upon this rocky knoll, the wind stirs and tears words into obscurity," Travail replied. "No one can overhear our conversation."

William studied the troll, wondering if he was lying. Maybe this was another sick test from the Servitor, Fiona, or Serena.

A moment later he realized it didn't matter. What if it was another test? What more could be done to him? By now he'd grown used to punishment.

"What do we do?" William asked.

"I teach. You learn. We break free."

William scratched at his scruffy face. "That simple, eh?" he asked with a wry smile.

"Simple, yes. Easy, no," Travail said.

———— ● ————

Later in the morning Travail took pity on William and ended the day's exercise. On their way back to the meadow the troll appeared lost in his thoughts, and William didn't want to talk much either. He struggled with putting one foot in front of the other and not stumbling in a heap. At least the hike back to Travail's field was mostly downhill. Nevertheless, by the time they got back, William wanted to simply flop down and fall asleep.

Fate, however, wasn't so kind.

Serena waited for them at the meadow. "Where have you two been?" she demanded.

"Where my fancy took me," Travail answered as he brushed past her.

Serena's mouth tightened with anger. "The Servitor said you were to answer to me about their training," she called to Travail's retreating back.

The troll paused. "And you believe his words compel my obedience?"

"I believe his words compel your good judgment," Serena answered. "If I were you, I would think very hard about whether you really want to make an enemy of me."

"Are you not already one?" Travail asked, his tone cutting despite its mildness.

William momentarily forgot his fatigue. The tension between Travail and Serena seemed to spark the air.

"I am not your enemy," Serena claimed.

William rolled his eyes.

"Pardon me. I mistook you for a mahavan," Travail responded.

Serena's jaw clenched, but she held silent.

Travail eyed her in disdain.

"Where have you been?" Serena asked again, this time her tone humble and undemanding.

Travail seemed to study her for a moment before he answered. "I began William's education," he said. "He had an incomplete knowledge of the relationship between *lorasra* and *lorethasra,* and none about anchor lines."

"I thought you already knew the basics," Serena said to William.

"Mr. Zeus might have taught me some things," William said, "but it was a long time ago. Another lifetime, when I was free." Pleasure washed over him when guilt flushed Serena's face. "Fiona never bothered telling me either."

"What did you learn about anchor lines?" she asked.

"They link *saha'asra*s," William said, choosing the simplest and most ignorant of explanations. Maybe it would irritate Serena further. Once again, he left off her honorific of 'madam'. She hadn't said or done anything about it before, and he wanted to see if she would now.

She didn't.

Serena wore an annoyed frown. "You knew that much before coming here."

William mentally grinned at her irritation.

"Tell me more," Serena commanded, "and this time, don't sound like a dolt. I know how smart you are. Impress me."

Or what? He wanted to ask, but that might be a step too far.

"No one knows how anchor lines are made," William began, "but they contain a thick foundation of Spirit, and on top of that exists a braid of Earth with Air and Water. To open one requires the right amount of flashing Fire, each anchor line's key."

"Very good," Serena said, in a tone sounding as if she were offering him a treat.

"Thank you," William said, letting a little sarcasm leak into his words.

"How fares Jake?" Travail interrupted.

"Better," Serena said. "Fiona says his urine is getting lighter. He's finally turning the corner."

William hid a frown. As if Serena really cared.

She must have seen something in his posture. "Believe it or not, I do want what's best for Jake."

"I think you and the Servitor are only interested in Jake because you think he's the chicken and I'm the monkey," William replied. *"Kill the chicken to scare the monkey."* He quoted the old Sinskrill saying that Fiona had once told him, the one she said the Chinese claimed as their own.

"That's not true," Serena said. "I do care what happens to Jake."

Her words almost unhinged William's self-control. *She cared?* *She actually dared to say she cared?* After everything she'd done to them? All the lies, the kidnapping, standing by while Jake was tortured, and she dared claim to care about them?

Anger boiled, and for a moment William saw red. He struggled to contain his rage. He wanted to hurt her every bit as badly as she'd hurt him and Jake. He wanted to . . .

His teeth clenched as he bit back his words.

Screaming at her would accomplish nothing, and the idea of a physical assault was laughable. He needed clarity of thought.

William imagined his fury as an untamed beast that he had to shove into a basement and slam shut the door. It still raged, but at least he could think again. "If you really cared about us," William said, "you would never have brought us to this hellhole. If you really cared about us, you'd find us a way off this island. Madam." He added the last, her title, through clenched teeth.

Serena might punish him for his honesty, but he honestly didn't care. She had earned every ounce of his hatred. Besides which, he had much more he wanted to say to Serena Paradiso. He'd spoken the barest trickle of venom he felt toward her.

Surprisingly, Serena didn't punish him. "Don't ever talk to me like that again," she warned.

"Or what?" William challenged, speaking the words he'd been too nervous to say before. "You've already punished me worse than any one ever could."

"I know you resent me," Serena said.

William laughed in derision. "That's putting it mildly."

"Regardless, while I wish my choices could have been different, I had no choice in the matter. I had my reasons to do as I did."

For a moment, William almost believed her, but then he remembered the truth: Serena was the greatest liar and manipulator he had ever met. He scoffed at her.

"Don't push me," she warned again. "I can ignore some of what you say in private, but let it become a habit and you'll make a mistake in public. Then you won't like my response."

"Do you suppose I'll like it any more than when you lied to me all those months?"

Serena rolled her eyes. "So what if I lied?" she said, her tone contemptuous. "You whiny child. Boo-hoo! I betrayed you. Who cares? Everyone betrays everyone. Grow up and stop being such an infant." She spun on her heel and stalked down the path toward White Sun.

William's fists clenched and unclenched as he watched Serena leave. He ground his teeth from suppressed fury and frustration. After everything she'd done, how had she managed to sound like the reasonable one?

"That was certainly interesting," Travail said as he came to stand next to William.

"What do you mean?"

"Not so much for your anger, but for the fact that she didn't swat you like a fly. I find myself wondering why."

———— ● ————

May 1987

Jake ran through the eerily silent forest. The only sounds were his footfalls and panting. He kept his focus on the path before him.

This early in the morning, the sun had yet to burn off the fog filling the surrounding hollows. A gust of wind whipped water off pine needles, and Jake took the drenching in the face, but he never slowed.

He had to run.

William paced beside him, and Jake sensed his silent scrutiny as they ran through the tall, evergreen forest. He understood the reason for it.

"I'm fine," Jake answered in reply to William's ongoing regard.

"You don't have to go so hard all the time," William said, his breathing even and relaxed. "The hill will still be there whenever you happen to reach it." He referred to Rock Hill, the talused slope Travail had them carrying stones up and down.

"It's not how I do things," Jake said. "Either give it everything you got or don't bother trying. That's how I take life."

"I'm just saying you can slow down a bit. I've been with Travail for five weeks and training with him for the past four. You've only been here one. You can't expect to catch up to us so quickly."

Jake shrugged. "Maybe not, but it doesn't change the way I see things. I need to get stronger and faster. Like you and Travail."

William snorted. "Have it your way," he said. "But no one's as strong or fast as Travail. If he went flat out, I don't think a motorcycle could keep up with him."

"Then like you," Jake said. His breaths came heavier, but he pushed past the sharp crimp in his side. "I have to get stronger as quickly as possible. I'm not going to be the weak link that fails."

"You aren't—"

"I'm the one who was lashed," Jake snapped. "Now shut up. I can't talk and run at the same time. Not yet." When William kept pace with him, Jake snarled at him. "Stop babying me. You have to get stronger and faster, too. Go. Don't wait on me."

William accelerated away, and Jake watched him go. Neither of them had spoken much about Travail's dream of freedom. *Why would they?* It was a vision they all shared, a precious flower in the midden heap of Sinskrill. Jake would rather die than see his hope for a life away from this hideous island falter and fail. The one time he'd tried to bring up the conversation with Travail, though, the troll had flashed him a warning sign. "Air hears everything," he'd said. "Only at Rock Hill might we discuss the matter."

The Walkers. The Air Master spies who used their abilities to bend the wind and bring distant sounds to their eavesdropping ears.

Jake mentally snarled. He hated them. He hated all the mahavans. He hated everything on this cursed island. The spiny hills and craggy ravines, the icy water of the White Sun River, and the crappy food and weather. He especially hated the weather.

Would there ever be a day without clouds?

Shitty island.

A second later Jake shook off his complaints. He could whine about it later. Right now he had to focus on his running. The lashing had burned him from the inside out, and a hollowness still existed within him, as if something precious had been ripped apart.

He had yet to figure out what he'd lost, but with every passing day since he'd come to stay with Travail that aching emptiness had slowly filled. He slowly recovered, but even past the unknown loss there had also been the searing pain of the lashing itself, deep and tearing. Jake's bones still ached, and his muscles often throbbed at the end of the day, weak as jelly.

Eventually they'd strengthen. Nothing to it but push past the pain and endure until they did.

Jake ran on and imagined himself in *Vision Quest,* with "Lunatic Fringe" playing in his mind. Nosebleeds, dehydration, going until he had nothing left to give. That's how he'd get through this, by being a hard-nosed son of a bitch.

Later in the morning, they finished their exercises and Jake and William sat before Travail as the troll began the day's instructions.

"William can source his Spirit," Travail said to Jake. "It took him two weeks to learn. For most, it takes several months. Do you think you can beat his time?"

Jake nodded. "Consider it done," he said in confident tone.

"You're certain you can succeed?"

"I'll do whatever I have to," Jake answered.

"No doubts infest your mind?" Travail persisted. "Even though you know William has it in him to be one of the most powerful *asrasin*s in hundreds of years?"

"No doubts," Jake said. "Precision beats power, and skill beats strength."

Travail tilted his head in consideration. "Either you have a fiery sense of confidence or an immaculate ability to lie to yourself."

Jake chuckled. "Maybe a bit of both."

Travail barked laughter and slapped his knee. "Very true," he said, "but in this case, you *are* mistaken. You cannot succeed more swiftly than William. Your *lorethasra* is only now starting to knit together. I fear it will be weeks yet before you can source your Spirit."

Jake scowled. "Then why'd you tell me you wanted me to go faster than William if you knew I couldn't?"

"I wanted a measure of your desire. For what you wish to achieve, only steely focus and hardened resolve will do."

Jake wondered if Travail obliquely referred to their shared dream of escaping Sinskrill or Jake's more personal desire for revenge against Sherlock Carpenter. *'No Shit Sherlock,'* as he'd taken to regard the Servitor's son.

"Apparently your resolve is not in question," Travail continued. "Which is good because you have something special to encourage your efforts, something shills and bishans lack. You have desire, need, and purpose." He stared Jake in the eyes. "Let them impel you to greatness."

"Yes, sir," Jake answered.

"Good. While physical exercise will aid the healing of your body, now we must work on healing your *lorethasra*. Close your eyes," he instructed both Jake and William. "Take in the wind rustling through the trees. Touch the dampness on the air."

Jake did as instructed.

"Smell Village White Sun's cook fires, the black smoke billowing," Travail intoned, his voice growing hypnotic. "Imagine the gray clouds scudding across the mournful sky. Feel the world, and find yourself."

Travail's voice trailed off, and Jake opened his senses.

His long hair stirred about his face as the air moved in fitful, moaning gusts. Dampness filled the meadow. Birds called from the forest. Branches rattled.

He lost himself to a vision he'd discovered several days earlier. He entered something not quite a dream, something other than consciousness. He imagined floating above the Earth, his being dispersed, spreading wide enough to encompass cloud, sky, rain, and mountain.

The aching in his bones eased. The throbbing of his muscles lessened, and the hatred clenching his heart loosened. Distantly, he recognized that his current peace was only temporary, that when he opened his eyes, all his hurts would resume. But for now, whatever he'd discovered was enough.

A bell tolled.

"Come home," Travail commanded.

The bell tolled once more.

"Come home," Travail said again.

Jake opened his eyes. As he'd expected, all the pains came back with his return to consciousness. His earlier peace fled, and he groaned in pain. Even his tongue hurt. Anger built within him. "When I've mastered whatever it means to be a *raha'asra*, I'm going to kill Sherlock Carpenter," he vowed.

"Then you'll have to hurry," Serena said. She stood nearby and must have arrived while Jake and William were lost in their visions.

Jake flushed and eyed her with a glower. *How he would like to punch her teeth down her throat.*

"Sherlock's dying," Serena said.

"What?" Jake and William both exclaimed.

Travail took a more tactful approach. He rubbed his chin and settled back for Serena to explain herself.

"Sherlock is dying. I learned about it earlier today. He has some kind of wasting illness. The healers don't think there's anything they can do for him."

"So it's true," Travail mused.

"What's true?" William asked.

"A story I came across in my investigations of lashing," the troll said. "I found it while perusing the Servitor's library. Therein I discovered an old account, five hundred years old, I believe, of a rebellious *raha'asra* who was lashed. The author claimed that the administrator of the punishment, the Servitor of the time, died of a wasting illness within weeks. Nothing could be done to save him, and he eventually withered away through his urine."

"What does that mean?" William asked.

"Exactly. What does it mean?" Travail shrugged. "There are several illnesses that can be described to kill a person by such means. At the time I read this account, I suspected the author was simply unaware of such diseases. After all, five hundred years ago many of those illnesses hadn't yet been categorized."

"You think whatever happened to that long-ago Servitor is happening to Sherlock?" Serena asked.

"The accounts do seem to mirror one another," Travail replied.

"Did they have any idea what happened to that Servitor?" Jake asked.

"The *asrasin*s of the time suspected that lashing a *raha'asra* somehow rebounds on the lasher. Remember, only two or three *raha'asras* are born each century. They create *lorasra*. They also purify it. *Raha'asras* are remarkable, and tearing into the *lorethasra* of someone with those rare qualities is bound to have a negative impact on the one doing them harm."

"You really believe this?" Serena asked, staring hard at the troll.

"Does it matter?" Travail asked. "If the healers from that account are to be believed, your brother will die whether what I posit is true or not."

CHAPTER 13:
SISTERS, TRUTHS, AND SELENE

May 1987

Village Bliss' pier consisted of a two-yard-wide span of wooden planks extending into a sheltered cove and held a dozen slips. Mid-morning, no boats remained berthed at the docks, as all the fisherman were out on the water. They went to sea at first light and weren't expected back until early afternoon.

Serena stared at the empty pier, but in her mind's eye she pictured herself elsewhere. She imagined Sinskrill's gloomy weather fading away, the dull clouds parting and replaced by a bright, vibrant sun. She stood atop basalt cliffs where a warm breeze played with her hair, swirling it about her face. The call of gulls echoed in her ears, and the scent of a different shore filled her nostrils. Serena lifted her face, closed her eyes, and let the images and sensations sweep her away.

Selene was with her in this dream, just the two of them. They left this new island at their leisure, sailing away upon their dhow; free to travel wherever their hearts took them.

Freedom. Such a dangerous word. Such a desperately, dangerously longed-for need, especially for someone born and raised on Sinskrill. Until meeting Mr. Zeus and the magi of Arylyn, Serena had always thought her fantasy of escape was simply that, a fantasy.

And now . . .

Serena exhaled heavily, opened her eyes, and let go of her dream. The world of Sinskrill returned, and so too did the confirmation of certain truths.

She couldn't stay here. She'd known it for a long time, and her time in the Far Abroad had only reinforced what had long been in her heart. More importantly, she wouldn't allow her sister to be raised on Sinskrill. The island would eventually break Selene, twisting her lovely heart into something grotesque and wicked.

They had to escape.

"Madam, should I paint this section of the dhow?" a soft voice asked.

Selene. A nub of paint smudged her sister's nose, and Serena wiped it off, causing the little girl to grin.

As always when they were alone, Serena didn't hold back her fond smiles or her affection. No matter what else the future might hold, she wanted Selene to know that she'd been loved.

"Yes, why don't you paint it," Serena said. The figurehead at the prow, a cat that reminded her of Aia, caused her to wonder where the strange calico kitten might be, what adventures she might have involved herself in.

"Madam, can I tell you how much I like being with you?"

"Of course. I like being with you, too. But remember, we can only speak like this when we're alone," Serena cautioned. "You remember the rule I told you about how you're to behave when others are around?"

"I remember," Selene answered. She straightened to attention and her face grew flat and unreadable like a drone's. "Never allow anyone to know your true emotions."

"And the reason?"

"Because emotions can be manipulated," Selene said in a drone-dull affect.

"And manipulation leads to slavery," Serena finished. "Good. Now let's get the painting done. The Servitor will still expect you to taste his food at supper."

"Yes, madam. What will you do with the boat when it's done?" Selene asked, her features transitioning into those of a curious little girl.

"Sail it," Serena answered with a smile. "I can teach you once you're my shill."

Selene's eyes grew wide and her face brightened. "Will I truly be your shill?"

"I promise you will," Serena said, although her heart's desire was that she and Selene would be long gone from Sinskrill by the time of her sister's Tempering.

William and Jake would be the key. Their longing for freedom was evident in every breath they took and every insubordinate statement they made to her—and that she ignored. They likely thought her forbearance due to guilt, but they were wrong. Need drove her, not guilt. She needed William and Jake to regain hope that they truly could be free of Sinskrill.

And if their needs required that she allow them to speak to her in ways she wouldn't allow anyone else, so be it. While they would always hate her, she didn't care. As long as they went along with her plan.

The strength of what she had in mind was its simplicity. Jason and Mr. Zeus had been able to dream to one another. Only those who loved one another or were closely related could do that, and William and Jason loved one another as deeply as any natural-born brothers. Or so Serena imagined, since such love didn't often occur on Sinskrill. Once William had further training, she reckoned he would be able to dream to Jason and tell the magi of Sinskrill's rough location. Then her plan could be implemented, and they could all be free.

Serena smiled at the notion before resuming her repair of the dhow. She hummed "Gloria", and the song momentarily startled her. How long had it been since she'd thought of it?

———●———

The night sky of Sinskrill could be a glorious abode of uncountable stars, of bright pinpricks and a smear of light on a vast canvas of darkness. However, for such a wondrous vision to appear, the island's infamous shroud of clouds had to clear, an infrequent event in any season according to Travail.

Tonight was one of those special occasions. Tonight, the clouds had parted, drifting into cotton-candy shapes lit from above by a half moon. Tonight, heaven's beauty became manifest, and William and Jake decided to stay up late to watch the evening's glory. Or at least what counted for staying up late on Sinskrill. It probably wasn't much past ten p.m.

Crickets chirped, coming forth from wherever they spent their winters as they sensed spring's arrival. For once the wind had also died down, the cold not as biting as usual. William still put his hands out toward the crackling fire, although he hardly needed its warmth tonight.

Travail lay nearby, an indistinct lump blending in with the other indistinct rocky shapes around him. "A beautiful evening, is it not?" he asked in a voice full of longing. "In times past, my elders would spend such a night in dance."

"How did you end up here?" William asked. He'd asked a variation of the same question a few other times, but Travail had never answered, always promising to tell him later. This occasion seemed no different as silence followed William's question.

He expected no response, but Travail surprised him.

"Curiosity and foolishness," the troll answered. "A deadly combination, especially in a child."

"What happened?" Jake asked.

"A lying mahavan told me of a book of surpassing wisdom, one holding all the secrets of the stars. I came here, enraptured by those false pretenses, intent on unlocking heaven's mysteries. And here I've remained, trapped since my foolishness led me astray." He sighed. "The stars have forever been my weakness. I long for them like a sailor longing for the sea."

"Who tricked you?" Jake asked.

"The Servitor's great-grandfather, the Servitor of his time. He is long since dead."

"That doesn't make sense," Jake said in confusion. "How old are you?"

215

"Two hundred and twelve," Travail said. "For my kind, it is early adulthood. I came here when I was fifty-five, a child then."

William whistled. "That's even longer than *asrasins* live."

"Yes," Travail acknowledged. "Trolls live up to five hundred years."

Jake looked back and forth from William to Travail in uncertainty, obviously wondering if they were joking.

"It's true," William said. "Mr. Zeus was born before the Civil War. Jason says that creatures of magic live long."

Rather than being elated by the news, Jake gaped in horror. "You mean we might end up being slaves for over a hundred years?"

"No, because we'll master what we need to learn and do what we must to earn our place," William declared. "No one's going to keep us in chains forever."

"In this, the two of you demonstrate far greater wisdom than I," Travail said. "I should have listened to my mother and remained in the mountains of my birth."

William couldn't imagine Travail as a youth, nor could he imagine the troll having a mother. "Is that where you . . . you know?" he asked, not stating the entirety of the question in case an eavesdropping Walker was listening to them.

"I don't know. My mother is likely dead by now," Travail said. "She was old when she spawned me, and I was the first troll birthed in centuries, possibly the last. I may be the last of my kind."

"What about your father?" Jake asked.

"I don't have a father. Trolls are born of obligate parthenogenesis."

William frowned. *Obligate what? Wait.* He searched his mind, certain he'd heard the phrase before. He smiled when he remembered, and silently blessed Mrs. Nelson and her boring biology lectures. "Isn't parthenogenesis an asexual form of reproduction?" he asked.

"It is."

"But I thought only plants and lower animals reproduced by parthenogenesis," William said.

"They do," Travail replied, "but how do you know the process is limited to those species?"

Silence descended as William and Jake digested Travail's words. Rarely did the troll fully explain his thoughts. More often he gave them snippets of knowledge, expecting them to puzzle out the rest on their own.

William stared into the fire as he considered Travail's words. "Are you a lower animal?" he finally asked the troll.

"Am I?"

William scowled. He hated when people answered a question with a question.

"You're a lower species according to the *asrasins*," Jake said, sounding sure of himself.

William shook his head in disagreement. "But he looks like a mammal. Look at his hair."

"Looks can be deceiving," Jake reminded him, and William's thoughts went to Serena. "Remember what he told us last week. Only *asrasin*s can create the woven, the beings of magic. And trolls are magical beings."

William remained perplexed. "Okay. *Asrasin*s created the trolls, but I don't get why that makes them a lower species?"

217

"Because all woven species were made by *asrasins*," Travail explained. "All were created lesser in some ways. For most it comes with our birthing. Parthenogenesis, the reproduction of the lower animals."

"All the woven are like that?" William asked.

"Not all reproduce by parthenogenesis," Travail said, "but all of us have a weakness. The unformed, witches, warlocks, banshees, chimeras, dwarves, and so many more. Even the proud nearly immortal elves. We're all lesser than *asrasins* in some way."

"Elves and dwarves are real?" William interjected.

"*Were* real," Travail said. "Most woven are gone from this world, destroyed when their *saha'asra* homes emptied of *lorasra*. Only a few such braided creations still roam the earth, those lucky enough to find themselves upon either Sinskrill or Arylyn, a *saha'asra* which can still support our kind, or those who can create their own *lorasra*."

"You mean some woven are like *raha'asras*?" Jake asked.

"Yes and no," Travail answered. "Yes, they can make their own *lorasra*, but no, they cannot share what they create. Their *lorasra* is all for themselves, to keep them alive."

"What about the necrosed?" William asked.

"The necrosed." A snarl leapt to Travail's lips. "Pray you never meet one of those abominations. But if you do, flee. Nothing but the long dead holders could kill such fell foes."

William and Jake shared a look of uncertainty. Jake gestured, as if inviting William to tell the story.

"We met one last Christmas," William said.

Travail startled. "Truly?"

William nodded, knowing the troll's night vision allowed him to see the movement in the dark. "His name was Kohl Obsidian."

Travail sat up, his interest piqued. "Was? As in past tense?" he asked. "Tell me what happened."

William explained what he, Jason, and Serena had endured. *Had it really only been five months ago?*

"A talking cat, a Shining Man, and a man with two minds," Travail mused. "What does this portend?"

William didn't know, nor did he care. Studying someone else's future, worrying about it when it didn't directly impact him, held no interest. Right now he only cared about the present, how to shape each moment so he, Jake, and Travail could escape Sinskrill.

Thunder rumbled, cutting off their conversation as heavy clouds rolled in. Heaven's brilliance was curtained away, and dampness rolled in as a misty rain pattered to life. The lovely evening ended.

"I know where I would go," Travail said, his words masked from listening Walkers by a rumble of thunder. "There is only one *saha'asra* where I could freely roam the land. Arylyn."

"Arylyn," William whispered in reverence. The name itself felt like a prayer.

———•●•———

Choices.

In nine-year-old Selene's mind, the notion of choices, of choosing for herself, was as foreign a concept as a cow with hands. It might be funny, but what would a cow do with hands?

Maybe it would make it easier for them to shove grass in their mouths?

Selene mentally shrugged. She didn't know, and she didn't care. Choices were for big people, like the Servitor. Little girls like her could only do as they were told, like fetch William Wilde, the new *raha'asra*.

Madam had asked Selene to bring him to Village Bliss to help her restore the dhow. Of course, Selene had done as she was told, and the two of them rode the rusted bicycles the Servitor maintained for such journeys on the Great Way. While they traveled, she tried to study William, eyeing him sidelong and hoping he wouldn't notice.

What a strange man, she decided. *Not a mahavan or drone. Maybe a shill or a bishan?*

Selene frowned, trying to figure out William's status. On Sinskrill, status meant everything. Those with greater status were better people, and those with less were obviously worse people. It was the core of Lord Shet's teachings.

Selene continued frowning, and eventually decided that William must be an enigma.

She drew herself up in pride.

Enigma. A word Selene had discovered while sweeping the Servitor's Library as part of her duties, serving the holy man who was also her father. *Enigma.* A good word. It described William Wilde perfectly.

She gave a firm nod. *Yes, that's what he was.*

"How old are you?"

William's voice startled her, not because he'd spoken but because of its curious, friendly tone. Only Madam ever spoke to her like that. "I'm nine. Sir," she added a beat later in case she was wrong about his status.

"William," he said with a smile.

Selene's puzzlement deepened. Whenever there was no one else around, Madam smiled at her like that. Warm and kind. Every time she did, it caused Selene's belly to tremble and made her eyes blurry with tears. She didn't understand what her reaction meant, but she knew the smile was something between only her and Madam.

William was someone else. He was a stranger, an enigma. Again, she puffed with pride at knowing the word. Selene's bike hit a pothole and almost sent her over the handlebars, but she quickly regained control of it.

"Are you okay?" William asked.

Selene flushed and gave a brief bob of her head. She'd have to be more careful with her riding, but thankfully, she and William were alone. No one had witnessed her near disaster.

Moments later, despite her decision to pay more attention to her riding, Selene's thoughts drifted again. She stared at the strange *raha'asra*, wondering what he wanted from her. Everyone wanted something—another of Shet's teachings. Everyone other than Madam.

So what did William Wilde want?

"Your name is Selene, right?" he asked, still wearing a smile.

Selene nodded, still puzzled by his behavior. He spoke to her like Madam, like she meant something to him even though she was only a drone.

Why?

"Yes, sir," she said in reply to William's question.

"I feel like stretching my legs," William said. "You want to ride harder?"

Selene tried not to frown as her confusion deepened. She didn't know what to say, and she hesitated. The *raha'asra* was offering her a choice?

"We don't have to if you don't want to," William added.

"I'd like to go faster," Selene hastily replied. Early on, Madam had taught her that the best answer to a confusing question was generally a form of 'yes'.

William grinned. "Good. Let's go."

The *raha'asra* set off, and Selene pedaled her hardest to keep up. She quickly fell behind, and William slowed to a coast, easing back next to her.

"Sorry about that," he said.

Selene remained silent, further put off by William's strange behavior. Now he was apologizing to her? How was she supposed to respond to that? Madam had never taught Selene what to do if someone of higher status demonstrated kindness. The lack of understanding had her scowling in frustration.

William must have noticed her frustration and he further slowed his pace. "What's wrong?"

Fear stole her words, and Selene tried not to tremble. He'd seen her scowl, seen that it had been aimed at him. Selene swallowed, terrified as she imagined his punishment. Her fear worsened when he looked upon her with concern rather than anger.

"Are you all right?" William asked, still showing none of the fury he should have displayed. Even Madam might have been upset with her had Selene looked at her like that.

"Nothing, sir. My side was cramping," she lied—a useful skill on Sinskrill, and one best mastered early in life.

William didn't notice her deceit. Instead, he nodded understanding. "Hurts like a knife stabbing you in the side, doesn't it?" he guessed. "It'll pass. Give it a few minutes."

Selene took the reprieve, and pretended to massage her side and flank.

They passed the rest of the journey talking about Selene's life. William wanted to know about everything: her parents, her past, her present, her friendships. He sounded genuinely interested, and throughout their conversation, he continued to wear a warm, open expression.

Despite Selene's best efforts, she couldn't help warming to him, even laughing when he showed her a rock covered in white moss and pointed out its resemblance to Fiona's head.

Several hours later, she was grinning non-stop when they finally reached Madam.

"I see you've met Selene," Madam said to William when they arrived.

Selene's face instantly went red. Guilt gnawed at her. She shouldn't have laughed with William, nor should she have enjoyed her time with him as much as she had. For some reason, it felt like a betrayal of Madam.

"Thank you for bringing him, Selene," Madam said.

"She's a sweet girl," William said, ruffling her hair fondly.

Guilt and pleasure warred within Selene. She liked the warmth of William's presence. Liked how kind he was, how he talked to her and listened and laughed. But she couldn't be his friend. Not with Madam staring at him like that.

"Selene is my sister," Madam said. "She's the reason why I brought you here. Without me, she might not become the person she should. You understand what I mean?"

Selene didn't understand, but William seemed to. A series of emotions flitted across his face. Distrust and anger, but eventually understanding. "Is this true?" he asked Selene. "Is she your sister?" He gestured to Madam.

"She is if I pass my Tempering," Selene answered. "Until then, I'm a drone like anyone else."

William turned to Madam, eyes glinting like he was mad at her. "You really came back for her?"

"I did, and I wanted you to meet her so you'd understand why I did what I did."

"I'll never understand that."

"What lengths would you go to for Landon?"

William's mouth shut with snap.

"You see my dilemma?" Madam asked.

William nodded slowly, but Selene frowned, even more confused than before.

Who was Landon? And what dilemma?

"How do you plan on making sure Selene becomes the person you want her to be?" William asked. "She's going to become a shill, then a bishan, then a mahavan and a slaver. There's no coming back from that. You know it better than most."

Madam stiffened, an almost imperceptible twitching of her shoulders. No one else would have noticed, but Selene knew her too well.

Selene pretended to work on a loose plank on the deck while they spoke, but all the while she listened closely.

"Maybe I do know," Madam replied, "but Selene . . . Once she matures to a bishan, she'll leave Sinskrill on her pilgrimage. Her Isha will accompany her."

"How will she leave?"

"The anchor line. Only the Servitor can open it on this side."

"You intend to be her Isha?" William asked.

"Yes," Madam said.

"And afterward? What's your plan?"

"I have none," Madam answered. "Now help me fix the dhow."

"You brought me out here to help you repair this little boat?"

"Yes," Madam said, "and when the dhow's ready, I mean to sail her into deep waters this summer. The fishing is supposed to be especially good there."

William pursed his lips and seemed to study Madam through considering eyes. "I see."

Selene hid a frown. The two of them had discussed something by not discussing it. But if she paid enough attention, maybe later on she could figure out what they really meant.

And what it might be worth to her.

CHAPTER 14:
PAST MYSTERIES

May 1987

Unlike the rest of the world, springtime on Sinskrill did not bloom beautifully. Stiff winds continued to blow down from the island's rugged northern hills and mountains and off the Norwegian Sea, but at least the air warmed, becoming merely chilly rather than frigid. More noticeable and welcome, however, was the sun's more regular appearance. For a few hours every day, brilliant sunshine beamed down, uplifting and vibrant. After winter's icy cold and seemingly interminable overcast, it felt tropical, like how William described Arylyn.

Unfortunately, because of the sunshine Jake and William were temporarily pressed back into farming.

"You will hoe while your partner plants the spring wheat," shouted the foreman, Josiah Dales. "Five rows each, to my satisfaction, before you're done."

Jake mentally scowled. "Why are we back to this anyway?" he complained after the foreman finished passing out the tools.

"Because Serena voluntold us."

226

"Sounds like something she'd do," Jake muttered moodily.

William didn't reply, and Jake noticed his friend staring at someone in narrow-eyed anger. Jake searched out the source of William's ire. Justin Cardinal, their former foreman, glared at them.

"You better move those eyes or I'll knock them through the back of your skull," William warned Justin. "You're a drone, and we aren't. Piss me off, and no one will stop me from beating you into the ground this time."

Cardinal's face whitened, and he bowed briefly before scurrying away.

"Would you have really put a beat-down on him?" Jake asked, hoping the answer would be 'no'.

William hesitated a moment before slowly nodding. "I would hate having to do it, but it's the way of this piss-hole place," he said. "If we let Cardinal disrespect us, everyone will. We can't afford to show weakness."

"Compassion isn't weakness."

"It is if it gets you killed," William said. "Besides, you did your fair share of bullying back home. This isn't much different."

Jake grimaced. "Yeah, but that was then. Now I actually understand those lectures from Father Jameson. Remember how he used to go on and on about the banality of evil? It all makes sense now."

William lifted his eyebrows.

"There's no mercy or grace here," Jake explained. "Only strength and weakness. The user and the used. I don't want either of us to end up like that."

William flushed in embarrassment. "Let's get started," he grumbled. "The sooner we're done, the sooner we can go back to learning what we really need to know." He cut into the ground with his hoe and broke up the soil as he started running a furrow along the edge of the field.

Jake measured the distance they'd have to cover. A hundred yards per row times five. A day's worth of work or more, but at least they'd already composted the field a few days ago. Jake sighed before following William, laying a long piece of wood into the furrow. Notches cut into the plank told him where to put the seeds. Stoop, drop some seeds, cover them up. Stoop, drop some seeds, cover them up. Over and over as fast as possible, because William's pace didn't slow.

Clearly, he meant to have their five rows hoed and seeded before lunch. William's hoe lifted and fell like a metronome, cutting through the dirt like a plow hitched to a bull. He never wavered as they made the turn at the far end of the field. Most of the other drones had yet to reach the halfway mark of their rows.

Jake privately marveled at William's strength and stamina.

Where did it come from? He never got winded no matter how hard the exercise, and the stones he lifted to the top of Rock Hill beggared belief . . . His frame shouldn't have allowed him to move any of those boulders, much less lift them to the top of the slope.

Even though he had the easier job, Jake had to hustle to keep up with William, and in the end, they *did* complete their rows well before lunch.

Jake plopped down next to William on a small rise and they had lunch: a tough hunk of beef, a raw potato, and a large piece of bread slathered in butter. Clouds rolled in, hiding the sun, and a drizzle fell. Fog blurred the distant borders of the broad valley housing most of Village White Sun's fields, especially the farther reaches, which butted against low-lying hills covered in heather and stands of pine.

"What's Serena keep calling you out for?" Jake asked.

"She wants me to help her fix a boat," William answered. "You know that little girl who comes to get me?"

Jake nodded.

"She's her sister. Sweet little thing. Only good thing on the island, and Serena wants her to stay that way."

Jake snorted in disbelief. "How's she going to stay sweet on Sinskrill? Weakness isn't tolerated here."

"No, it isn't," William agreed.

He said no more, and Jake mulled over William's words, trying to parse out what they meant. They held the feeling of a puzzle.

"You remember what Travail told us about anchor lines?" William asked a moment later. "How the one here is only operable by the Servitor?"

Jake nodded again.

"Out in the rest of the world it's different," William explained. "Every anchor line out there uses the same key, and if you know it, you can use all of them. That's how the *asrasin*s used to travel around, using the anchor lines to leap from one *saha'asra* to another. But sometimes it was easier to do an overland journey. That's what we did when Kohl chased us, but in our case, we drove."

Pieces of the puzzle clicked. A boat. A young girl, a sister. Innocent, and Serena wanted her to stay that way.

A picture built in Jake's mind. Serena meant to sail away from Sinskrill. She meant to save her sister by stealing her away from this island on a boat.

"When Kohl chased you, what kind of vehicle did you drive? How big was it?" Jake asked. He hoped William would pick up on the true nature of his question.

"Plenty big enough for what we needed," William replied with a wink.

Jake smiled. Steal a boat, and they might have a way off the island.

———●●———

Serena listened with half an ear as her father droned on about the many supposed virtues of her adopted brother, Sherlock.

Despite the warmth of the noonday sun, she clutched her black robe more closely about her. The docks below the Servitor's Palace held an assortment of mahavans today, and they reminded Serena of crows at a feeding, single-minded in their focus upon the dead. Serena stifled a shiver at the thought.

No weakness. Especially not now.

Her father spoke on, but his words were ripped away by the hard wind blowing off the gray waters of the Norwegian Sea and the surf pounding the docks. Of course, even if he could have been heard, it didn't matter. None of what he said was true, but on Sinskrill truth and lies were simply a matter of perspective. Her father—at a funeral his title as Servitor was held in abeyance—continued, and a stranger to Sinskrill would have assumed

Sherlock a saint, rather than the senselessly cruel man he had actually been.

With today's funeral, her brother's trek through this world ended. He'd wasted away through his urine exactly as Travail had predicted, and now he would supposedly begin his next journey. Her father would set alight the boat meant to carry Sherlock's husked remains to the gates of Lord Shet's home, and if her brother's spirit was judged worthy, he would pass on to Seminal, the heavenly realm of the valiant.

Despite her father's words, the sobbing of Sherlock's widow, and the sorrow-filled visages of the mahavans in attendance, Serena doubted any of them would actually miss her brother. As soon as her father finished his speech, the jockeying for position would begin. Every mahavan of note would fight for the Primeship of Paradiso. For all Serena knew, the jockeying had already started last night, or maybe even earlier.

Her father finally finished his speech and tossed his burning brand onto Sherlock's funeral boat. The torch was followed by those of everyone else in attendance, and the boat caught fire. A stern wind lifted its sail and sent it forth into the waters before the Servitor's Palace. There, it blazed higher and higher. Smoke billowed, and despite how Serena felt about Sherlock, she said a silent prayer for her adopted brother before his remains sank beneath the waves.

Afterward the somber crowd dispersed, most melancholy for reasons having nothing to do with the demised. Instead, their sorrow was aimed inward. Sherlock's funeral, like all funerals, reminded the people of Sinskrill that their long lives would eventually end, and they hated the reminder. In this they shared a similarity to people the world over, but for mahavans the idea of a second birth and a more glorious life to follow rested on a faint hope.

Very few actually believed in Seminal, and no one expected any sort of pleasant afterlife awaiting them on the other side of this one. At best, their religious devotions contained a polite pretense based on little more than tradition. Most mahavans reckoned this world was the only one, and they greatly feared life's final curtain.

"A distasteful spectacle finally ends," Walker Brandon Thrum said, coming up to Serena's side. His thick features were shaped in a smirk.

"A distasteful spectacle that offers us an unexpected opportunity," Rider Evelyn Mason said, approaching Serena's other side. Her striking auburn hair floated about her plain, pale face, and her blue eyes flashed with excitement.

"An opportunity not to be squandered by loose lips," Serena warned.

Evelyn didn't take the hint. "Only two other mahavans can gainsay our claim to the Primeship of Paradiso. We should demand—"

"Air carries all. Be silent," Brandon hissed. His thick jaw clenched and unclenched.

Evelyn and her stupidity, Serena thought. The fool had been about to blurt out for all to hear whatever thought or plan she had in mind following Sherlock's death.

"Sorry," Evelyn said, rightfully abashed.

"Next time, think before you speak," Serena advised, maintaining her composure despite her annoyance. "If a Walker had been listening . . ."

"No one will be listening now," Brandon said. "I braided a block. No sound will echo past our conversation."

"Good. You should have done that the moment you approached," Serena rebuked.

"How was I to know she'd start discussing our plans right away?" Brandon complained.

"You know now," Serena said before turning to Evelyn. "As for you . . . what were you going to tell us?"

"I was going to say that we should demand your brother's support of your claim."

Serena snorted. "No one demands anything of Devon." Her mouth barely moved. Some mahavans could read lips. "His services belong to the highest bidder."

"And what would he want?" Brandon asked, his lips barely moving as well.

"Support for his claim of the Servitor's Chair when my father's time is ended," Serena answered. "He wants to be made Secondus."

"The last Secondus was hurled from the Judging Line," Brandon said with a grim chuckle.

"That makes three in the past twenty years," Evelyn added. "It seems more like a curse than a title to desire."

Brandon nodded. "Besides, the Servitor is a healthy man."

"No one lives forever," Serena reminded them. "And a Servitor's life burns brighter than any other, but it's also shorter because of it."

"You think Devon will—" Evelyn began.

"Don't speak it out loud," Brandon shouted, cutting her off.

"I thought you blocked the Air," Evelyn complained.

"Yes, blocked, but many can read lips. I can."

"Oh." Evelyn flushed.

"Never mind that," Serena said. "I'll talk to Devon, find out if he's willing to support me. Meanwhile, both of you go about your duties. I'll call for you when the time is right."

The two of them nodded, but as they were about to leave Brandon paused. "What do you plan on doing with the dhow you're fixing up?"

Serena kept her face calm. "Sail it," she said. "Some people like horses. I like boats."

Brandon accepted her lie with a brief nod. "Your Isha's influence?"

Serena quirked a smile. "Of course."

They departed, and she watched them leave with a vague sense of guilt. Brandon and Evelyn had tied their futures to hers, and if she successfully escaped Sinskrill, their fortunes would tumble. Then again, as young as they were, they would have many years and opportunities to reclaim their lost status.

Alternatively, if Serena's plans to leave Sinskrill proved impossible, then what better means to protect Selene than from the office of Paradiso's Prime?

A few weeks ago, when William had sourced his Spirit, he had found himself floating on a slow, steady river of shining light. In this dream-like state he nonetheless remained aware of the world. More aware, in fact, as his mind languidly swayed upon an endlessly ebbing stream, white and shining. William recognized the wash of brightness as his Spirit, but it didn't glow from an internal light. Instead, it served as a mirror, reflecting something else, something vast and beautiful. Something like a song captured in light. Cradled in the mesmerizing stream, a peace unlike anything William had ever known descended upon him.

Later on he'd told Travail what he had seen and felt, and while the troll had read similar accounts from other *asrasins*, as far as he knew no one had a proper understanding of what such a happening meant. But having experienced that perfect peace once, William longed for it again.

This morning, though, wouldn't be one of those days. Not with Serena's presence. She'd come to Travail's home, wanting to test William's and Jake's progress. Of course, Fiona had decided to join her. The old *raha'asra* often showed up unannounced, helping with their instruction whether they wanted her there or not.

"I am the second set of eyes that the Servitor requires to properly determine your growth," Fiona had explained to them once.

When she had been the one charged with their instruction, she had been horrible to them, but ever since Travail had taken over their teaching, she'd been different. Pleasant and kind. William didn't know what had stirred the change in Fiona's behavior, but he was grateful.

Nevertheless, hard feelings died slowly.

"How well can they source their Spirits?" Serena asked Travail.

"They are progressing nicely," Travail answered. He had his face turned up to the morning sun.

William, Jake, and the two women waited for Travail to explain himself, but he said no more.

"What does that mean?" Serena asked. A breeze, warm and carrying the scent of the nearby pine forest, stirred her hair.

"It means what I said. I am satisfied with their progress, and so, too, should the Servitor."

"They're learning far faster than I did," Fiona said, with what on anyone else would have been a fond smile.

Travail nodded gravely. "Very true."

"That doesn't tell me anything," Serena replied, her tone irritated.

"They can source their Spirits with little effort," Travail said. "A few more weeks of practice and it should become as simple for them as taking a deep breath. Does that suffice?" Irritation suffused his voice as well.

"No, that doesn't suffice," Serena snapped. "When are you going to teach them to separate their Spirit into the other Elements?"

From behind her back, William rolled his eyes. Always complaints with her. Move faster. Work harder. He flipped her the bird when only Jake could see, and Jake coughed in his hand, hiding a smile.

"I won't teach them to do that for many more months to come," Travail answered. "What you mahavans do in the training of your shills is a farce. You push them too quickly, throwing them into deep waters when their minds and *lorethasra* are unready. It is why so many of them fail to advance as bishans." He narrowed his eyes. "I imagine Selene with her kind disposition will struggle in that regard as well."

Fleeting dismay flashed across Serena's face, brief and easily missed, but William had seen it.

Fiona had as well, and the old *raha'asra* eyed Serena with a face pinched in speculation. "Your sister has yet to undergo her Tempering, and you fear for her."

Serena had quickly regained her composure. "I fear nothing for a drone's future, and she only becomes my sister if she passes her Tempering."

She lied. William knew it. He'd seen the affection Serena had for Selene. The love. While Serena was a consummate liar, that kind of emotion couldn't be affected. Her love for Selene was real.

Fiona must have thought the same. "You raised her when her mother died. Don't tell me you don't care for her. A true mother always does."

"What would you know of a mother's love?" Serena asked, sounding contemptuous. "A mother's love is a weakness. You should know this better than most. After all, weren't you a broodmare to several children, all of them taken from you?"

Fiona sourced her *lorethasra* and a faint rose fragrance wafted. She gestured, and Serena's eyes widened. The world grew quiet, and William shared a look of confusion with Jake. Even Travail seemed to have no idea what was going on.

"The world without cannot hear us," Fiona said. "My braid will silence our words. We can speak freely with no Walkers to overhear."

William turned to Travail.

"I'll explain later," the troll murmured.

"How did you do that?" Serena demanded of Fiona.

"I remember being loved by my mother," Fiona said, not

answering Serena's question. "Before I came here. I remember her laughter and taking long walks with her through the park. I also remember my father holding me when thunder shook our house and how he kept me safe and loved me. My brothers and sisters, my family, I remember them all. I've never forgotten."

"How very touching," Serena said, "but none of that is important. Neither is Selene." She wore a sardonic smile, but a fleeting expression of longing seemed to wash across her features.

"You lie," Fiona whispered.

"And you're afraid."

"Of course I am," Fiona admitted.

"Afraid of what?" William ventured. "What's going on?"

Both women shot him scowls of annoyance.

"She's braided a block around all of us so no one can hear what we say," Serena explained before turning back to Fiona. "I thought only Walkers could do that."

"Or a skilled *raha'asra*."

"I thought you weren't supposed to be all that skilled," Jake said, hesitantly.

"So everyone was meant to believe," Travail replied.

"I'm missing something," William said.

Serena seemed puzzled, too. "I think we all are."

Travail peered into Fiona's eyes and whispered, "She needs to know."

"When I came to Sinskrill," Fiona said, "I poured every effort into finding a way off the island. "I even had a plan, one quite similar to yours: a boat."

William's head snapped to Fiona. *How did she know? And if she knew about the dhow, what else did she know?*

238

Even Serena couldn't entirely contain her shock.

"You have nothing to fear from me, child," Fiona said. "None of you do. When I failed in my attempt to escape, I was recaptured, and the Servitor of the time—your father's aunt—gave me to a drone with whom I was to breed. With him I had two daughters and a son. All three were stolen from me and given to others. But I knew them," she continued. "I watched them. I loved them whenever I could, and for that sin, the Servitor stripped my oldest child for some minor infraction when she was seven and ensured that my middle child failed her Tempering.

"When that punishment wasn't enough to ensure my fealty, the Servitor lashed me, a private punishment that ironically took her life a few months later." Fiona smiled in satisfaction.

Serena scowled. "Who are you?"

"Your mother's mother," Fiona answered. "Your true mother. Cinnamon, the one who taught you to garden."

William could have been struck by a flying pig and he wouldn't have been more stunned.

"You look very little like her, but thankfully not like your father either," Fiona continued. "But Selene does. She looks like Cinnamon, my daughter, the girl who I loved above all else."

Serena wore a stricken expression. Her mouth briefly opened and closed.

"I've always loved you as well, Serena," Fiona said, "but I could never show you my affection. After what happened to my children, I feared for you. I stayed away, but your mother had no such fears. Even as a child, Cinnamon had more courage than I. A bright light and a wondrous woman. She loved you as a mother should, without reservation. It was her love that helped you grow into a good, decent person."

William made a sound of scorn.

Fiona addressed him. "She isn't perfect, but she did what she had to for the one person she loves in this world: Selene." She returned to Serena. "While you're a decent person, Selene has a chance to be a good one, like Cinnamon. Selene must be treasured and saved from this place."

"And you'll help us?" Serena asked with a smirk, but William could see suppressed hope in her eyes as well.

"I will do whatever is needed to save both of you from this island," Fiona vowed.

"She speaks true," Travail said.

Serena stared Fiona in the eyes, and she must have seen something she believed because she nodded acceptance. "We have much to discuss," she said, still apparently studying the old *raha'asra*.

"A conversation we should have had long ago." Fiona gestured again, and the noises of the world resumed.

"You've done well," Serena said to Travail. "I will let the Servitor know that the new *raha'asras* are progressing well, but they really should be taught to separate their Spirits. It could prove useful."

"I'll consider it," Travail said.

"I'll let the Servitor know of their progress as well," Fiona added.

With that, the two women left.

"What just happened?" Jake asked, echoing William's own thoughts.

"I have no idea," William replied. He watched the two women make their way down the trail back to Village White Sun. It felt like a storm had passed overhead.

"Do you believe them?" Jake asked.

William shook his head. At the end of the day, they were both liars, no different from everyone else on the island.

"Fiona spoke the truth," Travail said. "Every word. I know. I trained her."

"I don't trust them," William replied.

"Same here," Jake said.

"But maybe we won't have to," William said. Walkers could hear everything, but they couldn't listen in on what they never saw. On a bare patch of ground, William bent down and wrote, *'Dream last night. Mr. Zeus coming on a boat.'*

Jake smiled.

———— • ————

Hours afterward, Serena still couldn't get the conversation with Fiona out of her mind.

Fiona was her grandmother?

Serena had never known it. Never suspected, and Cinnamon had never told her.

"What happened to my grandfather?" Serena had asked as they walked away from Travail's home. Once again, they spoke in the safety of a block. "The father of your children."

"He died," Fiona answered, her voice curt. "As soon as I was able, I no longer allowed him to use me."

She had briefly wondered whether Fiona was lying about their relationship, but Travail had vouched for her, so it seemed unlikely. As a justice, the troll's honesty was above reproach, which meant that as hard as it was to believe, Fiona spoke true.

During their walk along the curves and steep hills descending from Travail's field to Village White Sun, Serena had studied the old woman's face, seeking out the tell-tale resemblances in their features. She had found only one startling similarity. They shared the same eyes, the same hue and shape. How had she never noticed it before?

With those disturbing thoughts on her mind, she went to report to the Servitor. He waited for her in Lord Shet's Hall and sat in silence upon his Chair while she spoke.

"Travail believes they'll master sourcing their Spirits in a few more weeks," Serena said. "Soon, he plans on teaching them to separate it into their component Elements." She finished her account and hoped her distracted thoughts hadn't been too obvious.

The Servitor asked a few more questions before he eventually nodded approval. "Very good. Thank you, daughter. If what you say is true, then matters are moving as smoothly as I require." His gaze grew sharp. "I will shortly take Fiona's account as well. I trust there will be no discrepancies."

Serena shrugged. "I couldn't say. Her account is her own, but if you're asking if she will contradict what I told you, I find it unlikely."

"As you say," the Servitor said. He settled back in his Chair and waved Serena off in dismissal. "Send Fiona in."

"Yes, my liege," Serena said, her face remaining untroubled. She and Fiona had already planned what to tell the Servitor, making their accounts different enough that he shouldn't suspect they'd been rehearsed.

Serena bowed and made her way out of the Hall. As she did so, her eyes went to the stained-glass windows, and for some reason she remembered the church in Cincinnati she and William had visited all those months ago. Unfortunately, the images here weren't of a loving Christ or a saving God, but of Lord Shet and his bloody battles. The scenes, violent and savage, never brought Serena any comfort, and her lips curled in disgust.

As her gaze returned to the doors leading into the Hall, a trick of the light made a mirror of one of the iridescent columns lining the room, and Serena saw a distorted reflection of the Servitor on his Chair.

She almost stumbled when she beheld his visage. His mouth had elongated, and tufts of fur covered arms bulging with ropes of muscle. The Servitor had the appearance of a bear. Serena gave her head a slight shake, trying to disperse what she saw. It had to be a trick of the light or the mirror.

But the image persisted, and Serena barely held in a gasp as understanding came to her. The Servitor was an unformed.

Serena called upon every ounce of her training to keep her pace steady and smooth, her gait loose and unhurried, though she wanted to sprint out of the Hall. But all the way to the end, she maintained an eyes-forward posture, looking neither left nor right, and certainly not glancing back at the Servitor.

She finally reached the far doors and pulled them open. Until she exited the Hall, she didn't realize she'd been holding her breath, and she finally exhaled. A guard glanced at her and yawned.

"He wants you," Serena told Fiona, who stood waiting outside.

The old *raha'asra* must have seen something on her face. She quirked a questioning brow, and Serena shook her head, flicking her eyes toward the guard.

Later, her manner was meant to convey.

Fiona nodded imperceptibly and swept past as she entered Lord Shet's Hall.

Serena walked on, maintaining her steady, unhurried pace and forcing her face to the bland disinterest common to drones and mahavans alike.

An unformed sat upon the Servitor's Chair.

Serena's heart pounded, thudded loudly in her ears, and it surprised her that no one she passed in the hallways heard it or recognized her terror.

She made it to her quarters, and once there, she carefully shut the door, leaning against it before sliding to the ground. She closed her eyes while her heartbeat slowly recovered to normal.

Although not normally a religious person—she had absolutely no use for Shet—Serena certainly believed he existed. But how could he allow an unformed to fill the Servitor's Chair? Sacrilege.

Serena covered her face as a worse realization occurred to her.

Selene was around that monster every day. The girl was in constant jeopardy, and somehow, Serena would have to accept it and maintain the fiction that she didn't know the truth about the Servitor.

CHAPTER 15:
SCHEMES PUT INTO PLAY

June 1987

ARYLYN

Jason checked the straps of his pack one final time before lugging it onto his back. "Ready," he said to Mr. Zeus.

"Good. Let's get moving," his grandfather replied.

Mr. Zeus gestured, and Jason and the other volunteers—Daniel, Julius, Rukh, and Jessira—fell in behind him. His grandfather had chosen all of them for the mission to Sinskrill, thinking they possessed the necessary talents and skills to carry out their raid on the mahavans' home.

Julius O'Brien—a dreadlocked immigrant from Jamaica—and Daniel were Adepts in Water, a useful talent since they'd be sailing a boat to Sinskrill. Jason had skills in both Air and Fire, also useful abilities on a boat, while Mr. Zeus was the best Spiritualist on Arylyn. He was also good with Air and Earth.

As for Rukh and Jessira, although they couldn't do much more than source their Spirit, they already far outstripped Jason when it came to the sword or bow. Those skills might also come in handy on Sinskrill.

Of course, others had volunteered, but the Village Council had refused their petitions. These five were the only ones who'd been given permission to make the attempt.

When they reached Linchpin Knoll, the hill upon which all of Arylyn's anchor lines were fastened, the morning sun had yet to burn off the overnight dew. A fog, chilly and unusual for Arylyn, held the world in stillness. No birdsong or insects marred the hush.

"Gather close," Mr. Zeus ordered. "Let's go over the plan one more time."

This would be the twentieth time, and Jason tried not to roll his eyes.

Hawk-eyed Mr. Zeus noticed. "I see what you're pretending not to do," he said to Jason. "Pay attention anyway. I don't care if you think I'm being overly cautious. We're going over the plan again."

"With all due respect, I think we know what to do," Julius said. "We get to the Faroe Islands, figure out exactly where Sinskrill is located, and find out if William and Jake are still alive."

"They're alive," Mr. Zeus said. "Last night I dreamed to William. I don't think he realized it, but he answered. Jake is with him, and so is a troll, which is odd. I thought their kind had died out a long time ago."

"They're both alive? You're sure?" Jason demanded, a surge of excitement racing through him.

"I'm sure," Mr. Zeus replied. "Now, once we reach the Faroes, we need to proceed very carefully. We'll have to mask our *lorethasras* the entire time. For Rukh and Jessira, they'll both need an additional *nomasra* to do that. We can't alert anyone of our presence, and the mahavans might have someone posted at the Faroes to prevent exactly what we're trying to do."

"Do we have enough *nomasras* for William and Jake?" Julius asked. "Last week you weren't sure."

"We have plenty," Mr. Zeus answered. "We got the last two yesterday. But remember, once we're on Sinskrill, *nomasras* or not, the mahavans will be far more powerful than we are. They'll be braiding directly from their island, a *lorasra* they know quite well. We'll be at their mercy if we run into any of them."

"But if we do run into any mahavans, do we have to kill them?" Daniel asked, obviously unsettled at the prospect.

"The short answer is 'yes'," Mr. Zeus said with a grimace of distaste. "I don't like it, but if we want to rescue William and Jake, it might come to that. There can be no witnesses to spread the alarm." He met each of their gazes, probably wanting to impress the gravity of the situation on them.

Rukh whispered something to Jessira, who responded with a whisper of her own. She placed a hand on his shoulder, and he shook his head, his face growing pale.

"Is that going to be a problem?" Mr. Zeus asked.

"Not for us," Jessira answered. "We know what's required."

"Good. Because if you can't do what's needed, then you shouldn't come."

"We understand duty," Rukh replied in his oddly accented voice. He could have been Indian, but he didn't have the accent of someone from the subcontinent. Nor did he speak like a midwestern American. He and Jessira had an intonation all their own.

"Good," Mr. Zeus said, giving him a last, hard look before eyeing the others. "Our first stop will be Vijayawada, India. Remember, you'll be disoriented, but give it a few seconds, and it'll pass. After Vijayawada, we'll travel on to a *saha'asra* near Frankfurt, West Germany. Then comes the longest part of our journey, a car ride to Gdansk, Poland. Once there, we'll go straight to the Faroe Islands."

"The people of these other places speak different languages?" Rukh asked. "How will we communicate with them?"

"I'm sure Mr. Zeus has a magic spell up his sleeve to solve that problem," Jessira said in her confident contralto.

"I prefer knowing in advance the various aspects of our plan," Rukh said. He offered her a half-smile. "You know how I am."

"All too well," Jessira said with a faint smile of her own.

Jason shook his head. Those two always sounded as if they were carrying on a private conversation, one that only they understood. It was uncanny and weird.

Daniel and Julius must have felt the same. They gave Jason perplexed shrugs.

"It's been taken care of," Mr. Zeus answered Rukh's question. "We'll have no trouble communicating with the people we come across, not even in the Faroes. They speak a Germanic language there with a Norwegian accent." He looked about. "Any other questions?"

They shook their heads.

"Then it's time," Mr. Zeus said.

Jason felt his grandfather source his *lorethasra,* a rustling of leaves and the scent of brine. A line of sulfurous Fire rippled across Mr. Zeus' chest—a sight and smell only an *asrasin* could sense—and he triggered the anchor line. A black line slit the world and rotated on its long axis. It became a doorway filled with chaotic colors and patterns. The ringing of a bell heralded the doorway opening out onto a rainbow bridge extending into infinity.

"Tether to it," Mr. Zeus ordered. "Jason, bring Rukh across. I'll take care of Jessira."

"No need," Rukh said. "We've already learned how to tether to an anchor line. Lien taught us."

"She did?" Mr. Zeus shrugged. "Good. Then let's go."

SINSKRILL

Selene loved the long bicycle ride from the Servitor's Palace to the docks of Village Bliss where Serena had her dhow berthed.

Serena.

Selene still thrilled at the notion of referring to Madam by her first name, as though they truly were sisters, though she was only a drone. But Serena had confirmed and claimed the kinship a few weeks ago in William's presence.

Hearing the words, a number of things Selene noticed over the years finally made sense. She remembered Serena from long ago, when Selene had been younger. She also remembered a beautiful woman with a warm smile and loving arms. Their birth mother.

In those memories a younger Serena stood out—every bit as loving as their mother—and she'd promised to protect and save her. From what, Selene wasn't entirely sure, but she trusted Madam—no, her sister. Serena had been her truest friend all her life, and if she said Selene needed protection and saving, then it must be true. Her sister didn't lie.

As Selene approached Village Bliss' dock, her bicycle rattled on the uneven flagstones forming the twisting path, and she heard voices from around the final corner. They spoke in hushed tones, and Selene slowed her bicycle to a halt before hopping off. Bushes lined the stone walkway leading to the pier, and she hid behind a clump of them. Sunlight dappled the ground and glistened upon the glimpses of water she could see through the leaves and branches.

Selene eased forward, her feet squishing in the perpetually wet ground of Sinskrill. Two men spoke, and she strained to hear their conversation. One voice she didn't know, and the other belonged to William.

Selene liked him. He reminded her of Serena, kind and warm. Up to a point, she even trusted him.

Selene fingered the locket her sister had given her, the one with the picture of William and his family in it—at least she figured it was his family. She kept the charm with her always, hidden away in her smock, daring to stare at the photo only in the privacy of her small room. By now, she'd memorized every line on every person's face, the play of light on their hair, and most of all the love in their eyes as they stood with arms around one another. The locket and the photo were precious to Selene. It showed her a better world than Sinskrill.

"Hold on, Jake," William said. "Let me get this plank in place."

Jake Ridley then. The other raha'asra.

Selene crouched lower and crawled forward to better hear the two men.

"How much longer will it take?" Jake asked.

"I don't know," William answered. "Probably another few weeks."

"Then what's she plan on doing?"

Selene frowned. *Were they talking about Serena?*

"Sail it, I guess. She'll probably keep it close to shore and not risk the deeper waters until she's sure it's seaworthy."

It was Serena.

"You think she'll christen it first?" Jake asked.

"If you haven't noticed, these people aren't exactly Christian," William said, his voice sounding wry.

Jake laughed, open and friendly like William's. "I meant like breaking a bottle over the bow."

"How would I know?" William replied, sounding exasperated. "I never asked her, but maybe Selene could tell us. What do you think, Selene?" William called out to her.

Selene slowly rose from her hiding place, a knot of fear tightening her gut. William had always been nice, and while eavesdropping wasn't a sin on Sinskrill, getting caught at it was. They might beat her for doing so at their expense.

Selene slowly approached the two *raha'asras*, head low as she tried to keep her knees from shaking. She swallowed heavily before meeting William's gaze.

Some of her fear unclenched when he smiled at her, still warm and inviting.

"Who's this?" Jake asked, his voice friendly and curious.

251

Selene's fear diminished further, replaced by confusion. Neither of the *raha'asras* appeared the slightest bit annoyed at her.

"Selene," William replied, in answer to Jake's question. "Serena's little sister."

"So you're the reason," Jake said,

Reason for what? Selene wondered.

Jake opened his mouth, on the verge of saying more, but a sharp headshake from William must have changed his mind. "She looks like her," Jake said instead, and he held out a hand. "My name's Jake. We haven't been introduced."

Selene took Jake's hand, and they gravely shook. She still couldn't understand why they weren't angry with her. It made no sense. *They* made no sense.

Jake squatted, lowering himself until they were almost eye-to-eye. "What's got you so spooked?" he asked. "We aren't that scary-looking, are we?" He glanced at William. "Well, one of us is, I guess," he added with a grin.

"It's because we caught her eavesdropping," William said. "You're afraid we're going to punish you, aren't you?"

Selene nodded, staring at the ground again and unable to meet their eyes. Her fear surged.

Jake put a finger under her chin and tilted her head up. "It's all right. Just don't do it again."

"I won't," she promised in a whisper.

"Are you sorry for eavesdropping on us?" Jake pressed.

Selene vigorously nodded her head.

"Then you have to say it."

"I'm sorry." She looked Jake in the eyes. "I won't do it again."

252

Jake smiled, and the sun seemed to come out. "That's a good girl. Now, where I come from, once two people say sorry and forgive each other, they hug it out."

Selene frowned. "I don't understand."

"It's like this." Jake enveloped her in his arms, pulling her close and holding her.

Selene stiffened, but his arms were loose. She could break away anytime she wanted. He pulled her closer, and without thinking about it, Selene threw her arms around his neck and held him. She even rested her head on his shoulder. It felt like . . . only Serena had ever held her like this or made her feel so safe. Selene wanted to stay here forever.

"Well, isn't this an interesting sight," a voice noted in a dry, amused tone.

Selene stiffened.

Fiona.

She spun around to face the old *raha'asra*, sensing Jake straightening up.

Fiona smiled at Selene. "Don't worry, girl. I won't tell anyone what you were doing."

"There's nothing to tell," Jake said.

"Dawdling while on a mahavan's business isn't exactly nothing, is it, girl?" Fiona said.

William paced toward the old *raha'asra*, and Selene gasped. Never before had she sensed menace from William, but this time she could feel danger pouring off him like a fire. Violence simmered in the air, and Selene backed away from William until she ran into Jake. She looked up at him, and he laid a comforting hand on her shoulder.

"If any word of dawdling reaches anyone's ears, I'll break you," William vowed.

Selene remained pressed against Jake and stared at William in horrified fascination. It was like seeing one of the fat rabbits they kept in the kennels suddenly grow fangs.

Fiona held her ground, and Selene found herself impressed by the old *raha'asra's* courage. She would have fled if William glared at her like that.

"You mistake me," Fiona said, making a gesture.

Selene's ears popped.

"She's young, and accommodations can be made, but not for something like hugs when you aren't her family and she's uninjured. Then it's considered weakness, and you place her at risk."

William's anger slipped. "You aren't threatening her?"

"You know I'm not," Fiona replied. "You know why I never would."

The last of William's anger melted away, and he relaxed. "I'll never understand this island."

"Which is good, because the moment you do, that's when it has you and you become a part of it." Fiona held William's gaze, and he eventually nodded.

"Let this be a lesson," Fiona advised. "You have to be aware of where you are at all times and, just as importantly, who's around you."

———— • ————

Serena stood upon the cliffs near Village Paradiso while waiting for Brandon, Evelyn, and Isha. She had called them here, to a secluded, sloping finger of grass amidst a forest of trees, for a discussion about their futures. It was a necessary ruse, and she considered what she should say to them. They couldn't know the depths of her feelings for Selene or Fiona, and they certainly couldn't know her true plans with regards to the dhow. Nor could they know about the abomination of an unformed as the Servitor.

Serena chewed her cheek while she studied the steep descent from the clifftop to the narrow, tumultuous waters of Suborn Strait hundreds of feet below. Spiny rocks jutted like fangs and made passage of the channel treacherous.

On the far side of the strait an evening fog cloaked the island of Amethyst. Serena could barely make out Village Fealty, which stood in a valley where low-shouldered mountains formed a bowl. The buildings looked like broken teeth, abandoned and ruined like the rest of the island. A pine forest grew down the slopes of the hills and covered the fields that had once fed those who'd lived on Amethyst. Otherwise, signs of human habitation were absent. Fealty had been abandoned centuries ago.

Nowadays, the island's only inhabitants were grizzlies, elk, deer, and the occasional rabbit. Sometimes, though, the bears swam across the Suborn Strait and entered Sinskrill, usually near Village Bliss, where the island's eastern escarpment flattened into a series of gentle hills. It was the most easily accessible point by which to approach Sinskrill. Invariably, the creatures became a menace, and mahavans would be dispatched to hunt them down. It happened several times a year, almost always in the autumn.

Serena considered the bears while she waited for Brandon, Evelyn, and Isha. It had been a week since the discovery of her father's true nature, and she had yet to discuss the matter with anyone. After all, no one would believe her, and no one would be foolish enough to challenge the Servitor on the matter.

"Why are we meeting here?" Brandon called out, surprising her with his presence.

Her distracted thoughts and the booming surf had hidden his approach.

Despite Brandon's thick build, he moved easily and a smile split his bearded features. Evelyn accompanied him, short and slight next to him, and they marched up the short rise to where Serena awaited them. A mineral-iron smell told Serena that Brandon had sourced his *lorethasra*. He gestured, a wave of his hand, and out shot clear pulses of Air smelling of ice. They spread around the three of them and formed a block.

Serena's ears popped. "How goes recruitment amongst the younger mahavans?" she asked Brandon.

"Support grows. Your only challenger for the role of Prime is Park Alawah, the Isha to your own Isha."

Serena smiled faintly. "Once an Isha, always an Isha," she said, quoting the old proverb.

"Be that as it may," Evelyn began, "Many think Park is too old for the post."

"How many think I'm too young?" Serena asked. "I was only recently elevated to my position as a mahavan."

"Now you seek both citizenship and Primeship within a year of achieving your new status," Brandon replied.

Serena saw Isha break from the tree line, and she paused, waiting on him. She briefed him on their conversation thus far.

"Citizenship and Primeship can be yours," Isha told Serena, "but only if you're bold enough to claim the prize. Your best option is to convince Park to step aside. Even better if we can force him."

"How?" Evelyn demanded. "Park has many allies. It's said that he failed the Chair itself by only a few seconds. Had he been able to remain seated for a little longer, he might have become the Servitor."

Evelyn's words provided no new insight, and Serena instead focused on Isha's advice.

"Nor is Park a fool," Brandon said. "He lost out on the Primeship of Paradiso when he had to attend to his bishan's pilgrimage. He wasn't present when it became available, and he's probably done nothing but plan for every eventuality since then, in case another Primeship comes open."

Serena silently agreed with Brandon's assessment while still trying to understand Isha's counsel. A moment later she smiled at her mentor with unfeigned admiration. *Once an Isha always an Isha, indeed.* "Park's bishan died during his pilgrimage," she said, "and shortly thereafter, a posthumous decision granted him the status of mahavan. It happened years ago, but as far as I know, Park never completed his year of mourning."

Brandon immediately saw the opening, and he laughed. "He can't serve if he's in mourning while away in the Far Abroad."

Isha's eyes twinkled in apparent pleasure. "A simple solution, no? He steps aside or we send him off the island." He turned to Brandon and Evelyn. "Arrange a meeting with Park so we can go over the issue," he told them. "I have other matters to discuss with Serena."

The others left, and Serena raised a questioning brow. Isha complied, forming another block.

"What did you really wish to talk about?" he asked.

"The Servitor. I saw something when I met with him a week ago."

"What did you see?"

"An unformed," Serena replied. She explained what she'd witnessed in Lord Shet's Hall.

"Have you told anyone else?"

Serena shook her head.

"Good. Keep it that way."

Serena frowned, suspicion forming at Isha's lack of reaction. "You already knew."

"Only recently," Isha said. "When I became your father's Secondus. He elevated me shortly after Sherlock's death. He'll make the formal declaration in the next few days, and if I outlive him I will ascend to the Chair."

Serena gaped. "You'd become the new Servitor. But what about those other Seconduses who were thrown from the Judging Line? They failed the Servitor in some way and were punished for their failure. You've placed yourself at great risk."

"Only the bold can claim the prize," Isha repeated. "But I think I'll succeed where those others did not. They never knew the Servitor's secret. I do."

"You think it means the Servitor trusts you where he didn't trust the others."

Isha nodded. "The Servitor showed me a book. In it were secrets known only to the Servitor and his Secondus. His true heir. Those others were not."

"Meaning you're assured ascension to the Servitor's Chair."

Isha shrugged. "Not quite assured. The Chair rarely chooses someone other than the appointed Secondus." He moved to stand at the cliff's edge and stared out across the strait to Amethyst Island. "Mahavans once numbered in the thousands," he said, his voice solemn and sad. "The southern villages were the size of small cities, and four more villages populated the northern coasts of Sinskrill proper." He pointed. "Then there's Fealty across the water. Do you never wonder what happened to it?"

Serena shook her head. "I assumed we lacked the *raha'asras* to support such a population."

"No. It was far more stupid. A foolish Servitor brought a pack of unformed to Sinskrill, thinking he could control them. Instead, they took him and made him one of their own."

"But he would have been the Servitor," Serena said. "An *asrasin*. Unformed are woven. They shouldn't have been able to effect such a transformation on one of us."

"They can if Lord Shet wills it," Isha said. "An unformed Prime fears nothing in this world except a troll, a holder, or a necrosed. And while a Servitor is powerful, he's still human, slow and easy prey to those who hunt. For his hubris, Shet allowed the Servitor to be taken as a slave to the Prime of this pack of unformed he so foolishly allowed on Sinskrill. They swept over the island like a tide."

"Surely the Servitor isn't still a slave to the unformed," Serena said. She struggled to make sense of this secret history Isha revealed. "We sometimes hunt them."

"Eventually the mahavans of the time understood what had happened," Isha said, "and the Servitor who had loosed the unformed on Sinskrill was stripped of title and *lorethasra*. He became a drone, and his name forgotten for all time. A new Servitor arose, and Lord Shet sent her a solution: enslave the Primes. But by then there were many, many unformed and far fewer mahavans. It took decades to bend the various unformed tribes to the will of the Servitor's Chair, and by then, they'd nearly destroyed us." He pointed to Amethyst. "Many of the unformed live there now, as bears mostly. Or in Sinskrill's northern reaches as wolves."

Serena's mind reeled from all the information. "When did this happen? There are no accounts of such wars in our histories."

"Did you expect there would be?" Isha asked. "That we would allow such dangerous information to become publicly known? That our infallible Servitors are fallible? Remember, history is written by the victor."

"And in Sinskrill, the victors were the unformed?"

"No," Isha instantly replied. "The victor was Lord Shet."

A thought occurred to Serena. "The unformed who attacked William and Jake?" she asked. "How could they do so if they're tied to the Servitor's Chair?"

"I said most, not all," Isha reminded her wryly.

"And the ones who aren't?"

"They seek freedom from the Servitor's rule, to escape Sinskrill." Isha's eyes contained a speculative gleam. "I assume you've given up on such foolish ambitions."

"I never had them," Serena lied, grateful she hadn't told Isha about her plans, not when he was the Secondus. Her brows furrowed in thought.

Secondus. That word. Amongst the unformed . . .

She stepped back from her mentor, staring wide-eyed at him.

Isha never moved, but his eyes glowed and his teeth elongated. "The Servitor's bite made me what I am," he said. "Be careful no one else learns about this."

"Why tell me?"

"Because a Servitor doesn't live forever. Their lives, glorious as the sun, are shortened by their communion with Lord Shet, and your father grows old. In time, I will need my own Secondus, and who better than my finest bishan?"

CHAPTER 16:
SKILLS AND NIGHTMARES

June 1987

A s Sinskrill's spring warmed into early summer, the sun shone bright for longer hours in a vivid, blue sky and brought life to the green fields and budding purple heather near Travail's home. However, the weather remained cool.

On one such day, Travail took William and Jake to the shores of Lake White Sun. Fiona accompanied them, and they sat upon boulders strewn along the northern shore. To the south, the lake emptied over a cliff and down a laddered waterfall into the indigo waters of the Norwegian Sea surrounding Sinskrill. Farther out, as if demarcated by a pencil, the color transitioned to leaden.

"Source your Spirit," Travail instructed.

From where William sat, Lake White Sun appeared infinite, holding a depthless quality as it mirrored the puffy clouds floating across the sky.

"William. Pay attention!" Travail snapped.

William's attention wrenched back to the here and now.

"Focus," Travail rebuked. "Today you learn to create *lorasra*, and you won't succeed if you don't listen."

"You think you can teach them with words?" Fiona challenged with a lift of her brows. "As Jake would say, you can talk the talk, but of the two of us, only I can walk the walk."

Travail tilted his head in acknowledgement while William and Jake chuckled.

Surprisingly, the old *raha'asra's* presence no longer bothered William. In fact, he found himself looking forward to Fiona's visits. *Strange,* he thought, *given how cruel she'd been to them early on.* Maybe talking to Serena about their family ties had changed her, releasing some pent-up frustration or something. Whatever the reason, William and Jake felt grateful.

It didn't mean they trusted her. They hadn't yet told her their real plans for escaping Sinskrill and had no intention of doing so. Instead, they let her go on believing they were going to sail away on the dhow, not telling her that Jason's grandfather and several magi from Arylyn were coming to rescue them.

With any kind of luck, in a few days or a few weeks they'd be free of this piss-hole.

William couldn't wait. He still hadn't figured out what to do with Selene, though. She deserved a better home than Sinskrill. All the children here did. One day, he intended—

"Pay attention and observe," Fiona admonished, apparently noticing William's unfocused gaze. She sourced her *lorethasra*, and a rose scent briefly wafted. She drew out her silvery Spirit and from it separated the other Elements, each one a thick cord. Next, she wrapped the four threads in a thick, new layer of Spirit. "That was the forging," she explained. "Now we heat." She set the packet alight with a wave of crackling, yellow Fire made hotter by clear pulses of Air. A smell arose, a mix of boiled eggs and the glacial scent of Air. The packet wavered as if caught in a heat shimmer. It burned for several seconds before Fiona quenched it with rustling ivy-like tendrils of Earth and a wash of blue Water. A glowing golden ball remained in the air before Fiona. When she withdrew her Elements, it slowly dispersed into the ground.

William whistled.

"Only *raha'asras* have a touch delicate enough to manipulate Spirit in such a fashion," Fiona said. "Some Spirit Masters might come close, but they don't have the strength in the other Elements to do the heating and quenching."

"Why not have the Spirit Masters make those bundles of *lorasra* while you do the heating and quenching?" William asked. "Wouldn't it be, I don't know, more efficient?"

"I heard there aren't a lot of Spirit Masters around," Jake said.

"There are more Spirit Masters than any other kind of master," Fiona corrected. "All people who are stripped of their *lorethasra* become weak Spirit Masters. They can source their Spirit, but not much else. However, the bundles of *lorasra* the stripped could create would be like a drop of water in Lake White Sun compared to what I can manage."

"All the drones?" Jake said. "Every one of them is a Spirit Master?"

"Yes," Fiona replied.

"But we're masters of all the Elements?" Jake asked.

"Of course." Fiona smiled in satisfaction. "Did you think we were nothing more than jacks-of-all-trades?"

"That's what Mr. Zeus said," William replied.

"Well, this Mr. Zeus, whoever he is, is wrong," Fiona said. "The best of us are greater than any Walker, Tender, Rider, or Sere, but few people realize it. We spend our time creating *lorasra,* or all-purpose braids, and no one notices our true skill." She winked. "It's our little secret."

"What about—" William began

Fiona cut him off. "Enough. The Servitor intends on testing your knowledge in a few days and I won't have you embarrassing me, or worse, yourselves in front of him. In case you haven't noticed, he is not a forgiving man. You can't make mistakes with what you say to him."

Jake grimaced. "One day, I'll say exactly what I want to him. He'll hear it loud and clear."

"That day isn't today," Fiona reminded them. "Now. William. Tell me of *lorasra.*"

"*Lorasra* is created by a *raha'asra,* and from there it enters the ley lines of a *saha'asra.*"

"What are ley lines, Jake?"

"They're like arteries. They carry *lorasra* into every nook and cranny of a *saha'asra.*"

"I prefer roots as a metaphor rather than arteries, since roots penetrate the ground," Fiona said.

"Either will do," Travail said in a soft rumble. "This questioning is unnecessary. They know the theories behind the work of a *raha'asra* as well as you do."

"We need to make sure. We can't—" Fiona stopped, shook her head, and corrected herself. "*They* can't afford the slightest chance for the Servitor to find them unworthy. I won't have it.

Finish your explanation about ley lines, Jake. Surely you've learned more. What is a *raha'asra's* relationship with them?"

Jake frowned in concentration. "Ley lines corrode over time, and while other Element Masters can fix them, only a *raha'asra* can make new ones."

"What about Primal Nodes?" Fiona asked William.

William concentrated. "They're a kind of *nomasra*," he began, wracking his brain, "but they're only found in the bigger *saha'asra*s. The ley lines start at them."

"Good. You've progressed far and become much more than the dullards I knew when we first met." Her smile took the sting out of her words. "Have either of you heard of *therasra*?"

"Polluted *lorasra*?" Jake answered.

"Are you asking me?" Fiona asked with a glint in her eyes.

"No, madam."

Fiona turned to William. "What do you know about *therasra*?"

This William could confidently answer. Travail had discussed it with him during Jake's long convalescence. "Once *lorasra* is used, it becomes polluted. It becomes *therasra*. Trees and bushes become twisted by it. Same with some animals. *Therasra* also flows along a ley line, but it's collected in special vessels, *theranoms*, which are then cleansed by either a *raha'asra* or by a Water Master."

Fiona clapped her hands. "Excellent. You'll do," she said with a pleased smile.

William sat up taller under her praise.

THE FAROE ISLANDS

Jason bent over and heaved. Three transitions in less than twenty-four hours did that to a person. Mr. Zeus, Daniel, and Julius were similarly hunched over in misery, and a part of Jason was glad.

Schadenfreude. A word he had only recently learned, and one William would have liked. German. Taking pleasure in the misfortune of others. It was how he felt, taking joy for some reason in his grandfather's green-tinged face.

As Jason straightened, he glumly noted that Rukh and Jessira hadn't been nearly as affected as the others. While their faces had paled, neither had vomited. Already their color was restored.

How?

Jason shook his head in disgust before uncorking his canteen and taking a swig of water, warm now. He swished it around his mouth and spat it out before taking another drink. This one he swallowed.

"Let's get out of this alley," Mr. Zeus said. "I've made reservations at a nearby hotel."

He led them out of the narrow cobblestoned alley, and they entered one of the main streets of Tórshavn—Thor's harbor—the capital of the Faroe Islands. Jason peered about, getting his bearings.

Tórshavn was more of a small city or a large town than a metropolis. Probably fewer than twenty thousand people lived

here, but they obviously took pride in their homes. The buildings—
some wood and others brick or stone—were generally narrow,
three or four stories tall, and painted vibrant reds, blues, or
yellows. Despite the harsh ocean air, they were handsome and
obviously well maintained. The same care extended to the harbor,
where rugged boats bobbed in their moors.

A stiff wind blew, and Jason shivered. He wrapped his coat
more tightly about himself, heartened when Rukh did the same. At
least something made him uncomfortable. In their travels thus far,
the boy, a supposed freshman, had carried himself with confidence
and an eerie calm, even when the heavily armed border guards had
challenged their right to cross into East Germany. The rest of the
group had shifted about in worry, but Rukh had remained serene,
almost bored.

"What lovely weather," Jessira noted with a smile.

Rukh grimaced at her. "Why am I not surprised?"

She laughed, and Rukh shook his head.

Jason frowned. *There they went again with their weird, private
conversation.*

"You all have your *nomasras*?" Mr. Zeus asked, stopping at
the entrance to their hotel. "Before we left Arylyn, Cornelius
assured me they'll let us speak Faroese without any difficulty. We
should sound like one of the natives, even if we don't look like
them."

Of their group, only Mr. Zeus and Jessira had complexions
similar to the people of the Faroes, although neither of them could
be mistaken for natives. Both sported deep tans from their time in
tropical Arylyn, with Jessira's having a ruddy undertone. The rest
of them had skin with different shades of brown.

268

"I know I'm needlessly reminding you of what you already know," Mr. Zeus said, "but pardon an old man's worry. I don't want to take anything for granted."

They marched into the hotel and put away their belongings before meeting in Mr. Zeus' room. It held a narrow bed covered with a plush, down comforter, a pair of plastic chairs, and a dresser that took up an entire wall. Jason opened a drawer and caught the odor of mothballs.

"Is it always this cloudy?" Daniel asked, staring outside.

"I think so," Jason replied. "At least, that's what it said in an encyclopedia I read."

"What do we do now?" Julius asked.

"Now we figure out exactly where Sinskrill is," Mr. Zeus said. "I know it's north of here, but the Norwegian Sea is a big place. Settle in for a wait," he advised.

"Not too long, I hope," Julius said.

"It'll take as long as it takes," Mr. Zeus answered.

"Is there anything we can do to help?" Rukh asked.

"Find us a boat. Something with a motor and sails," Mr. Zeus answered. "We'll use the engine to get us most of the way there, but the sails when we get close to Sinskrill so no one hears us coming."

"Anything else?" Jessira asked.

"Start gathering supplies," Mr. Zeus said. "It's likely to be many hundreds of miles to Sinskrill, and we'll need food and water."

"We can't make do with fish?" Jason asked.

"You want to eat fish the whole way?" Daniel asked. "Nothing else?"

269

Jason grinned sheepishly. "Maybe we should take some vegetables with us."

————◆●◗————

SINSKRILL

Axel Carpenter, the Servitor of Sinskrill, tested Shet's Spear for what could have been the one-hundredth time this morning. He stared at the haft and a deep frown creased his face. His attention wasn't on the strange, white wood with its whorling patterns like Damascus steel, but rather on the dark runes carved into the haft. They flickered, burning with an intermittent red fire. *Strange.* They'd never done that before. In fact, as far as Axel knew, they'd never been reported to have ever done so.

What had changed?

Axel pondered.

The Spear was one of Sinskrill's great treasures, its secrets known only to the long line of Servitors who had ruled the island and handled by no one else. Even as Secondus, Axel had never guessed the weapon's importance, and prior to his ascension, he had believed the Spear to be but an emblem of the Servitor's authority, something akin to a scepter or a crown.

As a result, he'd thought the Servitor's Chair was the more important artifact. After all, the Chair was how a new Servitor was determined, and how Lord Shet communicated with His Voices, giving advice in the form of images, impressions, and feelings.

But once Axel ascended to the Servitor's post and actually held the Spear, he'd immediately realized how much more significant it was than the Chair. He also understood it was a secret no one else could know.

The Spear was a Primal Node unlike any other, the true source of Sinskrill's power, of the island's abundant *lorasra*. No one had ever guessed at its pivotal nature. Or did they all truly think that Sinskrill's might could be managed and maintained through the work of a single *raha'asra*?

Fools.

It was the Spear, a Primal Node that linked Sinskrill to Seminal, the world of gods and legends. Seminal. Not a final, heavenly home for the dead, but a living world of blood and battle, where Lord Shet waged endless war against the unworthy followers of Shokan the Befouler. From Seminal, *lorasra* poured forth into Sinskrill like Lake White Sun's waterfall cascading down into the Norwegian Sea. That same *lorasra* eventually dispersed past Sinskrill's shore into many of the world's *saha'asra*s, possibly including that of fabled Arylyn.

Axel set the Spear's steel-capped butt on the ground, and the leaf-shaped blade rose two feet above his head. This was a Spear meant to hunt bears, and the irony was not lost on him.

His totem was the bear, a choice made the day he'd ascended to the Chair and received the Lord's blessing. It had always been thus. Or at least, it had been since the unformed first came to Sinskrill. Upon their elevation, the newly forged Servitor chose an animal emblem, and for Axel it had been the bear.

Again the runes flared, and again Axel frowned while he studied them. Their secrets had been lost long ago, and he wondered . . .

He opened his mind, sourcing his Spirit, suffusing himself within its silver-white purity before he mentally reached out for the Spear.

Axel's eyes involuntarily rolled as knowledge flowed into him, dread, terrible secrets forged into the Spear through its mystic runes. His muscles spasmed, and his heart raced. He tried to let go of the Spear, but it wouldn't release. Lord Shet would soon return, with great fury and vengeance. An anchor line from Seminal to Sinskrill, one forged millennia ago and fastened to Shet's Throne, would open in five years, the first time it could be tethered in over three thousand years.

Axel's mouth went dry. The Spear burned in his fisted hand.

Shet the Indomitable, the Destroyer of Empires, the Murderer of Elementals, was coming.

With a gasp, Axel managed to release the Spear. It clattered to the floor, and he stumbled away from it, bumping against his desk. His knees gave way, but he managed to fumble into his chair before he fell on his face. Axel panted as if he'd run from Village White Sun to the peak of Mount Toll. Fear like nothing he'd ever felt coursed through him. Distantly he wondered if this was how a drone felt when he spoke to one of them.

Minutes passed, and the panic receded. His heart slowed, and his breathing came easier. His mind unlocked from its terror-induced paralysis, and thoughts flowed once more.

As much as the people of Sinskrill honored Lord Shet, none of them truly wanted to live beneath his dread shadow. Deadly, unforgiving, and dangerous to friend and foe alike, Shet was more a demon than a god. But he also provided the *lorasra* that kept the island alive and supported the uncounted Servitors through the unspooling centuries.

But when Shet's presence had been nothing more than a vague voice and impressions in Axel's mind, Sinskrill's god could be honored without worry. A distant ruler whose grasp far exceeded his desired reach.

But, now . . .

The Lord standing upon Earth was another matter entirely. A terrifying one. Axel feared much more than the loss of his station—and he had no illusions about what would happen to him when the Lord strode Sinskrill's rugged hills and mountains. After all, what need would Shet have for a Voice when he could speak for himself? Or the mahavans in general. Given the Lord's power, would he need any of them?

Disaster loomed, and Axel had no more than five years to find a way to save himself and Sinskrill.

He smiled then in grim amusement. Servitors didn't live as long as other mahavans, and in that moment, Axel wished he were older. Then he might have passed away before Shet entered their world, and the problem would be Adam's.

But life was never so simple.

Axel mused long over the terrible problem at hand, and an idea sparked within him.

Anchor lines were said to mostly be manifestations of Spirit. Only a powerful *raha'asra* could create one, and only a powerful *raha'asra* could destroy one. A powerful *raha'asra* like William Wilde.

Yes. William Wilde.

Axel sensed great potential in the boy. But how best to ensure his loyalty?

Axel nodded.

Mortal terror usually worked best.

CHAPTER 17:
TORTURE AND DREAMS

June 1987

William tried to suppress a shiver when the doors leading into Lord Shet's Throne Hall clanged shut behind him. For some reason, the Servitor required his presence, and William had no idea why.

The ruler of Sinskrill reclined in his Chair, the second step up on the dais, and his heavy features were twisted in a sardonic smile. The Servitor seemed to study him with a cold-eyed amusement, and William imagined a snake's scales slithering in the hushed room. His mouth went dry as he realized he had truly entered the serpent's lair.

The Throne Hall, dark lit and brutish, suited Sinskrill's ruler. Onyx flagstones formed the floor, and a line of thick columns supported a ceiling muralled with images of blood and battle. Little light from the afternoon sun penetrated the room, and that which did lit up the stained-glass windows bearing additional images of death and war. The entirety formed a tableau of barbarity and killing.

At the far end of the Hall—placed atop the dais—sat an empty throne. It was a blue-hued monstrosity with rune-written, broken spears forming the arms and legs, and a back surmounted by an arch of human skulls. Behind the throne loomed a monstrous statue, a commanding figure with six arms and a pitiless smile.

Shet.

William took a deep breath. *Here went nothing.* He marched across the hall, came to a halt before the Servitor, and fell to a knee. There could be none of the flippant disrespect he slipped into his conversations with Serena or Fiona. Without being told, William knew the Servitor would kill him for the slightest offense and feel absolutely no regret afterward.

"How may I serve you, my liege?" William asked.

"You believe you can serve me?" Amusement twisted the Servitor's features.

William's palms grew sweaty. He had no idea how to respond and decided on the truth. He prayed it wouldn't offend the Servitor. "I don't know the answer to your question, my liege."

"The query is simple. Do you think you can serve me?"

William chose his words carefully. "It is not for me to say."

The Servitor slowly formed a fist, and his knuckles cracked. He leaned forward, menace radiating off of him. "Do you presume to tell me what *I* must say?"

Fiery pain broke over William, a mountain of agony compared to Fiona's molehills. He collapsed. Muscles seized, and his mouth gaped. He couldn't even scream. The pain seemed to last for days, but likely only seconds before easing off.

William gasped in relief when it ended. Sweat drenched him. *Please let me survive this,* he prayed.

"I ask you again: do you presume to tell me what I must say?" the Servitor demanded.

"No, my liege," William quickly replied. "I am unworthy to tell you anything except the truth."

The Servitor leaned back in his chair, a half-smile on his face. "A good answer," he said. "For a coward. Serena has taught you too well in the ways of obedience."

William didn't show any response to the Servitor's observation, and honestly, he had no notion what reaction would be allowed. He didn't want a repeat of the earlier agony.

"Now answer my question. Do you think you can serve me?"

"I can attempt to serve you, my liege."

"Fly."

"My liege?"

"Step off the balcony there and fly," the Servitor ordered. He pointed to a terrace directly off the Hall with a face lacking any semblance of amusement. "Do it now, or I'll flay the skin off Jake Ridley's breathing body."

William's thoughts raced in muddy disorder. What was happening? Did the Servitor really mean for William to kill himself? What should he do? How could he live through this? Perspiration dripped down his face, and he looked to the Servitor, hoping to see some clue that the man might be joking.

He wasn't. The Servitor wore a visage as pitiless as the statue of Lord Shet.

William slowly climbed to his feet. He dragged his way toward the balcony, opened the doors, and stepped outside. A happy sun greeted him, but a hard wind kept the day cold. William struggled to keep his balance, leaning into the breeze. Sinskrill spread out before him. Green hills loomed directly ahead, while beyond them rose rugged mountains farther north. Village White Sun huddled to the left with thin columns of smoke rising from cook fires. A sliver of the Norwegian Sea sparkled to William's right.

He wondered if this would be the last thing he saw.

The Servitor had arisen from his Chair and stalked behind him. "Climb the balustrade," the old tyrant ordered.

William hesitated. "Why do you want me to kill myself? Is there no other way I can serve?"

"I want you to leap off the balcony for my amusement," the Servitor answered. "There is no other service I require of you." He gave William a shove. "No more dawdling. Climb. Do it now. This is your final warning. I *will* flay the skin from Jake. He'll live through it, too. This I promise."

William wanted to rage. He wanted to ask why, to demand answers. But he held silent, not voicing the furious questions. What would be the point?

Instead, he climbed until he stood atop the railing.

Regret filled his thoughts. So many things he wished he'd done differently. Spend more time with family and friends, laugh harder with them, love them more deeply. He sourced his Spirit, seeking its silvery, calming influence. A faint, distant song rang in the vaults of his mind, and peace settled over him.

William locked his knees. He would go no farther. If the Servitor intended his death, the old bastard would have to do the deed himself. A snarl of defiance formed on his face. The Servitor could go to hell with his threats. William would—

The Servitor flung him into empty space.

William screamed. The ground rushed toward him.

He slammed to a halt after falling no more than twenty feet. He twisted about and looked up. Above him, the Servitor waved and offered him a friendly smile.

Panic and confusion filled William as he floated upward. His arms crested the balcony's floor, and he made a desperate grab for a baluster.

The Servitor crouched over him and slowly unpeeled William's grasping fingers. *Shit!* His grip loosened, and he slipped. He scrabbled for the floor of the balcony. The Servitor stood and moved his feet, placing them on William's hands, but not applying much pressure.

"Understand this." The Servitor's weight slowly bore down. "I can kill you whenever I want." More pressure. "Your life is mine. Your friend's life is mine. Everything on this island is mine."

Grinding pain bore into William's hands, and he keened with the agony of it.

"You will obey me in all things, or the fear, pain, and shame you feel now will seem a balmy dream. I can make your life a misery unlike anything you can imagine. Am I understood?"

"Yes, my liege," William panted, panic stealing any semblance of pride.

"Good. Then we are understood." The pressure let up, and William heard the Servitor's bootheels ring as he strode away. "Perhaps you *can* serve me," he said from somewhere within the Hall. "You brought me amusement this afternoon."

His footsteps receded farther, and quiet followed. It told William he was alone. No one else was in the Throne Hall. He could climb back to safety. William levered himself over the balustrade and scraped his ankle heavily before flopping onto the balcony. Once there, he lay on his back and sobbed with relief and humiliation.

As the fear receded, a red haze took its place. Fury stole all thought. *The Servitor would die.* He would pay for what he'd done. No matter the cost, William would see the man dead.

———————◄●►———————

William limped back to Travail's field with his head down. He'd banged his ankle hard and scraped off a good chunk of skin during the Servitor's assault. His entire foot throbbed and could barely hold his weight. His hands ached from where they'd been stepped on, but the pain was the least of his concerns. He had much to consider. Foremost was that he and Jake had to escape Sinskrill as soon as possible. Tomorrow wouldn't be soon enough.

He passed Village White Sun's fields with the sun still shining, and distractedly acknowledged the greetings from the drones working the crops. They called out his name, and he waved to them before trudging on. Despite their training with Travail, he and Jake still took some of their meals with the drones. But because everyone now knew their status, it made things easier. Eventually he and Jake had gotten to know a few of the drones and formed what passed for friendship here.

Jake grinned when he eventually arrived at Travail's field. "About time you got back," he said. "I had to help Serena with her boat all by . . ." His voice trailed off when he took in William's ragged appearance. In addition to skinning his ankle, he'd ripped his pants getting back on the Servitor's balcony. "What happened to you?"

"The Servitor," William replied. He grimaced upon noticing Serena sitting there. *Great.* Fiona was there, too.

"What did he do?" Serena asked.

"Say no more," Fiona hastily gestured. The floral scent of rose wafted, and their world became silent as she formed a block.

"He threw me off the balcony next to the Throne Hall." William explained what had happened.

"He threw you off the balcony? Mother . . ." Jake raged, almost incoherent with anger. "That son of a bitch!"

"Control yourself," Travail said. "We need to examine today's events with a cold eye."

"You examine it with a cold eye!" Jake shouted.

"He's right," William said. He caught Jake's eye and shook his head slightly.

"Tell me exactly what the Servitor said, every motion, every expression, all of it," Serena demanded.

"Why do you care?" Jake asked, not bothering to mask his dislike or distrust.

William hobbled to a nearby boulder and carefully sat down with a grateful sigh.

Take off your boots," Fiona said. "I'll heal you while you talk."

William unlaced his boots and hissed when he tried to remove the one from his injured foot. Fiona took his ankle in both her hands and sourced her *lorethasra*. The sound of rustling ivy and surging waves briefly flared along with scent of rose and ice as she wove a complex braid of Spirit, Earth, Water, and Air, the basis of healing.

Coolness seeped from Fiona's hands into William's foot and brought immediate relief. Next, she worked on his bruised hands.

"I care because I need your help to get Selene off the island," Serena answered in response to Jake's earlier question.

"At least you're being honest for once," William muttered, while Fiona continued to pour healing into his hands. Again came the clean aroma of rose and ice.

"How can we help you get Selene off the island?" Jake demanded. "Why do you need our help? As soon as the dhow's fixed, you'll sail off without us."

"And go where?" Serena asked. "Selene and I can't live in the Far Abroad forever. The only safe place for her—for either of us— is Arylyn. Only William can dream to Mr. Zeus or Jason and ask for help so we can go there."

Her words jerked William upright and he shot Jake a look of alarm.

"So you don't really need *us*. You only need William," Jake replied.

"I'm not going anywhere without Jake," William said.

"You won't have to," Serena said in exasperation. "I promised we'd all leave together."

"We can worry about it later," Fiona said. "First, tell us what happened with the Servitor."

William told his story. Fiona and Serena interrupted often, pressing for more details. So did Jake, and by the time he finished, his foot and hands no longer throbbed and the swelling had receded. "Thank you," William said to Fiona.

"He wants something," Serena said.

"He fears something," Fiona corrected.

"Or both," Travail added. "That is the more likely scenario. Like all Servitors, he uses fear to demand obedience."

"Does he fear William?" Jake asked with a frown, obviously perplexed.

"No, he doesn't fear me. Or you, for that matter," William answered. "He thinks we're his slaves, scum."

"That isn't entirely correct," Fiona said. "He believes everyone is his slave and his natural inferior, but he does not hold you in contempt. Not when he needs you."

Serena nodded. "It's why he did what he did. The promise to torture Jake and the threat to your life. All of it had a purpose." She paced, head bent in thought. "He wants your unwavering fear and obedience, and more importantly, he wants you to master your skills as quickly as possible."

"But why worry about it now?" Fiona mused, tapping her chin.

"Is it because of your boat?" William asked. "Does he think you're trying to leave and take us with you?"

Serena shook her head. "Not if he's about to make me the Prime of Village Paradiso."

"Maybe he intends to fill that position with someone else," Fiona said, "and when you try to leave Sinskrill, he'll have proof of your treachery. All the excuse he needs to tear you down."

"Why bother?" Jake asked. "Why not just kill her? I mean, who'd actually care if he did? Would anyone actually miss her?"

Serena gaped at Jake in what might have been hurt, but William knew her too well. She cared about no one's good opinion, except maybe her sister's.

"Selene would," William said reluctantly, hating having to defend Serena.

"I wouldn't," Jake muttered. "She could fall into a volcano for all I care."

Serena's eyes flashed.

"What? You're going to lash me?" Jake asked. "Or toss me off the top of the Palace like your father did to William?"

"There are easier ways to hurt you," Serena said. "Say something like that to me again and you'll find out."

"Enough!" Fiona shouted.

"Whatever the Servitor's motivations, I don't see how any of this changes our plans," Travail said. "We all wish to be off this island."

"Selene comes with us," Serena said. "That's non-negotiable."

William privately wanted to free the child of Sinskrill's evil as well. In fact, he wanted to free all the drones and all the children, but that was a battle for another day.

"Then nothing's really changed," William said. "The Servitor's still an evil bastard, and he needs us for something we'll never do. Screw him. Meanwhile, Jake and I have to redouble our efforts and Serena needs to get her boat fixed. And when no one's looking, we steal Selene and get the hell off this rock."

"Amen, brother," Jake replied.

"There is one other thing," Serena said. "The Servitor is not entirely human. He's an unformed."

Her words elicited a shocked silence.

A few minutes after Serena's shocking revelation, she and Fiona departed. There wasn't much more to discuss because by then everyone knew what they had to do. Also, with twilight rapidly approaching and the ongoing threat of the unformed, the women needed to leave for their respective homes.

Afterward, William, Jake, and Travail built a fire and had a supper of cod, roasted potatoes, and a half-loaf of bread with butter. Night had fallen, and the stars shone as the clouds remained parted. The fire burned cheery and bright amidst the darkness, and leaves rustled in a gentle breeze.

During the meal, Jake addressed Travail. "Why's it so important if someone is an unformed? Does it make them evil because they're a type of woven or something?"

"Am I evil?" Travail asked with an arched brow.

"Err." Jake wanted to crawl under a rock. He should have thought out his question more carefully.

Travail harrumphed. "Remember what I told you about the woven, what I really said. I never told you they were evil. The woven were created through the art of an *asrasin*, and as a result mahavans believe the woven to be lesser beings. This includes powerful, deadly creatures such as the unformed, and according to *Shet's Counsel*, it is a sin for *asrasins* to be ruled by their lessers."

"Then why do they listen to you?" William asked. "Aren't you a justice? You tell them what to do."

"I am a justice," Travail agreed, "but the word means something less than what you believe. I see the truth. It is my purpose. When confronted with two conflicting views on an issue, I can see the heart of the matter, something few truly wish to know. Only occasionally am I asked to render such a decision because once I see the truth, I make it known so it can never be unknown. It's a power a mahavan respects and even fears, but it doesn't set me on the same footing as them. My status will always be lesser than theirs. I belong to them."

"You're also a slave," William guessed.

Travail nodded, regret etching his features. "To own another, especially a powerful woven, is how the mahavans measure their status, even the Servitors. It is why I was tricked and enslaved in the first place."

"We were all tricked and enslaved into coming here," William muttered.

"But, the Lord of the Sword willing, maybe not forever," Travail said, his voice a whisper barely heard above the murmuring leaves rustling in the breeze.

"Who's the Lord of the Sword?" Jake asked.

"Shet's enemy. The mahavans name him Shokan the Befouler. I can say no more."

Quiet fell amongst them, and crickets chirped while Travail stepped away from the fire. He repositioned himself with his back to a rock and closed his eyes.

Jake stared into the fire, not wanting to have the conversation he knew was long overdue. He mentally grimaced as he readied his words and arguments. William wouldn't like what he had to say.

"I think we should trust Serena," Jake said.

William eyed him askance, but with no anger or upset on his face. "Even after you told her she could fall into a volcano, and you wouldn't care if she did?"

Jake shrugged and relaxed a bit. "Just because I don't like her doesn't mean we can't work with her. You know. Keep your friends close . . ."

". . . and your enemies closer," William finished. "I still don't understand why you think we should trust her, though."

"Because since we've started working with Travail, she seems trustworthy."

"When Jason and I were running from Kohl Obsidian, I thought the same thing," William responded. "As long as our purposes were the same as hers, she helped us. But the moment they diverged, she betrayed us."

"She'll probably do the same thing again if we're dumb enough to give her a chance," Jake said.

"Not probably. She *will* do the same thing if we give her another chance," William corrected.

"I'm not saying we blindly follow her, but I think we should tell her about, you know . . ."

William picked up his unspoken reference to Mr. Zeus and shook his head. "Not a chance."

"But what about the girl? You really want to leave—"

"Be cautious," Travail warned.

Jake took the mild rebuke in stride. "I know you hate Serena, but remember she helped them kidnap me also," he said, "and I'm the one who got lashed. If I think we can trust her, then you should, too."

William might have given him a considering gaze, but it was hard to tell in the dark. "You really believe this?" he asked, and again Jake found himself relieved by William's lack of anger and upset.

"I'm sure," Jake said.

"What about you?" William addressed Travail. "What do you think?"

Travail appeared to take a moment to gather his thoughts. "She isn't trustworthy, but she isn't lying to you, either."

Jake smiled at William in triumph.

"Then we trust her," William agreed with a shrug. "But we only trust her as far as we can throw Travail."

"When you complete your training with me, you'll likely be able to throw me quite far," Travail said. "You'll have mastery of Air, after all." He hesitated a moment. "I should also mention my fear of deep water. I'll tell you about it tomorrow."

Jake wanted to know what Travail meant right now, but the troll had already closed his eyes and appeared to be asleep.

Jake and William shared a shrug. Both of them knew that at this point, other than a natural disaster, nothing would cause the troll to stir.

<hr />

"Is it supposed to tilt like that?" William asked, eyeing Serena's boat with a critical eye.

Serena scowled. "No," she said, trying to understand what had gone wrong with the dhow.

Blue Sky Dreams—the name she'd settled on for the boat—had been fine yesterday. Serena had even launched her a few days back to make sure the dhow had no hidden leaks, and everything had gone well. But now . . . What the hell?

Blue Sky Dreams floated and bobbed in her berth, in Village Bliss' shallow harbor, indigo-hulled like the surrounding waters with everything serene and perfect. Everything except the boat's pronounced list to starboard.

Serena continued to scowl as she crossed the dock to where she'd tied off the dhow. "If someone's messed with my boat, I'm going to—"

She didn't get to finish the thought. *Blue Sky Dreams* lurched, swaying as if caught in a series of waves. The dhow shifted, first listing to port and then to starboard before settling upright. A shaggy head thrust through the hatch and lumbered out from belowdeck.

Serena gasped.

An unformed bear of Amethyst, a huge male, old and scarred from many battles.

Serena sourced her Spirit, immersing herself in its silvery sustenance. Fear remained. Any unformed creature was dangerous, but especially those who'd survived to the age this one had.

She took quick stock of her surroundings. No one else lingered around the docks. The other boats had pushed off earlier in the morning. The streets of Village Bliss were similarly deserted. The drones were likely laboring in the fields on this sunny, spring day.

William remained behind her. He had no weapons, but there he stood, unarmed and unafraid.

His bravery would get him killed.

"Run," she shouted to him. "I'll hold him off."

"He'll kill you."

"He'll kill us both if you stick around."

William wisely retreated. She sensed him source his *lorethasra* when she smelled the fragrance of pine, the scent of his Spirit.

She involuntarily shot him a look of amazement. Serena had known he had great potential, but until now she hadn't realized how strong he'd grown.

"What?" William asked, noticing her shock.

Serena didn't bother answering. If Isha, the most powerful mahavan she knew, other than the Servitor, was a lantern, then William was an inferno.

She gritted her teeth a moment later when she realized he'd only withdrawn a few feet. She wanted to scream at him, tell him to get going, move, but she couldn't risk turning her back on the bear again. The unformed creature would break free of the dhow any second.

Serena drew Air, wrapping the thread around itself into a compressed knot before linking it to Sinskrill's *lorasra*. Her braid expanded.

The bear lumbered down the dock toward her.

With a gesture, Serena hurled the fist of Air at the creature. The bear grunted and easily shook it off, not slowing in the slightest. *Fine.* Serena had another braid ready. From her hands spurted a gout of fire.

The bear twisted aside but caught a glancing blow on the chest. The unformed roared in anger.

Serena hurled another blast of fire, but this time the creature seemed to eat it. The bear glowed brightly for an instant, and Serena's flames snuffed out. Her mouth dropped open in shock. The beast slammed down on all fours and rumbled forward.

Serena snarled. She brought up ropes of water from the bay. They twisted, long, sinuous, and serpentine. The ropes whipped at the bear, too many for him to avoid.

He roared and leapt into the water, disappearing from view.

Serena backed up. Her heart pounded. The unformed hadn't retreated. Of this, she was certain. *Then where was he?* Her eyes darted about.

He surged out of the bay as a dolphin and transformed in mid-air. He landed with an earthshaking thud, a bear once more. His leap had carried him to within feet of her.

Serena fell on her butt. Fear held her paralyzed. The unformed was going to kill her.

At the last instant, a sputtering pulse of fire knocked the bear back.

William!

Serena scrambled to her feet and got precious distance between herself and the creature. She faced the bear again, mind racing. *What would it take to stop the thing?*

The unformed came at her. The dock rattled beneath his weight.

Serena shouted and clenched a fist. Sand from the beach behind her slammed into the bear from both sides, pinning him in place. Still he struggled against her braid. He clawed the sand, disrupting her weave. Serena pulled in more sand, straining to keep the beast back. He pushed forward. His jaws slavered, and he lunged forward, breaking through her prison of Earth.

Serena curled into a ball. Instinctively, she encased herself in Air and Water. The bear beat at her armor, slamming her to the ground. Through the Elements surrounding him, she saw him rear overhead, ready to smash her flat.

She rolled as his heavy paws struck the dock's wooden planks and smashed them into kindling. He reared again. She tried to spin out from beneath the creature's paws.

She couldn't.

The unformed creature hammered her into the dock, and her breath went out with a whoosh. Pain bloomed in her chest. The bear had broken at least one of her ribs. The planks splintered beneath her, snapped apart. She screamed.

Her head slammed into a spar of wood, and she fought to retain consciousness as she plunged through the dock. Her flight halted when the bear snagged her shirt with his six-inch claws and threw her on to the dock.

Serena rolled over and over. Her ears rang. She tasted blood. Breathing came hard. The pain and disorientation—

She was going to die.

A core of resolve that wouldn't allow her to quit reared up. Serena gritted her teeth. *Hell no!* She snarled at the bear as he stood over her.

Eat this!

Serena hit the bear with a blazing line of fire. It caught the creature flush in the face, and the unformed roared. Serena didn't let up. She poured out more flames. The heat blistered her skin. The bear reared up, roaring in anger and pain. Her hands throbbed, and she gritted her teeth.

The bear continued to roar.

Fire hot enough to melt metal blazed over Serena' head. It hit the bear in the chest and punched through him. The unformed screamed in mortal pain, high-pitched and disturbingly human. A second later, the bear fell over, and from his muzzle and ruined chest, smoked curled.

Either the world held quiet or her ears didn't work. Serena didn't care. She'd survived. That's all that mattered. She lay on her back and tried to stifle the sobs. Her broken ribs couldn't take much more than shallow breaths.

William stood over her. "You hurt?"

Still in shock, Serena sat up, grimacing when her broken ribs sent a stab of pain through her. "Who shot the fire?"

"I did."

"You?" Surprise forced her to claw her way upright. "Who taught you to do that?"

"I taught myself," William said, kneeling at her side.

Serena viewed him in disbelief. *He taught himself?* "William. If you hadn't been absolutely precise in your braids, the fire would have burned you instead."

He shrugged. "Then it's a good thing I was absolutely precise." He sounded entirely too nonchalant about the matter.

Serena shook her head. "You hardly have any training. How did you know the fire wouldn't hurt you when you aimed it at the bear?"

"How do you know I was aiming at the bear?"

Serena stared at him, wondering if he was serious. She couldn't tell. His time on Sinskrill had served him well. Back in Cincinnati, she could read his every thought and intention without any difficulty. Now he was a cipher.

Serena continued to stare at him, wondering about his intentions. "You aren't serious," she declared, hoping she was right. *Did he really hate her so much that he'd murder her?*

"Maybe not, but the thought did cross my mind," he said with a sardonic smile. "Do you want me to get help?" He gestured to her chest. Her ribs ached, and blood leaked from a long runnel on her forearm where the bear had cut her.

"Fiona," Serena said. "She's supposed to be in Bliss' fields today."

"You trust her?"

"About as much as I trust anyone," Serena replied.

William snorted. "Fiona. She's an odd one. I wonder if she would have liked Mr. Zeus. They would have made an interesting couple."

Serena stared at him in surprise. His voice had held a puzzling tone. Her eyes narrowed in thought. William meant for her to know something. A secret lingered in his mien, something about Mr. Zeus, Jason's grandfather. "Only if they ever met," she said.

"What a meeting that would be," he said with a laugh.

Insight bloomed. *Mr. Zeus. He was near, and he was coming.* A well of gratitude filled her. *Maybe William wouldn't hate her forever.* "Thank you," she said softly.

"Make sure you don't betray me again. I don't think you'd do as well next time." William rose to his feet. "I'll get Fiona."

Serena watched him depart before she rested her head on the dock and stared at the blue sky. She breathed out her gratitude at being alive, and for the first time in weeks she hummed "Gloria."

CHAPTER 18:
SEMINAL

July 1987

Selene worriedly chewed her bottom lip as she stood outside Serena's quarters. She fisted her hand and raised it, ready to rap upon the door.

Courage, she told herself.

But it's wrong, another part of her argued.

She needs to know.

You'll betray the Servitor, the other part of her insisted.

Selene might have stood there for hours, held still by indecision, but approaching footsteps made the choice for her. She couldn't afford to be caught standing around in the Servitor's family quarters for no good reason. A mahavan might punish her if she was discovered here doing nothing.

Selene quickly knocked on Madam's door.

The footsteps drew closer, and Selene flicked a fearful glance at whoever approached.

Secondus Adam, the Servitor's brother and her uncle, turned the corner, and Selene dropped a curtsy. Secondus Adam never noticed. He passed by, not bothering to acknowledge her presence, before he entered his own quarters.

Her sister's door opened, and Serena stood there with her hair haloed about her head and shoulders in an untidy mess. She rubbed her side. The broken ribs from the attack by the unformed bear must have still bothered her.

"I'm sorry to disturb you, Madam," Selene said.

"What is it?" Serena asked.

"The Servitor wants to see you."

Something in her tone or her posture must have given away her nervousness because Serena stared at her so intently that Selene began fidgeting. "The Servitor wants to see me?" Serena repeated with an arch of her eyebrows.

"Yes," Selene said, trying to make her voice sound certain rather than filled with fearful uncertainty. "In his study."

Serena stared at her a moment more before shrugging. "Lead the way."

Selene nodded and darted back the way she'd come, glancing to make sure Serena followed.

"What's the hurry?" Serena asked. "If I didn't know better, I'd think you were nervous."

"I'm not nervous," Selene said.

"I'm glad to hear it," Serena said. "By the way, is the Servitor actually in his study?"

"No, Madam. The water in Village White Sun's well went muddy this morning. He went to purify and bless it."

"Then he'll be gone for a few hours," Serena mused, "and he wants me to wait for him in his study the entire time he's gone?"

Selene winced. Her lie sounded so obvious when put like that, but she made herself nod in assent. "That's what he said."

"I see."

Selene changed the subject. "Are your ribs getting better?"

"Slowly but surely," Serena answered. "It's only been a few days, but maybe in a couple more I'll be back to normal."

Selene barely paid attention. She rushed them through the Palace, and exhaled in relief when they reached the door to the Servitor's study. "We're here," she announced, rapping once to make sure the Servitor hadn't unexpectedly come back. No sound came from within, so Selene opened the door and ushered her sister inside. "He said for you to wait here," Selene reminded Serena before darting out of the room.

Hopefully, her sister would notice the ornate case standing open in a corner. The case that only the Servitor could unlock. The one he'd mistakenly left open when he had gone to take care of Village White Sun's well. The case that held Shet's Spear, the holy object carved with runes that glowed, and when touched led to a place of terror.

After the Servitor had set off to cleanse Village White Sun's well, Selene could have walked away. But she hadn't. Instead, she'd glanced about the Servitor's study, wondering if this might be some sort of test to see if she'd reach for the forbidden Spear.

But there hadn't been anyone around, and Selene had been unable to help herself. Curiosity had always been her great weakness, and she'd touched the Spear. Even worse, for some immensely stupid reason she'd sourced her nascent Spirit while doing so.

Idiot. Why couldn't she have left the Spear alone?

Selene darted to a small alcove down the hall from the Servitor's study and waited there.

At least this way she could warn Serena if the Servitor came back early. He'd be furious if he found her sister alone in his study, since he'd never actually asked her to be there.

———————◆———————

Selene clearly meant for her to see something in the Servitor's study, and after her sister left, Serena searched about, wondering what it might be. At once, she spotted Shet's Spear standing upright in its case, which unaccountably stood open.

Serena frowned.

The Spear glowed. No. Not the spear itself. The small runes carved into it.

Serena carefully approached the open case. Only the Servitor could open it, and only the Servitor was meant to handle the Spear. But Selene must have as well. The girl had curiosity carved into her bones like the runes cut into Shet's Spear. But what had her sister discovered? Something terrible for her to have risked lying to bring Serena here.

Serena carefully studied the Spear, while her instincts screamed at her to leave the study as swiftly as possible. The Servitor would be furious if he discovered her here without his consent, especially with the case open.

Her heart pounded as she continued to study the Spear, trying to figure out what had spooked Selene so badly. Why was it glowing? Serena hesitantly reached out a hand, but paused with her fingers a paper's thickness from the Spear's haft.

She really didn't want to do this.

Serena swallowed heavily before lightly gripping the Spear. She waited a beat for a reaction, but nothing. More seconds passed, and still nothing happened. She cracked open her eyes, having involuntarily pinched them shut. The study remained unchanged, and Serena tightened her grip on the Spear.

"Source your Spirit when you touch it," Selene whispered from the doorway.

Serena almost shrieked as she snatched her hand from the Spear. Her attention had been so inwardly focused that she hadn't heard the door open. Her heart thudded, and she shot a glare at Selene, but the girl had already scampered away, shutting the door behind her.

Serena exhaled heavily, calming herself before doing as Selene suggested. She sourced her Spirit before reaching again for the Spear.

This time when her hand touched the rune-carved wood, knowledge poured into her as a voice—ponderous, proud, and terrifying—laughed.

A rainbow bridge—an anchor line wider than any she had ever heard of and leading into deepest night—opened in her mind rather than in the physical world. It drew her in, carrying her involuntarily forward before she could think to resist.

She traveled a vast distance, but only her mind and Spirit, not her physical shell. Farther and farther she journeyed, pulled onward by a force like gravity. The journey appeared to have no end. She blurred along the bridge, and her mind stretched to fraying. An endless rush of noise filled her eyes, and Serena lost all sense of herself, her purpose, her very name. Emptiness clawed at her heart, but at her utter breaking point it ended with a jarring halt.

Serena's mind snapped back, annealing with a shuddering force as a world opened before her, one of long, lost fantastical creatures. She viewed this land as if from high above, but wherever she chose to focus her attention the world came into bright clarity.

Proud elves strode forest empires while dwarves and gnomes contested for rule of the mountains amidst deep caves. And humans scurried about everywhere, fearful denizens of unlovely kingdoms of stone and metal, but more often as slaves to elves or other unknown species.

And throughout the entire world, uncountable monsters existed. Rotting necrosed, shape-changing unformed, courtly yet sadistic vampires, and an entire mountain range with every dell and valley webbed by spiders the size of elephants. A dragon soared close by. Even more creatures out of antiquity and legend.

A sense of unreality filled Serena, but she knew this world she gazed upon hadn't been dredged from her nightmares or fantasies. This world was as real as her Spirit, and as Serena studied it more closely, she noticed titanic statues standing in forlorn majesty, lost, fallen over, or broken, in fields, forests, and seas. Thick chains were wrapped about their torsos, arms, and legs.

A few she recognized from ancient stories. *Verde the Valiant. Duval of the Lightning. Tomag Shield-Render.*

Titans all. Gods and demigods in the service of Lord Shet. His mightiest generals.

The voice from earlier laughed again, and Serena sought its source.

In the shadow of a lonely peak, a cavern opened into the heart of the mountain. There another titanic figure waited. This one still lived. The right side of his face contained a horrible burn, a still seeping wound. He stood within the eaves of the cave, straining against smoke-black chains binding him to the deepest stone. He must have sensed Serena's regard because he paused in his exertions.

"I see you, child," the titan said. "I have already greeted your sister, and now I greet you. I will greet you both in the flesh soon enough."

Serena shuddered. This was a being of power and malice, a creature who could tear apart suns as easily as a child might snuff out a firefly. *Lorasra* poured off of him like smoke from a forest fire, traveling to where Serena watched. It passed through her, along the anchor line in her mind, all the way back to Sinskrill.

"You have many questions," the titan said.

Fresh terror seized Serena. The being's words grated against her mind like razors.

"I will answer them anon," the titan continued. His good eye twitched, and a glow ignited in his burned-out socket. "For now, understand that I am your lord, and I will rule you with a firm but gentle hand when I resume my rightful place."

"Who are you?" Serena asked, her voice reflecting the panic coursing through her.

The titan cast her a disbelieving gaze. "You don't know me? Truly?" He sneered, a grotesque twisting of his face as it crossed to the burned right side. "Then know that I am Lord Shet, and this world is Seminal."

No. Shet might be true, but the world of Seminal was a story, a myth. It couldn't be real.

"And yet it is," the titan answered Serena's unspoken thoughts.

A whiplash of pain bloomed within her mind, and Serena screamed. She fled back along the anchor line.

Shet's voice chased her. "Five years, child. Five years, and these chains break. A half a decade, as you measure time, and I travel back to the world where I was birthed. Mark my coming, for on this occasion there will be no Befouler and His Bride to save the world!"

———— ● ————

Along the north shore of an island in the Norwegian Sea stood an empty, shingle beach within a darkened, sheltered cove. The sun had yet to fully rise, and mist softened the features of the lichen-covered boulders and the scree littering the shore. A rugged escarpment, made mystical by a wreath of early morning fog, loomed over both beach and water. Farther inland, a range of tall, granite-shouldered hills marched south. An eagle cried out from high above.

Sinskrill.

Jason imagined menace emanating off the island, with hidden warriors ready to strike them down the moment they reached shore.

Sinskrill.

The name itself evoked fear and excitement. This was the home of the mahavans, the legendary enemy of Arylyn's magi. This was the home of Shet's followers, still active all these thousands of years later. This was where they would—God willing—find William and Jake and escape home.

"We'll drop anchor here and take the canoe in the rest of the way," Mr. Zeus announced.

The sailing yacht they'd rented couldn't approach closer than fifty yards from shore, and Jason, Daniel, and Julius got to work readying the canoe.

While they transferred their backpacks into the small boat, Rukh and Jessira had binoculars to their eyes. The two of them studied the cliffs with youthful faces furrowed with frowns.

Jason scoffed. Rukh and Jessira might appear young, but they didn't act young. In fact, they didn't even look like freshmen anymore. They looked like seniors, or even older.

He'd mentioned his observations to Mr. Zeus, but his grandfather had brushed him off. "I took their measure, and I trust them. Trust that, if you trust nothing else."

"You saw them?" Jessira asked Rukh, interrupting Jason's thoughts.

"I only caught a flash."

"But they're up there," Jessira said, sounding sure of herself.

"What did you see?" Mr. Zeus asked.

"Wolves," Jessira answered. "Big ones. Two or three of them."

"You're sure?"

"Positive."

"I knew we should have brought some guns with us," Daniel muttered.

"I already told you why we couldn't," Mr. Zeus said. "Sinskrill is like Arylyn: anything entirely encased in metal is rendered inert. That includes the chemicals needed to fire a bullet."

"We still have our bows," Rukh said. The tall Indian, or whatever he was, gestured to a recurved bow and a quiver full of arrows strapped his back. "We can take out the wolves if we have to, and no one will ever hear it."

Jason might have once doubted anyone's ability to hit a running target with a bow, especially a wolf, but he'd seen Rukh shoot a mackerel swimming close to the water's surface from a hundred feet away. This from the rolling deck of a yacht, with a slender fishing line tied to the arrow.

"Let's go," Mr. Zeus said.

They clambered aboard the canoe, and Jason smelled pineapple. Julius had sourced his *lorethasra* and reached for Sinskrill's *lorasra*.

"Gross," the other man said with a scowl of disgust. "Do you feel that? It's like the Elements are covered in a layer of slime."

Jason sourced his *lorethasra* and linked it to Sinskrill's *lorasra*. Immediately, he understood what Julius meant. Every *saha'asra* had a different flavor to its *lorasra*. Arylyn's was fruity with a touch of salt, but Sinskrill's tasted foul as a sewer.

"No wonder the mahavans are demented, feeding on this *lorasra* all their lives," Julius said.

"Nobody source the *lorasra* unless you absolutely have to," Mr. Zeus ordered, his face tight with worry. "We get ashore, get our boys, and get the hell out of here."

Julius nodded, and the canoe darted forward under the impetus of his braid of rushing Water and pulsing Air. As soon as they reached the shingle beach, Jason jumped out and pulled the canoe the rest of the way in.

When his feet hit the rocky beach, thoughts of wolves, disgusting *lorasra*, and mahavans left him. Instead, a sense of soaring accomplishment filled him.

Sinskrill.

Against all hope of success, they had found it.

He grinned.

"We need to get our bearings," Mr. Zeus said.

They'd taken a long, circuitous route to get to their current location. After weeks spent in the Faroes, they'd sailed toward Sinskrill. But, miles from shore, a village on the southern coast of the island became visible. As a result, they skirted west, passing through a sea littered with jagged reefs and needle-like rocks thrusting up from the water, before discovering this sheltered cove.

"There's a cut in the cliffs there," Daniel said, marking a narrow pass leading through the escarpment.

"It's going the right direction," Rukh noted.

"We'll take it," Mr. Zeus said.

They lugged their packs out of the canoe and began the ascent up the pass. All of them but Rukh and Jessira were huffing by the time they crested its lip. They paused at the top before slowly descending on the other side. Rocks slid out from beneath their feet, threatening to spill them down the hill.

Strangely, Mr. Zeus deferred to Jessira, and allowed her to lead them. Hours later, they reached a long, north-south valley, forested and headed in the general direction of the village they'd seen from afar.

Before continuing onward, Mr. Zeus called for a halt in a small glade. All of them—even Rukh—needed the break. The rugged terrain made traveling slow. The evergreen forest covering the valley appeared virgin and passage was difficult.

Jason slipped off his backpack and slumped down next to Daniel and Julius with a relieved groan. The forest canopy hid the sun, but here sunbeams dappled the ground. Birdcalls filled the air.

The three of them sat with their backs to a massive cedar, and Jason fanned his chest. Despite the cool weather, he sweated profusely.

"That was one helluva walk," Daniel said.

"How much farther do you think it is?" Julius asked.

Jason shrugged and took a long swig of cold water from his canteen. "No idea."

"Does anyone remember how to get back to the boat?" Daniel asked.

"I've been leaving breadcrumbs," Jason said.

"Ha, ha."

"I left a *nomasra* in the yacht," Mr. Zeus said. "I know the way back."

"Jessira can get us back, too," Rukh said. "She never gets turned around."

"How?" Jason asked.

"It's a skill I learned," Jessira answered.

"When?" Jason asked. "When did you learn to find your way through the woods? And when you came to Arylyn, both of you looked younger than me, but now you look older. How?"

"I learned what I know like everyone else. Those with the knowledge taught me," Jessira said. "That is all I can tell you."

Jason eyed her with distrust.

Rukh's head snapped up. "Someone's coming. Off the trail."

Jason hadn't heard anything. He opened his mouth to ask what Rukh had heard, but the strange Indian had already vanished. So had Jessira. Both had darted out of the glade. He spotted Jessira behind a tree, an arrow nocked to her compound bow. Rukh stood close by, similarly ready.

How the hell had they moved so fast?

Hoofbeats, slow and steady, echoed toward them, and Jason shared a slack-jawed look of fear with Daniel.

"Shit!" they said together before scrambling out of the glade. They concealed themselves behind rocks and trees. Mr. Zeus and Julius hid nearby, too.

Muffled voices rose, and two riders—a man and a woman—came into view. Armed with swords at their hips and bows cased to their plain saddles, both appeared bored. They wore leather armor and chaps along with goofy hats with red plumes.

"I heard one of those new *raha'asras* burned a bear last week," the man said.

Jason stiffened with excitement. *William and Jake. It had to be them.*

"Which one?" the woman asked.

"The dark one."

Jason grinned. *It* was *William.*

"Yeah?"

"Yeah. And I heard the Servitor wants a demonstration soon. If they don't pass, one of them dies."

Both riders laughed at this and moved on down the trail. Their voices faded away.

Jason's heart soared. He wanted to shout in triumph and relief. "They're alive!" he whispered to Daniel. He shared a grin with the others.

"I told you they were," Mr. Zeus said with an answering grin. "Let's follow those riders. Maybe they'll take use where we need to go.

Half an hour later, Jessira signaled them off the trail. "What did you see?" she asked Rukh.

"In the trees." He pointed with his chin while puzzlement marred his features.

Jason stared to where Rukh indicated. He squinted, straining to see. All he could make out was a dark bird.

"What about it? It's a bird," Julius said, sounding as confused as Jason felt.

"It's a hawk," Rukh said. "A moment before it was a wolf, big and lean. It might have been watching us, but I saw it slip behind a bush, but a hawk winged out the other side."

"You're sure about this?" Mr. Zeus asked.

Rukh nodded.

"We're in trouble," Mr. Zeus said. "If it really was a wolf that became a bird, it means it was an unformed."

Jason paled. *Unformed were only one step below necrosed in terms of deadliness.*

"It'll track and attack us?" Rukh asked.

"Worse," Julius said. "It might tell the mahavans where we are."

"Not this one." Rukh nocked an arrow. He barely took time to aim before he loosed a shaft. An instant later the hawk cried out, and a plume of feathers erupted from where it had perched as it fell from view.

"Stay here," Rukh said. "I'll make sure it's dead." He set off into the trees, ghosting through them. A minute later he returned with a bloody arrow in hand. His eyes were red, and Jessira briefly squeezed his shoulder.

Jason shook his head. It had only been an unformed.

"We can't go anywhere if unformed patrol the island," Mr. Zeus said. "We should go back to the boat and figure out a better plan."

A howl rose from a nearby hill as if to underscore the danger all around them.

———◆———

William sourced his Spirit, and from it he carefully unbraided the other Elements. Four strands—hissing Fire and pulsing Air roped across his chest and torso while susurrating Water and slowly rustling Earth coiled down his arms and filled his hands. They threatened to re-twine around one another, and he pushed with tiny nudges of Spirit to keep them separate. A thrill of accomplishment coursed through him when they remained untangled.

He took a deep breath, inhaling the scent of pine and heather. Travail's meadow bloomed purple, and the forest stood dappled in the afternoon, summer sun. It was a beautiful, unseasonably warm day, and William had discarded his jacket. Jake concentrated on his own threads of *lorethasra* while Travail appeared to nap with his back against a boulder twice his standing height.

William reached for *lorasra*. Its power pulsed into him, but before he could unbraid the Elements from it, his threads trembled. He chased the flaw, steadying it, but the moment William reached again for *lorasra*, the Elements of his *lorethasra* fused together in a glitter of light and ringing bells.

He slammed a fist into the ground. *Damn it!* He'd been so close that time.

After the attack against the unformed bear, William had thought it would be easy to combine the Elements of his *lorethasra* with those of *lorasra*. After all, he'd done it during the battle. However, his actions during that encounter had been instinctual and fear-fueled and he had yet to replicate his prior success.

As a result, without the ability to braid the Elements of his *lorethasra* with *lorasra*, his abilities remained limited to no more than temporarily draining *lorasra* out of small area. A useless skill he'd accidentally discovered. Fiona had never heard of it, which was a small consolation since William couldn't do anything else. He silently snarled at his ongoing failure.

"Fiona and Serena are coming," Travail murmured.

"I held it for a minute that time," Jake said, grinning as he opened his eyes.

William tried not to scowl and failed miserably. Jake wasn't having nearly as much trouble in linking the Elements of his *lorethasra* to their respective threads in *lorasra*.

"Serena appears upset," Travail noted.

William studied the approaching women. They hiked the trail from Village White Sun and walked side-by-side. He frowned. "No. Fiona's upset. Serena looks . . ." His eyes widened in surprise. "She looks scared." He found it difficult to imagine what could frighten her. Other than when she'd faced off against a necrosed and the unformed bear, she'd always remained calm and cool.

"What could scare *her*?" Jake echoed his thoughts. "Other than the Servitor, she's the scariest person I know."

William shrugged, but the notion of a fearful Serena stirred his own anxiety.

Fiona gestured as soon as they arrived, and a block of Air formed around them. "We have many things to discuss."

"We're in trouble," Serena announced.

William chuckled nervously. "And here I was hoping you were about to tell us that the Servitor's dying."

"We aren't so lucky," Serena said. "The old crocodile has decades more life ahead of him."

"I thought mahavans lived for a really long time," Jake said.

"They do, but not the Servitors," Serena explained. "Fifty or fifty-five years into their reign they suddenly start aging. In a matter of years they go from middle-aged to infirm. But none of that's important."

"Then what is?" Fiona asked. "You were awfully mysterious down at the village."

"Lord Shet," Serena said. "He's coming. I touched Shet's Spear, and—"

"But only the Servitor can handle the Spear," Fiona protested. "It's locked in its case."

"I know," Serena said. "My father left the case open when he went to fix Village White Sun's well this morning. I touched it, and while I did so, I sourced my Spirit." Serena swallowed heavily, as if in fear of what she had to say next. "I traveled along an anchor line, a different kind of one. Only my mind made the journey, but I still went somewhere."

Serena described a world of humans, elves, dwarves, and monsters, of dragons, vampires, and dead gods in chains.

All but one. One god lived. Lord Shet.

"He's chained with black bands of Spirit that extend into the heart of a mountain," Serena continued, "but he says the chains will soon wither away, and when they do he intends on coming here."

"Impossible," Fiona declared. "Shet is a myth. What you saw must have been an illusion or your own imagination."

"*Lorasra* poured off him," Serena insisted. "It joined the anchor line connected to the Spear

William tended to believe the old *raha'asra*. Serena had seen something that had clearly rattled her, but it didn't make it real.

"I saw him," Serena said in a quiet voice. "I was there. Seminal is real. Lord Shet is real."

"You say *lorasra* poured off him and joined the anchor line you traveled?" Travail pressed.

Serena nodded. "I think it's linked to the island through the Spear." She hesitated. "It might disperse to the island from there."

Travail rubbed his chin in thought. "That explains much."

"Explains what?" William asked.

"The unnaturalness of this island and its people," Travail said. "Parents with little devotion to their children. Absent familial ties. Love, decency, friendship. . . . Tender emotions and relationships are so rare on Sinskrill that when they do occur they are deemed a weakness and hidden away." He turned to Fiona and Serena. "The two of you are rare in that you can still love. Think of the world beyond Sinskrill's shores, though. How common love and friendship are out there. Why is Sinskrill so different?"

"How does her vision explain this?" Fiona asked. "The people here are hard and cruel, but so are people throughout the world."

"Not like this," Travail declared. "Even in the worst places, the basic instincts of people to love one another shines through, to care for their weakest, to protect those they love, to actually love and devote themselves to their children. But not in Sinskrill. I've often wondered why."

"You actually believe this?" Fiona asked.

"The answer to the ultimate mystery of Sinskrill is one that has eluded me for decades," Travail said. "For instance, how is the *lorasra* of this island so potent? It shouldn't be. Not with a single *raha'asra* to fund it. Have you never wondered why *therasra* collects so readily here? Your production of *lorasra* isn't prodigious enough to account for it."

Fiona shrugged. "I can't gauge *lorasra's* strength the way you can."

"Then trust me when I tell you that no single *raha'asra* can supply the depth of *lorasra* Sinskrill possesses."

"But a god can," William said.

Travail nodded.

"You've never made mention of this before," Fiona accused.

"It had no relevance before," Travail replied. "Now it does. If Serena's vision is correct, then the source of Sinskrill's *lorasra* lies with Lord Shet. As such, it is likely as poisonous as the god himself. His book of supposed morality, *Shet's Counsel*, and his many murals of death and torment, should be proof of his underlying wickedness. I would guess his *lorasra* twists a person's mind, changes those who live here until love, sacrifice, compassion, empathy, the graces given to you by God, wither away."

William reflected upon Travail's words, and he studied Serena, wondering about her. She had loved her mother, and she loved Selene even more. That love had driven everything she'd done. No matter all her other lies, on this he was certain.

It left him debating whether he should still hate her.

"If Lord Shet is real," Jake mused, "and he comes here, can we stop him?"

"If we're on Arylyn, do we care?" William asked, hating to be callous.

"We must care, because Lord Shet is the god of *raha'asras*," Travail said. "That is one of his ancient titles, and if his power can fuel this island from a distant world, imagine his puissance when he stands upon Sinskrill's soil. No place will be safe from him."

"Then we have to close the anchor line," Jake declared.

"No one knows how," Travail said. "Knowledge of the creation and destruction of them is long lost."

"A worry for another time," Serena said. "We have to get out of here first, and sooner than we planned. I think we should leave tomorrow."

"Why?" William asked. "You learned something terrifying, but why not wait until we're ready?"

"Because we're ready now," Serena said. "The longer we dawdle, the greater the chance for someone to figure out what we're planning."

"I can't come with you," Travail said, his tone nonchalant.

William bit back an oath. He knew why. Travail had explained it to them earlier, but it didn't mean he had come to terms with it.

"I'm afraid of open water," Travail explained. "The last thing you want is a terrified, two-thousand-pound troll on a wooden boat in the middle of the ocean. I can only leave Sinskrill the same way I came, by the anchor line."

"Now you tell us," Serena growled in obvious frustration. She glared at the troll.

Travail gazed back at her impassively.

She muttered something under her breath.

A realization came to William, and his eyes widened.

"What?" Jake asked.

"Serena's right. We have to leave Sinskrill as soon as possible."

"Why?"

"Because if what she said is true, and Travail thinks it is." William looked to the troll, who nodded affirmation. "Then Sinskrill's *lorasra* is poisoning us. We'll end up like everyone else here."

"Will Mr. Zeus be here by then?" Jake said.

"Who's Mr. Zeus?" Fiona asked.

CHAPTER 19:
FLIGHT

July 1987

Serena had called for Selene's attendance, and she tried not to pace about her quarters while waiting for her sister.

A knock on her door had her breathe out in relief. *At last. Only Selene knocked so softly.* She opened the door and ordered her sister inside.

"How can I help you, Madam?" Selene asked. Her face held an open expression of innocence and trust, and Serena mentally scowled, hating lying to the little girl.

"I need you to go to the dhow," Serena said. "William and Jake should be there. The bear damaged the boat worse than I thought, and I've sent for them to help me fix it. I want you to make sure they're not wasting time and are actually working. I'll be along shortly."

She figured if she and Selene departed the Palace separately, they would be less likely to be noticed.

"Yes, Madam."

"Good girl. Now go and make sure to hurry."

Selene left, and Serena gathered a few belongings, including the anklet William had given her for Christmas. She fingered it for a moment. Regrets, long suppressed and ignored, arose, and her eyes welled.

She mentally snarled at her weakness. Work needed doing, and she blinked back the tears. Her features firmed, and she dashed away a few unspilled tears and shoved the anklet inside a small bag, imagining her regrets being thrust away as well.

She turned to leave.

Isha stood in the doorway. He gestured, and the world grew quiet.

Serena's stomach hollowed. "How long have you suspected?"

"Since we returned to Sinskrill."

"Yet you said and did nothing."

"I'd have continued to say and do nothing until you were gone," he said, "but matters are no longer so simple. The Servitor spoke to me this morning. He told a strange story about two girls who confronted Lord Shet and showed him disrespect. He has his suspicions of who these two girls might be."

"Lord Shet?" Serena cursed under her breath. *The Spear.*

"The Servitor wants these girls stripped and questioned, possibly in that order, and any who are closely associated with them may find themselves similarly punished."

"Unless they give over the ones who supposedly offended Lord Shet?"

Isha nodded, regret filling his face. "I wish it could be otherwise, but your actions put my own life at risk, to say nothing of my position."

Sorrow rose like nausea in Serena's chest. She didn't want to see Isha harmed, but she also couldn't let him take her or Selene. Serena gazed outside at the sunny day. *What to do?* She turned back to Isha. "What did the Servitor have to say about Lord Shet?"

Isha's brow furrowed. "You know something more?"

Serena briefly explained what she'd learned about the Spear.

Isha rubbed his chin. "Even if what you say is true, it changes nothing. We . . ."

He tumbled bonelessly to the ground, and Serena gaped.

Fiona stood in Isha's place in the doorway, a large hunk of firewood in her hands. She sourced her *lorethasr*a, and her silvery Spirit flared. She formed a braid too complex for Serena to follow. "Hurry! I've numbed his mind and his Spirit, but he won't be out for long."

"You heard what he said?"

"Yes. Now hurry. The Palace is about to become a beehive. In addition to learning that you and Selene visited Seminal, the Servitor also claims magi have landed on Sinskrill's shores. He rallies the mahavans."

Serena startled. "Truly?"

"Truly. Come!"

Instead, Serena bent to check on Isha.

"Leave him!" Fiona hissed. "You must flee."

"Do we have to kill him?" a cold part of Serena asked. Horror filled her mind even as she voiced the question.

"It will be for you to decide," Fiona said.

"Sometimes we have to decide who to hurt if we're to save the ones we love." Isha had once spoken those words to her.

"Then he lives." Serena couldn't kill Isha—not now, not ever—but leaving as she intended would certainly hurt him.

"A merciful decision," Fiona said, her eyes shining with what looked like pride.

Serena snatched up her *jian* as well as a longsword, and allowed Fiona to lead them down the hall to a cross corridor, and from there through the drones' quarters. They reached a doorway opening onto a small yard behind the stables. They skulked inside and quickly saddled a pair of mounts. Serena went to help her grandmother mount up, but Fiona shook her head.

"I can't leave," she said.

"Why not?" Serena asked, nervously glancing about.

Fiona fingered a gold necklace at her throat. "Only the Servitor can remove this. If I make an attempt, or if I ever leave Sinskrill without permission, it removes my head." Fiona shrugged helplessly. "I can't go with you, child." Tears filled her eyes. "But my life will have been well-lived if I know you and your sister have broken free of this place."

Serena's eyes blurred. "But . . ."

Her grandmother's eyes softened. "I loved your mother so much. I've loved you, too. But this isn't an island made for softness. It's a cruel place, evil and hard, and I could never show you how much I cared for you and your sister. You have my eyes but Cinnamon's soul, and you make an old woman glad. Now go! Flee."

Serena made to argue, but movement from a nearby door ended all conversation. Mahavans poured out. They hadn't yet seen her.

"I love you," Fiona whispered, before running in front of the onrushing mahavans and gesticulating wildly. Her actions slowed them. "Hurry!" the old *raha'asra* cried. "The Servitor rallies us. Magi on the island, north of Lake White Sun. Get to your horses!"

Serena used the distraction to mount up, grab the reins to the second horse, and sprint past the confused mahavans.

"Hurry up! Twenty magi descend upon Village White Sun and a single mahavan won't be able to stop them!" she heard Fiona shout at her retreating back.

She grinned at Fiona's lies while she surged through the front gate and raced north toward Village Paradiso.

The cobbled road passed beneath her gelding's hooves, and as she left behind the Servitor's Palace—hopefully for the last time— Serena found herself wishing that she could have known Fiona better, laughed more with her, and loved the old woman as she had her birth mother.

Those regrets would have to wait. Right now, she had to ride.

Leaving Sinskrill turned out to be unexpectedly hard for William, all because of Travail. They had to leave him behind.

William hugged Travail one last time and blinked back unbidden tears. He'd forgotten how good it could feel to cry for love rather than pain and hatred. "I'm sorry," he whispered, while the troll held him off the ground.

"There is no need for apology," Travail said softly.

"We should have figured out a way. We could still try and . . ."

"You cannot." Travail cut him off and set him down. He bent so his great, horned head drew level with William's. "If your dreams are true, you know what you must do. You may not have another opportunity."

"We wouldn't have survived without you," Jake said, his eyes wet as well.

Travail smiled. "You are both stronger than you know, and I don't mean just your *lorethasra*. Go swiftly now."

"I'll never forget you," William said, "and I won't leave you here. We'll get you free of this place."

Travail nodded gravely. "I certainly hope so."

With the sun barely risen over the eastern hills, William and Jake made their final 'goodbyes' to Travail and left his home. They had no belongings to their names and they set off, each armed with nothing more than a stout staff to fend off wild animals they might come across.

"I want to get to the dhow as quick as we can," William said. "I've got a bad feeling about today."

"Why?"

"I don't know," William replied. "Something tells me we should hurry."

They'd already claimed two of the bicycles available at Village White Sun for today's journey, and as soon as their path intersected with the Great Way, William pushed the pace. They rode hard, and soon enough, neither of them had the breath to talk. They pedaled in silence toward Bliss, working up a sweat as the crisp, cool morning felt like it would lead into a warm-for-Sinskrill day.

"I wish a necrosed had touched me," Jake huffed during a break when they had slowed.

While the months spent with Travail had hardened them both, William could have gone faster and they both knew it.

"No you don't," William said, breathing heavily but still with plenty of stamina left in his tank. "Then you'd either turn into a necrosed yourself, die, or have to run like hell to get away from the damn thing."

"Blah. Blah. Blah," Jake said. "Let's go."

William pushed the pace again, and a couple of hours later they entered the huddled cabins and cobbled streets of Village Bliss. A few querulous dogs fought over a bone while children dashed around, somehow finding a way out of their work. Otherwise, the place lay quiet. Wood smoke drifted on the air as drones prepared lunch, which they would deliver to their fellows in the fields in a few hours.

"We go straight through," William told Jake. "No stopping, and if anyone asks, we're on orders from Serena."

Jake nodded, and William slowed them to what felt like a crawl as they passed through the quiet alleys and shadowed streets of Bliss. The sun had yet to burn off the dew glistening on the village green, and puddles of water from last night's rain pooled in ruts.

They left Bliss behind, but William nervously studied the Prime's castle in the distance. It stood upon a hill to the north, pennons flying and nothing amiss. He breathed easier when they passed it.

They biked through the tree and bush-lined pathway leading to the pier. A few final curves, and the empty docks opened before them. A golden sun shone in a blue sky filled with cotton-candy clouds above the indigo waters of the Norwegian Sea. The scent of brine and fish carried on a stuttering breeze. And straight ahead of them, floating in her berth at the end of the short pier, lay *Blue Sky Dreams*.

William grinned. Part of him—a huge part—had been convinced that Serena would leave without them. Or that her entire plan would turn out to be another lie.

But there floated *Blue Sky Dreams* with only fifty yards to safety and the journey to freedom.

Jake spotted the problem first. Two unfamiliar people stood upon the deck of the dhow.

"Who are they?" William asked, flickers of anxiety sparking through him.

"Can't tell from here," Jake replied, sounding as nervous as William felt, "but based on their clothes, it looks like a Sere and a Walker."

William eyed the mahavans and silently cursed. *Damn it!*

"Think they're here for us?" Jake asked.

"Who else?" William answered. He dismounted his bicycle, and Jason did the same. They waited on the stone pathway leading to the pier. The tall bushes rising all around them reminded William of a prison.

The two mahavans stepped off *Blue Sky* and onto the dock. They approached, relaxed, unhurried, and confident.

"You are bound by order of the Servitor," the Sere announced when he and the Walker were no more than ten feet away. All four of them stood on the stone-and-sand path leading to the pier. "Do nothing, and we won't hurt you."

"We were ordered to *Blue Sky* to fix a few things the unformed bear damaged," William said, hoping they could lie their way out of the situation.

"We know why you're here," the Sere smirked. "Magi have been spotted on Sinskrill, and the Servitor figures they're here for you."

William sensed both mahavans source their Spirits. Fiery lines coursed across their chests, and the smell of burnt wood and mildew emanated off them.

He and Jake sourced their Spirits as well.

One of the mahavans smiled. "So you want a fight."

A torrent of flame raged toward William and Jake. Tendrils of Earth poured off Jake's hand, and into the ground. He pulled up a mound of dirt. The fire dashed against the earthwork. William hunkered down, wishing he could do more, but he still hadn't figured out how to unbraid the Elements of his *lorethasra*.

A hissing whisper and a glacial scent heralded a howling wind that bit at Jake's mound. The braid of air threatened to rip it away, and another torrent of flame blistered toward them. This one took a high, arching path. Jake shouted. Clear pulses of air surged down his arms, into his hands. With a gesture, he blasted the fire aside.

The Walker used the distraction to further tear into Jake's earthwork, and it exploded in a fountain of mud and dirt. William dove to the side, avoiding another blast of fire.

Jake wasn't as lucky. He took a gut-punch from a fist of air, and it sent him flying.

"You should have taken the easy offer," the Sere said to William with an evil grin. "Now I get to pain you."

William did the only thing he could, created the only braid he knew. His Spirit coursed along his body. Into it, he sucked in the *lorasra* all around him for a distance of twenty-five feet. It felt like inhaling sewage. His gorge rose, and he emptied the foulness out of him in a silver-white stream only a *raha'asra* could see. It poured forth to the side and contained a red tinge like blood. The drained *lorasra* brushed against a tree, instantly withering it.

The Sere's wicked grin faded when his flame shivered and went out. The Walker cried out in confusion as his fist of Air wisped away.

William twirled his staff. Maybe he couldn't fight with Elements, but with a stick he could do some damage. He roared a challenge and charged.

The mahavans drew their swords and stood loose and ready. William raced forward. At the last instant, he leaned aside from the Sere's diagonal slice. A flick of the staff slapped away the Walker's blade. A twist of his wrists blocked the Sere's return thrust.

The Walker aimed a vertical slash, and William stepped back, evading the blow. He parried and retreated, all the while studying his opponents. They were good, and while he hadn't trained in months, William knew he could take them.

But he had to be fast about it. While he'd drained *lorasra* from the surrounding area, it was already starting to fill back up. He might not have time to try that trick again, not while fighting off two swordsmen.

The Sere pressed forward.

A mistake. His movement left him unsupported, and William rapped aside a horizontal blow and followed up with a thrust. He stepped closer, into the pocket, and delivered a heavy knee. The air blasted out of the Sere's lungs, and he collapsed, face white and gasping.

A fist of air hammered William in the stomach, and he landed flat on his back, pinned there and immobile. The *lorasra* had recovered. William cursed as the Walker leered in triumph, sword raised.

The killing blow never landed. The Walker tumbled away. A burst of air sent him flailing, and William found himself able to move again.

Jake reached his side. "Get up!"

William surged to his feet. He sourced his Spirit and drained the *lorasra* once again, discharging it into the water.

The Walker and the recovered Sere faced off against him and Jake with murder in their eyes. Their fight moved onto the narrow, stony beach in front of the dock. Footing became treacherous.

William flicked his staff and pushed aside a thrust. He blocked a horizontal slice before lashing out. The Walker tried to stumble back. He slipped on the loose stones. William adjusted his aim, and the butt of his staff caught the Walker in the chest. The mahavan crumpled and cried as ribs broke. Jake hammered him into unconsciousness.

The Sere shouted defiance and attacked. William let him come. He blocked. Blocked again before stepping out of range. He circled to his right. Another block. Another evasion. Twist to the left. The mahavan spun with him.

Too slow.

The Sere managed to block the first of William's blows, but not the second. That one, a thrust, caught him flush on the temple, and the mahavan collapsed like a felled tree.

Jake grinned. "Not bad for a couple of half-trained *raha'asras*."

William grinned with him. "We better tie them up and get them out of sight."

"Do you think we should—?" Jake made a slitting motion across his throat.

William hesitated before shaking his head. "Not yet." He hoped not ever.

———— • ————

At its core, the plan Serena and the others had come up with had simplicity as its strength. They'd avoided unnecessary tricks and misdirections, and instead had gone for the straightforward approach: repair the dhow, launch it, and sail away from Sinskrill with no one the wiser. Best of all, since Mr. Zeus really was lurking about the island, they could try to reach him and make their way to Arylyn.

All that was out the window now.

Serena cursed when she thought about how their fine plan had come unglued. All because the Servitor had to grasp the Spear, speak to Shet, and find out about her and Selene's travels to Seminal. She cursed again before taking a deep breath and quieted her furious thoughts. There was no help for it now. What was done was done, and they had to deal with the consequences.

A new plan was needed, the outlines of which quickly took shape in her mind as she galloped the gelding along the Great Way and toward Village Paradiso. She'd tied the reins to the other horse—a mare—to her saddle, and the animal galloped without complaint. The Great Way remained empty of any other travelers.

First she had to reach Selene, who should still be on the road to Bliss. Second, the two of them had to reach the dhow. Third, she needed to rest her horse. The gelding couldn't handle the fifteen-mile journey from the Servitor's Palace to Bliss at a gallop.

Serena pulled back on the reins, and the gelding huffed in gratitude.

And fourth, she had to hope William and Jake had left for Bliss even earlier than they'd initially planned. If not, yet another plan might be needed.

Part one of her scheme came to fruition when, a few miles later, she caught sight of Selene. The young girl had chosen to walk her bicycle instead of ride it. Selene stepped off the road and grinned upon seeing Serena's approach.

Serena reined in alongside her. "Why are you walking?"

"Chain broke."

"Get on," Serena ordered.

Selene's face went white with fear. "Drones don't ride."

"Do you trust me?" Serena asked.

Selene nodded.

Serena offered her sister a hand. "Then get on. We have to go. Now."

Selene clambered aboard.

Serena waited until her sister settled in behind her. "Hold tight," she advised, and Selene's small hands clutched about her waist.

Serena pushed the gelding as fast as she dared, and they soon reached Paradiso. She stared at the village for a moment, searching for anything out of the ordinary, but a few moments of study revealed nothing worrisome. The village appeared unchanged. No columns of mahavans waited for her, and she wondered why. Maybe Fiona's alarm about magi on the island had actually worked. Or maybe a message hadn't yet been sent along the lightposts used to transmit emergency warnings from village to village.

Whatever the reason, Serena breathed out her gratitude to whatever deity might be listening.

She and Selene passed through Paradiso, and all the while Serena kept an ear pinned, listening for the hoofbeats of onrushing horses.

No sounds came, and they pressed on, stopping only when they had to switch to the mare. The gelding's mouth frothed, and he heaved.

Serena continued to fret as they traveled, and her worry didn't let up even when Bliss hove into view. They were almost there, almost to *Blue Sky Dreams*. Again, Serena eyed the village and offered another silent prayer to whatever God might be listening. *Please don't let there be mahavans waiting for us.*

Her prayers must have been answered because they swept through the village unchallenged.

"Where are we going?" Selene asked.

"To the dhow," Serena answered.

"What are—"

"I'll explain it all when we get there," Serena promised.

"Yes, Madam."

A few minutes later, Serena's worries dissolved when they reached the docks. *Blue Sky Dreams* bobbed in her berth, and a pair of familiar figures stood on deck. Laughter bubbled in Serena's throat.

Almost there. Almost out. And there was absolutely no one to stop them.

She and Selene dismounted, and they rushed to the dhow.

"We have to leave," Serena ordered as soon as she climbed aboard the boat.

William's happy grin withered away. "What happened?"

"Somehow Lord Shet—damn him forever—told the Servitor about our visit to Seminal." She gestured to include Selene. "I'll explain it all later, but right now we have to cast off. There might be pursuers behind us."

"What should we do about them?" Jake asked, pointing out a Sere and Walker laid unconscious on the deck of the dhow.

Until that moment Serena hadn't noticed the two trussed-up mahavans. "What are they doing here?"

William shrugged. "Your father sent them. Something about magi on the island, and him being suspicious we'd try to escape. They were waiting for us when we got here."

"Well, get them off my boat. I don't care if you toss them in the sea or dump them on the dock. Your choice."

CHAPTER 20:
PURSUIT

July 1987

William and Jason quickly dumped the Sere and Walker on the dock.

"Move it!" Serena shouted. "We've got company."

William's head shot up. A half-dozen horses had crested the final hill leading to the pier. All bore mahavans and even from faraway, William could tell they were mightily pissed.

"Shit!" William scrambled to untie the lines securing *Blue Sky Dreams* to the dock.

"They're coming!" Serena called out. She braided something. William heard a whine of air emanating off of her.

The hoofbeats thundered closer, no more than fifty yards away. His fingers seized. Panic bubbled. *So close to freedom, and they'd be undone by his clumsiness.* He fumbled with the rope and cursed when it slipped out of his hands.

"Hurry up!" Jake called, already done with his line.

William remembered to breathe, bit down on his fear, and got his fingers working again. The rope unwound from the cleat. He tossed it aboard and scrambled after it.

The mahavan warriors dismounted and raced across the sandy beach. They shouted and fell in a clatter when their feet went out from under them.

Serena chuckled.

"What did you do?" Jake asked.

"I put pockets of air under the sand. They slipped on them like they hit a banana peel," Serena said.

William silently applauded her trick while urging the dhow to get going. *Faster!* The single, lateen sail puffed out, and the boat eased forward, sluggishly picking up speed. William measured the distance back to the pier. They hadn't gone nearly far enough. *Come on!*

The Sinskrill warriors rose up from where they'd fallen with angry shouts. They tore down to the end of the pier and readied bows.

The dhow headed toward the mouth of the harbor, and William implored the wind to blow harder. A second later, his hopes dashed as *Blue Sky's* sail luffed. She slowed to a crawl.

"The Walkers are disrupting the wind," Serena said. She frantically trimmed the sail, hauling it closer to the ship.

"Get down!" Jake warned.

William ducked, and a flight of arrows passed overhead. Most thunked into the hull, but one slammed into the mast, luckily missing the sail.

As soon as the arrows landed, Serena stood up. A ripple of sulfurous fire arched around her chest, and a bloom of fire burst from her hands. It exploded the support posts of the dock. Half the mahavans tumbled into the water. Only a few managed to leap clear of the damage.

William shouted in triumph, but his victory proved short-lived.

Some of the mahavans who hadn't fallen into the sea had jumped off the broken pier. William's jaw dropped. Walkers raced toward *Blue Sky*, bouncing along the sea's surface like crazy lizards that ran on water.

"We can't let them land on *Blue Sky*!" Serena shouted.

"They won't," William said. He sourced his Spirit, and focused like he had against the Sere and the Walker. He sucked away all the *lorasra* around the dhow and poured it out along the side of the boat, into the harbor.

The Walkers shouted in panic when their jets of Air cut off. Nevertheless, with momentum on their side they all managed to make the leap onto the boat.

Serena had her *jian* out, and William drew the longsword he'd noticed in her belongings. Jake held his staff at the ready.

The dhow continued to drift toward the mouth of the harbor, the sail luffing again.

Three mahavans faced them. William recognized them from his time on the island: Brandon Thrum, Samuel Ingot, and Preeti Amal.

"I trusted you," Brandon snarled at Serena.

"Trust no one," Serena replied. "Lord Shet's advice."

Samuel, a whip-thin and whiplash-fast Walker, opened his mouth. "By order of the Servitor—"

William didn't let the man finish. He swept his sword in a horizontal slash followed by a thrust. Samuel parried. William angled away, struggling with his balance on the bobbing boat. He managed a diagonal cut that Samuel blocked. William twisted at the wrists and pinned the mahavan's blade against the deck.

He was about to hammer an elbow into his opponent's face when Selene snuck up and cracked Samuel over the head with an oar. The mahavan stumbled, and William gut-kicked him. Samuel flopped out of the dhow, splashing into the water.

William spun, looking for another opponent.

Brandon had Jake hard-pressed. "You should have learned your lesson at your lashing," the Walker growled. He smashed aside Jake's staff, his blade poised for the final stroke.

William slashed into Brandon's thigh. The mahavan fell back with a grunt. William kicked away the Walker's sword, grasped him by the collar, and flung him off the boat. He hit the water with an inarticulate shout.

Serena had already dispatched her opponent. Preeti slumped over *Blue Sky's* bow. William couldn't tell if she was alive or dead. A groan gave him his answer, as Serena shoved her overboard as well.

William watched Preeti float away in their wake, and sighed with relief that they'd survived the Walkers.

Movement in the corner of his eye caught his attention, and William blinked. He shook his head. *It couldn't be.* Some of the mahavans who had fallen into the water at the docks were coming after them. They surfed waves of water.

"Riders," Serena said, sounding disgusted. "We aren't out of this yet. Help me trim the sail."

Jake jumped to where she pointed and followed her crackling commands as best he could. William moved to help.

"Watch out!" Jake shouted.

The boom swung about and William ducked. It grazed his back. Serena called out more orders. The sail filled with a whoosh, and *Blue Sky* leapt forward.

William watched the Riders rush onward. Even as they rapidly closed the distance, he couldn't help but admire the way they rode the waves. The glided back and forth across the water as if it were ice, surfing with one hand down to maintain balance and the other grasping a bow. It was so cool.

"Pay attention!" Serena yelled.

William snapped out of his admiration as Serena called more instructions. They trimmed the sail again, and this time the wind was with them. The sail snapped full, a thudding whoosh as *Blue Sky Dreams* jumped forward. She picked up speed and finally cleared the harbor.

William stared ahead. Nothing but open sea. The dhow thumped over water and wave. Cold, salty spray splashed his face, and wind whipped his hair about.

He glanced back, measuring the distance to the onrushing Riders. Four of them, three men, all bearded and ranging from young to middle-aged, and an older woman. They had sheathed swords on their hips and the woman had a bow in her hands. Their clothes and hair streamed behind them as they leaned forward over their surging waves.

"Where are they?" Serena asked, facing forward at the tiller.

"Closing fast," William answered. "Fifty yards or so. Drifting in and out of our wake."

"Can you do what you did with those Walkers?" Serena asked.

"It's only good for about twenty feet," William answered.

"Look out!" Jake warned.

One of the Riders, the oldest male, had a strong talent for Fire. His hands glowed, and a gout of flame blasted toward the dhow.

William instinctually sourced his *lorethasra*, separated his Elements, and connected them to *lorasra*. In less than a heartbeat, he braided air and drove the flames aside. He even managed to smack at the Rider. The mahavan struggled to maintain his balance when the air battered him about, and he eventually had to break off his attack.

Elation filled William, but it died away when he lost his connection to *lorasra*.

"Do that again," Serena demanded. "But this time aim it at the Riders. Knock them off their waves. Or better yet, aim it at the sail. I want us going faster."

"I can't," William replied. He mentally berated himself and pounded his thigh in frustration. "I can't consciously separate my Elements."

Serena glared at him.

An arrow hissed past his head and thumped into the inside hull.

William viewed the oncoming Rider—the woman—in dismay. She'd closed to no more than twenty yards away, and her bow held a nocked and ready arrow. The mahavan sighted along it.

"Not this time," Serena muttered. She held the tiller between her knees and twisted around. She pointed. The stench of sulfur filled the dhow as fire surged down Serena's arm and exploded toward the Rider with the bow.

The mahavan threw up her hands, covering her torso in a shield of water. It absorbed most of the flame, but some of it penetrated. The woman lost control of her wave and smacked into the water. She bounced over the sea like a stone—five, six, eight times—before flopping to a rest. She momentarily disappeared underwater before surfacing again. She screamed at them, but William couldn't make out the words.

"Only three more," Selene crowed from her spot at the bow, hunched low and hidden beneath Serena's coat.

She'd been so quiet that William had almost forgotten about her. He shucked off his coat and tossed it on Selene. She needed the protection. Jake quickly followed suit.

Blue Sky raced before the wind, but the Riders continued chasing them. One cut in front of them. He gestured, and their sail luffed, flapping in the wind. The dhow shuddered to a stall, its bow digging into the water.

"Get ready!" Serena warned.

The three Riders rode separate surges of water toward their boat.

No chance they'd make it on board. William sourced his Spirit and drained the *lorasra* all around *Blue Sky*. He reached as far as he could, stretching twice as far as he'd ever done before.

The Riders' storm surge collapsed beneath them, and they fell into the ocean. One managed to clutch *Blue Sky's* railing. Selene popped out of her hiding place and rapped his knuckles with her oar. The Rider shouted in pain and promptly let go. William laughed at the Rider's comical scream right before he splashed into the ocean.

"Get back on the sail," Serena barked. "I need the sheet to starboard."

The sail filled with a boom, and the tell-tales flapped backward. *Blue Sky Dreams* accelerated, and Serena shifted the rudder. The dhow changed course.

"Haul the sail perpendicular to the dhow," Serena ordered.

The dhow kicked forward again as they ran before the wind. The Riders grew distant and eventually disappeared. No other pursuers chased them. There was nothing behind them except for empty water and Sinskrill itself.

But it took minutes more of sailing with no further pursuit for William to finally relax. *Blue Sky Dreams* rode the sea, thudding as it slammed over the waves. William's shoulder-length hair streamed behind him like a tell-tale, and salty spray filled his mouth. He squinted, protecting his eyes from the ocean water as it splashed into his face.

As further time passed, the first stirrings of optimism, of real belief that they would escape, kindled to life. William's spirits lifted, and he shared a grin of triumph with anyone who happened to look his way.

"Shouldn't we go south?" Jake asked. "Isn't that the quickest way to get clear of the island?"

Serena kept them headed east. "We aren't going through Suborn Strait," she said, referring to the channel separating Sinskrill and Amethyst. "We'd end up too close to the Servitor's Palace. We're heading east and then north. It's the longer way but safer."

Through the next hour, Serena kept William and Jake busy. They carried out her commands, keeping the sail trimmed and doing whatever she needed to maintain *Blue Sky's* easterly course.

"Bring in the sail, toward starboard," Serena ordered.

William and Jake did so, and the dhow swung north.

Shortly afterward, Serena noticed William clench his stomach and groan. He swayed and his face held a green tint.

"I think I'm going to lose my biscuits," Jake moaned. He and William both looked nauseated.

"We've left Sinskrill's *lorasra*," Serena explained. "You're suffering from the lack of *lorasra*, not seasickness." She passed around *nomasras*—smooth pieces of white marble—leftovers from her time in the Far Abroad. She'd saved them after her pilgrimage, and no one had asked her to give them back.

The instant their hands closed on the *nomasras*, William, Jake, and Serena's expressions cleared.

"Thank God," William said fervently.

"Amen to that," Jake said.

"Where are we going, Madam?" Selene asked.

Serena smiled at her sister. "If we're lucky, we're going to a place where you don't need to be afraid anymore, where you can call me Serena whether we're in public or in private. We'll be true sisters, and you won't have to worry about any more Temperings or strippings."

Selene studied her with solemn, judging eyes. "Where's that?" she finally asked.

Serena's smile faded, and she called her sister to her side. She took Selene's hands in hers. "Do you trust me?" she asked, repeating a question she'd asked Selene earlier that morning. *Had it really been only a few hours ago?*

Selene nodded.

"Then trust me now," Serena said, giving the little girl's hands a squeeze. "You'll find out when we get there."

"Stop bothering her with talk like that," Jake said, lifting Selene and moving her to the bow. The little girl squealed when he tickled her before setting her down. "Make sure to stay low," Jake advised. "You don't want to get knocked off by the boom."

"Yes, sir."

Jake smiled at her. "Jake. You call me Jake, remember?"

"Yes, sir . . . I mean, Jake."

He ruffled her hair. "Watch out for flying sharks and mind what I said about the boom. Last thing we need is a drowned cat."

Selene trusted Jake enough to stick her tongue out at him, and he grinned at her, ruffling her hair again.

Serena watched their interaction in amazement. Jake was so gentle with Selene, and she obviously adored him. What a change from the arrogant ass she'd known back in Cincinnati.

"If we're past Sinskrill's *saha'asra*, can the Walkers still hear us?" William asked.

"No," Serena said.

"Then stay on this heading," William said, grinning with excitement. "Mr. Zeus dreamed to me last night. They're here, on the northwest side of the island. They've been trying to figure out how to get to us, but all we have to do is sail over to them, and we can all leave together."

Excitement and trepidation warred within Serena. Excitement for leaving Sinskrill, and trepidation for how the magi would react to her. Would they save William and Jake and maybe Selene, but leave her on Sinskrill? "Do they know we're coming to them?" Serena asked, pushing back the anxiety.

"I don't know," William replied. "I tried to dream back, but I couldn't tell if Mr. Zeus heard me."

Serena nodded. "Then we try to find them, but I'm not waiting around Sinskrill any longer than absolutely necessary. If they aren't where you think they are, then we head to the Faroe Islands. There's an anchor line there that we can use to get somewhere safe."

"We'll find them," William replied, sounding confident. "Mr. Zeus showed me where their boat was docked. There's a bunch of white cliffs and a small island in the harbor."

"Does this island have a peaked hill on it?"

William nodded.

"Then I know where they are," Serena said.

Jake whooped, and he and William danced about.

"Watch it! You're messing with the sail," Serena said. She laughed even while she warned them.

William's grin faded when he noticed something Selene was holding.

"What's wrong?" Serena asked.

William didn't answer. Instead, he approached Selene. "How long have you had that?" he asked.

Selene closed her fists, holding tight what she'd been staring at, but Serena had seen it. The locket holding a picture of William's family.

"Madam gave it to me," Selene said, her voice soft yet fierce.

William bent low. "It's my family. My father, my mother, and my brother. I loved them. It means a lot to me."

Selene's eyes filled with tears, and she wordlessly offered William the locket.

Serena's heart broke at Selene's generosity. She wanted to do something for her little sister, protect her somehow, but she didn't know how.

William closed Selene's hand about the locket. "Hold on to it for me," he said with a smile. "I know you love it, and you'll keep it safe."

"Yes, sir," Selene promised.

William pulled her into a hug. "William," he said to her. "You know that's my name, right?"

Jake came up to Serena's side. "We might hate you," he said, "but she's a sweet girl who deserves better than what she's received."

Serena silently agreed. She loved Selene, but her sister *did* deserve a better parent than the one fate had left her. Serena saw it now. William and Jake loved Selene more easily and truly than she ever had. She wiped at her eyes.

The boat fell quiet, other than the orders she called out from time to time.

Soon after, they swept past Sinskrill's northern edge and tacked west. Nothing but open water lay before them.

William scanned behind them with her binoculars. "We've got company," he said.

"A ship?" Serena guessed.

William nodded. "It's flying the Servitor's flag, a white throne on a black field. It's carrying a lot more sail than us, too."

"*Demolition*," Serena said, making the name of the other ship sound like a curse.

———— • ————

"Get the ship moving," Mr. Zeus said to Daniel and Julius, their Air and Water adepts. "The *nomasra* is moving too quickly to still be on land."

"Where's it going?" Jason asked while he helped uncoil the lines and run the sails out.

"I don't know. Somewhere east, and moving fast," Mr. Zeus answered.

"A ship?" Jessira asked.

"That would be my guess," Mr. Zeus said, "Maybe they're making their own break for freedom, but I won't be happy until William and Jake are with us and we're all back on Arylyn."

Moments later, the yacht's sails unfurled, filling under the power of Daniel and Julius' braids of Air. They could have also run the engine, but Mr. Zeus still feared giving away their position.

Eventually they slipped out of the harbor, and Jason took them northwest, on the closest course to intercept where Mr. Zeus sensed William's *nomasra* moving.

"Stay on this heading," his grandfather said. "Be on the lookout for a ship with a single sail. It's the image William sent me last night when I dreamed to him."

"How could he send you anything?" Julius asked, sounding skeptical. "He's untrained."

"He *was* untrained," Mr. Zeus said. "He's been on Sinskrill for five months, and I'm sure the mahavans haven't had him sitting around doing nothing."

"If he's already on a boat, he's probably figured out a way off Sinskrill," Jason said.

"He's not free yet," Rukh said.

Jason tried not to scowl. "Which is why we're going to get him," he said, hoping he didn't sound too condescending toward the man.

An instant later he muttered in disbelief.

When had he started to think of the freshman as a man? Then again, he did carry himself like one. And Jessira, standing at the prow with a hand on her sword and the wind streaming her hair like a golden pennon, was all warrior woman.

"When did they learn to sail, anyway?" Daniel asked.

"Who cares?" Julius answered. "As long as they keep on coming to us, and we can get out of here."

Daniel's question, though, raised doubts in Jason's mind.

When had *William and Jake learned to sail? On Sinskrill? Why would the mahavans have taught them? They'd risk having their prize* raha'asras *flee the island, which was exactly what they were apparently doing.*

"There are others on the boat with them," Jessira said, apparently working through the same set of questions as he. "They are the ones sailing the boat."

"But probably not enemies," Rukh said, "unless this is all a ruse. William and Jake might be bait meant to capture us."

Jessira briefly pursed her lips. "We may have to fight."

"Isn't it always the case?" Rukh said to her.

An hour later, Mr. Zeus snarled again in frustration. "Now they're tacking south. Whoever's sailing with them must be drunk."

"Or they're being chased and are trying to throw off their pursuer," Rukh countered. He glanced at Jason. "Can we go faster? I have a feeling they'll need us there sooner rather than later."

A chill passed down Jason's spine at Rukh's softly asked question. It contained a promise of violence all the more menacing for its quiet tone.

"We can push harder," Julius said.

"Do it," Mr. Zeus ordered, "and fire up the engine."

Jason did as instructed, and the engine rumbled to life. The yacht picked up speed while Daniel and Julius sourced their *lorethasras* more deeply. Clear pulses of air rolled across their torsos and punched from their hands. The braids had the sails straining, and their boat jumped forward.

Jessira laughed, holding her arms out to the wind, the waves, and the spray. "I'd almost forgotten the joy of being cold," she said.

"I wish I never remembered it," Rukh complained.

Jessira laughed again. "Your Pureblood blood was always too thin," she said in a voice full of affection.

Jason shook his head. *What the hell was that about?* He decided it might be best to stop paying attention to the weird freshmen.

Half an hour later, a single-masted ship came into view. Several hundred yards behind it rode another ship, much larger and with many more sails. As they watched, the bigger vessel slowly gained on the smaller one.

———— ● ————

William shot a glance at the Servitor's ship, *Demolition*, and cursed.

An hour was all they needed. A short but endless hour to circle Sinskrill's north coast and rendezvous with Mr. Zeus. Only an hour, some luck, and they'd have escaped the mahavan's island. But, like everything about this island, the only luck here was bad. With every passing second, the Servitor's ship gained on them.

How the hell was it moving so fast?

Jake and Serena had thick braids of Air pumping into *Blue Sky's* sail. They gave the dhow every last bit of speed they could manage.

"My *nomasra* is almost out," Jake panted.

"Mine, too," Serena replied, also gasping.

A feverish idea percolated in William's subconscious. "If we sail closer to Sinskrill, we'll be able to draw from the *saha'asra* again."

"So will they," Jake countered, "and they've got Walkers."

"But the Walkers won't be able to do squat if we drain the *lorasra* behind us. We create a dead zone, they sail into it, and the only push they get is from the wind."

Serena brightened. "If we leave braids of turbulence, they'll lose even that."

"It's only going to get us a few minutes of extra time," Jake replied.

I know, but maybe in those few minutes we can find Mr. Zeus' ship," William countered, "or he can find us."

"We'll head south," Serena said. "Bring the sail to port."

Blue Sky swung about toward Sinskrill.

Demolition tacked with them, keeping pace to starboard.

As soon as they re-entered Sinskrill's *saha'asra*, William knew it. *Blue Sky's* sail snapped and the dhow leapt like a horse straining at its bit. More importantly, his senses heightened and his fatigue faded away. He sourced his Spirit, ready to drain the *lorasra* in front of *Demolition* when Serena waved a hand in warning.

"Not yet!" she shouted. "Wait. I want them to hit the dead zone absolutely square."

William studied *Demolition*. Mahavans crowded the bow. Shouts, taunts, and threats carried across the rapidly closing space between the two vessels. Bowmen stepped forward.

He glanced at Serena in worry. *When would she give the signal?*

He turned back to *Demolition*, and his eyes widened. "Incoming," he shouted as a volley of arrows whistled toward them.

Jake shrugged them off with a pulse of air.

The distance between the two vessels closed to no more than thirty feet. Lances of fire reached out from *Demolition*. They roared like wide-open incinerators.

"Now!" Serena shouted.

William hit the Servitor's ship from starboard while Jake took port. They drained the *lorasra* along *Demolition's* leading edge, extending it like an unfurling carpet.

The Servitor's ship shuddered to a halt. The lances of fires wisped away. Shouts of confusion came from the mahavans on its deck. A mad scramble took place as mahavans raced about to trim their sails. The Servitor, visible on *Demolition's* bow, glared murder at them.

His outrage grew when Serena hit his ship with a funnel of air and *Demolition's* sails luffed. To add insult to injury, she also sent a torrent of fire at the Servitor's ship. Riders put out the flames but not before she burned a huge hole in the mainsail.

Adam Paradiso—Serena's Isha—and Fiona moved to stand beside the Servitor. "You will not escape!" the ruler of Sinskrill shouted while the old *raha'asra* gave William the barest of smiles before she schooled her features to stillness.

William flipped everyone on *Demolition* the bird.

Blue Sky Dreams pulled ahead, and they gained desperately needed yards.

"They'll be back," Serena warned.

"And we'll be ready," William countered.

The Servitor's ship drifted to a full stop, and it took them precious time to get back to full speed. Minutes later *Demolition* picked up the chase again, but William and Jake continued draining *lorasra* along the other ship's path. *Demolition* would run with full sails, close the distance for a time, then sputter to a halt without warning.

Jake's face reddened, taxed by continually sourcing his *lorethasra*. William felt the burden as well, and his heart pounded.

"Save your strength," Serena advised. "We've got a bit of a lead on them now. We'll try that trick again the next time they pull close."

William nodded, and kept his eye on the Servitor's ship, willing it to slow on its own. Or better yet, capsize and sink.

"I see another boat!" Selene called.

William stared to where the little girl pointed. In the distance a ship raced toward them, blue-hulled, built for speed, and obviously modern.

"It's Mr. Zeus," William crowed. "It's got to be." He searched for *Demolition* and quailed. Once again, the Servitor's vessel had closed on them.

He drained *lorasra* before the other ship's path, but this time it bulled through, not slowing at all. He gasped in consternation.

"Fiona," Jake snarled. "It's her. She's doing it."

"Doing what?" Serena demanded.

"She's pulling *lorasra* and filling the places we empty."

William twisted about, staring forward to Mr. Zeus' boat. So close, but so was *Demolition*. It quickly became apparent that the Servitor's ship would reach them first.

They needed more wind, but Serena and Jake were already giving all they had.

William stood by feeling useless.

Damn it! They couldn't go down like this!

William sourced his *lorethasra*, teeth clenched in determination. *This time it would work. It had to.* He separated the Elements and took a deep breath. *Now came the hard part.* His heart pounded as he slowly, carefully linked the Elements of his *lorethasra* to the corresponding ones in *lorasra*.

The construction trembled, threatening to fall apart. William stiffened, praying for it to hold. The connections steadied, grew firmer. He took a tremulous breath, smiling at his success.

"Hold on," he advised the others.

To increase their speed he had to increase airflow against their sail but also decrease the boat's friction as it passed over the water. William created a braid of Earth and reached for the hull and keel. He smoothed the flow of water against both, making it less turbulent.

Blue Sky's speed increased. She skipped over the waves.

"Whatever you're doing, keep doing it," Serena encouraged.

Now for the sail. William concentrated, pushing more air against the lateen sail. It creaked, straining against its stays.

The dhow accelerated. The wind whined as the hull thudded against waves. They began pulling away from *Demolition.*

Lights flashed on Mr. Zeus' boat.

"It looks like Morse code," Jake said. He quirked a grin. "Thank God for Boy Scouts." His eyes narrowed with concentration. "North," he translated. "They want us to go north."

"You sure?" Serena asked.

"Positive," Jake said.

"All right," Serena said. "Then ease the sail to full out."

William went to trim the sails, but Serena called him back.

"Not you. Your job is to keep us running fast. Jake can handle the sail."

"Use my *nomasra* if you have to," Jake said, passing William his white, marble stone.

"You can have mine, too," Selene said, handing William her stone.

"I need mine to pilot the boat," Serena said with a regretful shrug.

William clenched his fists about Jake's and Selene's *nomasras.* "I'll get us out of here."

The moment they passed out of Sinskrill's *saha'asra,* he felt it. His senses deadened, a lethargy settled on his thoughts, an uncomfortable weight dragged at him, and *Blue Sky* slowed.

William grimaced.

Jake and Selene both paled, looking sickly.

349

"You going to be right?" William asked.

"Get us to Mr. Zeus' ship, and I'll be right as rain," Jake said.

Selene gave him a thumbs-up.

William grinned at her, before focusing on connecting his Elements to the *lorasra* contained in the *nomasras*. It took what felt like ages to figure it out, but when he did *Blue Sky* regained her lost speed. The axe-like prow cleaved the water, the wind keened, and saltwater sprayed in their wake.

William shifted his gaze from Mr. Zeus' sleek yacht to the Servitor's ship.

"I think we're going to—" Jake began.

"Don't jinx it," William cut him off.

They had a good lead on the *Demolition*, but once they reached Mr. Zeus' yacht, they'd have to transfer over. Who knew how long that would take?

As the minutes passed, *Blue Sky* extended her lead over *Demolition*. The Servitor's ship had fallen more than a half-mile back.

"Come on," Jake urged.

Mr. Zeus' boat had already swung about to match their course, and Serena had Jake trim the sail again. They pulled along the starboard bow of the yacht.

William waved when he saw Jason, Mr. Zeus, and Daniel, all of whom were grinning.

"Closer!" Mr. Zeus shouted. "I need you inside thirty feet."

"Pull the sail close in," Serena ordered.

Blue Sky slowed.

William glanced at *Demolition* charging at them. "Hurry!"

Clear pulses distorted Mr. Zeus' arms. He made a lifting

gesture and separate weaves of air, like cold, spongy baskets, lifted William and Jake. They floated over the water to Mr. Zeus' boat and landed on the deck.

Both of them laughed in ecstatic relief. Until this moment, William hadn't truly believed he'd ever be free of Sinskrill.

"What about those two?" Mr. Zeus asked, pointing to Selene and Serena.

"Bring them," William said without hesitation.

"Make it quick," an unknown man urged Mr. Zeus before quirking a grin at William. "I'm Julius, by the way."

Demolition closed, no more than a hundred yards away.

William sourced his *lorethasra. There was no way he was ever going back.* He passed Jake a *nomasra.*

Serena and Selene landed on the yacht.

"Go!" Mr. Zeus shouted.

The yacht's engine rumbled to life. Daniel and Julius pulled in air and filled the boat's sails. They punched forward.

Demolition raced after them, closing the gap. "Prepare to board them!" the Servitor shouted.

"Down!" Rukh shouted.

William did a double take. *Rukh and Jessira? What the hell were they doing here?*

Arrows arched toward them.

A swirling wind from Mr. Zeus and Serena sent the volley astray.

Lines of yellow fire, hot enough to haze the air, erupted from the mahavans and toward their yacht.

William snarled. *Enough. No more running.* He formed a susurrating braid of water and set it loose. From the sea exploded a cyclone. The throbbing lances of yellow fire snuffed out.

More.

William created a braid like the one Mr. Zeus and Serena used against the arrows. Walkers tried to stop him. William pushed aside their efforts, using his braid of air to smash theirs aside. The way to *Demolition's* sails stood open. William flayed them.

Demolition slowed.

"You will not escape me," the Servitor cried out. A conflagration exploded from his hands. It blasted into the yacht's mast, tearing it into splinters.

William gaped in shock.

Rukh pushed him aside, out of the way of burning spars of wood.

Pulses of air rippled across the Servitor's chest. He extended his arms and the yacht lurched to a halt.

William lost his footing. He fell to the deck. Selene screamed.

"The bastard's holding us," Jason said. The yacht's engine whined, and he throttled down.

William studied the thick braid against which the yacht strained. He sent out a tendril of rustling earth, seeking to weaken the weave of air holding them in place. He might as well have tried to chew steel.

Demolition inched forward on momentum alone. She closed to within twenty feet of the unmoving yacht.

"Whoever you are, you're trespassing," the Servitor shouted at Mr. Zeus. "You've also stolen my property, and I demand you return it."

"I don't recognize your authority, and I don't recognize your claim of ownership."

The Servitor smirked. "Your recognition is immaterial. I rule

Sinskrill, and before this hour is ended, you will kneel at my feet." His hands glowed. "Or I can simply immolate the lot of you where you stand."

"I thought Lord Shet ruled all," Serena shouted in defiance. "You're nothing more than his puffed-up servant."

The Servitor reddened. "Daughter you may be, but be silent or I will forget our familial bonds and slay you where you stand."

"My family is with me," Serena said, putting her hand on Selene's shoulder. "She's all the family I've ever needed."

"Foolish girl," the Servitor replied in a cold voice. He flicked a glowing finger in their direction. Arrows thrummed.

Rukh and Jessira's swords blurred, and five arrows fell broken to the yacht's deck.

William's jaw dropped. He hadn't even seen them unsheathe their weapons.

Rukh offered the Servitor a smile as cold as the older man's words. "You see. We are not such easy meat." He stood relaxed and confident, but in that pose, he and Jessira reminded William of hungry predators unexpectedly met in the wild.

He inched away from them.

"There is no need for bloodshed," Mr. Zeus said. "Let us sail away in peace, and your people and mine will both live to see another day."

"No," the Servitor disagreed. "I will not allow you to sail away with my two *raha'asras,* both my daughters, and Sinskrill's location."

"You'll never see us again," Mr. Zeus promised.

"On that, you are correct," the Servitor agreed.

Rukh and Jessira stepped toward the stern, toward *Demolition.* They held bows.

William didn't know what they intended. Braids of air would easily stop their arrows.

Rukh and Jessira's hands blurred. A scream split the air. An arrow sprouted from a mahavan's calf. Another appeared in another mahavan's arm. Another scream. Three more mahavans went down.

The air tying the yacht in place frayed. William reached out with a braid of earth mixed with fire. He burned at the weave of air holding them. It snapped apart with a crack.

The yacht shuddered forward.

"No!" the Servitor shouted. Pulses of air traveled down his arms and chest. He obviously intended to recapture their vessel.

Jason gunned the engine.

William shot a stream of fire at the Servitor, hoping to distract him.

Jake and Serena joined him. They sent out bolts of air, hammering at the Servitor. Daniel and Julius snapped with whips of water.

The Servitor shrugged aside their attacks. His mahavans sent out bolts of fire.

Mr. Zeus used air and water to blunt their attacks. Fires broke out on the yacht. Daniel and Julius quickly put them out with streams of water. Jason sent lightning coursing at the Servitor's ship.

Serena's Isha held up a fisted hand. The lightning crackled around *Demolition*, but passed the ship by on either side.

William attacked with fists of air, surges of fire, walls of water thrown up from the Norwegian Sea, and even tendrils of earth meant to tear apart *Demolition*'s planks.

Adam thrust his hands forward. A braid of Spirit, Fire, and Air whipped out.

William's breath went out. He collapsed and screamed. His blood felt like it had caught fire. It boiled in his veins and arteries. The same punishment Fiona had often administered early in their time on Sinskrill. Vaguely he noticed the others crumpled in pain as well.

The yacht shuddered again. It halted and slowly *Demolition* drew closer once again.

William gritted his teeth. *He wouldn't be taken again.* He fought against the pain. Inch by inch, he rolled himself over. He bore down and got to his knees. Up to his feet. He pulled in air and earth and cut Adam's weave in half. The pain receded. William stood on unsteady legs but managed a grin. He gestured Adam on. "Is that all you got?"

The others stood alongside him, looking shaken.

William's breathing came easier. He sourced all the water he could, connected it with his fading *nomasra*. He sent a storm surge at *Demolition*.

Walkers frantically tried to blunt his attack.

The air rumbled with lances of fire. Bolts of air crisscrossed the short distance between the two ships. Tendrils of water tore at *Demolition's* planking or sought to sink the yacht.

The stench of sulfur and a glacial chill filled the air.

Rukh hurled a ball of fire. It punched through the Servitor's defenses, and he screamed. As one, the mahavans seemed to gasp, as their ruler disappeared from view.

Jason gunned the engine again, and the yacht pulled ahead. Dozens of yards opened up between the vessels.

The Servitor pushed to the fore of *Demolition*. Fire coursed down his arms. With a shout, he sent a ball of white-hot fire at them. It roared like a furnace and shimmered with heat haze.

William drained his *nomasra*. If the fire hit, the yacht would go up in flames. He aimed a stream of water. It struck the Servitor's fire. Steam exploded. Thunder rumbled from the impact. More sulfur stench. The fire dissipated but continued to push forward. Daniel and Julius joined him. They added their braids of water. So did the others. More water hit the fire.

With a grunt of triumph heard over the intervening distance, the Servitor punched through. His flame had cooled considerably, a muted red now.

William gripped the gunwale. The fire was going to hit.

Something glowed like a dull green web around Rukh. It spread, enveloping the stern of the yacht.

The fire impacted against the webbing and dissipated harmlessly in a shower of sparks.

The yacht pulled farther away, and *Demolition* grew small in the distance.

For a time, no one said anything.

"Are we free?" Selene asked from the hatch where she'd taken cover down below.

Her question seemed to spark jubilation.

William whooped in victory and shared hugs with everyone he could lay hands on.

CHAPTER 21:
REUNIONS AND
NEW CHALLENGES

July 1987

After sharing several rounds of hugs with Jason, Daniel, and Mr. Zeus, William settled down to tell them everything he and Jake had lived through. While he did so, they worked to sort out the wreckage of the mainmast and repair what damage they could from the battle against the mahavans. Jake piped up every now and then, clarifying some point.

"I can't believe you survived such a shitty place," said Julius. He was a Jamaican immigrant to Arylyn.

"We wouldn't have made it if it hadn't been for Travail," Jake said. "We'd have died without him."

"There were a couple other people who ended up saving our asses," William added. "Fiona for one, and even the two of us. We saved each other."

Jake gave him a playful shove. "You turned out all right, Wilted."

"Yeah, but you're still a jackass, Jake," William answered.

Jake's mouth dropped. "Wait! Is that what you guys used to call me? Jake the Jackass?"

Jason laughed. "No."

Jake relaxed.

"We called you that Jackass Jake." Daniel laughed.

"And if we were *really* mad at you, we called you that Sumabitch Jackass Jake," Jason added.

Jake groaned.

"A troll," Mr. Zeus said, returning to the topic of Travail's role in their escape. "You gave me an image of him in a dream but I wasn't sure what to make of it. Everyone's always believed trolls were extinct." He shook his head in disbelief. "I suppose your friend is the last one."

"He's not the last," Serena said, speaking up for the first time. Until then she'd sat alone in the bow, staring ahead and saying nothing. Selene had fallen asleep in her arms. "There are more. At least, there are on Seminal."

"Seminal is a myth," Mr. Zeus scoffed.

"It's real," Serena replied. "I saw it." She explained about Shet's Spear, how the runes on it had glowed, and why their escape from Sinskrill had proven far more difficult than anticipated. "Isha—Adam Paradiso, the man you thought was my father—said the Servitor knew Selene and I had gone to Seminal, that we'd spoken to Shet."

"Or maybe you're lying again," Jason said, eyeing her with antipathy. "Like you lied about who you were for all those months."

Serena shrugged. "You'll all know the truth in five years," she said. "That's when the anchor line between Seminal and Sinskrill opens again. That's when Lord Shet returns, with no Shokan the Befouler, the Lord of the Sword, to stop him."

Rukh stepped forward, and once again William was struck by the way he moved. Deadly and graceful. He flowed across the moving deck like water. Jessira, too.

Who were they, really? They couldn't just be freshmen. They were something more. Something dangerous. William hadn't decided whether to trust them.

"This Lord Shet, describe him," Rukh told Serena.

She flicked an assessing gaze at him, and William could imagine her thoughts. She, too, had noticed the changes in Rukh and Jessira. "Shet is a titan," she said. "He's a god. He's taller than a troll and has hair so dark it seems blue. He only has one eye, though, black and pitiless. The right side of his face is burned and ruined."

"Like Two-Face," Daniel said.

"Two-Face is burned on the left side," Jason corrected.

"Stop being pedantic," Daniel said. "You know what I meant."

William smiled. *How typical.*

"Burned on the right side," Rukh repeated. His brow creased as he flicked a questioning glance to Jessira, who shrugged in response.

"Why? Do you know something about him?" Serena asked. Her question mirrored William's thoughts.

"No." Rukh shook his head before returning to Jessira's side.

"You think the mythical Lord Shet will return to our world in five years?" Mr. Zeus asked.

"Don't tell me you actually believe her." Jason sounded betrayed. "She's a liar. She's the entire reason for William and Jake's suffering."

"We were tortured," William said to Jason. "Don't bother sugarcoating it. We lived through it, and we won't ever call it anything else."

"Then why aren't we tossing her off the boat?" Jason demanded.

"By 'her' you really mean 'that bitch'," Serena said.

"If the name fits," Jason countered.

"Let it go," Jake said. "She wanted to save her sister, and we never would have escaped without her help. All she wants is for Selene to be happy."

"And that makes what she did okay?" Jason demanded.

"It doesn't make it okay, but we've taken a shine to Selene," William said, pointing to the sleeping child.

Daniel snorted. "You thinking of adopting her?"

"She already has a mother," Serena said, drawing the child closer to her. "Me."

"You?" Jason sneered. "Liars who get their friends tortured won't make mothers."

"I've been all she's had since our mother died," Serena said. "I raised her. I'm the one who tried to mold her into someone good, like our mother."

"Enough," Mr. Zeus said. "It's done." He glowered at Serena. "But you'll never leave Arylyn." He made the vow sound like a threat.

"What if she dreams the location of Arylyn to her father?" Jason demanded.

"We won't let her," Mr. Zeus said.

Serena paled. "You're going to strip me?"

Mr. Zeus' face creased in confusion. "Make you take your clothes off? What kind of perverts do you take us for?"

"Stripping is when they burn out someone's capacity to source their *lorethasra*," William explained. "It's why they have so many drones on Sinskrill to do all the menial labor."

"You think that's what we're going to do to you?" Mr. Zeus asked Serena.

She nodded.

"Disgusting," Mr. Zeus said with a shake of his head.

"Then what do you intend?" Serena asked.

Mr. Zeus' *lorethasra* flared, and the smell of vanilla drifted on the breeze. "It's already done," he told Serena. "I've bound your use of Spirit. You won't be able to dream to anyone, and you'll lack the ability to use an anchor line."

Serena sourced her *lorethasra* and her eyes widened in consternation. "But—"

"The other choice is leave you in a life raft," Mr. Zeus said.

"What about Selene?" Serena demanded. "Will she be bound as well?"

"Selene will be tested," Mr. Zeus said. "She'll be watched. We'll see who she truly is before deciding what to do with her."

"Selene is an innocent, little girl," William said.

"We'll see," Mr. Zeus repeated, his tone unyielding.

By the set of his mouth, William knew he wasn't interested in hearing more about Selene. Nor was he willing to make a commitment about her future.

"I'm beat," Jake announced.

"There's a bunk down below," Julius offered. "Couple of cots."

Jake moved to take Selene from Serena. "I'll put her in one of the beds," he told her before glancing at the others. "Someone wake me up when we get to the Faroes?"

———•———

July 1987

Serena watched as Selene played in the surf, calling out to her favorite friend, Jake. In the weeks since they'd arrived on Arylyn, her sister had sprouted, filled out, and darkened, with a rich nut-brown hue to her skin. More importantly, Selene had learned to laugh without reservation. She laughed even now at something Jake had said or done.

Serena smiled, delighted to see her little sister thriving and happy, but some of her pleasure was wistful. She wished she could feel the joy Selene seemed to experience every day here on Arylyn.

Serena's own time hadn't been nearly as wonderful. Distrust followed her wherever she went, a cloud of whispered comments and dark looks. In the past none of it would have bothered her. But in the past Serena would have been back home on Sinskrill.

Back home.

Serena mused over the notion. Did she truly have a home? She didn't think she did, but on Sinskrill she wouldn't have cared what others thought of her, especially her lessers. On Sinskrill she would have shrugged off anyone's poor opinion of her with a dismissive indifference.

But here on Arylyn, life marched to a different beat. Here, people genuinely cared about one another. They loved one another and shared friendship and family ties.

And here, other than Selene, Serena had no friends or family. The loneliness stung, especially when she witnessed the gladness of others, a joy in which she couldn't take part. It left Serena wondering if she should have sent Selene alone to Arylyn and remained behind on Sinskrill. At least then she wouldn't miss what she didn't know.

Of course, events couldn't have occurred like that. William and Jake knew nothing of sailing. They and Selene couldn't have escaped Sinskrill without Serena to pilot *Blue Sky Dreams*.

Her dhow.

Serena had only had one chance to really sail her boat, and she wished she could have sailed her much more. If she still had the dhow, she could have at least sailed her out into Arylyn's turquoise waters and lazed the days away.

Anything would have been better than her current existence, sitting around like an unwanted guest, ghosting about the island, unloved and unliked in a world of friendship and happiness.

Serena grimaced, embarrassed by her self-pity.

Enough.

She stood up and dusted the golden sand off her loose-fitting clothes. The sun shone bright and warm, and while every day saw a number of brief showers, for the most part Arylyn was an island of light and rainbows.

Literally.

A double rainbow arched from the sea to the red-veined set of cliffs upon which Lilith, the only village on Arylyn, perched. The magi had built their homes there, a mystical place where a river broached the escarpment in dozens of locations. The cascades laddered hundreds of feet downward in a series of wispy waterfalls and tumultuous cataracts. A permanent mist fell in places while scant feet away, sunshine beamed. Dappled shadows of many colors, shaded homes and majestic bridges carved with mythical animals crossed canyons of spray and beauty.

Arylyn glowed golden and glorious, loveliness given life. Even the island's *lorasra* tasted of fruit, something far better than Sinskrill's wretched stink. Nevertheless, a part of Serena still ached for white-capped, rugged peaks, fields of heather, and indigo waters.

"You ever going to build another dhow?" William asked, stepping to her side.

His month on Arylyn had treated him well. He'd filled out a bit, regaining some of the weight he'd lost on Sinskrill, and browned up. He'd also shaved off the awful scruff on his face and gotten a proper haircut. He looked far better for all the changes.

"I've thought about it," Serena said.

"Would you try to sail her back to Sinskrill?" William asked.

Serena looked his way, but he was staring at Jake and Selene where they practiced bodysurfing under Jason's amused eye.

She went back to watching her sister as well. "You know I can't," she replied. "Lilith's Council would never allow it."

"But what if you could leave?"

"That part of my life is over," Serena said. "I don't want to go back."

"But you miss it."

"I miss the island," Serena admitted, "but not the people. I miss the weather, too. Arylyn is too warm for me. I miss Sinskrill's mist and cold. I even miss the clouds."

William's mouth curled upward in sardonic humor. "I miss nothing about Sinskrill, except Travail and Fiona. We need to go back for them."

"You've been talking to Rukh," Serena said.

"Rukh and Jessira." William frowned. "They won't explain themselves. Mr. Zeus knows something, but no one else believes they're fifteen-year-olds who happen to be supremely gifted with any kind of weapon. And they sure act a lot older than high school freshmen."

"There *is* something about them that draws you in, though, isn't there?" Serena said. She'd felt that same attraction.

William nodded. "Even Jason has started trusting them." He hesitated. "I like them, too."

"Rukh thinks we need to go back to Sinskrill?"

"Rukh and Jessira believe you about Lord Shet."

"They're the only ones," Serena said, not letting her bitterness show. How ironic. For once in her life she was telling the unvarnished truth, and no one believed her.

"I believe you."

Serena eyed him in surprise.

William shrugged. "I don't like you and I don't trust you, but in this one thing, I do believe you. If nothing else, Selene says the same thing."

"How generous," Serena said. This time she did let the bitterness show.

"You brought this on yourself," William reminded her.

"I own the responsibility for my current situation," Serena admitted. "But I won't apologize for what I did to you and Jake." She gestured to Selene. "I had to save my sister, and I did."

"I know," William said. "I might have done the same thing if it was Landon's life at stake."

"Really?" Serena said in disbelief.

"I love Landon, and I'd do almost anything for him," William said, "but I'd have told the truth about who I was and what I needed if our roles had been reversed. I would have been upfront about my motives. Maybe honesty doesn't make everything right, but it helps."

"Thank you for the advice," Serena said, letting him hear the sarcasm, "but it really doesn't matter now, does it?"

"Nope. But if you really *are* willing to listen to some advice, then take this. Stop with the drone expression."

"The drone expression?"

William flattened his features, making them unreadable and tight yet somehow also arrogant.

Serena rocked back. "Is that what I'm doing?"

"No one knows how to react to you," William said. "You lock yourself away. Try being friendly, smile because you mean it—I know you can at least fake that much—and maybe then you'll actually make some friends. I know you can fake friendship, too. Your way, though, makes you look like a moron."

Serena pursed her lips. In every conversation between them now, William insulted her and she had no answer. She couldn't respond. She didn't know how. Too much guilt at the harm she'd done him sealed her lips. Despite her unwillingness to apologize to him or Jake, it didn't mean she wasn't sorry.

"Anyway, if you ever decide to build another dhow, let me know," William said. "I'll help you out. So will Jake and a few others."

"Why would you help me?" Serena asked.

"Because we'd expect you to help us," William said. "I meant what I said before. Even if your story about Lord Shet is a bunch of bat guano, we still have to go back to Sinskrill and rescue Travail and Fiona."

"Fiona can't come with us," Serena said. "She wears a necklace she can't remove. Only the Servitor can. If she tries to do so or if she steps foot off Sinskrill while wearing it, the necklace will cut off her head."

William's features hardened. "One problem at a time."

His intensity surprised her, and she eyed him in consideration. "You really expect to build another dhow, sail her to Sinskrill, and escape with Travail and Fiona."

William shook his head. "I expect to sail a ship to Sinskrill, but I expect to take the anchor line off the island. Travail is afraid of the sea, remember?"

Serena laughed. "No one can open the anchor line except the Servitor. Only he knows the key."

"The key can be learned," William said.

"How?"

"Are you willing to risk yourself to save Travail and Fiona?" William asked instead of answering.

Serena nodded.

"Then we'll need to build the boat. And this time you're going to teach me to sail her."

THE END

ABOUT THE AUTHOR

avis Ashura is a legend...in his own mind. He resides in North Carolina, sharing a house with his wonderful wife who somehow overlooked Davis' eccentricities and married him anyway. As proper recompense for her sacrifice, Davis then unwittingly turned his wonderful wife into a nerd-girl. To her sad and utter humiliation, she knows exactly what is meant by 'Kronos'. Living with them are their two rambunctious boys, both of whom have at various times helped turn Davis' once lustrous, raven-black hair prematurely white (it sure sounds prettier than the dirty gray it actually is). And of course, there is the obligatory strange, calico cat (all authors have cats – it's required by the union). She is the world's finest hunter of socks, be they dirty or clean. When not working – nay laboring – in the creation of works of fiction so grand that hardly anyone has read a single word of them, Davis practices medicine, but only when the insurance companies tell him he can.

Visit him at www.DavisAshura.com and be appalled by the banality of a writer's life.

www.ingramcontent.com/pod-product-compliance
Lightning Source LLC
Chambersburg PA
CBHW051218120726
47905CB00004B/1168